Manufactured in the United States of America

ISBN: 978-1-886591-35-6

$16.95 — Copies of this book may be purchased from your local bookstore, online at bluecreekpress.com and amazon.com or from Blue Creek Press by writing to P.O. Box 110, Heron, MT, 59844

Inquire at books@bluecreekpress.com

Blue Creek Press

Book designed and published by
Blue Creek Press of Heron, Montana.
www.bluecreekpress.com

Something About Miracles

Something About Miracles

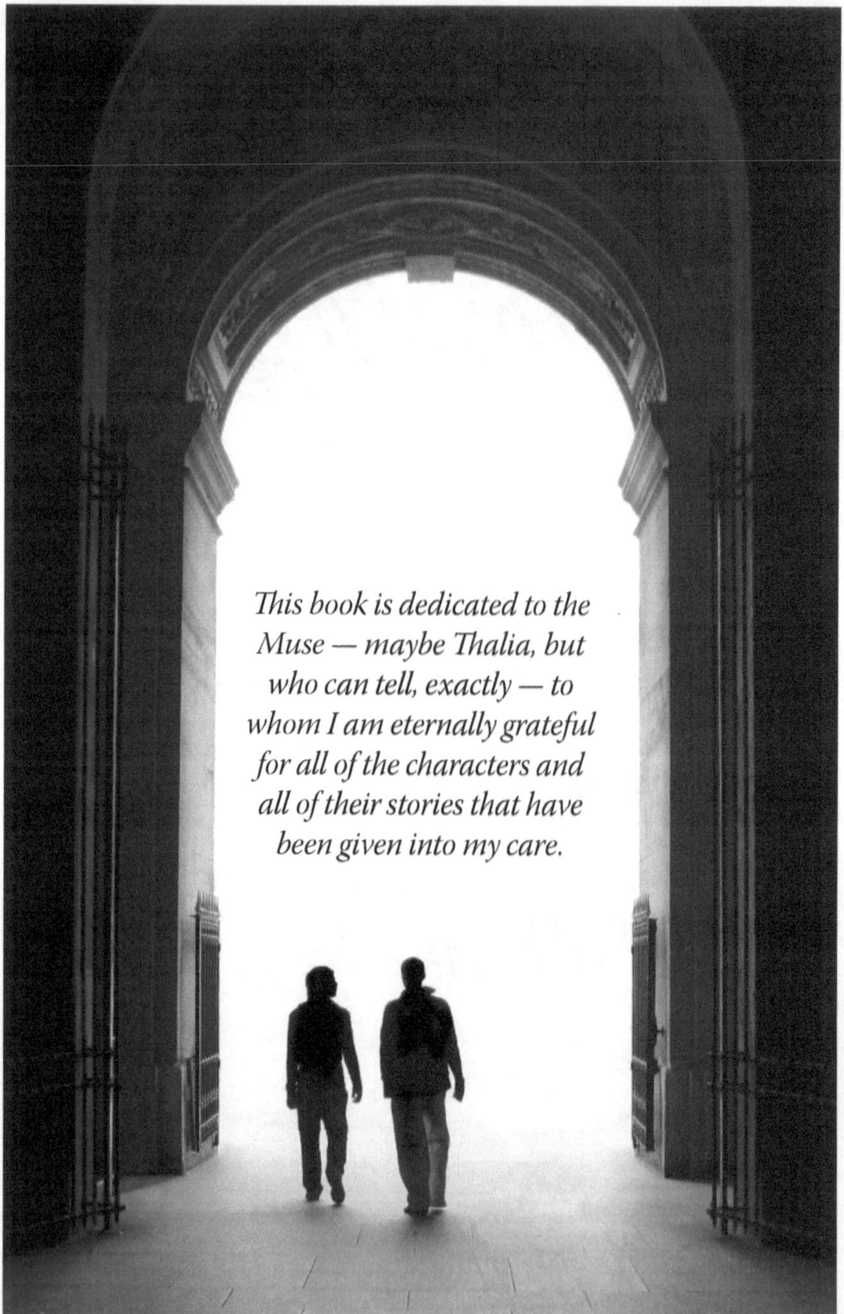
This book is dedicated to the Muse — maybe Thalia, but who can tell, exactly — to whom I am eternally grateful for all of the characters and all of their stories that have been given into my care.

Something
About
Miracles
A Mary Magdalene Miller Trilogy
Sandy Compton

The *friction* of Desire

Larry Longquist, world traveler, depressive, recovering addict, and freshly 60 years old, cashes his tiny 401K and engages the services of Mary Magdalene Miller, MD, specializing in psychiatry. Object — clarity.

Prelude
In the Beginning

Once there was a man who couldn't do anything else very well, so he became a writer. That is not to say that writers are incapable of doing other things well, but just that he was not. He wasn't such a great writer, either, but of all the things that he couldn't do well, his writing was at least mediocre, sometimes good, but not often stellar.

It took him a long time — nearly three decades — to conclude these things about himself, but when he finally did, he wasn't surprised. He had suspected it on one level or another for a long time. However, through the art of denial, he had kept acceptance at bay for just as long.

Acquiescing to his own mediocrity was not as difficult as he had thought it might be, but in so doing, he was presented with a somewhat formidable task: deciding what to do next.

That's where I come in. I'm his therapist. Or, more accurately, was.

I must say up front that the conclusions and assertions above are those he made himself and not mine, confessed in our first "meeting" — he refuses to call them "sessions." I'm not making judgments here, nor is it my place to do so.

My job, I thought, was simply to help Larry decide what to do next. I believed that Larry was deciding what he believes, and it was my opinion that to make that decision, Larry had to come to terms with his self-image and decide whether it was accurate or not.

"As you believe, so shall it be for you."

I'm still not sure what came out of all of this, but something did, though it wasn't necessarily what I had in mind. And, the only way, I think, that I can clarify that for myself is to process it through writing. Bear with me as I sort this out.

So, there. I've given away the plot. Another thing I will give away is method. Some of this is written in retrospect. Some of it was lifted directly from my notes. And some of it was transcribed from recordings of our, um, meetings. So don't get tense about tense, please. He's the writer, after all, not me.

His name isn't really Larry Longquist, anymore than my name is really Mary Magdalene Miller. But, those will have to do, because the AMA gets right upset when doctor/patient confidentiality is breached. So, pretend for a while that this is just fiction. Not that there is really anything just about fiction, as Larry himself once said.

Larry turned 60 last year, whatever year that was, and that may be as much of his problem as anything. The big six-oh is not an easily passed moment. Sixty is not for sissies, I don't think — though I personally won't know for a while, I guess. I do know that sometimes, about the time that life should be treating you with some respect, it instead kicks the crap out of you. Not always, admittedly, but that's what seemed to be happening to Larry when I first met him.

Since, I've found out that life was kicking the crap out of Larry for a long time before he turned 60.

"For Christ's sake," he says, in that self-same first meeting, "I'm still journaling about the same frickin' thing I was 25 years ago."

Stuck, I think. *He is very, very stuck.*

The question, of course, was what is he stuck on — or in?

"So, what happened 25 years ago, Larry?"

"That's a good question, Docta."

He says it like he's from Boston, which he is not by at least half a continent. But, that, with the Bostonian inflection, immediately became his nickname for me. Larry gives everyone nicknames — everyone he likes, and it's obvious he likes me. Larry likes most people. There are a number of institutions he's not fond of, but people, he likes.

He sits quietly for a moment, and then says, "I got divorced for the second time. My dad died. I went into recovery." He pauses for a moment, as if adding something up in his head. "Not sure, though, all that means very much, 'cause truth be told, I'd been journaling about the same thing for five years already, so it's really 30 years."

Larry, I'm thinking, *I'm thinking all that means very much, but we'll go with your train of thought. For now.*

"OK. So what happened 30 years ago, Larry?"

"Besides turning 30? Hmm. I was just divorced from my first wife — I hate that term, 'first wife' — I was just divorced from Julie, I just lost my job, and I just decided that I was going to be a writer."

"Why do you hate 'first wife'?"

" 'Cause she was a *bitch*!" he exclaims in a rough voice, and then he starts laughing. This is when I begin learning that Larry's sense of humor is off the wall, spontaneous and sometimes on the gritty side. His laugh is infectiously uninhibited, more like a kid's than a 60-year-old's.

"Not really," he finally says, with a giggle. "Julie was a good girl when I met her and a good woman when we parted company. 'First wife' sounds like an object or a phase of life or something. Julie's a person with a name."

"Why'd you get divorced from Julie?"

He doesn't hesitate an instant. " 'Cause we got married."

It's obvious he thinks this is obvious, and I would have asked him to explain, but it made so much sense, I snorted. My caught-unawares laugh it not so delicate.

"Jeez, Docta. Be careful with that. You could deviate a septum or something."

Snort two.

"All right, Larry. I will try to be more careful. So, what have you been journaling about for 30 years?"

Again, there's that pause, as if he wants to make sure he gets the right answer. "Money, relationships, anger, addiction, loneliness, frustration — and my inability to figure out how this world works — or even how *I* work."

"That's a lot to journal about," I say.

"I have lots of journals," he says.

"How many?"

The pause. "I don't know. Dozens."

"And, they're all about" — I consult my notes — "money, relationships, anger, addiction, loneliness, frustration and your inability to figure out how this world works?"

He gets a little smile and a faraway look.

"No," he says.

September 1
Uncouched

Larry doesn't like the couch, and categorically refuses to lie on it, unlike most of my other patients, who often choose to lie on it in more manners than one.

This aversion to the cultural symbol of psychotherapy is chancy for us both. The couch and chair are the way they are for a reason, and much of it has to do with preserving professional distance. Larry doesn't know that, probably. He definitely doesn't care.

The couch and chair remind me somewhat of the parent-child relationship, the bedtime ritual of story and prayer; but here, the child tells the story while the parent prays. What do we "parents" pray for? A next answer to our last question and then for a next question to grow out of the last answer. Curly punctuation is a hallmark of our profession, while definitive punctuation like periods and exclamation points are reserved for either end of the session — um, meeting.

On that first visit to my office — the first Thursday in September — he walked carefully around the couch, examining it as if for land mines. "I'm not here for a nap," he said bluntly. So, I sat in my chair while he stalked around the room examining my knick-knacks, heirlooms and diplomas, of which I have not a few. He was not *not* paying attention to me, but exploring my office while I began exploring him. He was indulging his curiosity, but it felt as if he was looking for something, and I'm not so dense as to not recognize some symbolism in that.

"What did you come here to find, Larry?" I ask him.

He puts down — gently, thank God — a very expensive piece of porcelain he had been peering at and looks at me for the first time straight on, reminding me by doing so about the couch and its place in psychotherapy — the eye-contact thing. It's best if the patient doesn't fall in love with the doctor. Or vice-versa. Eyes. Windows on the soul. All that.

Which strikes me odd, just now, because that is what we are trying to do in that chair and on that couch, expose a soul, see what's out of whack, and see if it can be fixed. Maybe that's why psychotherapy can take so damnably long — we are often working in the dark.

His answer to the question is delivered in a manner of pause that's since become familiar: an initial jolt of blue-gray eye contact, then an averted gaze, a tiny smile and a quiet voice. "Clarity."

"And you think you'll find it here?"

"It's my great hope," he says. He lowers his voice. "Confidentially, Docta, I don't think I'm all that screwed up. I just can't see the forest for the trees anymore, it seems like. You know what I mean?"

"Tell me what you mean, Larry."

He sighs and looks away. "Ten, twelve years ago, I was still full of hope, piss and vinegar. Life's never been easy for me. I think I know how to make every mistake possible. But then, I was still on track, I felt like. Now, I feel lost a lot of the time. It's hard to remember what the hell I'm doing sometimes, much less why I'm doing it. The goals and plans I had a decade ago have sort of dissolved. Or dissipated. Like fog, or something. Or, maybe it's that a fog has descended. I sure as hell can't see very well these days. I don't even really know what I'm looking for anymore."

"What were you looking for? I mean before the fog descended."

"I'm afraid to say," he says. "Not so much, really, but a great deal, too. A good partner. A way to make a living with my writing, and some other related talents. A life in which the daily struggle was well-enough rewarded that it seemed worth it."

"When you say 'partner,' what do you mean?"

"What do I mean? Someone to share life with. A companion. Lover. Friend and collaborator. A cohabitor."

"Is that the right word? Wouldn't it be cohabitator, as in 'cohabitate'?"

He laughs. "No. Actually, it would be neither. 'Cohabitate' isn't a word. The word is 'cohabit,' and it's a verb, and it really means to live together without benefit of wedlock. So, maybe that's not really what I was looking for because I thought I would like to be married again.

"How many times have you been married?"

"Twice."

"So, you've been divorced for 25 years?"

"I suppose you could look at it that way."

"How do you look at it?"

"I've been single for . . . " he looks away " . . . a long, long time."

"No girl friends, no romances during all that time?"

"Oh, yeah. Girl friends and romances, surely." He laughs. "Some fine, fine moments — and some really nasty ones, too." He pauses. "It's my fault. I'm kind of picky, and somewhat self-destructive sometimes. And, I tend to fall in love with Jenny."

"Jenny. Who's Jenny?"

He laughs. "Remember the girl who was the love of Forrest Gump's life, the abused girl who couldn't let him love her until she was dying of AIDS or whatever it was."

"Yes," I say. "I remember."

"Jenny."

"Why do you suppose that is? That you would fall in love with Jenny?"

"I don't know. Maybe because Jenny needs at least one person in her life who really loves her with no other agenda."

"And that's bad?"

"No. Not really. But it doesn't lead to domestic bliss very often."

He had me there.

"I think the best relationship I've had in those years was with a woman who was like you in some ways."

My professionalism radar begins to go "beep — beep — beep — beep."

"She was a professional counselor — not a psychiatrist, though — who made a pretty good living. Beautiful. Sexy."

The beeps are getting closer together. I am sure he is projecting. I give him a glance, and he's not looking at me, but toward the window.

"Lots of fun. Sensible. Divorced. Somewhat domestic." He laughs. "God, could she cook."

I suddenly realize he is actually talking about her. The beeps begin to get farther apart and fainter. *Be still my foolish ego,* I think.

"And she had three kids, who were great. A bit crazy from having a mom who was a counselor, I think, and a dad who was sort of a macho jerk, but not completely out there.

"We had a couple of really good years together," he says, emphasizing "we." "I would say we loved each other a lot."

There is a prolonged moment of silence.

"So, what happened?" I ask.

"She wanted to get married," he said.

"Oh," I said, "and you didn't."

"It wasn't that I didn't," he says.

"Were you afraid to commit?"

"In a way, I suppose I was."

"In a way?"

"I couldn't afford her," he says.

"What do you mean by that?"

"She didn't have expensive tastes, necessarily, but I didn't have a big income then any more than I do now. She wanted to build a house, get her kids out of high school and send them to college. I wasn't in any position to help her do that."

"So, you broke up with her over money?"

He laughs. "Not really. I just didn't propose, and in the end, someone else did."

"Really. How did that feel?"

"In one way, it was sad, but it was also a relief, if you know what I mean."

"You were off the hook?"

"I suppose you could say that. But, I was also happy that she found what she wanted, especially because he's a good guy. And, they built a house together and put her kids through school — with a bit of help from the ex."

"So, you've kept up with them?"

"Sure. We were friends."

"You and the woman?"

"Yes."

"Were?"

"Were. Are, I suppose, we just don't get to express our friendship very often."

"Why's that?"

"We've gone on to different places. At one point, she chose to stop corresponding. It was not any big thing, but more like a decision on her part to move on or something . . . "

"But you still consider yourself her friend?"

"No, I consider her *my* friend. I can't decide for her if I'm her friend or not."

"You can decide to be a friend, can't you?"

"Being a friend is sort of passive, Docta," he says. " 'Friend' is defined as 'a person whom one knows, likes and trusts.' I happen to know, like and trust the counselor. So, she is still my friend. If I have failed that test for her, and maybe I have, then I am not her friend. I guess you can act as a friend, but only the other person can decide if you are or not."

"And how do you act as a friend, then?"

"Jeez, Docta. Aren't you paying attention?" He laughs. "Pretty simple, really. You have to be knowable, likeable and trustworthy."

He gets his considering look.

"I haven't always been that," he says.

September 15
Money, money, money, money

Keeping up with Larry's thoughts without benefit of a notebook — something that will be explained more fully in a chapter or two — is a challenge that I have attempted to solve by carrying a small digital recorder, but the recorded conservation is mostly one-sided. I can hear my questions, but more often than not, his answers sound like the adult voices in the "Peanuts" animated cartoons, a remote "wah, wah, wah." But, if I listen to the questions, I can remember his answers. I find myself doing homework, which reduces my real rate to Larry by about half. I don't mind, but don't tell my business manager. She will have a fit.

"You're giving yourself away," Madeline would say, which really means, "You're wasting valuable time that you should be charging for." As if we don't both make enough already.

As we went through the initial exercise of establishing rates when I began my practice seven years ago, I was amazed at how much I could charge. And how much I needed to so I could pay the rent, pay my business manager and pay myself enough to pay back the student loans and have a life. Now that the student loans are history — well, I do very well. Anyway, the extra hour — or two — a week that I spend on Larry is my deepest business secret.

Madeline informed me in the beginning that Larry was not such a great risk as a patient because long-term therapy was not likely. No insurance. Mediocre income. In fact, she tried to dissuade him after he filled out the initial paperwork, and offered him a referral to another, less expensive, therapist — one who worked in a public health clinic — which I would have blithely signed if she hadn't been in the midst of trying to dissuade him and he hadn't been insisting that I was the one he wanted to see when I came to work one morning.

"You're Dr. Miller," he said and held out his hand.

Behind his back, Madeline gave me a bug-eyed look and mouthed the word, "No."

Madeline, great business manager that she is, can piss me off, as she forgets sometimes — but not always — that the business of being a therapist is dependent on honesty and, to a great extent, compassion.

"Yes, I am," I say and shake his hand, firmly, as I was taught to do when I was ten years old. Madeline rolls her eyes.

"I'm Larry Longquist. I hope you'll be able to see me. You come highly recommended."

"That's nice to hear," I say. "Who sent you?"

"Alice and Adam Whitmore," he answers, which surprises me. Neither Alice nor Adam is a patient — client. They are, first of all, too healthy for therapy, and second of all, dear friends of mine.

"How do you know the Whitmores?" I ask

"Through church," he says.

That's funny, I think. *I've been to church with Alice and Adam several times and never noticed this person.*

"Yes," he says, "I've seen you there with them. Third pew from the front on the left."

Did he just read my mind? I think. And, he's right about where the Whitmores sit, and I with them.

I happen to know that I have a place in my schedule at two on Thursdays that opened recently when a certain Mrs. Gotrocks decided she was cured of all her piled-on neuroses and booked a lover for that time slot instead. This may not have been a bad thing for Mrs. Gotrocks to do, as her lover is probably a cheaper distraction than I am, and might even help her fulfill the fantasies that she's always on about.

"Does two o'clock on Thursdays work for you?" I ask.

I can almost feel Madeline clinch her butt-cheeks together.

"See you then," he says, and he turns to walk out. At the door, he turns back and says "Thank you."

"You're welcome," I say, take my coat off and hang it up. As the door closes behind him, Madeline is giving me the ugly eye.

"What?"

"Good luck collecting from *him*," she said.

"I don't do the collections," I said, and flounced into my office. I didn't feel bad, either.

When Larry came to the office that next Thursday, he came early and first of all got Madeline to tell him all about the billing process, what kind of time it takes to fill out insurance forms and horror stories about collections. Then, he made a deal with her. At a 15 percent discount, he paid for 30 sessions up front. She is still shaking her head when she tells me about it at the end of the day.

"If he's such a bad risk," I ask, "how could you take a check for that much from him?"

"He paid cash," she says.

"What?"

She opens the drawer where such things are kept and levers out a stack of $100 bills.

"Cash."

September 22
The Doctor Will See You Now

There is something about timing in Larry's ses . . . — meetings — that I find interesting. Just about when we are going to get into something really interesting, it's time to stop.

I admit that I very nearly always have 15 minutes between sessions, and sometimes a half hour. One of the reasons that I charge so much — I'm in the top range of doctors by fee in the city — is that I give folks a full hour instead of the customary 45 or 50 minutes. We get more done. I see fewer patients in a week. Less paperwork for Madeline.

A typical day starts at 8:30 with prep and Madeline consultation. I see six patients between 9:45 and 5:45 p.m. or seven between 9:00 and 6:30, depending on the day. So, the average time per patient (counting breaks in between) — of which they get a full hour — is between 80 and 100 minutes, again depending on the day. On my seven-patient days, I snack in the trenches. We start appointments on fifteen minute marks, so at some time during my seven-patient days, I get an extra fifteen minutes between patients. Which means I get a 10-minute nap.

Ah, the power nap.

Thursday is a seven-patient day, and the patient following Larry is one of my most challenging. Even though there is a half-hour directly after Larry, I can't intrude into that break. Besides avoiding getting the riot act from Madeline, I need to a.) get ready for Hildegard the Horrific (not her real name) and b.) scratch out a few notes about Larry before the conversation of the day is washed away.

This is what I wrote after his 4th visit: *L. is not delusional. If anything, a bit too much of a realist in waking life. "No dreams left," he says. Not disillusional, though. Very pragmatic approach. "Dreams are for young guys," he says, "and they should have them." He is speaking of lofty goals.*

Sleeping dream life is rich and varied. Chasing wife one (Julie) through multi-storied department store a couple of nights this week. "Chasing" not right term, but "following" not either. "Tracking?" "Stalking?" Not in contemporary terms. Like a hunter, maybe.

"I'm afraid if she sees me she will run," he says, "so I just stay back and enjoy her from a distance."

Bird watcher?

Apparent he still cares about Julie. Interesting. Nothing ever said about wife two.

Asked him today why he chose a psychiatrist instead of a -chologist or a life coach.

Direct quote: "What the hell's a life coach?"

Some ways, he is sooooo out of touch. Where has he been culturally for the past 10 years? (Note to self: Ask Larry what happened a decade ago.)

Says he "chose the professional, not the profession," at the advice — again — of his friends and mine, the Whitmores. He doesn't say more except that he admires and trusts them, and I was first mention, first choice. Never says what the question was. (Note to self: Resist temptation to ask Alice and Adam about Larry.)

Talked about depression, but not much. Know he suffers, but it doesn't seem to be his priority. It's more about direction, which is why I mentioned life coach.

In an hour, that's about all I get from Larry, but I have an idea that I'm not supposed to be "getting" a lot from Larry, but that Larry is getting a lot from — well, from Larry. I'm just holding the mirror, I think. But, I've already alluded to that.

Something about this makes me a little — what's the word — apprehensive? About what? The outcome, I guess. Is this really helping Larry, all of this mirror-holding, or is it just feeding into a deep-seated and nearly invisible narcissism?

"And who's narcissism is it?" McElroy might ask. He is such a pain in the ass, sometimes. A helpful, bright, compassionate pain in the ass, but a pain in the ass.

We who choose this profession are sometimes in the worst need of healing, which of course, is why we do it. It can be very demanding, facing ourselves. And, we are soooo freaking interested in how humans work, even watching ourselves work can become fascinating. Thus the narcissism of McElroy's question. When I start wondering why *I'm* apprehensive about the outcome, I have ceased to be intent on the problems of the patient — client. I think. Maybe. Oh, who the hell knows?

It's Saturday morning, and I am writing about just one of my 30 or so client/patients, which Madeline would be on my tail about. So I will desist.

I think I'll go for a walk. Maybe there are some birds to watch out there.

October 6
A Walk in the Park

In place of the couch, Larry likes instead to walk, and we have sometimes strolled up and down the hall of the office building, or slowly clambered up and down the stairs, though acoustics in the stairwell suck for psychotherapy — all the little echoes and the "scuff, scuff, scuff" of our feet on the metal treads.

Occasionally — OK, often — he talks me into walking with him outside, including to the park near the lake, which is more than a few blocks from my office.

The first time he suggests this, we are strolling down the hall toward the staircase, he in his fleece jacket and I in a light coat. It can be cool in the stairwell in October.

"We don't have time," I protest.

"We do if we don't argue about it," he says, and takes off down the hall.

"I'll get cold," I call.

"It's a beautiful day," he calls back.

"Fine," I say to his back. "But only this once."

He doesn't answer, and I almost have to run to catch up, but not quite.

As we turn into the street — where it is a beautiful fall day, one made for walking — he slows down and we begin to walk abreast.

"Larry," I say, trying not to pant too obviously, "we'll lose a lot of precious time by doing this."

He looks at me like *I'm* the crazy one, and I realize that, at that moment, I am. I'm letting a patient — client — make me that way by trying to control *his* craziness. Not that Larry's really crazy. He's not. He's a struggler, is all, and he wants to know what, after all these years, he's been struggling for. And, even though he assesses himself somewhat incompetent, he is used to doing things his own way.

As we stride toward the lake, Larry tells me about his home. He lives in the country on a place he's occupied for decades in a house that's slowly falling apart; which, according to him, will continue to do so.

"It's beyond redemption, I'm afraid," he says.

I'm tempted to ask if the house is symbolic of him, but instead ask why he feels that way.

He laughs. "Other folks think it's a great little house," he says, "but I know too much. I know all its little secrets: what's rotted, what's broken beyond repair, and where the vermin live."

"Vermin" is not a word I expect him to use.

He looks at me and grins. "Are you gettin' this all down, Docta?"

My notebook is in my purse. I can't write and walk at the same time.

"Tell me more about your place," I say.

In his back yard is a structure he describes as a "botched hodgepodge of bargains, gifts, salvaged supplies and misplaced labor." He built it over the last two summers between debilitating bouts of depression, and finished it just before he started seeing me.

With that same wry smile, he says that it resembles his life; a bunch of odd pieces slung together by someone with only a vague idea of what they are doing; working with no real plan and a pile of materials that don't match, trying to build something out of nothing. Ruminating on that, he says it is, in a word, inelegant, but he also admits that it's "hell for strong," and he fully expects it to outlast him.

"Longquist architecture," he jokes.

I haven't seen it, so I can't be a judge of its elegance, but if Larry says it's hell for strong, I will have to believe him. Larry is possibly the most honest patient I've ever had.

Many others — I won't say most —never really want to really know what's really going on, as one of my instructors in college used to say. They only really want to know that they are seeing a therapist — one who's not very helpful, in their opinion — so they can continue to foster the illusion that they are trying to cure their angst and become better people.

The great thing about these people is that I have no problem keeping professional distance or charging them for every second they spend in my office. They spend most of their very expensive hour lying on the couch and lying to me and lying to themselves about the real problems they face, and I spend most of my very lucrative hour being bored out of my skull with their blathering, occasionally saying "uh-huh" or "tell me more" and sketching dog cartoons in my notebook.

Don't tell the ethics committee.

And, just so you won't think I'm a totally mercenary bitch, I wish to say that I have many patients who don't fit this mold, who are really there to get something done, and whom I really care about. Just not all of them.

Larry, on the other hand, is not boring. Nor, as I said, does he lie. He is so good at not lying, in fact, that he often says, "I don't know," an ultimately truthful statement not enough people are willing to say.

"When you say, 'hell for strong,' Larry, does that refer to you, also?"

"Hmm," he says. "Maybe. I don't know."

"You seem to have survived quite a life, Larry."

He laughs. "So far, anyway."

Larry's moods change quickly sometimes, and he is suddenly sad.

"Survival's not all its cracked up to be," he says.

"It's better than the alternative," I assert blithely, missing the question mark all together. (I think the fresh air was getting to me.)

He looks at me, then, and says, "We don't really know that, do we?"

My therapist brain comes immediately back online.

"Have you ever considered suicide, Larry?" I ask in my best gentle-helper voice.

He looks at me again, this time with that little grin on his face. "I think we're talkin' about two different things, Docta." He rolls his eyes to the sky and says, "Of course I've considered suicide. What truly sane person hasn't in this crazy frickin' world?"

He makes two fists and grabs two imaginary bars in front of him, shaking them like a prison grate.

"Let me outta here!" he growls. "I didn't do it. I didn't do it!"

He presents me with a new grin, a bit bigger and somewhat crazed. He has one eyebrow, his right one, elevated. "James Cagney," he says.

I'm trying to stay on task, here, so "What didn't you do, Larry?" I ask. I am sooooo creative in my questions.

He is suddenly serious and sad and angry, but not overwhelmingly so. Just mad enough to let me know that is how he's feeling, for which I am grateful, for some reason.

"I didn't ask to be born," he says.

I search for another question to throw out there, but the best I can come up with is, *What did you ask for, Larry?* which I mercifully leave unasked. Even savvy therapists such as myself are at a loss for something to say sometimes. This is one of those times.

The discussion is stalemated, and I take a moment to let things be. We are now walking in the park by the lake, and it is a grand fall day. The predominant color beside the blue of sky and water is brilliant, unabashed yellow.

Traffic is hidden away, a low background hum almost like white noise. Silence lies between us, and I become conscious of our measured steps, not quite in cadence. His stride is longer and slower than mine. The pattern of our footfalls is chaotic and accented by flutterings of fallen maple leaves thrown aside by our progress. Geese chatter their way across the sky.

"Today," he says finally, sweeping his arm toward the lake, "I can say I'm glad I was."

Me, too, Larry, I think. *Me, too.*

I look at my watch and say, instead, "I think it's time for us to head back." I stop.

He stops, too, but doesn't turn. "Go ahead, Docta. I think I'll just keep walkin'."

"You still have 15 minutes left," I remind him.

"Keep the change, Docta," he says, still looking away. He turns and grins. "See ya next week."

A few minutes later, I look back and try to spot him in the park. Way out on the sandbar, separated from the shore by a small bay, is a person who could be anybody, but I'm pretty sure it's him. Then again, Larry could be a lot of anybodies that I know. He's just decided to try to clarify his anybodiness.

October 13
Larry Longquist, Architect

"I once wanted to be an engineer," Larry tells me one day. We are walking — again — down Seventh Avenue toward the Circle, and he is looking at the buildings looming overhead. "But, now I think I would have rather been an architect."

"Why?" I think of his comment about his botched hodgepodge, and "architecture" grows a capital "A."

"I don't really know," he says. "I don't know enough about architecture to know why I'd want to be one, but I know that I find all the styles and structures of buildings fascinating. Don't have a clue what style is what, and couldn't recognized a Wythe from a Wright if I had to."

"Wyeth, as in Andrew? He was a painter."

"No, a Wythe, as in Joseph. Sort of obscure as an architect, but real edgy with materials and placement — like Frank Lloyd, but without the public relations department."

"You seem to know a little about it."

"A little. My favorite, I think — at least the favorite that I know about — is Kirtkand Cutter. He worked primarily in the Northwest and did incredible things at the cusp between the Victorian Age and the twentieth century.

Lots of big houses for the nouveau riche of Spokane, Seattle, Tacoma, Olympia. Train stations. Hotels. Theaters. He wasn't a specialist.

"There's this tiny little town up in northeastern Washington State that has two of his beauties; a private residence built for a mine owner (I think) and a theater. Both in Metaline Falls."

"Metaline Falls? How do you know about that?"

"I went to look at them once. Sort of a private Kirkland Cutter tour. I got onto him when I went to the museum in Spokane, Washington, when I was on a trip out West a few years ago. They have this big house next door that Cutter designed and was the original museum. The guy wasn't a minimalist. To hell with those modern, low-feature, slick steel buildings. He loved wood and stone. And detail. You could spend an hour in one room — or longer — and still not comprehend all the details. Anyway, I started looking for Kirkland Cutter designs and sort of collecting them."

"Do you think you could be an architect?"

"Now?" He starts laughing. "Honey," he says, "have you forgotten why I'm here?"

I'm not sure I like him calling me "honey." I give him "the look," set on medium-low and try to sound a little frosty. "As I recall, you said you were looking for clarity."

He laughs. "Yes. Sorry."

"The look" doesn't phase him much, though I *think* he thinks he has committed a faux pas, even though I'm not really sure it was. While I'm still sorting that out, he keeps going.

"I wasn't lying when I said that, you know," he says. "But it's more than just clarity. I'm looking for something that might not be available. In fact, it probably isn't."

"What's that?"

He looks at me, and then away, and I suddenly realize that Larry is shy, in a profoundly elemental way; that each time he tells me something deep and meaningful, he's taking a deep breath and jumping off a higher ledge into deeper water. And maybe that's why the recommendation of the Whitmores means so much to him. They trust me. He trusts them. Ergo. . . .

I also realize that I don't know Larry not because the Whitmores haven't introduced me to him but because Larry is not someone who easily lets himself be known. I am suddenly aware of that as privilege and responsibility. I want to cry, but I can't right now.

"I'm looking for the end game, Docta." He says it very seriously.

"End game?"

"I'm looking for a clear view to the future. At least in intention." He laughs. "Even though, God knows, intention is not the future."

I'm not convinced of that. "Explain, please."

He takes a deep breath. "I have 25 years left, tops. Any more than that, I will be outliving my genes. I'm looking for a good path to follow into that quarter of a century."

"Clarity of vision, then."

"Yes, Docta. You just nailed it."

I don't know why I asked the next question. It just popped out. "Have you ever experienced that before?"

"Yes. When I was ten, maybe. But, not since then that I can remember."

"Why do you suppose that is?" I ask, expecting some sort of self-revealing answer which he goes inside to ferret out; some nugget of understanding that is a breakthrough for him.

" 'Cause it storms a lot where I live," he says, nearly immediately, "and I've never had a very good compass."

"So, how do you navigate?" I ask. I am truly curious.

He laughs. "Most often," he says, "by dead reckoning."

"Don't you think there might be better methods of navigation?"

"Depends on whether you know where you are starting from or not," he says.

"How would you not know that?"

"Ever been in a big storm at sea?"

"No."

"Me neither, but I can imagine what it might be like. I have storms, episodes of depression or angst, during which all I can do is hold on to the wheel and try to keep it headed into the wind. I often come out of one wondering where the hell I am and which way is up, much less north. All I can do then is take a guess about where I am and start for wherever it is I think I was headed before the storm hit."

"When was the last time this happened, Larry?" I ask.

"Counting this one?"

"You're in a storm now?"

"Worst one of my life."

I'm stunned. How could I not know? "What are you doing about it?"

He starts laughing. "Docta," he says, "I'm here talking to you!"

"Oh," I say. "And, is that helping?"

"It ain't hurtin'," he says, and before I can sort on that, he adds, "I'm also trying something else I've never tried before."

I'm not sure how I feel about "It ain't hurtin'," which feels sort of like a backhanded compliment, but I ask, "Something else?"

"Besides talking to you," he says.

"What's that?"

"I've let go. I've turned downwind, and I'm running with it."

"And your intention is?"

"To see where it will take me."

October 20
Voluntary Exposure

While he is careening downwind, Larry volunteers a lot of information that at first I thought might not be useful. As our meetings have continued, though, I have begun to suspect more and more that I am not really the therapist in this relationship; he is. His own, that is. If I needed a therapist, it probably wouldn't be Larry. It would probably be James McElroy, M.D. — also specializing in psychiatry — and his office would probably be a couple of floors up and on the other side of my building.

I don't see Dr. McElroy professionally very often, but there are moments when, as Larry knows, a little clarity is in order. Dr. McElroy is very good at providing that when I can't find if for myself. Yes — shrinks need shrinks, too. At least this shrink does. Sometimes. Not all the time, but sometimes.

With Larry, I sometimes think all he needs are my credentials. I'm someone he can trust to talk to, and he's paying for the privilege, although at first I was not sure how.

But, money is one of the things he has confessed to journaling about for 30 years, plus or minus, and that puts it on the table for discussion. I find out that he has a part time job, half time to be exact, that almost makes ends meet.

I am curious about how he paid for 30 sessions — meetings — in advance. He knows that I know, intuitively. It's not like I work for some huge clinic where Peter and Paul have offices on opposite sides of the building.

"If that's the case," I ask, "if money is such a struggle, how can you afford therapy?"

"I've had at least one pretty good job in my life," he says. "They had a small retirement program — a 401k — that survived the fluctuations of Wall Street. I cashed it."

I know enough to know he's old enough to cash a 401k without paying a penalty but not old enough to cash it without having to pay income tax on it.

He laughs. "Desperate times call for desperate measures." He's reading my mind again.

"Are you desperate, Larry?" I don't see him as being so, even though he has confessed to being in the worst storm of his life. If that's true, he's being very calm about it.

He sighs and slows his pace — we are walking up Seventh from the lake — then stops. I think he's being dramatic, but then I'm glad he's paying attention. I haven't been, and the light says, "Don't walk."

"Not yet, not all the time," he says, and that grin plays across his face, "but I wanted to avoid the rush."

I'm not sure what that means, but the light changes and I have a moment to decide that I want to think about that before I ask another question on that line.

He tells me more about his money situation. He supplements his half-time income by selling a piece of writing from time to time, but not very often. I think he grosses in a month less that what I net in a week.

He has a mortgage on the house beyond redemption with the hodgepodge in the back yard that takes at least a third of his income, plus credit card payments and a car payment.

"I'm underemployed," he says, "and grateful to be so." I understand that to mean that he doesn't want to work full time.

"You don't want a full-time job?" I ask, making sure that I don't accuse him of slacking with my tone of voice.

"Well, that's true, too," he says, "but what I meant was that I'm grateful to have this job at all. Times are not exactly great in our world."

I once again miss the point entirely, except in retrospect. Sometimes the next question is not really an answer to prayer, but a kneejerk. "Why don't you want a full-time job, Larry? Don't you think it would get you back on track with money?"

Larry doesn't rise to the bait, and maybe he doesn't get my point any more than I got his the first time around.

"Maybe. If I could survive it spiritually. It would have to be an incredibly satisfying job. And, I might have to give up writing. Which may not be a bad idea, and which may be one of the things I'm trying to decide here, you know."

Yes, Larry, I think, *I think I knew that.*

"What do you mean by 'survive it spiritually?'" I ask.

"I've never had a job that gives back as much as it takes," he says. He gets that look of his, his considering look. "But, maybe I've failed my jobs. I've always been afraid of them — afraid that they would just suck me dry and leave the empty shell behind."

"Why do you think you feel that way?"

"Maybe from watching my dad work." Pause. I am learning to wait for that next thought.

"My dad liked to work, I think, even though his jobs were pretty much the kind I am afraid of. Eventually, they killed him. But, he liked many of his jobs. Loved some of them.

"Maybe my problem comes from working for the wrong people," he says, "and being afraid to quit, even when the circumstances are rotten. That was one thing the old man was never afraid to do. 'I was lookin' for a job when I found this one,' he would say."

"Why are you afraid to quit?"

Pause. "I don't know. Why am I afraid to do anything?"

"That is a fine, fine question, Larry. Why are you afraid to do anything?" The double *entendre* of the question bursts into my mind just a bit late to take it back for a rephrase. I grit my teeth. *Dammit.*

He looks at me, and then away. We are walking under the archway that leads into the courtyard behind my building, the one Dr. McElroy's office overlooks. In spite of the ambiguity of the question, he nails the answer. "I don't know," he says, "but sometimes I am. Sometimes, I'm afraid to get out of bed."

I think about this later, when I am doing my Larry "homework," and I wonder how a man who looks as competent as Larry, and who presents himself so well, and is so articulate and funny sometimes, can, first of all, be that way in the middle of "the biggest storm" of his life; and second of all, be afraid to get out of bed.

"How is that possible?" I ask Dr. McElroy.

"I can't advise you about a patient I"ve never met," he says.

"I'm not talking about him specifically," I counter. "How is that possible in general?"

"You know the answer to that," he says.

Yes, I do. There are answers upon answers upon answers. Denial. Psychoses. Neuroses. Paranoia. Schizophrenia. They just keep getting worse. But, I don't want Larry to have those kinds of problems. I want his solution to be simple and timely and complete. And obvious. He came seeking clarity. And he paid for it up front. I want him to have it.

I don't tell McElroy that. He would, I think, advise me to refer Larry to someone else.

NOVEMBER 3
The Friction of Desire

It's early November and pouring rain outside and cold in the stairwell, and we are both bored to death of walking in the hallway, so this is a rare, um, meeting in my office. Larry is sitting in my therapist chair — at my invitation — and I'm lying on the couch — at his suggestion. We've had a good laugh about that, and I'm feeling somewhat giddy. *I've never done* this *before,* I'm thinking. Larry isn't the only person being taken someplace they've never been before these days.

Just one of the interesting things about therapy with Larry is the continued feeling that I've never done this before. He fits no preconception of mine.

"Tell me, Docta," he says, "Do you ever get depressed?"

"Wait, Larry. Just because you're there and I'm here doesn't mean you get to ask the questions."

"Shucks," he says. "Well, it was worth a try."

He moves the chair so he is now seated in front of me. The chair is turned a bit to his right so I see him in quarter profile. For some reason, his posture and position make him seem very vulnerable. Some of my giddiness subsides. Some.

"Do you ever get depressed, Larry?"

"Nah," he says. "I just stay that way." He laughs.

"What's depression like, Larry?"

Dr. McElroy knows full well that I know the answer to this question on a personal level, but nobody experiences it the same.

He thinks a moment. "It's like a wall between me and everything else," he says, "The wall is made of 'I can't.'"

He pauses. "That's not a very good description, is it? As a writer, I should be able to do better than that."

I don't know, Larry, I'm thinking. *That was a pretty damned good description.*

I don't see a question to ask, so I don't ask a question. I'm learning. Silence.

"The wall's made of hard rubber," he continues, "so not much will make an impression on it. Things bounce off of it, including me when I try to penetrate it. Sometimes the only thing to do is ignore it. Then, it might go away. If that doesn't work . . . hmmm. What do I do? I might try to climb over it by action. Sometimes that works. But, you can't approach anything on the other side of the wall without great effort, because the friction of desire is very hard to break. That may be what it's like."

"What do you mean, 'the friction of desire?' "

He laughs. "The more you want something, the harder it is to get."

"Where'd you get that phrase?"

"It's the name of my latest book," he says.

"You're working on a book?" I'm genuinely surprised. "What's it about?"

"It's an autobiography," he says.

"How far along are you?"

"I have the title." He laughs.

"And that's all?"

"Yeah. That's all." His mood swings hard right and the resignation in his voice surprises me. Then he brightens. "The title alone is depressing enough. And it's all mine. I don't need to go further."

Sometimes I want to say things to Larry that might be considered inappropriate for a therapist to say. Today, I want to say something a friend might say, like, *Larry, why don't you get off the pity pot and actually write the book?*

I'm thinking of it as a declarative statement, not a question, but then I realized that there is, in fact, curly punctuation at the end.

"Larry," I say, "why don't you get off the pity pot and actually write the book?"

He turns sideways in the chair and looks at me with that funny, contemplative look of his. "Docta," he says, "that is the question of a sponsor, not a therapist, I think."

"What do you mean, 'sponsor?' "

He turns away again. "You're familiar with the 12-Step Program, Docta. Sure you are. You know about the sponsor thing, don't you?"

I did. "A person with more time in program — an advisor," I say.

"Correct," he says. "A mentor."

"Do you have a sponsor, Larry?"

"Me? No. Not now. I've been one. And, I had one once when I first went into recovery about a jillion years ago. Turned out he was more interested in 13th-stepping my wife than he was in being a sponsor."

"Thirteenth-stepping?"

He gives a rough laugh. "Seduction of new folks by folks with more time in the program. My wife was pretty seduceable."

"This was your second wife?"

He swivels his head and looks at me like I have two. "Yes. Second wife."

"What was her name?"

He looks away. "Mary."

"Same as mine?"

"Yes."

"Anything else about her that you might wish to say?" I ask.

"Not at this time," he says, like Perry Mason would say when asked if he wished to cross examine a witness but he was waiting for Paul Drake to bring back information critical to the defense.

I realized later, as I reflected on Larry's answer, that the question might have sounded flippant. OK. It might have *been* flippant. I was lying on my own couch and feeling somewhat giddy, after all. After that answer, it got very quiet in the office. Very quiet. Larry just looked away at the far wall. I could see his back and the side of his face, and that was all.

"What are you thinking now, Larry?" I ask. It's an old icebreaker we savvy therapists often use to get things moving again.

He looks at his watch. "I think that's all the time we have today, Docta."

He was right.

November 10
Fear of Rising

"Are you always afraid to get out of bed?" I ask. It is a couple of meetings later, and we've been dancing around the fear thing.

"Not always, but I'm often scared to death."

"So, you're not very brave?" I ask.

He laughs. "Not true. I might be the bravest person I know. I spend much of my time doing things I'm afraid to do."

"How do you do that?"

He grins. "With trepidation."

"I mean, how do you force yourself into doing things you're afraid to do?"

"I know, I know. Just kiddin,' Docta." He thinks for a moment. "I guess I don't really force myself as much as I lead myself into it. There's this little kid in me that doesn't want to, and sometimes, he is really loud, but the adult in me just keeps moving into it."

"So, the adult isn't scared?"

"Still scared, just not as scared as the kid."

"What are you afraid of, Larry?"

"Everything."

I don't think he's kidding. "You're even afraid of me?"

"No, no. I'm not really afraid of people. Though sometimes, I am afraid of what people will think of me. Not you, of course. I'm *bribing* you to like me." He laughs, and then gets quiet. "I guess what I'm afraid of most often is what's going to happen next."

I'm suddenly confused here. I don't know what to do with that little aside of his, his joke about bribing me to like him. I'm not sure why, but this has hurt my feelings. I actually happen to *like* this person. I mean, Larry. I like him. Interesting revelation for me, and somewhat unsettling because of the professional distance thing. I'm supposed to remain detached, you know, so I can *analyze* — that is why they call it *analysis*, after all — the confessions and assertions of the patient against a clinical set of criteria that should lead me in the direction of some sort of treatment.

But, now I'm sitting here on the window ledge of the downtown Macy's store (we have taken shelter from a sudden rain storm), and wondering why my feelings are hurt. I see the next thing coming, and I want to hold up my right hand, the one with which I took the Hippocratic oath, and stop it, but it is already too late. In direct violation of the personal pronoun rule, it leaps off the end of my tongue.

"So, you don't care what I think of you because you're paying me."

Three strikes in one pitch: first person beats second person, three to two; assertive statement assuming the intention of the patient; and curly quotation is missing in action. *Nuts! That was not good.*

He looks at me, surprised, I think, at the tone in my voice. Me too. I sound half pissed. I see a flicker of something like panic in his eyes, but then, he looks away.

Banned for life, I'm thinking, *at least from Larry's presence.*

"Docta," he says gently, looking at his feet, "that was a joke, and I can see that you felt it was unkind. I apologize."

I want to accept that apology really, really badly, but I also want him to tell me that he cares what I think of him. *Dammit!* I am not *supposed* to care what he thinks of *me.*

"Shall we go back?" he asks. It's stopped raining, and the sess . . . meeting is nearly over.

"Yes. That would be good," I say.

We walk back to my building in silence. At the entrance, he stops.

"See you next week?" he asks.

"At your regular time." I don't know what else to say.

"Good," he says. "Good."

He turns and walks away. It begins raining. He pulls the hood of his parka up and keeps walking. It begins to rain hard. I watch until he turns the corner. He does not look back.

I hear him say, "I guess what I'm afraid of most often is what's going to happen next."

Dammit!

December 1
Ironic Expectation

"I had this theory, once," Larry says. "I guess it wasn't really mine, but it was someone's — that things go wrong because we expect them to. One day, I decided to test the theory, and over the course of several years, I proved it not true."

I'm a self-determinist, I guess. I'm a little skeptical when I ask, "How so?"

"I quit having any expectation that things would go one way or the other, and you know what I determined?"

"What did you determine?"

"After living without expectation and watching things go wrong anyway, you begin to expect things to go wrong." He gives a little laugh. "The suspected cause has become the proven effect, you see?"

I don't know quite what to say.

"Do you know what Longquist's Addendum to Murphy's Law is?"

"No."

He laughs again, "At the worst possible time."

"And you think that's funny?"

He sighs. "Yep, I do."

"Why is it funny?"

"Irony is always funny," he says. "I once knew this writer who wanted to write a story in which life for one of the characters was so ironic that the irony was threatening to kill him. The best irony of all was that he would survive by laughing about it."

"Were you the writer, Larry?"

"Oh, hell, no!" he says. "If I could write that story, I wouldn't have to be talking to you."

"You did say he wanted to, didn't you? Did he write the story?"

"I did. And he didn't, at least I don't think he ever did. But he was a good enough writer to make bank with it. You gotta be good to even think up an idea like that."

We walked for a ways in silence. Then, he says, "Not that I don't like talking to you, Docta."

He's been careful with my fragile ego since the I'm-bribing-you-to-like-me incident. We are not quite recovered from that. Neither he nor I. I want to ask him about it, but I'm unsure of what it really means to him; which in itself is inexplicable logic.

"How can I know what it means to him if I don't ask?" I say to Dr. McElroy.

"Good question, Miller," he answers. He doesn't go any further.

"You're a big help, McElroy," I say.

He says nothing. Just takes a sip of his old-fashioned. This is after-hours therapy.

"Mary," he says, gently, so I know this is serious. We rarely call each other by our first names. "You got yourself into this mess. You will have to get yourself out. And you will."

He lifts his glass and taps it against mine. "Courage."

"Larry," I say, "If you haven't written about the guy who was dying of irony, what have you written about?"

"Where should I start? The state of the world, I suppose, in an insipid sort of way. I have these great thoughts, but when it's time to put them to paper, they get diluted."

"With what?"

"Worry. Tears. Sweat."

"Are you sure those are dilutants?"

" 'Diluent,' " he says.

"What?"

" 'Dilutant' isn't a word," he says. "The word is 'diluent.' Something that dilutes is a diluent."

"OK," I say, "are you sure those are diluents?"

"Actually," he says, "one could say 'Are you sure those are diluent?' It's an adjective, too. Means 'capable of diluting.' "

"Are you sure those are diluent?" I ask.

"Why would you ask that, Docta?"

Because you have left me no room to ask anything else, Larry! I want to yell at him.

Instead, I say, quite calmly, "It seems like things like that might be spices for the stew, as it were."

"Depends on how they land," he says. "Sometimes, they miss the page entirely."

I suddenly realize that Larry, maybe for the first time since we have begun this process, is being evasive. Not just bluntly uninformative, like he is about Mary the Second, but evasive. I'm somewhat shocked. And then, I'm not so shocked. Larry is still afraid of what might happen next.

A lot of people I know — maybe most people I know — would have blown that whole bribing-you-to-like-me thing off. It was a joke, meant to be funny, and it hurt someone's feelings. Mine. There was an apology issued. I was not very gracious about accepting it. Most folks would have said somewhere inside, "Get over it, Mary," I would have and we would have eventually both forgotten the whole thing.

But, I knew that Larry was not forgetting it. And, neither was I. But, I also did not have a clue how to explore all that without — without what. Making it worse, I suppose. And then, it came to me in a flash of insight. Larry has abandonment issues.

OK. That's not much of a flash. Most of us have been left behind on one level or another. But, it seemed to me that Larry was more than a little worried that I was going to desert him over his joke.

The real flash, and what was really interesting, was that I was also more than a little worried that he was going to abandon me over my response.

I stop abruptly in the middle of the sidewalk, which causes him to swing around to look back at me, eye to eye. "Larry," I say, "why are you being evasive?"

"That's a good question, Docta," he says, much in the same way McElroy said the same thing. And, it's apparent he's not going to answer me either. He looks at his watch.

"Time's almost up," he says, turns and keeps walking.

He's right.

I suddenly know exactly what to say. "Larry," I call after him, "have you stopped trusting me?"

He swings around again. He has his funny little smile on.

"Not completely," he says, and we both start laughing. People are looking at us strangely. I move to catch up and we begin down the sidewalk together.

"That was brave," he says.

"Funny you should say so," I say. I let out a big sigh.

"Larry, I'm sorry for letting my feelings be hurt over your joke about bribing me to like you."

"Good," he says. "Thanks."

There is a huge sense of relief settled between us, and we walk down Seventh toward my building in silence. After a few moments, he says, out of the blue and matter of factly, like there is no connection with my earlier question entirely, which makes it almost hilarious. "I was afraid you'd stopped trusting me."

"McElroy," I say, later, and stop.

He looks at me across the table. "All better?" he asks.

I take the cherry out of his old-fashioned and eat it. He smiles.

December 8
Encountering Monica

We are walking up Seventh away from the lake, and we approach the office of one of the last surviving travel agencies in our little city. The agent, who I know casually, is coming out of the office, and she spots Larry beside me and comes unsummoned to give him a hug. She's a bit on the rotund side with a jolly edge to her. Her hair is silver, bouffant. She wears a teal and burgundy silk scarf against the cold. She is a woman much closer to him in age than I am, one who likes her food and wine, I suspect. I suspect she likes Larry, too.

"You haven't called me lately," she says.

"Sticking close to home these days, Monica," he says.

"You haven't started dating Travelocity, have you?" Monica is teasing. Sort of. It's hard to compete with the internet. She's now looking at me somewhat expectantly, as if she's waiting to be introduced.

He throws me a glance, lowers his voice, raises his eyebrows and says, "Spending my money on a therapist instead." He's got his goofy grin on, and I know the joke is somehow on her.

She looks at him in surprise, and then me, trying to see if he's serious or not. Then I see the synapse close as she recognizes me.

"Hello, Ms. Adams," I say, and hold out my hand. "Mary Miller." I am tempted to add, "M.D." but I restrain myself. One joker in a crowd is enough.

"Yes," she says, and takes my hand. "I remember your Costa Rican vacation. Three years ago."

Still, she seems confused, and I watch her try to sort out whether Larry is teasing, and in what manner he might be spending his money.

"Oh," she finally says, in a manner that makes me think her hand will fly to her mouth. Instead, she has made a flying leap to a conclusion. "Well, if you ever plan to go anywhere," she says to me — I think — "remember to call me. Have a good day." And she bustles away down Seventh.

We watch her go, and Larry says, "Now there's a rumor waiting to happen." Then, he looks at me, and says, "Sorry, Docta. I couldn't resist. Some people just want to know too much."

"You didn't lie, Larry," I say.

"Docta," he says with a short laugh, "I think you are part enabler."

I think that is interesting from a therapy standpoint. "Why do you say that, Larry?"

The game is back on, and he knows it. He picks up the ball effortlessly. "You have just helped me indulge my addiction to getting people to mind their own damned business."

"You're a very private person, aren't you?" I say.

"Yep. And, we all are, in our own way," he says.

"What do you mean by that?"

He gets the grin. "Are you being defensive, Docta?"

"No!" I recognize the trap I have fallen into even before he starts laughing. I have no choice but to join him.

"Alright, smart . . . aleck," I say. "Let's go back to work. Please to answer the question."

He sobers. "Sorry, Docta. OK. I don't think anybody really exposes themselves very much to the rest of the world, at least until we know we are somehow embedded in another person's life. Ever notice how anger begins to crop up in a relationship only after the courtship is pretty well cemented?"

Yes. I had noticed that. Especially in relationships that turn abusive.

"Why do you use the example of anger?" I ask.

"What's a better one?" he says.

I am nonplus for an answer.

"Jealousy might be close," he says, " but it often manifests itself in anger."

"Insecurity," I venture.

"Which manifests itself in jealousy," he says.

"Have you ever had any problems with any of those emotions in relationships, Larry?" I'm thinking tha maybe Larry should be a therapist.

"I have a theory," he says, "that no second child should be born until the first one is well weaned, and so forth and so on."

So I really *am* right about those abandonment issues. I will pat myself on the back later.

"So where are you in the birth order?"

"Numero uno," he says.

"How old were you when your next-oldest sib was born?"

"Eleven months."

"So, you know why, anyway."

"Yep. But knowledge doesn't necessarily make it immediately better. Old habits die hard. Embedded defense mechanisms are hard to disarm."

"This is part of what you've been journaling about for 30 years?" I ask.

"Da."

"What?"

"Russian for 'yes.' "

"Of course. How foolish of me." Sarcasm is splattering onto the street.

He laughs. "Remember when I told you that money, relationships, anger, addiction, loneliness, frustration and my inability to figure out how this world works were not the only things I wrote about in those dozens of notebooks?"

"Yes."

"There's also a great deal about adventure in those notebooks."

"Adventure?"

"Oh, yeah." He sighs, and gives his patented short laugh. "Adventure."

"What kind of adventure?"

He gets his goofy grin. "Ask Monica," he says. "She knows."

December 15
Rooftop Russian

During our next meeting, Larry leads me up the staircase in my own building to the rooftop, where there is a garden with benches and a greenhouse, inactive at this time of the year. I'm astounded, because I knew nothing about it, even though I have been in this building for five years.

"How could I not know about this?" I ask him and myself. I would ask anybody else, too, but there is no one to ask. We are seven stories up, two above McElroy's office. The lake is gleaming over there in weak December sunshine, and I am wondering if even he knows about this.

"Not many people know about this, comparatively speaking," Larry says — in the mind-reading vein. "I only know because I'm willing to try doors to see if they are unlocked. The door at the top of the stairs was unlocked."

"When did you find this?"

"A few weeks ago. I was restless, I guess. Haven't been on adventure for a while."

"Finding this was an adventure?"

"Just a little one," he admits, "but an adventure, nonetheless. Let's see if *this* door is locked."

He tries the greenhouse door. It's open, and we go inside, where it is 20 degrees warmer. I do not object. There are two benches at the far end, and we sit on them. The shelves that hold plants in the warmer seasons are empty, the glass is clean, and we have a view of the rooftop. It's very quiet, and our voices come back to us off the glass undisturbed.

"Tell me about some of the big adventures," I say. "The ones that Monica arranged."

"Monica hasn't arranged all of my big adventures," he says, "just the ones that took me out of this country."

"Like to Russia?"

"Yes. To Russia."

"Where else?" I ask.

"Germany, once, on my way back from Russia. Now, there's a contrast. Go from a place where many things don't work to a place where everything works. Everything." He laughs. "Not really sure I liked it better, though."

"Why do you say that?"

He thinks for a moment. "I think it's because Germany is predictable. Russia is the real adventure, or was when and where we went. You never knew what would happen next."

A bell starts ringing in my brain. "But, Larry, aren't you the guy who. . . ."

He starts laughing. ". . . . the guy who's afraid of what's going to happen next? That's hilarious, Docta. Yes. That's me." He sobers. "Hmmm. So, what the hell's that about?"

"Seems like you have a contradiction, there, Larry."

"Yeah. Interesting." He is truly perplexed. "I'll have to think about that."

"Why do you suppose that not knowing what's going to happen next is OK when you are in Russia, but not when you're at home?"

"It's not just when I was in Russia. It's any time that I'm out."

"Out?"

"Traveling. On adventure."

"Why do you supposed that is?"

"I don't know, Docta. I said I'm going to have to think about it."

"Will you?"

"Think about it?"

"Yes."

He laughs. "Probably not as much as you will," he says.

"Why do you say that?"

"It doesn't seem to me that there is any great secret lying there," he says. "Will knowing why help me not be afraid to get out of bed sometimes? I don't think so. But you might think so."

He hesitates. "Not that that is a bad thing to think, you understand."

This makes me laugh.

"I like that sound," he says, and then he continues. "Am I braver on adventure than I am when I'm not? I don't think so. But, I seem to be more able to handle surprises. Does that mean that I need to do nothing but be on adventure? I don't think so, although I would probably love it — for a while.

"Maybe," he continued, "when I'm out traveling, I'm not depressed as easily or as often — because of the newness of everything, you know. And maybe I expect things to happen differently when I'm out; no, I have different expectations of daily life, maybe. . . ."

He stops talking suddenly, and I think he's gone into his considering mode, but when I look at him, he's looking out the window. A couple has appeared on the roof, and we can see them quite clearly. They seem mismatched. She is slender and young and lovely, and he appears to be at least 25 years her senior. Nonetheless, it is easy to see that she is in love. She clings to the man's arm and leans against him, smiling and chattering on about something we know not what. We can only hear the timbre of her voice, which is melodic with happiness and seems to carry an accent. His answers are deep and make her laugh. They walk around the edge of the roof looking down, and then come to the door of the greenhouse.

Larry gets up as they open the door, and I learn that my impressions were correct. He is much older than she, and she is beautiful. We surprise them, and they begin to retreat.

"No, no," Larry says, and beckons them in. "*Pazhalsta*. We're just leaving. Please come in and stay a while."

They hesitate, and I get quickly to my feet. They come into the greenhouse, and we pass each other as Larry and I leave. He is reserved and somewhat embarrassed. She is shy, but pleased we have given them the place.

"*Spacebo*," she says, in an accent that seems purely Slavic.

We walk across the roof to the stairwell. As Larry opens the door for me, I ask, "What did you say to each other?"

"I said 'please,' and she said 'thank you.' "

We begin back down the stairs. I stop at the landing. We have a few minutes left, and I think something important has just happened, but I don't know what.

"How did you know she was Russian?" I ask.

"How could I not know?" he asks, with a tremor in his voice I can't quite interpret. He looks back up the stairs, and there's an expression on his face like I have never seen before; pensiveness, longing, regret and joy. Somewhere in the midst of all those, perhaps. He is somewhere else, I think. Maybe back in Russia?

I don't press for a better answer. I think we both have plenty to think about already today.

December 22
Lucky Schmucks

Larry has come to me now for sixteen meetings, and the seventeenth visit is a few days before Christmas, a fine holiday for depressives. I'm not so much worried about how Larry handles Christmas as I am interested. It is one of the few meetings during which we don't get out of the office, and we don't talk much about Christmas.

He brings me a gift, which does not surprise me. What surprises me is that I have one for him, too. We sit on the couch to open them, at opposite ends with our knees quartered toward each other, each with our gift in our lap.

"You go first," he says. So, I do. I unwrap what I know undoubtedly is a book. An ornate tome, *The Collected Works of Sigmund Freud*, comes to light. It is edited by "Jas. Boodles, PhD." I am puzzled, first of all, because I have never heard of this book or "Jas. Boodles, PhD.;" and second of all because I am more of a Jungian, and I think Larry knows that.

"Open it," he says, and I do, expecting some sort of inscription. Instead, I find molded into the ample interior a cavity containing a carafe of what smells like very good gin, a pair of delicate apertif glasses and a miniature bottle of dry vermouth.

"For that perfect ending to a hard day at the office," he says. He's grinning. I am pleased, and I get up and look for a place for it in the bookshelf. As I look, I feel somewhat ashamed that my gift is not so fine as his.

"I found it totally by accident," he says, then. "I love junk stores, and that was sitting on a book shelf with a bunch of other real books. The title intrigued me, but when I opened it, I just started laughing. I knew it was for you."

I feel better. A preordained gift seems better than one that someone has put endless thought and effort into. More fitting. Easier to accept.

"And the gin?"

"That was easy to find, too." He laughed.

"Now, you," I said.

He carefully unwraps his gift, using his tiny Leatherman to cut the tape so as not to ruin the paper. He gets that slight smile of his when he sees what it is, and I am pleased. It struck me as perfect when I saw it at the import store, *St. Petersburg by Night*, a Russian calendar, featuring many of the great architectural triumphs of the city. I've never been, but even I was captured by the pictures of the Kazan Cathedral, which looks like it belongs in Paris, and the Hermitage, positively Florentine to me. Really, only the Church of the Resurrection looks completely Russian.

He holds it lightly, flipping the pages. "Thank you," he says. He pauses at the Church of the Resurrection. "It's just as glorious inside," he says. "No. Magnificent. It's really called 'Our Saviour-on-the-Spilt-Blood.' Built in honor of Alexander II, who freed the serfs. He was a progressive, and for that, plus the small crime of being Czar of Russia, he was murdered by an anarchist with a bomb. The Cathedral is built upon the spot where the attack took place. I think it took almost 30 years to finish, just in time for the Soviets to close it and turn it into a warehouse or something. They could never bring themselves to destroy it, though, as they did thousands of other churches and cathedrals in Russia.

"I always found it interesting that in the very heart of the Soviet empire, within the Kremlin in Moscow, where Stalin and Molotov and Beria and all that murderous mob made their plans and carried them out to kill thousands upon millions, the Soviets didn't tear down the churches. The Cathedrals within the Kremlin walls stood all through the Terror and The Great War and the Khrushchev era unscathed, as did St. Basil's."

"St. Basil's?"

"The most photographed Orthodox church in Russia. You've seen pictures of it, I'm sure, with its purely colorful onion domes standing at the east end of Red Square. The first time I saw it, I was surprised at where it was. And, how small it is. Looking down the square from there, Lenin's tomb and the Kremlin are on the left, the State department store G.U.M. is on the right and the Moscow Gate is dead ahead. All of the Mayday parades rolled right past it."

"How many times have you been to Russia?"

"Twice."

"Those are part of your adventures — the ones beside money, relationships, anger, addiction, loneliness, frustration and your inability to figure out how this world works in your notebooks."

"Da," he says. He sounds sad.

"I may be mistaken, but you sound sad," I say. "Why are you sad about that?"

"About what?"

"Don't be evasive, please."

He closes the calendar and lays it on the window sill behind the couch. "Sometimes, Docta, life combines events in an odd way to give me something that is exactly what I don't want. The final result might even be made up of things that I do want, but constructed in such a way that the final structure is so ironically and sadly misshapen that it proves a painful fit, but I have to put it on and wear it for a while because the parts have become so important to me that I can't lay them down immediately. I would call it bad luck, but I really don't believe so much in luck any more, and particularly the maxim that we make our own. Tell that to the millions who died in slave camps and gulags and torture chambers dragging Russia into the modern age. It wasn't bad luck that killed them.

It was the state of the world that they lived in and the time and place they occupied in it. Luck is for schmucks," he says. He sounds angry.

"Why are you angry?"

"I am, aren't I? Hmm. I don't really know."

He gets his considering look. "I guess I'm angry because luck is one of the many illusions that I've had to divest myself of in the past decade. I used to believe in it. Even if it was bad luck I was suffering from, there was always good luck to believe in, waiting just around the corner. I have come to understand that both are as illusory as predestination or the idea that we here in America can grow up to be anything we want to be — even though, of course, children in other cultures can't. Some people believe that and it happens. Some people believe that and everything but happens. It's a damned shame to live long enough to find out that Walt Disney, sitting on the corner of his desk on Sunday night in all of his sincerity — and in living color — lied to us."

"What do you mean, 'lied to us' ?"

" 'Fairy tales can come true,' " he sings, " 'they can happen to you, if you're young at heart.' You can only be young at heart for so long. Eventually, you will find out that it's not true."

"So, you believed that growing up?"

"I did," he admits, "pretty much wholeheartedly. I believed it for a long time, in fact, all the way through my addiction and beyond."

He is very sad, now. I think he might cry.

"And you don't any more?" I ask softly

"And, I don't any more." He turns and picks up the calendar, and finds September, which features a picture of the Hermitage. He runs his fingers across the picture, as if trying to catch the corner of the building. "As much as I sometimes still want to."

"You know, Larry," I find myself saying — I'm about to give advice, I realize, but I don't stop — "you could allow yourself that. You could just believe it anyway. It doesn't say they will come true; it says they can."

He looks at me, and we both have shiny eyes. "I suppose you're right, Docta," he says. "I suppose you're right."

He takes a deep breath, lets it out and looks at his watch. He gets the Larry grin.

"Ya know, Docta," he says, "I'm not addicted to alcohol."

I laugh and look at my watch. It's 50 minutes to Hildegard. "Martini?" I ask.

"I thought you'd never ask," he says.

"What are you addicted to, Larry?" I ask. We are sipping our small martinis.

"Among other things," he says, "hope."

He holds out his glass in toast, and I touch mine to his. "But many of us are," he adds. "Many of us are. Merry Christmas, Docta."

Later, I find myself humming that silly song. And thinking of the cathedrals inside the Kremlin walls. And how much they might resemble hope.

Merry Christmas, Larry, I think.

January 12
Ice Cream Freezer

I never found out anything more about Larry's second wife — about Mary. It's the last time he's been married, and it was a long time ago and that is all I am able to figure out, even though I asked him one time quite bluntly to tell me about that time in his life.

"Tell me about Mary, Larry," I said once, in my best concerned therapist voice.

We were, for a change, inside. It was mid-January and the Arctic Express had arrived full force. It was about 20 below outdoors, and even Larry was not in a walking mood. Instead, we hiked down the hall from my office and down the walk-in freezer of a staircase to the lobby of my building, where there is an ice cream shop.

"Great day for a sundae," Larry announces, and heads through the doors.

I am so surprised that I drop my guard so far that it hits the floor. "Larry! It's colder than a well-digger's . . . " I let that trail off.

Larry squints down his nose at me with his right eye. "Docta," he says, "you surprise me." Then, he laughs and turns to the girl behind the counter. "A strawberry sundae, please, and whatever my friend is having."

She looks at me expectantly. I look at Larry, who is also looking at me expectantly. "Did you know," he says, "that Russians eat ice cream no matter how cold it is outside?"

The girl — her name is Sherri, according to her name tag — says, "Really? Have you been to Russia?" She seems kind of star struck.

"Yep," says Larry.

"Wow. What's it like there?"

"A lot like here," says Larry. Then he lowers his voice. and leans forward. "Except they talk funny."

She laughs. "You talk funny," she says.

"C'mon, Docta. What will it be?" Larry is looking at me again.

"Hot fudge sundae," flies out of my mouth unheeded.

"Have a seat," Sherri says. "I'll bring 'em out."

We sit at one of those ice cream parlor tables with twisted metal legs and tiny round tops. "These were designed specifically for two people to eat ice cream off of," Larry asserts. He's reading my mind again.

Sherri brings the sundaes. She's quick and she's good at building sundaes. I have to admit they are just the thing for a day like today and I do.

Larry just smiles and spoons portions of his into this mouth.

That's when I ask him to tell me about Mary.

His spoon is about halfway to his mouth. It stops. Then, after a full second, it continues.

"No," he says around his mouthful of ice cream.

"Why not?" I ask.

"Because I don't want to," he says, and he says it in such a way that I know I will not convince him to, no matter what I say, but just the way he says it — it pisses me off.

We eat our sundaes in silence, while I try to think of some way to take my foot out of my mouth, some way to start a productive conversation again. Finally, it occurs to me.

"Then what *would* you like to tell me about, Larry." I say it like a teacher who is not very happy with one of her students, one who is acting stubborn and uncooperative. He looks at me in surprise, and I see a flicker of what looks like anger in his eyes, but then it fades and something gentle replaces it.

"Docta," he says, "it's nice to know that you give a damn about what you do . . . and me. Mary — just so you know — was a non sequitur, a flash in the pan, an illusion. I thought she was the panacea. She was, instead, the disease at its worst. I was the addict. She was the drug. And vice versa. We used each other badly. My abstention from her includes giving her no more thought that the fleeting. And that is why I say 'No.' And will always say 'No.' Don't ask about her again, please."

And, I didn't. But I sat there thinking, *You should write that down, Larry,* and wondering about her. How could I help if I didn't know about what appeared to be an incredibly important episode in Larry's life? Who was this illusion, and what about her was Larry addicted to? What was it about Larry that she was addicted to? On top of that, what if this was some textbook case that I really needed to know about to gain a fuller understanding of the human animal and its foibles.

I really, really, really wanted to know about Mary.

"It's driving you crazy, isn't it?" he asks. He's scraping the last of his strawberry sundae out of the plastic dish.

"How do you know that?" I ask. I'm kind of tired of him reading my mind. I'm the mind doctor around here, after all.

"You haven't asked a question in three minutes." He points at my dish. "And, your hot fudge has gotten cold."

I don't laugh at his joke, though I really want to. I won't give him the satisfaction. "Maybe I can't think of a question."

"You could if you decided to think of something other than my relationship with Mary."

I say nothing.

I have already realized that what I really am is still pissed. I want to know about Mary because I think it's important, and that his refusal to discuss it is standing in the way of his own good health, and I'm pissed because he is being obtuse. *Obtuse!*

I look at him, and he's looking back at me like my patient old uncle or something, waiting for me to come to my senses after a short lecture on the vagaries of the human spirit.

"You're pissed," he says. And then, he starts laughing.

"What's so damned funny?" I ask. I am really, really tired of him reading my mind.

"Everything," he says. "You're of the opinion that I need to talk about Mary for my own good. I know for certain that to talk about Mary is to indulge in addictive behavior, and I refuse. You can't understand that, partly because I haven't explained it fully enough for you to understand, and that is because no matter how fully I explain it, you will never fully understand. Still, you think it's important to talk about. And, still, I know that it is important not to talk about it. It's the irony thing. And irony is funny."

He turns serious and quiet. "You wish to root out the truth" he says. He is looking out the window, and not at me, but I can hear him perfectly.

"I tell you that the truth in this matter is so imbedded in me that to root it out will produce so much pain that it will cause me serious harm or kill me. It's like a cyst wrapped 'round part of my soul, and to remove it is to threaten my being. I have managed to turn that tumor benign, but to disturb it will bring it back to malignancy. You are the doctor, but in this case, I know best."

He says the last three words emphatically, distinctly, one, two, three. Period. End quote.

I take a deep breath. I pick up my spoon and fill it with vanilla ice cream and what is now cold fudge. I want to flick it at him. Instead, I stick it in my mouth. It's really, really good.

"You're not my father, you know," I mumble through the ice cream, much to my own surprise.

"I know," he says gently. He's not surprised at all, I don't think. He sighs. "I'm not."

He's still looking out the window where there are steaming cars passing by and the occasional mummy-wrapped pedestrian hurrying toward the next bit of heat. There is something in his face that I can't quite identify at the moment. On reflection I will know that is because it is not what I want to see. My ego has gotten in the way here, and I know it. I want to be right, dammit, because I'm the gal who spent ten years and a quarter mil so I can tell people what I think about what they are thinking and their deepest, darkest secrets and here's a guy who won't play fair.

Later, I remember that expression and realize that it was one of peaceful assurance.

Larry may not know all that he wants to know, but he knows how he feels about Mary.

January 19
A View of Purgatory

"When you quit indulging your addiction," Larry told me in the next meeting after the sundaes, "you are exposed to the trepidations of the world, and you begin to understand why you were hiding in the first place, immersing yourself in sex, drugs, rock and roll, or television – whatever. After you quit, if you stay quit long enough, you eventually learn that you have a couple of choices. Learn to live with terror or reenter the addiction. Some folks just switch addictions. I did. A couple of times. I was at one time, addicted to 12-Step meetings. Couldn't live without 'em. Lots of addicts entering recovery become that way."

Speaking of addictions, it's NFL playoff week, which means my dad will be nearly incommunicado on Saturday and Sunday. The Pack is playing someone on Sunday, and I will be forced to witness the violence no matter what I do. I could feign terminal illness, but the television in my hospital room would be tuned to the green and gold. It is one of the few things my dad is unreasonable about.

Maybe "unreasonable" is the wrong word. "Unconscious" might be better. It never occurs to him that someone with his genes might not relish football as much as he does. If he found out how I really feel, he might wonder if I'm really his child. Then, my mom would have some 'splainin' to do, as Ricky Ricardo used to say. It's a good thing that I love my parents.

A thaw has followed the Express into town. It's a balmy 35 degrees. We are slicing through town on the bias, following Park toward Fourth, where we will turn and begin back toward the office.

"Admittedly," he continues, "that is not such a bad thing for someone who is just getting started in recovery. Fills the hole in the soul with something that is at least pretty much benign. There are, though, unhealthy meetings. As you progress, and get the principles down, you begin to smell those out. And the funniest thing of all is that you might be the only one that a particular meeting is unhealthy for.

"And, then, you can invoke the Serenity Prayer and either do what you can to change the direction or move on to another group.

"Eventually, you might remove yourself from that world altogether. I did. And after a few years, I began to indulge the addiction a little here and there, and then I flat relapsed. But even as I did, I knew it wasn't going to lead anywhere except back to hell. I eventually opted for purgatory."

"Purgatory. How so?"

"It sure as hell ain't heaven," he says, "at least not on my side of the tracks."

"Can you explain?" I ask.

"Maybe." He thinks for a while. A long while. That is one of the things that makes walking seem to work better between us than the chair and couch thing. Sometimes there are these long silences during which, if he were on the couch and I was in the chair, there might be a tendency to believe that one or the other — or both of us — had fallen asleep.

We are approaching a bus kiosk, the kind with a bench under the sort of roof that offers the bare minimum of shelter. He motions to the bench, one end of which is occupied by a man who has a paper bag that quite obviously has a bottle in it.

"Let's sit for a minute," he says.

I am hesitant. He's not. He just sits down, mid-bench. I sit on the other side of him, as far from the man with the bagged bottle as possible.

"So," he says, in a very clear voice, "the major problem with being an addict is that most people can't afford it. So we do all sorts of despicable things to support our addiction. Steal, rob, lie, deny, manipulate. We sell our bodies, souls, family heirlooms. Some people sell their children. Some people don't have children to sell, but if they did, they would sell them. Instead, they might try to sell their pets. Or their sister's children."

The man on the end of the bench is listening. Intently. He is making no attempt to be subtle about it. He's staring at Larry with a bleary, stupid look. "How can ya just sit there and talk about me that way?" he asks.

Larry looks at the guy like he's seeing him for the first time. "Who says I'm talking about you?" He asks. "Maybe I'm talking about myself."

The man laughs and holds out the bag with the bottle. "Wanna drink to that?"

"No thanks," Larry says. "Not my bag. When was the last time you were in jail?"

"Last we — hic — last week."

"How you doing today?"

"I'm great!"

"Where you going to sleep tonight?"

"Shelter."

"Won't let you in if you're drunk."

"Hell," the man says. "I know that. I'll be sober by dark."

"How'd you buy that bottle?"

"I have always relied," he says grandly, "on the kindness of strangers."

Larry gets up. "See ya around, Frank."

"Yeah, Larry. You know where to find me. Thanks for stopping by." We are walking away. "Hey, Larry. Got a buck?"

Larry doesn't answer. We keep walking.

I look back at Frank, and he appears to be talking to himself, swinging his arms around and waving the bag in the air. "You know that man."

"Frank. Good guy. Non-violent. Thinks he has his addiction figured out. Thinks he can afford it. Begs a couple of bucks by 10 or 11. Buys a bottle of really bad wine. Drinks it and gets good and drunk by 2. Sobers up and goes home to the shelter by 7 for a bed and a hot meal. Helps clean up after dinner. Reads his Bible. Prays with the other guys. Wakes up in the morning and does the same thing again.

"I never was Frank," Larry says. "For one thing, my addiction isn't alcohol. Different stuff, but still the same. Frank's gotten to equilibrium. He doesn't have any illusions of taking responsibility for himself or growing up spiritually. He knows he's going to wake up dead someday, and probably from drinking, and that's OK. He wants and expects no more. He has a wife and kids who know where to find him, but they don't, and he doesn't go looking for them."

"So what does this have to do with living in purgatory?"

Larry smiles and slows his pace. In a schoolyard across the street, a group of young boys are caught up in a game of pick-up football. Their chatter and bravado filter across the street to us.

"One of Frank's kids is over there playing football," Larry says. "If he were mine, I'd walk over and cheer him on, and then we would go get a soda and something that would almost ruin our dinner, but not quite. Then, we'd walk home, where his mother would greet us and point us to the pot roast.

"That's what I wanted when I quit my addiction and went into recovery. That's what I thought I had coming. Twenty-five years later, I'm still alone as I was the day I quit. I think I'm better off, and I think I'm a better man, a better person. I've worked and worked and worked on myself. I've had some great relationships, but they never panned out, and maybe that's my fault. Sometimes things have gotten sideways through no real fault of anybody, but they've still gotten sideways. And, then, there's Longquist's addendum, you know.

"I think I could be a good father and partner and mentor. But, I don't know because I've never got to try. Not since I went into recovery, anyway. So, I can see heaven from here, but I don't seem to be able to get there from here. Purgatory. You see?"

"I think I do," I say.

There's a ruckus across the street. One of the boys stretches to catch a long pass. He barely hangs on and then outstrips the others, beating them to the telephone pole goal line going away.

"That's Frank's boy," he says, and heads across the street.

"Hey, Frankie," he says when he catches up with the youngster.

"Hey, Larry! How's things?"

"Nice catch, kid. Good one."

"Sometimes you get lucky," Frankie says with a big grin. "Hey. You seen my dad?"

Larry turns cagey. "I see him once in a while."

"Tell him you saw me make a touchdown, OK?"

Larry's face changes ever so subtly, and the boy notices. "OK, Larry?"

Larry smiles, then, and whatever that was disappears. "OK, bud. I'll tell him."

"Thanks, Larry! See ya." He is already running after the others.

Larry and I turn back toward the office. Our time is nearly up.

February 9
Knowing What We Know

Larry, I find out, loves to ski cross country.

"Once," he says, "I thought I might like to ski across Siberia, but then this happened."

"This?"

He grins and points at his head. "My hair started to change color."

Larry's hair is not going to be gray when it is completely changed, but more likely silver, like the streaks that are in it now. And, it seems a ways off, although I know it happens fast sometimes. My own dad went from full-fledged brunette to silver-gray in about a year. That was the year that I finally graduated, and he blamed me – in a good-humored, teasing way, of course.

"Look what you've done to your poor old father," he would say, pointing at his head, much like Larry did. For Christmas, I got him, among other things, a comb and a bottle of Grecian Formula. Cracked him up.

"Did you actually think you might do that?" I ask Larry.

"Well, not *across*, but certainly *in*. Across is a long damned ways. It would be like skiing across America. Twice. With a range of steppes and mountains three times as daunting as the Rockies, to boot. No, skiing all the way across Siberia would be a months-long, incredibly hard and dangerous endeavor. By the time I grew up, it was already too late to try anything like that. What I mean by "across," I guess, is "across the surface" of Siberia. Western Siberia is made for cross country skiing."

"What do you mean, 'by the time I grew up?' "

We are walking along a freshly-shoveled sidewalk in a tiny leftover of our historically Victorian city, an eight-square-block enclave tucked between downtown and the lake. Commercial space looms across the street, but the neighborhood, once one of the wealthiest in the city — the state for that matter — holds it at bay with zoning ordinances and National Historic Registry plaques. It is populated by a few old families who claim ownership back to the original foundations and a hodgepodge of students, single folk and young just-getting-started couples who rent rooms and apartments in mansions now given over to tenancy. Larry loves this neighborhood.

"These are all from the Cutter era," he says as we stroll under huge oaks and maples lining the streets and wrinkling the walks with their roots. "I think that a couple of these houses might even be Cutters."

I repeat my question.

He takes a deep breath, then plunges forward. "Here's another theory of mine. When you start acquiescing to your addiction, you stop growing up. Wherever you are at that point, you remain emotionally and spiritually. If you are an immature, selfish 13-year-old when you begin acting out — as I was — then, when you stop acting out and enter recovery, that's where you are when you begin growing up again. No matter how old you are physically, you still have to learn to take care of yourself, think for yourself, take responsibility for your actions, be an adult. You have to grow up.

"OK," he says, "you don't have to. You can remain dependent and juvenile if you wish. Some do, claiming abstinence as recovery, but staying away from the rest of it. Abstinence isn't recovery. Growing up is recovery and recovery is growing up. It means facing life one day at a time and doing your best, doing your part, and letting the rest of the world do their best, their part, without trying to control or fix or countermand. It means minding your own business, and at the same time, holding out your hand to others who might need it. It means commitment to growth and learning to let go.

"Growing up is a very complex thing to do in our culture, and it's hard enough if you are relatively healthy. That, I think, is why, when we get sick, when we begin to grow the addiction, we stop growing ourselves. It's too hard to do both, and growing the addiction is infinitely easier, so we who are inclined to be that way pick the addiction over growing up. And, once it is rooted, it is one hell of a weed to get rid of. It grows fast and grows strong and drops its roots into our very souls. Pulling it out is hard, hard work.

"But, truly working to pull it out teaches us to work hard, and working hard teaches us to do our best, take our lumps, get our asses kicked and still keep going, keep trying, keep moving, keep learning — in other words, grow up.

"But, wherever we were when we stopped growing up is where we must begin when we start again. There are no skipped grades in recovery."

We walk in silence for a while. I'm thinking of arrested development from my point of view. His analysis is different, more organic somehow. I find myself wondering just how smart this guy is. Because that seemed sort of genius.

"I don't think you have to be a genius to figure this stuff out," he says. I'm kind of getting used to him reading my mind, but it still surprises me. "What you have to be is diligent and vigilant and tenacious. All good qualities in a responsible adult.'

"*Why* are you talking to me? Why are you even seeing me?" I ask. "I mean besides the fact that you are paying me?"

This makes him laugh.

He stops and looks out toward the lake, now fully frozen over

"So I will know what I know," he says without looking at me. "It's very helpful to know what you know."

February 16

Ulla

It's two days after Valentine's day, and it's snowing, but we are out walking anyway. Neither of us got hearts and flowers this year, I don't think, though McElroy did slide a card under the office door that morning.

He's soooo romantic.

Not that I mind. I've always known, I think, that whoever my life partner will be — besides Madeline, that is — will appear when time is right. Sometimes, I get a bit impatient, but I remember that my folks didn't get married until their early forties. My dad teases that I was their desperation Hail Mary pass. But, then, he always goes, "Touchdown!" I love my dad.

It's not snowing hard, really, just big, beautiful flakes perigrinating out of the sky almost one at a time. If this beginning lives up to its potential, it will be snowing an inch an hour by the end of the day, but now, it's like snow on a movie set or a ballet stage.

Larry and I are talking about nothing in particular — the oddity of the snow, for one thing — but that's because I haven't asked him a relevant question yet, and the reason for that is that two seemingly separate incidents in my time with Larry have been poking at me for the past couple of weeks, and this morning I recognized them as being somehow connected. I'm looking for an opening, you might say.

"Sometimes, Docta," Larry said before Chrismas, "life combines events in an odd way to give me something that is exactly what I don't want" — I'm paraphrasing here — "but I have to wear it because the parts have become so important to me that I can't lay them down immediately."

For some reason, I have come late to the conclusion that this relates to the young Russian woman we met on adventure in the greenhouse on the roof before Christmas. And her — what? Lover? Husband? Boyfriend? Lothario? OK, not Lothario. If there was any seducing done, I don't think it was by the guy she was clinging to.

Anyway, remembering Larry's expression when we met her — them — in the greenhouse has convinced me that there is some connection between the Russian woman and the odd, painful gifts that life gives Larry sometimes. I think. Or feel. There was something in his face as he looked back up toward the roof that day — seemingly as complex as one of those gifts might be. And, today seems like a perfect day to ask about such a connection, what with the snow falling like it might in . . . in what?

"*Dr. Zhivago*," I say. "This snow looks like it's falling in *Dr. Zhivago*."

"Really?" Larry says. "Hm. I never saw that movie."

"What? You never saw *Dr. Zhivago?*"

"Not yet, anyway," Larry says. "There's still time if you think it's that important."

This makes me laugh. "I'm just surprised you've never seen *Dr. Zhivago*, having been to Russia and all."

"Where do I begin," he sings, "La la la la la la la." He stops and grins at me. "Omar Sharif and Julie Christie in a movie about Russia, and the Revolution to boot? I don't know how valid that is to Russian history."

"You have a nice voice, Larry," I say.

"To be fair, I must admit that *Dr. Zhivago* came out a long time before I went to Russia for the first time. I guess I just wasn't intrigued."

"Did that Russian girl on the roof remind you of someone you know in Russia?"

He turns to me, and I expect him to be surprised at my astuteness, or ready to tell me it's not any of my business, but instead he wears that same expression I couldn't identify when we were leaving the roof. I detect a bit more this time, a hint of grief.

"Yes," he says, "Yes, she did. Except she doesn't live in Russia any more."

He sighs. "You know, Docta, as you already know, I don't talk about some things to anybody, not even a great listener like yourself. Some things just hurt too much, and it's just as easy to leave them where they lie. Those damned sleeping dogs, you know. But, I'm sort of tired of tiptoeing around this one. Maybe if I wake this dog up, it will go away and leave me alone."

He looks at his watch. "This could take a while."

I say nothing, but inside I am chanting, *Go, Larry, go!*

"The first time I went to Russia, I went with a friend who travels there a lot on business, and we ended up in an oil town out in the middle of Siberia, Nezhnevartovsk. It's like the end of the road at the end of the road, this big Soviet-modern city out in the middle of freakin' nowhere, 1500 klicks north of the Trans-Siberian railroad even.

"My buddy works for a humanitarian NGO, and a group of us was there to check out the environmental procedures of oil companies in Russia, which we found to be pretty much nonexistent. We were able to report — without a lot of covert observation for that matter; just look around and talk to anybody — that Big Oil, including Western-based companies, was running rough-shod over the land and the indiginous cultures that live there. Still is, because there is not much that anyone is empowered to do about it. No environmental legislation and not an ounce of corporate consciousness about what was happening to the place or the people. Of course, a corporation can't have a conscious, and the uncaring development of the fields is evidence that neither do the boards of directors."

Larry is straying from the point, I feel. Or has lost it altogether.

"What does this have to do with the girl on the roof?" I ask.

He glances at me through his eyebrows and gets his little smile. I think this is his version of "the look." I put the questions on the back burner.

"We met with a lot of different groups," he continues, "including many church groups, and though my friend speaks Russian, we always had a translator with us. Ulla. She was a great conversationist, well-informed, idealistic and had a fine sense of humor. When she wasn't translating, she was unassuming, thoughtful and prone to quiet observation. When she was translating, though, she was often the center of attention, as it were, for through her, the conversation of 10 or 12 people would flow. She would sit and listen intently, then pass on what had been said in whatever language it hadn't been said in. She was like a traffic cop of conversation, holding up her palm to stay someone who tried to jump in, holding out a hand to invite the next person to speak.

"Between conversations, our group acted like tourists, and Ulla and I spent a lot of time together, which did not make me unhappy. She was — is — a lovely, happy, faithful woman who still believes in the power of individual action and works daily to make the world a better place. There came a moment, in fact, when I was given a choice of whether to love this girl — and she was a girl, comparatively; just 24 — or not. I chose to let myself love her. It was easy, even though I knew that it would probably go no further than the end of this sojourn in Siberia.

"After ten days in the outlands, we were about to go in different directions, and she came to me and said, 'You will visit me when you come to St. Petersburg.' It wasn't a question, nor was it an order or an assumption. It was a statement of her wishes, given in classic Ulla style.

"It was dark, as it often is in Siberia in the winter, and we were standing in the entry of one of those innocuous tenement apartment buildings every Stalinist city contains. She was headed for the airport, and I was off on a drive to another city 350 klicks to the west. She was looking at me with luminous eyes, and practically holding her breath for my answer. I was surprised and highly pleased.

" 'I will visit you when I come to St. Petersburg,' I said, as if I had a choice.

"We had a four-day stop in St. Petersburg for a few more meetings and to be tourists on our way out of the country. We spent part of every day together. I found out that she had certain requirements for a man in her life, and that I didn't meet the requirements. He had to be 'not-boring,' not Orthodox, willing to live in Russia (ah, the catch).

"Eventually, I got back to America, and found myself laughing at myself, being the only guy I know that could go to Russia and come to love — and be loved by — the only young woman I met in Russia who didn't want to live in the United States. OK. She was probably not the only one, but there were a number that I met who displayed little interest in me until they found out I was from America. Then they would stand up straight and stick out their chest and become very attentive."

He laughs at the memory. "It was just a decade after the Iron Curtain came down completely and the Soviet Union dissolved, and pretty close to the height of the Russian mail-order bride era. Not that it's over, but it has subsided considerably. Ulla, who had been to America, held that practice in disdain. I learned this not because we talked about it with the idea of her becoming one — which she never would have really been — but because of a single comment she made one day as we were walking along one of the canals."

"We came upon an older guy and younger woman having their picture taken together. She was not quite all over him, but looking very happy and very possessive. Ulla said, with her teeth set, 'This is so immigration will see how much they belong together and let her go to America with her new husband.' The way she said it told me she found it to be revolting. When I asked her to explain, she said, 'There is not much love there for him, I think, just love for the idea of going to live in America. She is betraying herself. And, him. Old American men come and look and pick one. They are always amazed at how well they have picked, for she is "perfect." It is not so hard to be perfect for a while, when the stakes are high, and the "connection agency" has coached you how to act if you want to catch an American.' "

"We left it at that."

"But you loved each other?"

"Yes, Docta, we did."

"OK, Larry, I know you are not-boring" — he smiles — "but what does it mean, not orthodox? Although, I would say you're not very orthodox, either."

He laughs. "Thank you, Docta. Nice of you to say so, although I'm feeling like I'm blathering here. Not-Orthodox means not of the Russian Orthodox Church. Ulla is Russian, and all Russians are Orthodox by default, almost. But she grew up on the cusp between the USSR and the Russian Federation — she was a teenager when the empire collapsed and expression of faith in something other than the State became acceptable in Russia again. Her family was Orthodox, but when she was in America shortly after that, she discovered Protestantism. There is much more room for women to be active in Protestantism than in Orthodoxy, and so she chose not to be Orthodox any more. She didn't want an Orthodox husband, either."

"So, evidently, you didn't want to live in Russia."

"I might have tried it, but I knew I wouldn't ever want to live there full time, and that wasn't really the point, anyway. Ulla was determined, I thought, not to appear to be a mail-order bride, someone who was betraying herself for security or whatever it is that Russian women who desire to live in America are looking for, and I wouldn't have asked her to do something she didn't want to do."

The snow is falling a little more seriously now, and we are approaching the entrance to my building. We are nearly out of time.

"I told you this could take a while," Larry says.

"Well, what happened?"

"One day, Ulla got married."

"To a not-boring, not-Orthodox person who wanted to live in Russia?"

"Two out of three isn't bad," he said.

"What does that mean?"

"Her husband is from Scandinavia, northern Sweden. She moved there to live with him. From what I can determine from mutual friends, he is a very nice man. In pictures I have seen, she looks very happy." Larry pauses.

"You're going to be late if you don't go soon," he says, pointing at his watch. He's right. We are already ten minutes over, but I know there is something else, some other bit of discomfort in this odd, painful gift Larry has gotten.

A funny question comes to mind. "What was the other shoe, Larry?"

He laughs. "You're good, Docta. Very perceptive today."

"Maybe it's the big snowflakes," I say. I know he's teasing me. "Don't make me wait until the next meeting, please."

"Look at your watch, Docta," he says. "You don't have time for me to finish this. Not in good order."

He's right. It is getting imperative that I get back upstairs. I can imagine that Madeline is getting a bit panicked.

"Go on," he says. "Thanks for the opportunity to put it out there. I'm fine, really. This, too, shall pass. And probably quicker because it's been brought to light. Go."

I do.

Madeline is very relieved — if somewhat annoyed with me — when I come ramming through the office door.

"You have fifteen minutes until Mrs. Rich," she says.

"Thank you, Madeline," I say. I am sure I sound preoccupied.

She softens. "Was it a good session with Larry? Mr. Longquist?"

"It was. At least I think so."

But I also think that there is something else to know about Ulla.

February 23
Hopelessly Helpless

My curiosity has gotten the best of me — again. "What were you addicted to, Larry?"

"You mean, 'What are you addicted to?', don't you?" he says.

"Do I?"

"How much have you studied addiction, Docta?"

"Quite a bit. Enough to know it's a mental disease that manifests in uncontrollable or compulsive behavior that is often self-destructive."

"Mental disease. Maybe. I prefer to think of it as a spiritual disease. Cancer of the soul."

Yes. I believe that we have a soul. But I'd never thought of addiction in those terms.

"Do you know that it's incurable?" he asks.

I don't really know this. "I've seen addiction cured, I think."

"How?"

"Well, psychotherapy, for instance."

"What's the prescription?"

"Self revelation. Analysis."

"Abstinence?"

"At least temporarily."

"Remember Frank?"

"Yes."

"Do you think he could be cured by that regimen?"

I consider. "I think Frank might be hopeless." This makes me sad.

"Frank isn't hopeless," he says. "He's helpless. Helpless over the problem. He can't help himself, not while he's drinking. His only hope is to realize that, and stop — to abstain — forever."

"Then, why doesn't he?"

"He doesn't want to, doesn't think he can, is afraid to try for fear he might fail again. It could be any of those reasons. Or any of a bunch more."

"What about an intervention?"

"You want to try one?"

"We'd have to get his family to help," I say.

"They're done," he says.

"Done."

"They've done the first — and possibly most important — step in the 12-Step program."

I know what the first step is. The twelve steps of recovery are familiar enough from my days as an intern in a mid-city clinic in Milwaukee. It was a common prescription for those who hadn't enough money for other forms of treatment, which was most of our clientele. I don't say this, but I don't have to. Larry reads my mind again.

"The problem with the 12-Step program," he says "is that it's pretty much free. Therapists would have a hard time making a living if all they had to do was point potential addicts into the program. And the problem with addicts who can afford therapy — present company excepted, of course — is that they can often afford to be addicts, too. At least financially."

He had me there. I had seen it too many times. "But not spiritually," I say.

"Or mentally," he says, which makes me smile. Larry has a way of affirming others — or at least me — that is very subtle.

"Is that the case for Frank," I ask, "that he can't afford therapy?"

"I can't reveal too much about Frank — there is that anonymous thing, your know — but his wife — to whom he's still married, and who still loves him, even as she prepares to divorce him for obvious reasons — makes about as much as you do every year. His family could afford therapy for him, but, as I said, they are done."

"I don't get you."

"Frank's wife and kids are involved in their own 12-Step processes, and it's working for them. The first step is to admit that you are helpless over the problem. Frank, in a sense, is the problem. They have had to admit that they are helpless to do anything about Frank if he isn't willing to work at it also. So, they have let go. 'God grant me the serenity to accept the things I cannot change.' "

"Do you remember that Frankie didn't ask me where his dad was? He probably knew. But he also knows that his dad's still drinking, and until he quits, things won't get better for him. For Frank."

"OK, Larry. We have been meandering all over the place since my original question. I think I see your point. I think. Once an addict, always an addict. I'm not sure I agree with you, but you're the one with the experience here. What are you addicted to?"

He starts laughing. "You are going to have a hard time figuring this out," he says.

"Try me."

"Food."

"What?" I am incredulous. I am thinking of his obvious relish with the strawberry sundae.

"I'm a food addict. When I went into OA about a jillion years ago, I weighed 280 pounds."

Larry is sort of normal-sized. I would guess he weighs 160 pounds soaking wet.

"How do you abstain from food?" I am still incredulous.

"The same way you abstain from anything if you are in recovery," he says with that grin of his. "Perpetually." He laughs.

"Explain."

He sobers. "You don't abstain from food," he says. "You abstain from overeating. It's a delicate little dance, sometimes. It's possible, as you can see."

"So, for 25 years, you've been abstaining from overeating?"

"I've been in recovery for 25 years. My abstinence is — hmmm." He goes into his considering mode. "Sixteen years, 10 months and 26 days old. I'm a frickin' teenager!" he laughs. "I haven't said it out loud in a long time."

"So, for nine years — or so — you were in recovery but not abstaining?"

"Abstaining, yes. Completely, no. In and out of trouble, and back in again. The last shot was the worst. It was building back to full-on. I gained 12 pounds in 12 days. On the morning of the thirteenth day, I woke up, went to the refrigerator, started to plan a binge, and something said, 'You are a total addict. There is no controlling this for you. You have to give the control of this away or this will kill you.' Long-winded something, huh?"

"The something really said that?"

"Those were my thoughts at that moment, placed in my head by something other than the disease, and at that moment, the disease had all of me. It had to have been something else."

"What did you do."

"I said, 'Alright. Here. Take it then.' And I closed the refrigerator door — and have never overeaten since."

"How do you not control your eating?"

"By letting my body tell me when it's time to eat, and when not to eat."

"As opposed to what?"

"What do you mean?"

"What other than your body tells you to eat?"

"Let me count the ways," he says. "Fear. Anger. Sadness. Grief. Loneliness. Being horny. Stress. Depression. Even joy or great happiness." He pauses, and laughs. "In other words, being alive."

"Being alive."

"Yep. Bein' alive, bein' alive," he sings Bee Gees style, "and not knowing quite what to do with it. Probably the biggest trigger of all is ambiguity. You remember."

"I do?" I ask. I'm mystified. But then, I do. "Being afraid of what's going to happen next."

"Bingo."

"But why?" I ask.

"I used to think that mattered," he says, "but it doesn't. It doesn't matter why. I tried for all those nine years to figure out why I'm an addict, and the most I got was vague theories about childhood incidents and how they might have affected me. What matters is what is."

My psychiatric mind comes on line, and I miss the point entirely. "What sort of incidents, Larry?" I gently ask.

He looks at me like I've grown an extra arm. And then he starts laughing. He laughs long and hard, until I am somewhat uncomfortable with his laughter. He finally subsides with a giggle, and takes a deep breath and lets it out in a long sigh.

"Thank you, Docta," he says. "God. I could kiss you right now."

I'm afraid he's going to, and then I'm a little disappointed that he doesn't. Oh, McElroy would have a great time with that, should I tell him, which I won't.

"That was one of the greatest things you have ever said to me," Larry says. "It doesn't matter what sort of incidents. They are all passed, all gone. Forgiveness has been extended and accepted by the quick and the dead. There is no reason to dig further. The coffin of the past is lowered and the shoveling in commenced long ago. Dandelions may even decorate the grave by now. I visit so seldom that I don't even know." He sighs a happy sigh

"That was beautiful," I say.

"Thank you, Docta," he says. He has that goofy grin of his on. "I wrote it just for you."

I don't know what to say, so, for once, I say nothing.

"So," I say a few minutes later, as we are approaching my building, "you've never figured out why you're an addict?"

"Docta," he says, "we're going to run over if we get into all that."

March 1
Ulla Reprise

Do you have a picture of Ulla?" I ask. I'm very curious, suddenly, to know what she looks like.

He is startled. "Why would you ask that?"

"Just curious," I say. I'm afraid I've blind-sided him.

"I do," he said. "Somewhere. Including a couple of wedding pictures. My buddy who I travel with was at the wedding. He shared some of his."

We are back up on the roof, and the sun is shining through the greenhouse windows. It is warm enough to make us both drowsy. In a funny, Larryesque reversion to traditional therapy, he is stretched out in the sunshine on one of the benches with his hands folded across his chest. I am sitting at his head about a foot away, feeling slightly jealous that he is more comfortable than I and yet unwilling to go lay down on the other bench. *This is how things need to be right now,* I think. I don't know why I have awakened the dog again, but it seemed like a reasonable thing to do, and I knew there was more to know.

He sighs, and that expression — the one I first saw in this place — appears again. "I wasn't invited."

"This really hurts, doesn't it?"

He gives his patented short laugh. "It really hurts. Yes."

"Is it OK to talk about this today?" I ask.

"It is a good day to talk," he says, like Chief Dan George in *Little Big Man.*

I want to laugh, but I think this is too important to laugh about. Larry might not agree, but I'm the one who woke this dog up. It's important to watch it.

"You loved her very deeply," I say

"Ya think?" he says. "You must be reading my mind."

That's a new twist, I think. "Why is that?"

"This week is the anniversary of our meeting in Nezhnevartovsk."

"This week. But, that was a long time ago, right? Have you seen each other since you spent the time in St. Petersburg?"

"Oh, yes. We spent a week together when I went back to Russia five years ago. We exchanged thousands of e-mails, and sent gifts back and forth with my buddy and other friends. We talked on the phone. We really, really liked each other.

"About two years ago, though, I noted a change in behavior, and I deduced she had met someone she thought special. I joked with her about finding a not-boring guy. She didn't try to hide it, but she also didn't share a lot about it. She became — what — less communicative, less open with her affection. Finally, she asked me to become more formal in our communications, and I figured out she had opened her entire life to this person, whoever he was, including her relationship with me, and she was asking me to respect that. I did. And, our communications slowly dwindled to nothing.

"All this was OK with me. It was really what I had expected would happen eventually — and let's not get into expectations versus reality today — because I knew that she would find what she was looking for. Not-boring, not-Orthodox and willing to live in Russia. She had displayed great patience in this and I admired that, in fact, even though. . . ."

"Even though it precluded you."

"Yes. I felt she was staying true to herself, and I admire that." He pauses "Did you know that's what it says on the back of the AA anniversary coin?"

"What?"

" 'To thine own self be true.' "

"Were you being true to yourself, Larry?" I ask.

"Yes." He says it with complete confidence. "I was doing my part. Part of my personal mission is to do my part and let other people decide what's best for them. So, when I found out she was getting married, I sent her a congratulatory e-mail, and she responded with a very heartfelt thank you. I figured we were done, then. And, I began to — what — put her away, I guess."

"Put her away?"

"I put all of the pictures and letters and little gifts and stuff like that into one of the boxes she sent things in. It's a beautiful, little, green, completely Russian box. My Ulla box, I thought of it as, packed with the idea that I might or might not revisit it someday. It was a good exercise, a letting go exercise."

"That sounds very healthy, Larry. A great way to let someone go, a loving way."

He suddenly swings into a sitting position, ending up about three feet away. "Yep. I thought so, too."

There is something else, I think. "What else, Larry?"

"What else, what?" he asks.

"What else about Ulla?"

"Docta," he says, "I know that you know there is something else. And there is. But, I confess that I am feeling very fragile this week and I don't want to break, at least not in front of you."

I open my mouth to assure him that breaking is fine, but he holds up a hand and slides closer to me on the bench.

"I will break later, in the privacy of my own home," he says. "I promise. It will do me a lot of good, and you can ascribe it to your caring therapy."

He smiles and pats my hand, which is lying on my knee. I think this surprises us both.

"All is well, Docta. All is well. Sometime soon, I will tell you the rest of the story."

I have this urge to give Larry a hug. No, hold him. McElroy would frown on that, I bet. I will never tell him. And, I will have to resist the urge. *Dammit.*

March 8
Knowing What We Can Do

The first week of March has rolled in like a lion. Or a polar bear, I guess. It's been consistently 10 to 15 below for a week. Larry and I are holed up the in the ice cream parlor. Sherri is making sundaes for us. It is apparent that Larry has visited here without me. Several times. It is also apparent that Sherri is in love with Larry, who doesn't mind a bit. She's about 19, I think. Hero worship takes many forms.

In fact, Larry has a glow about him that makes me want to fall in love with him, too, though I know better. I'm a bit too close to his age and somewhat too well trained to do something foolish like that. We might both take it seriously.

He tells me he's been skiing a lot.

"Did you ever get to ski in Siberia?" I ask.

"No," he says, regret dripping from his words. "But, I've actually dreamed about it."

"Why is that, do you suppose?" I am actually expecting the rest of the story about Ulla, but with Larry, there is always something more simple, it seems.

"Western Siberia is a cross-country skiers paradise. Flat or rolling low hills. A savanna-like combination of birch and spruce forest and open taiga. Huge chunks of public land. A horizon that just keeps moving away. You could ski all day and not see anybody."

"Taiga?"

He laughs. "Swamp, in the summer time. No, 'bog' is probably more accurate. In the winter, though, frozen solid with a couple of meters of snow on it, and as smooth as a rolling prairie.

"Wouldn't that be dangerous, skiing where there is so little chance of contact, all alone in big, bad Siberia?"

"Well," he says. "There *are* wolves. And it does get damnably cold. And, then there are the Russian militia, who might think you are a spy or something. So, yes. It could be dangerous. But, I think we need a bit of danger in our lives — even if I *am* afraid of what's going to happen next. It makes us appreciate the safety in which we live and gives us an idea of the conditions that other people live in, for one thing. It also keeps the adrenal gland from atrophying."

This makes me laugh.

"It must be hard to find danger around here."

"Not really," he says.

"How so?" I ask.

"You can always ski across the lake."

Our lake freezes over each winter — very solidly. Folks drive their cars and pickups out to ice houses a mile or more off shore. The lake is about ten miles across, and people ride their snowmobiles anywhere on it with impunity.

"How's that dangerous?" I ask. It seems rather Milquetoastesque to think skiing across our lake is dangerous.

"You have to wait until there's a good blizzard," he says, "and you have to go by yourself."

I look at him to see if he's serious. He is. I can tell. He's not looking at me, but out the window and away toward the lake, and he has that funny little smile of his on.

"Now, that can be an adventure," he says.

"You've done that?" I ask.

"Not this year," he says, "at least not yet, but, yes, I've done that. The first time, . . ."

"The first time?" I interrupt.

"I've done it lots of times," he said. "Every year since I finally achieved abstention. The first time, there was no blizzard, but it was at night under a full moon. I skied to the other side and then skied back to the city lights. It didn't take very long, about five hours. It was glorious. I decided that I would do that every year from then on. The next year, the weather was not so great, but it was reasonable and I did it again, this time in a snow storm that came and went. A couple of times, when the lights on shore disappeared, I got a bit nervous, but I had a compass and I did OK. It wasn't as glorious, but somehow it was more fun.

"I began to pick times when I knew the weather would be challenging, preparing better, taking more stuff in my pack, just in case. I think my favorite crossing was seven years ago. Do you remember the storm that lasted four days with big winds that dropped about three feet of snow on the city?"

I did. It was my first year of practice. It shut everything down. Everything. We lost power, in fact, for a couple of days. It was a huge mess.

"It took me a long time that year," he says. "Quartering into a north wind, it took seven hours just to get to the other side. When I got there, I was tempted to find a house, knock on the door and ask for sanctuary; but I couldn't find a house because it was nearly dark and the power was out. The only reason I knew I had achieved shore was because the surface of the snow began to rise.

"So, I put my headlamp on, turned and started back across. The wind was pushing me to my left all the time, and I tried to compensate by taking a compass reading every five minutes. Once in a while, I was 30 degrees off course. I was getting frustrated and a bit scared, until it occurred to me that the wind *was* my compass, that all I had to do was keep the wind hitting me at a certain angle and I would be fine. If I didn't freeze my right ear off. It was mighty cold."

Twenty below, I recalled. *Yes. Mighty cold,* I thought, *you crazy person.* Not that we are supposed to use the word 'crazy' with a client.

"I had to clear plastered-on snow off of my right side every few minutes, and it felt as if I was skiing in an arc to my right all the time. My left leg and arm burned from pushing harder than with my right, and I was getting scared, which is not a good thing to be in the middle of a blizzard. I was beginning to think I should sit down and get in my bivvy and ride it out when I literally smacked into one of the ice shacks. Ran right into it."

He laughs. "Thank *God* it wasn't locked. I have never been so grateful to find anything in my life. I got inside, and even though it was probably 6 feet square and colder than — what was it you said? A well digger's you know what. — it seemed absolutely palatial. It *was* absolutely palatial. Had a propane heater, which I figured right out, and a Coleman lantern, which took a little longer.

"It wasn't until I got the heat working and the light on that I allowed myself to look at my watch. It was one in the morning. I'd been out for almost fourteen hours.

"I stretched out on a bench as best I could and went to sleep; stayed there until it got well light. Then, I got out and tacked my way back to shore. I don't think I have ever been so happy to get home as I was that morning. I also don't think I have ever been so happy to have done anything in my life. I probably had permagrin for about a week. Every once in a while, I would remember plodding along, being buffeted by the storm and just start laughing."

"Why would anybody do something like that on purpose?"

I didn't say that. It was Sherri.

We both look at her in surprise. She has been eavesdropping from behind the counter. OK, not really eavesdropping. Just listening to Larry tell his story.

"To see if it could be done," Larry says.

"But what if you died?"

"Yeah, Larry," I chime in, "what if you died?"

"I didn't," he says.

Sherri is willing to leave it at that. She goes to the back counter and begins doing some sidework. She looks over her shoulder a few times, and her expression is one of consternation and something else — worry, maybe. Or is it disillusionment? She doesn't understand.

I don't either. Larry understands that Sherri and I don't understand.

"Remember that I told you I was about 13 emotionally and spiritually when the addiction came to live in me?" he asks quietly.

"Yes."

"So, when I crossed the lake in the blizzard seven years ago, even though I was about 53 physically, I was about 23 emotionally and spiritually. That's the 'see-how-far-I-can-push-this' age. It was the average age of the Texas Rangers who went *looking* for Comanches in West Texas in the 1830s and '40s, and probably the age of the majority of Lewis and Clark's men.

"I'm a piker compared to them. All I did was ski across a big flat place in a blizzard. But, I wanted to know if I could do it. Not if I would, but if I could. Of course, I would."

He stops and looks at Sherri. He knows he has upset her.

"Hey, Sherri Lee," he says. I have no idea how he has found out her middle name. "I promise not to do such a thing again, OK."

She turns and gives him a big grin. "OK." she says, emphatically.

"Unless, of course," he adds, with the Larry grin on, "I have to."

She turns away, looking somehow pleased, even with the caveat. I sort of feel the same way. But, I hope he never has to.

"Remember that I told you that it's good to know what you know?" he asks.

"Yes."

"Well, it's good to know what you can do, too."

MARCH 17
Sweet and Good

It's St. Patrick's Day, and we have yielded Seventh to the parade. In fact, we are over on Fifth in the new Starbucks — finally, one has come to town. Larry is not especially thrilled with its appearance in our fair city, but I've been waiting on pins and needles. I lived across the street from a Starbucks in college, and developed an addiction to their chai. Well, not a real addiction, I suppose, but a great fondness, certainly. I'm buying.

If you've been paying attention, you will know that St. Patrick's Day is not on Thursday in this year, whichever it is, but a Saturday; and that this is a Leap Year. Which, of course, narrows down the years in which Larry might have turned 60. Take your best guess.

The reason we are meeting on Saturday is that on Thursday of this week, just before I had to go deal with Hildegard the Horrific, I bought a house. It's not a Cutter, and it's not right on the lake, but it is in Larry's favorite neighborhood.

It was built later than most of the mansions — in the 1920s — and is somewhat modest comparatively speaking; a bungalow with three upstairs bedrooms, one downstairs, a bath and a half, a beautiful kitchen that faces on a big back yard and a huge front room that will double as living and dining room. No basement, as the builders of that neighborhood figured out long ago that basements tend to have a foot of water in them almost no matter what you do. It has sniped gables — Larry tells me — and a big front porch.

Just the thought pulls me away from what I'm doing here, I am so excited, so I try not to think too much about it. I'm in heaven.

OK. I'm really in Starbucks with Larry, and trying to be present. I expect him to order a drip coffee, but he surprises me by asking for a double vanilla latté. "Once every six months, whether I need it or not," he says and takes his first sip. "Mmm. That *is* good."

We take our drinks to a window table. As I sometimes do when we are beginning a meeting, I am worried that we are not "doing" anything. I put my house away and begin mentally sorting notes, trying to find something to appropriate with which to start our "real" conversation.

Larry, on the other hand, is reading my mind again. "How's your house?" he asks, which sets me back on the new-homeowner track.

"Glorious," I say. He's the only patient — client — who knows why I took four hours off on Thursday. In fact, it's his fault that I am in this elevated state of being. He told me to buy the house.

"That thing is built like a brick, um, outhouse," he said one day as we walked by it with its Remax sign out front. I'd not asked for his comments, but with Larry's mind-reading ability, I guess I didn't have to. I'd looked lustfully at this beautiful little home — I should have known I was in trouble when I stopped thinking of it as just a house — numerous times, but never confessed it hardly to myself.

He pulls a brochure out of the rack on the sign. "Hmm," he says. "Great price. You should buy it."

"Do you worry about my sensibilities, Larry?" I asked. I was not about to let that dream enter my brain while I was working.

"Not really, Docta. At least, not just yours. I've had a potty mouth in the past. Just working on cleaning it up some. Someday, I may meet a woman who has kids and less than good sense about men. Don't want to screw up the deal by saying 'shit house' in front of the five-year-old."

This makes me laugh.

"Nice redirection, by the way," he says. "C'mon. Let's go look in the windows."

"Larry," I protest, "we're supposed to be working here."

"Fairy tales can come true, they can happen to you, . . ." he sings, as he leads me up the front walk. "Docta, it's time for you to settle down and quit flitting from apartment to apartment."

Another thought, stolen directly from my brain. Or heart. Or soul. Or something.

We climb up on the front porch and look in the big picture window to the left of the front door. Larry goes into a phase I've never seen him in, the appraiser phase.

"New windows, double pane. Good." He taps the glass. He points to a series of what appear to be round plugs up nearly under the eaves. "That's double good. They blew in insulation recently, and the finish is ugly. You get to save money on heat and by whining about how ugly those plugs are. Nice."

"I don't whine," I said, and looked in the window. The living room has a medium-knap green wall-to-wall covering that looks like 1970. "That carpet is absolutely revolting," I say, in my best whiney voice. I'm trying to find something wrong with this place.

"Good. Another whining point. Just don't use that tone of voice on the realtor. They will throw you out. Dispassionately list everything wrong about this house — we'll find more — and then make them an offer. By the way, under that ugly stuff is a hard-wood floor just waiting for hours of refinishing."

"You think?"

"I can hear the orbital sander now," he says.

Hardwood floors gleaming in the dining area. The big oriental rug that I inherited from great aunt Millie on this end of the living room. The thought that this might work is creeping into my head. In the meantime, we are getting absolutely nothing done. Except looking at a house. I should be paying him.

Ya know, Docta," Larry says as we walk around the house to the back, "you should be paying me."

We both crack up.

"Tell you what, Mister Appraiser. After I buy this house," — I can not believe I just said that — "I will make up for this by making you an incredibly good dinner. And giving you another hour of meeting time." I may have finally learned not to say "session."

He gets a funny expression on his face, and I realize that, in my enthusiasm for the house, I've pushed too far into his personal space — and invited him way too far into mine. McElroy would fire me, I'm sure. Maintaining professional distance with Larry is hard enough without me issuing invitations that might be perceived as very personal.

Perceived, hell, I think. *That was a* huge *error.*

He gets his considering look, and I expect him to say something, but instead, he smiles and climbs up the back steps to a small covered deck that was obviously added on.

"I don't know if this deck is redeemable," he says. "Make it a whining point. Tell them your consultant feels it compromises the architectural integrity of the house and will either have to be removed or remodeled."

"Should I be writing this down?" I ask.

"We'll make a list later," he says. "Look at this. You won't be able to use this as a whining point, I'm afraid."

He motions me to a window that turns out to be above the kitchen sink. Whoever lived here before loved their kitchen. I know that because I do as soon as I see it. It's not huge, but it's big enough to cook in. Tile. Copper. A gas cook top with a commercial grade hood over the top. Lots of counter space. What appears to be a walk-in pantry. And a breakfast nook that looks like it will seat four. Now, I really want to get inside.

"When you have your house-warming party, I fully expect an invitation," he says. "You can cook for me then. And, I'll take that extra hour when you get inside. Don't let the realtor 'show' the house. Get the key and tell him you and your consultant want to look at the place alone. Be very professional about the whole thing."

I realize he has let me off the hook I have hung myself on, but I'm not sure why.

"How," I ask, "is another hour of consultation going to make up for this hour?"

He grins his Larry grin. "I love poking around in houses like this," he says. "Total self-indulgence. Worth every penny to me, believe me. This is grand."

"See this?" He points to the back door. "These doors are brand new. Completely energy efficient. And installed just right. Perfect, too, because you can whine that they need to be painted, which they do."

Inside, I sigh in relief. I don't have to confess to McElroy after all. But, I wonder why Larry, who knows so much about this house, is not interested in fixing up his own. I frame the question, but he has something to say first.

"Docta," he says, "one of the things I like about you is that you have the ability to let things work themselves out over time, instead of forcing the issue. I bet a lot of your clients appreciate that."

I withdraw the question.

"Thank you, Larry," I say, and we continue appraising the house.

Later, though, I am still mystified that he would have the perception that other clients would appreciate that approach. Many of them are in such a hurry that I have to hold up my hand on their confessions, like Ulla, the conversation traffic cop.

I have been waiting for him to tell me the rest of the story about Ulla. I've not pushed it, because, as Larry pointed out, I have the ability to let things work themselves out over time, instead of forcing the issue. Hah. My curiosity over this has sometimes threatened to kill me.

On St. Patrick's Day in Starbucks, though, for some reason, he broaches the subject.

"I think we might wake that dog up one last time," he says, after my enthusiasm for home ownership has subsided somewhat.

"That dog?" I'm not quite sorting on that.

"The Ulla dog," he says, "though she certainly isn't."

"Oh," I say, somewhat surprised.

"I've practiced this," he says, "so I don't lose it completely."

"What do you mean, 'practiced?' "

"I've imagine that you were in the room while I told you the rest a few times. Very helpful. Sort of like practicing reading a tear-jerker so you can do it publicly without choking up."

"You've imagined that I was in the room. . . ."

He laughs. "Sort of a perverse kind of fantasy, don't you think?" He has his crazy Larry grin on.

"Mr. Longquist, if you don't mind. . . ." I'm pushing back, for some reason. This seems somewhat compelling and somehow inappropriate at the same time.

He subsides. The fun goes out of him, it feels like, and I'm ashamed for breaking his enthusiasm. *Help, McElroy!*

"Sorry, Docta," he says. "Just trying to break the ice. And avoid the unavoidable."

He looks away, out the window. I want to cry.

"Larry, I'm sorry," I say. "Please tell the rest of your story." *And, I'll keep my big mouth shut.*

He looks at his hands, which are wrapped around the grandé Starbucks cup.

"OK. So, they got married, and I know they didn't — she didn't — think about this. In fact, I know it was a matter of convenience. Ulla's favorite church was only available on one day within their timeframe, and so that was the day they picked. It happened to be my 60th birthday. And even that was OK. I just figured that was a really good wedding present for Ulla, loaning her my birthday to get married on.

"My traveling buddy — he's my best friend — he knew how I felt about Ulla, right down to the fact that I really felt that it was good she had found her right guy, so, when he got home a few weeks later, he was more than happy to share the pictures he had taken at the wedding."

He pauses, and looks again out the window, so I can't see the tears in his eyes, I think.

"The guy from Sweden?"

"Yes," I say.

He looks at me now, and his eyes glisten. "He's my age."

Ouch, I think. "And that hurt."

"Only a lot," Larry says.

So this is what I suspected it was in February — what began to pour out of him during the *Dr. Zhivago* snowstorm — one of those ironically twisted things that life gives him to put on: his young, lovely Ulla marrying a man who might have been him, and on his birthday. As prepared as I thought I might be, I cannot even be self-congratulatory about my perceptiveness. I am stunned. There is nothing I can say, and so I wait, resisting the urge to touch his hand, mute with understanding. I can't even say, "I'm sorry."

"My heart's not easily broken at this end of my life," he finally says, "because it's just one big scar anyway from all the times it has been. No, that's not true. My heart is really pretty pliable because it has been broken so many times. But, it has healed in such a way that I thought it was pretty much immune to major breakage. But this did some damage, and I've not had much luck putting it away, as I wish to do.

"At least, now, I'm closer to being able to, so thank you for that."

Somehow, I don't think I can take credit for this. He's the brave one at this table.

"I was prepared for her to marry a Russian her own age, or a Swede her age, or even an American her age. In my own mind, the difference in our ages was the major thing that kept us apart. It turns out that it was something else, her reluctance to live in America, maybe, or maybe more specifically not to appear to be a Russian mail-order bride in America. I don't know because we never got through that challenge because I didn't think there was a way to get through it. I believed by her own statement that it was a non-negotiable, and now I understand that it may not have been."

He stops talking and takes a sip of his latté. A single tear runs down his cheek, and I resist the temptation to wipe it away. So does he.

"Mmm. Not bad even cold," he says, and give me a wobbly smile. "One of those gifts, Docta. One of those gifts."

"Why do you think of them as gifts, Larry."

"What else would I think of them as?"

"But they're very hurtful, aren't they?"

"Yes," and he laughs. "But even so, they are also sometimes sweet and good. Sort of like this cold latté."

"How so?" I ask. I really want to understand this.

"Remember that I said that part of my mission is to do my part and let others make up their minds about what's best for them."

"I remember."

"Although I might have done things differently with Ulla if I had understood better what the true circumstances were, I still did my part. I was true to myself."

"And Ulla," I said.

"Yes, I suppose so."

"Larry," I say, "You are a good guy."

"Funny you should say that," he says.

"Why?" I ask.

"It was one of Ulla's favorite idioms. I was her good guy. Thank you, Docta, for reminding me."

Larry looks out the window and takes a sip from his cold latté. I find that I really, really like this man at the table with me, this good guy. I am hoping that he is liking himself better than he has sometimes in the past.

My chai is cold, too, but it is still sweet and good.

March 22
Purgatory Preferred

We are poking around in *my* new house. Larry is almost as pleased as I am.

"You stole this place," he says. He jumps up in the air and thumps down onto the floor. Nothing rattles or bounces. "Brick outhouse!"

"And you helped me steal it," I say. I'm sure my grin matches his. The day we got in — without the realtor — we went through the place with a fine-toothed comb and my whining list got relatively long, even though it was all superficial. And, as it turned out, worth about $40,000. Holy cats!

My desire to buy the house and Larry's approval grew steadily with each unsuperficial discovery. New wiring. Both bathrooms replumbed. Hardwood under the carpet, most certainly. (Don't ask how we found out. Larry was somewhat invasive in his investigation.) No termites. A great foundation. Beautiful little touches in the finishing which includes an incredible bannister — which Larry promptly slid down upon discovery.

"Just testing," he cried.

Floor joices that might well hold up the planet, as Larry is demonstrating by jumping on the floor.

"Back to work, Larry." I say.

"Oh, alright. If you insist." He's contemplating the carpet. "Shall we pull it up?"

"No! Someone else will do that, thank you."

He looks disappointed.

"Have you thought of using some of this kind of energy on your own house?" I say.

I'm not sure that I've asked the right question, but I do want to get back to work. His work, not mine. I'm concerned that Larry is not getting his money's worth.

He gets his considering look. "Touché," he says. "Maybe I should."

"C'mon," I say.

He follows me into the kitchen and we sit in *my* new breakfast nook. Again, I'm in heaven. I love *my* breakfast nook.

Thank you, Larry, I think. *Thank you, thank you, thank you!*

But I say, leaning toward him across my new breakfast table, "You said not long ago that it didn't matter why you are an addict? How can that be?"

I have been thinking about this a lot, for it makes no sense to me. How can it not matter why? "Why" is the reason, and the reason, once discovered, can be dealt with. It's much of what my job is about, unearthing reasons for things, particularly behaviors, thoughts and actions.

He pulls himself out of his Mister Appraiser role and melts back into Larry again, sitting in the sunshine pouring through the window of *my* kitchen. He looks out at my back yard with its huge Norwegian maple tree. "Remember the story about the day I quit indulging my addiction, the day I began my abstention?"

"Yes."

"That was the day I also realized that it didn't matter why I was an addict. And, that made the whole abstinence thing absurdly easy. It doesn't matter why I am, what matters is that I am."

"That seem sort of nihilist."

"Not really," he says. "Nihilism is a belief in nothing. I believe that I am an addict."

"And therefore, you are?" I am careful to put curly punctuation on the end of that sentence. His choice.

He gets quiet, and for a moment, I think I might have pushed a button that may have been better left unpushed.

"This is how much of an addict I am," he says. "When you said that — and that is not to say you shouldn't have — there was this brief surge of thought that maybe if I were to believe strongly enough that I wasn't an addict that I wouldn't be one any more. Then, I would be able to go on a binge every once in a while. Not often, you understand, but maybe after a stressful couple of days, I could just sit down and eat a whole broasted chicken — and a half-gallon of ice cream."

He starts laughing. "That's the kind of thing I start thinking when I start thinking that I'm not an addict. So — I don't think that. Are you beginning to understand?"

I'm certain that Larry is thinking he could plant corn in the furrow between my eyes.

"Maybe not, huh? Hmm. Think of it this way. In a very real way, that moment in front of the refrigerator was my real first step. I admitted I was helpless over the problem, and not only that, there was no finding out why. That's real helplessness, isn't it?

"The really cool thing about that, though, is that once you make that step, once you say it doesn't matter why, that it just matters what is, you gain a huge amount of power in the situation. With the death of denial comes the birth of sanity. Asking why, why, why and continuing to do so when there was no answer, and still thinking if I did find out why that I could somehow not be an addict was the ultimate form of denial. 'I can figure this out,' I told myself, a thousand times. My ego — OK. Let's not get into that — my pride was keeping me from what then became blessedly obvious: the key to my salvation."

"Salvation. But didn't you tell me that you were living in purgatory?"

"I did."

"And that's salvation?"

"Ever been to hell, Docta?" he asks.

"I don't think so," I say.

"Well, I have," he says, "and believe me, purgatory's not so bad."

I look around my kitchen. *Heaven's not so bad either,* I think.

"Thank you for this house, Larry," I say. I have tears in my eyes.

"Jeez, Docta," he says. "I didn't think I was paying you *that* much."

This makes me laugh.

March 29
Larry's Birthday

I realized one morning that Larry's 30th session was that day when I came to work and there were 29 roses waiting on my desk. They were arranged in a casual spiral and of every different color I could ever imagine roses to be, excepting red. Madeline said it was the most schizophrenic bouquet she'd ever seen and that I should keep an eye on whoever sent it (it arrived anonymously). It struck me funny that she didn't guess Larry had sent it, especially when I knew almost the moment I saw it that it was from him. Almost. I had to count the roses to be sure.

I didn't know how I felt about this. Or didn't want to know how I felt about this. OK. I didn't want to admit how I felt about this, but, in fact, I was somewhat — I think the best word is "frightened." What was I afraid of? Something, but I knew not what.

Life was going to change today. I knew that. Larry was either going to sign on for another stint (and probably pay in advance) or say "Thanks, Docta," and move on with his life. Give up writing, maybe. Sell that place and travel, maybe. Or maybe he wasn't going to change a thing. Maybe he would just keep being Larry, keep being afraid to get out of bed some days, keep fighting the friction of desire. I wanted him to not do that. I wanted him to tell me that he was feeling better than he had ever in his life since he was ten years old, even better than the day after he survived his lake crossing, and thank me profusely for all my help, so I could tell him that I wasn't the helpful one here, but he was.

OK, I don't really know what I wanted. And, I didn't then, either. It was indefinable. And, maybe that's why I was afraid; fearing that same monster that we all live with and handle more or less successfully, the same one Larry fights to keep from overeating, and gives in to over and over again. Ambiguity.

I didn't know what was going to happen next.

Two o'clock comes and Larry is in the waiting room, looking perfectly like himself — just as the day I first met him — blue jeans, hiking shoes, button down shirt, fleece jacket, baseball cap. It's spring, now, and his parka is back in the closet with his skis.

I put my coat on, and we head for the door. He stops in front of Madeline's desk.

"Madelina," he says. "It's been a pleasure."

I see something pass over her face. "Don't be a stranger," she says, and pointedly looks back to her work.

Soon, we are on the street, walking up Seventh, away from the lake. He says, "It's my birthday today."

I remember from his paperwork that his birthday was in June. I say as much.

He laughs his Larry laugh. "Glad you're paying attention, Docta," he says. "Yeah, the anniversary of my birth is June 29, but today is the 17th anniversary of my abstinence."

"Today, today?" I ask.

"Funny how that's worked out, huh? Yep. It was 17 years ago today that the something said what it had to say."

"Wow."

He giggles. "Wow, indeed."

"What shall we do to celebrate?" I ask.

"Let's go for a walk," he says.

And, we do. We walk all the way up Seventh until it turns into Poindexter and around the little park and back down Sixth to Maple and then back to the office. We don't talk about much, even though I want to ask him a couple of dozen pointed questions. I want to see if he learned anything. I want to know if I helped. He wants to show me the new building between Ash and Sycamore, which he thinks is hideous.

"I'm no architect, but if I was, and I design something like that, just shoot me."

"It's not a very attractive building," I admit.

"Did I ever tell you about the ugliest building in Russia?" he asks.

He had not, but now he has. It's a good story.

We walk up to the front of my building precisely as his hour is up.

"Thank you, doctor," he says, looking me in the eye and holding out his hand. I take it and shake it firmly, as I was taught to do when I was ten years old, and say, like a good psychiatrist, "For what, Larry?"

There is that familiar loss of eye contact, and his grin, and then a reconnect.

"For everything," he says. Then, he winks at me and turns and walks away. I want to run after him and ask, "What do you mean, 'everything'? What the hell does that mean? Give me some specifics, here. Did all this help? Did it make your life better? Are you going to be OK, now? Are you, dammit?"

He just keeps walking, and I watch him until he turns the corner onto Maple.

After a long while and a hot fudge sundae in the shop downstairs, I go upstairs. Madeline is at her desk. She doesn't look at me. There is a single red rose in a vase on the receptionist counter. Number 30.

"Mrs. Rich is waiting," she says, nodding toward the session room.

"She can wait," I say. "You OK?"

She doesn't look at me, but she says, "He always came 10 minutes early." She gets up and goes and starts fooling around in the top drawer of one of the file cabinets.

With her back still to me, she says, "He's a really nice man, OK? I like him. Thursdays are not going to be the same."

You're telling me, sister, I think, and go to my office for a good cry. Hildegard may stop coming to lie on my couch, but worse things have already happened today.

May 28
Whitmore's

So, two months later, I'm at a Memorial Day weekend cocktail party at Whitmores' — which is along the shore in Larry's favorite neighborhood, *my* neighborhood — and I look across the pool area and there's Larry. He's got a glass in his hand and the Larry grin on his face. He's facing me and talking to a woman in a slinky dress. She is quite shapely, and I am hesitant to interrupt. So, I don't. But, I really, really want to.

McElroy might tell me that this is a very adult way to act, this not interrupting, but I feel sort of like a 10-year-old.

I turn away and "Tell me about your father," runs across my mind with Larry's voice on. I almost start laughing. Yes. Larry could be my father, if I needed a father, and if I close my eyes just right. He would have been a young father, but in some sort of daughterly fantasy, I think he would have been a pretty good one. Until I remember all I know about him. No. If Larry had been my father, instead of my loving, steady-Eddie, dorky, sort-of-boring, terrific real dad — I mean within the restraints of real time — he pretty much would have sucked. But now — now that he's all grown up — I think he would be great. He is great. I'd go to him for advice any time. I've never told him that, but I might.

I glance back across the pool, and this time I catch his eye. He says something to the slinky, shapely gal — "Excuse me, dear, I see an old friend," maybe — and heads my way. Slinky, shapely gal turns and picks me right out. She's pretty — in an anorexic sort of way — that is to say, very slim and very fit. I get the once-over and then she drifts off to join a knot of folks more her age than Larry. I'm surprised, somewhat, by my own cattiness. I check my claws to see if they are presentable.

"Hello, Docta," he says, and holds out a hand, which I take and shake as I was taught to do when I was ten years old.

"How are you, Larry?" I ask. I try not to gush.

"Good," he says. "I'm well. And you."

"I'm well, also," I say, "though I must admit my Thursdays are not quite the same as they once were."

"Ha," he says. "Mine, neither. How's the house coming?"

"Really well, except I can't figure out what to do with that deck."

"Maybe I should consult," he says.

I'm not sure how I feel about ex-clients consulting, and I want some time to think about it, so I redirect. We therapists are experts at redirection.

"I don't want to take you away from your friend," I say. He knows I have redirected, but he is willing to allow that.

"Beautiful chicks are a dime a dozen," he growls in his fake Cagney accent. "Give me one with some brains."

I'm not sure how I feel about being "one with some brains," as opposed to a "beautiful chick," but he continues, "Better yet, give me one with both. C'mon, Docta. Let's see if the Whitmores will buy us a drink."

We start walking to the bar, and he says, "Besides, she's my niece."

This makes me laugh.

"I like that sound," he says.

At the bar, I get a lemon drop and he orders a double old-fashion.

When he gets his, he swirls it in the glass and holds it out in toast. I clink mine against his and we both take a sip. "Don't even think about stealing this cherry," he says. He's reading my mind again.

"C'mon, Docta. I'll introduce you to a friend of mine." He says conspiratorially, "I think he could use your services, personally, but maybe it's just me."

"Hang on, hang on," I say. "I want to know about you."

"About me?" he says. He is genuinely puzzled. "Docta. You know all about me."

"But how are you doing?"

"Didn't we do this already?" he asks.

I must have had a very interesting expression on my face, and it's reflected in his, a bit of distress, concern, maybe even confusion. Then came that considering look of his. He looks away, and then hits me with the momentary eye contact.

"Mary," he says and looks out across the crowd on the pool deck. It's the first time he's ever called me anything but Docta or Doctor or Doctor Miller, and I become very quiet inside, hyper-vigilant, even — *What does this mean?* I think. He bites his lower lip.

"Mary," he says it again, and what's left of the professional distance — not much, I admit — is blasted away. He's telling me, I think, that we are done with all that now, and he's not paying me to listen to him and I don't get to ask those kinds of questions any more. Or need to. I'm off the hook, he's saying, and he still wants to talk to me. I don't know if he will ever call me "Docta" again, or that I would ever want him to. But then he does.

"Docta," he says quietly, "life didn't get any easier. You gave me opportunity to sort some things out. And walk around town with a great person — and a beautiful woman, to boot. You listened. You didn't judge. You didn't try to fix me. One of the things I learned with you is that I may be bent and banged up and rusty in a few places, but I'm not really broken. Just gettin' old and beat up and tired. And I don't like it much. But, it happens to everybody that lives as long as I do.

"If you want me to tell ya that I'm all better, that I have gained the perfect vision for the future, that ain't gonna happen. But, I'm not all worse, either. I'm OK." He sighs. "I'm OK."

I don't know what to say to this, so, as Larry has taught me, I say nothing. We stand at the bar in companionable silence, watching the rest of the party orbit around us.

Finally, I ask, "Did you decide what to do next?" I want to know I did something for this man.

He laughs and takes a sip of his old fashion. "Continue. Keep going. Keep getting out of bed even when I'm terrified. Stay with my abstinence. Keep fighting the frickin' friction of desire. Figure out how to make a little more money or spend a little less. Maybe even try to fix my house. Maybe even write a book, for Christ's sake."

He looks at me again. "Continue. Not too glamorous, huh? But, functional, at least." He gets his Larry grin. "Now, c'mon. I really do want to introduce you to a friend of mine."

I'm not sure I want to meet his friend, but he leads me across the patio to a man standing alone at the edge of the lawn, looking at the lights across the lake.

"Hey, Bill," Larry says, and Bill turns to meet us. He's about the same age as Larry, though he looks older — Larry doesn't look his age — a big, florid man with huge hands and a somewhat childlike expression on his face. "Bill, this is the gal I told you about. Doctor Miller, this is Bill Warren. He's been in recovery for a little over 5 years now, and he's looking for a little help sorting some things out."

"Pleased to meetcha, Doc," he says, like a prize fighter might say it in a James Cagney movie. He holds out his right hand, and I take it and shake it like I was taught to do when I was ten years old. My fingers can almost bend around the side of his palm.

For all of his size, he is shy as a three-year-old. He hasn't a clue what to say next. Larry speaks for him.

"Bill's a bit on the reserved side," he says, "but he has a big story. He was a prizefighter once, and a cop and a sailor, but most often a drunk. But, not any more, huh, Bill?"

"Nope. No more." he says.

There is nothing more to say, it feels like, and we stand there in a triangle, each waiting for one of the others to say something. Larry is looking at me expectantly.

"Do you live in the city, Bill?" I ask.

"Yeah. Way out on Ash. Almost to the river."

He talks in stops and starts, like a car piloted by someone learning to drive a clutch for the first time.

'Are you interested in seeing a therapist?"

"A shrink, you mean. Larry says you're a shrink."

"I'm a psychiatrist," I say, giving Larry "the look" set on medium. He just grins.

"A psychiatrist," he says, like a five-year-old learning a new word. At least, he's getting older.

"Yes," I say. "A medical doctor who specializes in mental health."

"So, you're a real doctor?" he asks. He is truly surprised.

"Yes."

"But, you're a doctor of the mind," he says.

"I guess you could say that."

"Larry could be right, then," he says. "Maybe I do need to talk to you."

The ridiculous image of this huge man lying on the couch in the session room comes into my mind. "Do you like to walk, Bill?" I ask, and Larry laughs.

Bill looks at Larry, then at me. He doesn't get the joke. "Yeah. I like to walk," he says.

"What if we walk, and you talk and I listen? Would that work for you?"

Bill hesitates. He looks at Larry.

"Bill," Larry says, "this young lady is the best listener I ever met."

Bill looks first at Larry, and then at me. I see a little spark in his eye, as if some small flame has been ignited inside him. I want to think it's hope, but I don't know. I am going to find out, though. Because I'm the best listener Larry ever met.

And there's my reward. It's just like Larry — simple, honest, and yet piled with layers of meaning I may or may not ever get the whole of. I may not have changed his world, but at least, I listened to him talk about it. And, now, it appears, he will be bringing me his friends so I can listen to them, too.

Madeline is going to love this.

September 1
Housewarming Surprise(s)

It is September 1st, the anniversary of my first meeting with Larry. I realize this as I look at the very expensive piece of porcelain he investigated that day, now on display in *my* living room with its gleaming maple floor sporting Aunt Millie's plush oriental rug. It's the Saturday afternoon of Labor Day weekend, and I am hosting my housewarming party.

McElroy is here, along with a mass of other friends and a select few clients who have "graduated." He is standing in the corner of the deck overlooking the back yard and fending off one single woman after another with his wit and charm. I sometimes wonder if he's gay, but I have yet to wonder long enough to ask him. Solving that little mystery one way or the other might ruin things between us, I think, though I don't know why I would think that. It is also none of my damned business, as he himself might say.

Larry has been invited, but he's not here yet, and the party's been on for an hour. I don't know why I'm so intent on his lack of presence. In fact, it's making me ***not*** present, and I don't like that. I need to get out of my head and pay attention to my guests.

My parents are here, seams bursting with pride at their "little girl" all grown up. Both have said almost exactly that; my mother, in the refinished kitchen with Grandma's china standing in the cupboards and *my* cast-iron collection hanging above the range; my dad, a half hour later, in the more private expanse of my back yard. We are looking back at *my* house, full of friends. Their silhouettes show in the windows and a colorful jumble of them clutter the deck. Madeline flits among them with a tray of hors d' ouvres in one hand and a martini in the other. Dad puts an arm around my shoulders and pulls me to his side, as he has always done when I've done something exceptionally well, a stance from which we can both admire whatever it might be.

"I'm very pleased for you, Mary," he says. "This is a wonderful house. I heartily applaud your good sense and diligence." That's my dad. Mr. Formal.

"I've had lots of help with it," I say.

"And they have done a fine, fine job," he says. He's talking about contractors who have helped refurbish it, but I'm tempted to tell him about Larry, Mister Appraiser, without whose encouragement and assistance I would have never had the gumption to do this.

I open my mouth and close it, realizing that introducing my Dad and Larry will be a surreal experience. I'm not sure I'm going to like it. My dad is — oh, my God — nearly 20 years older than Larry. I have to look at him to make sure that could be true, and, yes, it could be. He will be 80 on his next birthday, and so will Mom. I suddenly want to cry, but I don't. Instead, I take his arm and walk back toward the house with him and tell him that I love him.

He laughs. "Hail Mary, full of grace, I love you too," he says, and pats my hand. "Got any significant men in your life?"

He often asks this, and I often say "No," but today, I say, "Yep."

"Really?" he says, "And who would that be?"

"There's you," I say. *And Larry. And McElroy,* I think.

He laughs again. "OK. No more questions."

At that moment, Larry appears on the deck, which he himself redesigned. "My finest architectural triumph," he calls it, with his crazy grin on. He waves at me, and I wave back. In his wake materializes a slim, pretty, forty-something woman. *Who's that?* I think.

Larry's appearance reminds me of when he's been skiing a lot. He's not quite glowing, but he is well-lit, and the slim woman is too. She very deliberately puts her hand into the crook of his arm. "*My* Larry."

My heart doesn't exactly sink, but it does drop a couple of feet and starts taking on water — fast. They begin toward where I am standing quite flat-footed, floored by my own feelings. I begin to panic. Whatever is written on my face I do ***not*** want Larry reading, much less this woman he has in tow.

No, she's not in tow. He's not having to drag her anywhere. She has come alongside — under her own power. They're not in step, and they don't have to be. They're not joined at the hip, but willing fellow travelers.

It never occurred to me that *this* would happen, that Larry would move out of purgatory without even sending me a change of address. How could I not know about this? Or how I would feel about it? *Dammit!*

They are ten feet away, now, and I glance at McElroy, standing serenely in his fort on the corner of the deck. A little after-hours therapy will be in order sometime soon.

"Hello, Docta," he says, in his best Larry voice, and a crack forms in my heart. Not a very big crack, but a tiny fissure that runs in a jagged line right down the front, top to bottom.

"Hello, Larry," I say, and I'm surprised at the sound of my own voice. I sound so freaking normal and happy. How can I sound like that when I feel like *this*?

"Doctor Miller," he says, "I'd like you to meet Grace."

"Grace," I say, and then, "Mary," and hold out my hand. She laughs, a completely grown-up laugh with no holds barred, and takes my hand.

"Anna Smith," she says. "Larry tells me that in some *obscure* language. . . ."

"Hebrew," he says

"OK, I guess it's not *that* obscure. Larry tells me that in Hebrew, 'Anna' means 'grace.' "

"Anna," I say, still holding to her hand. "I'm pleased to meet you."

I'm not even lying. This is one special person, this Anna. She must be. She better be. She has the good guy, after all.

"You OK, Docta?" Larry asks. He's looking at me with concern. I may not look my best right now.

"A little overwhelmed, is all. It's a very full day. And, I'm sorry, but I need to go take care of something right now. It's very nice to meet you, Grace — Anna." She laughs that laugh again. "I'll talk to you both soon."

I do not look back. I go into *my* kitchen and fix myself a drink — three parts gin, no parts vermouth. I go upstairs and lock myself in *my* bathroom. I look at my watch and give myself fifteen minutes, as long as I dare. In fifteen minutes, if you were somewhat sane before, you can become somewhat sane again. I have never been ambushed like this before, even it is by myself, and it might take every second to get back to me.

I take a slug of gin. Thank *God* I don't have any Valium.

"So, Docta," I ask myself, "how long have you been in love with Larry?"

"I don't know," I answer. "It just snuck up on me. And I'm not 'in love with Larry,' 'cause, as Larry once pointed out, wordsmith that he is, to be 'in love with' someone, the other person has to be there too. And he appears to be 'in love' with Grace. Anna. Whatever her name is."

"Point taken," I say, "but you're avoiding the question. How long have you loved Larry?"

"I *said*, 'I don't know!' " I answer, with my teeth stuck together. "It doesn't matter how long. What matters is what *is*."

"That right there seems kind of Larryesque," I say.

"Doesn't it though?" I parry.

I look in the mirror. "You are acting *crazy*," I say.

"Well right now, I sort of am." I admit.

I sit down on the toilet seat, which is closed — no men in this bathroom! *Stupid* men! — and, for five minutes, maybe longer, I bawl. It feels very, very good.

Then, I blow my nose, wash my face, Visene myself, fix my freakin' mascara, put on fresh lipstick and make myself smile at myself in the mirror. I'm sane again. I think. I test by thinking about Larry and Grace — Anna — together downstairs.

Where in hell *did she come from?* I think.

It wasn't hell, I answer. *Larry has been to hell, and he didn't find her there.*

Thinking of them together, I feel a little teary. This won't do. I can't be teary. I practice. I imagine walking up to the two of them and being cheery. I check myself in the mirror. No tears. Good. I *am* sane again. I look at my watch. Three minutes to spare.

"OK, Mary," I say to the gal in the mirror, "you can go back downstairs and join the adults." I sound very much like my dad. I don't mind. He's the first person I plan to seek out when I get to the ground floor.

As I descend the stairs — gracefully, I hope — I see Larry in the corner talking to Adam Whitmore. Larry is animated and Adam is laughing very hard. Over against the living room window, Anna Smith is talking to my mom. My mother is smiling and nodding. For a couple of folks so far apart, they look to have it very much together. This thought makes me smile, which makes me feel extra sane, and I decide that I will join my mom and, um, Grace.

"This is a really great house, Mary," she says. "I was just telling your mom that Larry advised you to buy it. Of course, he would never quite say it that way." She laughs.

I join her. "Yes, sometimes he does seem to speak his own language." Anna gives me an odd look.

My mom excuses herself. "I need to go see what your father is up to." I know without looking that she has spotted him fixing himself another drink. I am alone with "her."

"Where'd you get this rug?" she asks. "It's lovely."

"From my great aunt," I say. "It's really the only reason I bought the house, so I could have someplace to put it. That, and Larry's advice, of course."

She laughs again. I am beginning to like this woman, and I wonder how much she knows about Larry and me. Our meetings, I mean. She looks out the window in sort of a considering mode, and it makes me wonder if they are related and don't know it.

"Larry tells me that if it weren't for you," she says, making eye contact, "that he and I would have never met."

"How so?" I ask.

"He says you helped rebuild him, helped him remember who he was."

"That's nice to know," I say, and it is. I'm practically jumping up and down inside. *Confirmation!* I shout to myself. At *least* I get that.

"When *did* you meet?" I ask.

She laughs. "Do you remember that freak snowstorm we had at the end of March?"

I did. It was the last day of March, two days after my last meeting with Larry —*finally,* I am used to that word. A norther blew in and dumped eight inches of snow on the city that immediately drifted into traffic-stopping piles. The crocuses in my new front yard were taken by surprise, as was everyone else.

"Yes," I say, and she tells me this story. I didn't have my notebook, but I will try to remember it as best I can.

Anna has a place on the other side of the lake, and she had been trying for several hours to get out of her driveway to go pick up her kids from their father's. He is not so tolerant of *anything* about her, which she really doesn't give a tinker's damn about, she says. But, for the sake of the kids, she wanted very badly to pick them up. She knew he would use her lateness as an excuse to go ballistic, no matter what the reason.

Out of the blizzard on his cross-country skis comes her white knight. At least she says he was white; plastered with snow. She just happens to see him out the front window of her house as she is trying to call her plow guy to come rescue her. For some reason, she knows this crazy person will help her. And, "crazy" is her term, not mine. Although, Larry's blizzard habit is something Sherrie and I — and now Anna — might use the term in reference to.

"He said he wouldn't do that again," I say.

"Go skiing in a blizzard?"

"More specifically, ski across the lake in a blizzard," I say.

"Across the lake?" There is surprise in her voice.

"You didn't know?" I feel like I have betrayed him.

"Across the lake." She is looking across my shoulder at her guy standing across the room, and I see something in her eye that tells me that Larry is going to get a talking to.

In a mitigation attempt, I say, "But aren't you glad he did?"

She laughs, and the look changes. "It must have been something he had to do," she says.

Exactly, I think. "So then what happened?"

She leaves her living room, wades into the drift on her front deck and yells at him, "Hey! Can you help me?"

He yells back, "You talkin' to me, lady?" like there's a hundred people out there with him in his blizzard.

"Yes!" she yells back. "I'm talking to you!"

He changes course and skis up on her lawn and she explains to him the problem, like someone is always skiing up on her lawn in the middle of a blizzard.

"Can you put the chains on my car?" she asks

He takes his skis and parka off, brushes himself off as well as he can and apologizes for melting on her floor as he walks through the house to the garage. He finds the chains for her car and starts to put them on. While he's doing this, he asks her if she thinks it prudent to go get her kids in a blizzard. She explains to him the problems with the ex.

He's laying on the floor of her garage with his arms wrapped around the left front tire of her car. He looks up at her and says, "So, maybe I should go with you. Then, when you get stuck, you will have someone to suffer with you as you slowly freeze to death."

"He didn't say 'if,' he said 'when,' " Anna says, "and for some reason, I thought that was the funniest thing that anyone had ever said to me. I found myself thinking, 'This is a very interesting guy.' "

I want to say, "You're preaching to the choir, sister," but I don't.

Larry's concern makes her reconsider, and while he is working on the chains, she calls Bob — her ex — and tells him she just can't make it, that she is stuck until the roads are cleared, and he will just have to deal. He's horrible to her on the phone, and she becomes frantic. She goes back and tells Larry she *has* to get there. Larry holds up a hand, and says "Don't do that. It's not good for you. This isn't your fault, and don't let him make it yours."

Then, he goes around to the other side of the car and starts putting the other chain on.

While he's laying there, he asks, "How long's he been blaming you for his problems?"

She doesn't answer, and after a while, he says, "That long, huh?"

"This too, was hilarious," Anna says. "I thought that I might have found an honest man."

Amen, I think. "Then what happened?" I ask.

Larry finishes putting on her chains and gets up off the floor.

"When the storm clears, you'll be ready," he says. "And, now, I better head back for home."

"Are you crazy?" she said. "There's a blizzard going on."

"No, I'm not crazy," Larry answered. "I thought I was for a while, but my therapist convinced me otherwise."

I can imagine him telling her that, with his sort of crazy Larry grin on.

"He had this manic little grin on," Anna says — she's been taking mind reading lessons from the master, I see — "that made me think that he *might* be a little crazy, but in a good way. If I'd known he'd just skied across the lake, though . . . "

"I think that was probably the last time he'll ever do that," I say, in his defense. "He might have finally found what he was looking for out there."

She gives me that same odd look, and I suspect she has become suspicious about how I feel about Larry.

"What happened next?" I ask.

He starts getting ready to go back out into the blizzard and Anna pulls her trump card. "If you can go out in this blizzard, why can't I?"

"He didn't miss a beat," she says. "He said, 'Because you have children.' "

"And you don't?" she asks.

I can imagine what happened next. Anna Smith suddenly finds herself standing at her front window watching this crazy guy ski off into the white, growing dimmer and dimmer until he is gone, gone, gone. But she is remembering the last thing he said to her, and how he said it. He looks away, out into winter, and then looks back at her. He makes the by-now-famous momentary eye contact, and her heart lurches just a bit. Then, he refocuses on his blizzard and said. "Nope." One beat. Two. He looks back at her and says, with his sort of crazy Larry grin, "At least not yet."

Anna is now smiling past me, and I know Larry has approached. He is standing behind me, and I turn, wondering how long he's been there.

"Now, Docta," he says, with one hand up, as if to hold off my questions, and maybe hers, "If you are wondering why I've not told you about this great fortune that has befallen me" — and I was — "it's because we didn't see each other again until about two months ago."

"Oh," I say. "*After* the deck consultation."

"The what?" Anna asks.

"Larry redesigned my deck for me," I say. "And, I haven't seen him since."

Anna gives me her by-now-familiar odd look, and I *know* she knows how I feel about Larry. I also know that she will keep it to herself, and I silently bless her.

"I've been busy," he says, with his not-so-crazy grin on. "You know where we found each other?"

"Where?"

"Starbucks." He laughs. "Not that I didn't go looking for her a few times before that. Do you know how many houses on the other side of the lake have two-car garages?"

"And how hard it is to find someone when you only know their first name?" Anna chimes in. "After we had each given up on finding the other, I went into Starbucks to get a chai one day, and here was this guy ordering a double vanilla latte. . . ."

"It was my birthday."

"... and we ended up not leaving Starbucks for *hours*."

"It's your fault, Docta," Larry says. "I never would have gone into Starbucks if you hadn't insisted. Thank you."

I make a mental note to kick myself later, but not too hard.

I am suddenly very happy for this good guy and his gal, Grace. Even Sherrie Lee will forgive him this, I bet. There is something solid here, despite the youth and tenderness of their love, as if two well-rooted beings are joining to form an arbor.

Larry will tell me later, after I've introduced him to my Dad, and while Anna is off talking to McElroy, "Don't worry, Docta. We aren't going fast, but we *are* going."

He will look across the room at her and say, "Her kids are great. Especially the five-year-old. And I haven't said you-know-what in front of her yet."

Later still, after dinner, nearly all the others have drifted away to home and dark is coming to shore from across the lake. Madeline is in the kitchen cleaning up — for which she is going to get a big bonus this year, though she would never guess that was the reason — and McElroy and I are sitting on the deck watching night come on.

"Nice place, Miller," he says, and holds out his glass.

I clink mine against his and say, "Thanks."

After a while, after it is well dark, and after I can see stars through holes in the branches and leaves of the big maple in the back yard, I say to the tree, so as not ruin things between us, "McElroy, are you gay?"

He starts to laugh. He laughs for a long time. Finally, he says, "Who wants to know?"

The End

Scars On Top Of Scars

Arrested development meets recovery. Can they coexist? Mary Magdalene Miller, savvy therapist, thinks not. But how do you get a 220-pound ex-cop to give up acting like a scared five-year-old and grow up. Especially when his 55-year-old girl friend is exactly the same age emotionally.

Opening Round
The Boxer

Once there was a man who was punched in the face so many times as a kid that he became a boxer. He was a big boy and he learned in his youth that if he just kept getting up and wading in, eventually his opponent quit. He learned upon becoming a boxer that what he had learned as a youth was not a universal truth. But, true to his style, he kept boxing and he kept wading in.

Bill boxed in high school and then in the Navy, and then as a professional in the heavyweight class, or whatever they call it. I'm not up on boxing, nor do I really want to be. What I know of his boxing career is that he won over half of his fights, and every win was by knockout. The matches he lost were all by decision of the judges.

"Had my head handed to me lotsa times," he says. "Never stayed down."

He made the most money boxing as a sparring partner for more famous fighters. He was a favorite because he never backed off, never quit. Never. Larry says he thinks Bill actually knocked a couple of famous guys out, but Bill will never say one way or the other whether that's true.

"Some days'r better than others," Bill says, if you ask him about that.

When Larry introduced Bill and me, it was an act of kindness — toward which of us, I'm not sure, but maybe both. Kindness is one of Larry's long suits. When he first met his soon-to-be wife Grace — um, Anna — in a blizzard, he was being kind, and she was taken with that, as I had already been.

You might remember Larry Longquist. He's the guy who cashed his 401 K and paid for 30 sessions with yours truly up front and got a discount from Madeline the office manager for paying cash. He was kind to Madeline, too. She remembers him more fondly than any other patient I've ever seen. Not that he was a patient, you understand. He was, at his own insistence, a "client." And we didn't have sessions. We had "meetings."

This is making me laugh, just thinking of Larry, who is, without doubt, one of my most interesting and dearest, um, clients. I love Larry.

McElroy should never learn this. It's in violation of all the rules of psychotherapy to love your patients or clients or whatever in the manner that I love Larry. If you don't keep your professional distance, how can you be objective and effective and analytical and a good therapist? Good question, huh, Dr. McElroy? Not that I'll ever ask you.

Larry's name is not really Larry Longquist, nor is Bill's name Bill Warren. Same for James Fitzpatrick McElroy, but this bunch of made-up names will have to do for this little exercise, appropriately used so I can tell this not-so-made-up story. And, my name is ***not*** Mary Magdalene Miller. *Nom d' plume*. Or, maybe alter ego.

Larry gifted me with my writing style, you might say. When I wrote his story, some was pulled directly from my notes, which were made in the present tense. And some came from memory, by default in the past. Bill's story is put together in the same manner. I ask you, again, not to get tense about tense.

Larry introduced Bill to me at a summer cocktail party on the lake a few months after Larry's prepaid sessions expired. Maybe "cocktail" is an inaccurate descriptor, because Bill wasn't drinking a cocktail. He's an alcoholic. In recovery. Which adds significantly to the meaning of his made-up name. I stole it directly — almost — from the AA Big Book. Bill has been in recovery for a while, over five years, and he was ready to talk about it. Or, at least, wanted to. "Ready" is arguable.

For the first few sessions, I don't think Bill was "ready" to talk about anything. He was shy, reticent, and sometimes monosyllabic. "Yep." "Nope." "Hmm." "Could be." Getting him to "open up" might result in a sentence with six words. "I guess you could be right." It's like chipping away at an iceberg with a pen knife.

Once in a while, though, the berg calves somewhat unexpectedly. Then I have to keep the bow of my thought kayak pointed into the ensuing wave or I get washed away. The best example might be the calving that was the first significant event in the eventual dismantlement of Bill's iceberg.

We are walking along the lakefront bike path that is part of an irregular therapeutic loop we populate during Bill's sessions. Bill doesn't mind them being sessions, nor does he mind being a patient. I'm a doctor, after all, a "doctor of the mind," he called me the day we met. And, he confessed later, he had been feeling "sick in the head."

Bill spots a quarter lying on the trail and stretches down to pick it up. It amazes me how lithe Bill is. For a man over 50 who's a few inches over six feet and around 220 pounds (I'm guessing here), he is very supple. He just leans over from the waist and picks the quarter off the asphalt.

"Lucky day," he says.

"How so?" I ask for reasons I can't fathom. Obviously, finding a quarter is lucky, right? But for some reason, I ask. Intuition, maybe? OK, more likely divine intervention.

Anyway, he shows me the quarter, holding it up with his left hand, heads forward. George gazes out from behind the end of Bill's massive index finger.

"Look," he says, like the five-year-old I will come to understand he is.

I am looking, but not at the quarter. I haven't noticed before, but Bill has no pinky on his left hand, just a third knuckle where the finger used to be. It is obvious that it has been gone for a long time. I'm surprised that I've not noticed.

"What happened to your finger, Bill?"

He jerks his hand back as if he's been caught stealing and stuffs it into his coat pocket.

"Lost it," he says.

Obviously, I think. I have to be careful about being a smart, umm, alec, around Bill. Sometimes, he doesn't get it, and sometimes, he gets his feelings hurt, whether he gets it or not. For such a big guy, he has a thin skin.

So, I'm gentle with him, or try to be.

"*How* did you lose it, Bill?"

He starts to chew on his lower lip, which is one of the ways I have learned to tell when he's stressed. I don't say anything for a while. We just walk along. It's a nice fall day — sunny and not too warm, not too cold. Just right. We come to a bench facing on the lake. He slows and then suddenly sits. He's hunched at the shoulders, and I think that if his legs were shorter, he would be swinging them like a nervous little boy. Instead, he rocks slightly at the waist, and I see he's in anguish.

I sit down. I say nothing. I just wait. Bill's friend Larry taught me this trick.

"You never tell nobody, do you, Doctor Mary?" He's called me "Doctor Mary" since our third session.

I hesitate. "Sometimes, I might ask another doctor his or her opinion, Bill," I say carefully. "And sometimes, I use patient stories in publications, but I never tell who they really are."

He thinks very hard about this for a minute or so. "Like AA," he finally says.

I don't immediately get the connection, but then the word "anonymous" pops into my head.

"That's right."

"When I's a little boy," he begins softly, "maybe five — bein' little wasn't easy in my house, so I don't remember 'xactly — my dad cut my finger off."

"What?" I am incredulous. Bill is holding himself and rocking on the bench.

"I was pinchin' a quarter off the kitchen table an' he caught me. Took the butcher knife an' cut it off. I never took nothin' again. Never."

I am just trying to stay on top of the wave, here, paddling as hard as I can. So he *had* been caught stealing.

"Said it was the punishment for stealin' in the Bible, an' the next time he'd cut 'nother one off. He's really drunk."

"Nobody told?"

"Mama told the hospital I caught it in a car door."

"A car door."

"Old man woulda beat her if she told."

The wave subsides, and I'm able to reduce speed.

"You OK?" I finally ask.

"Yep," he says.

The sun is warm on our backs and it's quiet. A couple comes by on bikes and she laughs at something he says. Bill turns his head and watches them pedal away.

"Never told nobody that before," he says to them as they ride off.

I'm glad he isn't looking at me. It gives me time to wipe the salt spray off my face.

Round 2
Scars On Top Of Scars

Bill has many scars beside the one where his little finger used to be. He has scars on nearly every exposed surface, which isn't much more than his hands and head most of the time. I've seen him in short sleeves, though, and he has scars on his arms, too. I wonder about the rest of him, whether there are scars all over him. I wonder, sometimes, if each of his other scars has a story like the one where his little finger used to be; if he's like Bradbury's illustrated man, only it's the scars that come to life when he sleeps instead of tattoos, of which Bill has none visible. I wonder if I were to start with the bright white line under his right jaw and work my way around to the reddish stretch mark just forward of his left ear, how much of his life story I would learn. I wonder.

I decide to ask a careful variation of the question.

It's a week after he told me about his finger. It's raining and cold. We're bundled up and I have my Goretex jacket on — with the hood up. He's wearing an old blue pea jacket and some sort of woolen tam-o'-shanter, and rain is dripping off the tam onto his neck. I've already asked if he wants to go in, but he assures me he's fine.

"Nice weather," he says, without a hint of sarcasm.

Compared to what? I think.

It's hard to hear with my hood up, though, unless we're facing each other, or without talking loudly enough to violate confidentiality by default. And, I want to ask him this question.

So, I say, "Bill, I need to get out of the rain."

He looks around and then points across the street to an antique mall, one of those places where a few dozen sellers rent 10 by 10-foot booths in a big, old building and see how much stuff they can stuff into their space. I love these places. But, I don't spend a lot of time in them because my house is already full of stuff. Still. . . .

I nod my approval and we jay-trot across the street during a lull in traffic. For a guy who is 50-plus and has been pummeled by other guys as big as him for much of his life and has scars everywhere, Bill is in remarkably good shape.

He opens the entry door, and a jingle bell announces our arrival. A matronly woman about Bill's age is just leaving. She is surprised and happy to see Bill.

"Hello, Bill," she says. "How are you?"

"Fine," he says, nodding. He's a bit shy. "How's things at the shop."

"A little slow, but Christmas is coming, you know."

"Yep. Well, nice to see ya," he says, and she nods at us both and ducks out the door.

"Runs th' quilt store on Fifth an' Sycamore," he says.

And it's obvious she's kind of fond of you, Bill, I think. I'm curious, but everybody in therapy has a life outside of therapy. Hopefully. ***None of your business, Doctor,*** I tell myself.

It's quiet, dry and warm inside, and nearly empty except for us, all of which I am grateful for. Bill takes his tam off and stuffs it in a pocket, and I put my hood back. We walk down the first aisle looking at this and that, the small collectibles I never collect. It's the stuff holding up the collectibles that are my weakness, big oak or walnut pieces from a century or more ago. *Thank God I don't have anywhere to put them,* I think. Having thought that, I remember I have a new house.

I stop in front of a glass front bookcase, the kind where the front of each shelf slides up and in like a miniature garage door. It's lovely. *Maybe in the office,* I think. *I can take the credenza home.* I am now smiling.

"Nice," says Bill.

"You like it, too?" I say.

"Really pretty," he says.

"Do you remember how you got each of your scars?" I ask. *So much for timing, Dr. Miller,* I think.

I expect him to jerk or look at me in surprise, maybe, or at least pause to let the question sink in before he answers, but he says immediately, "Nope," and nothing more. He lifts the door on the top shelf and it slides flawlessly out of the way.

"Nice," he repeats, and then closes the door again.

"Not all of 'em," he says. "Some I's pretty drunk. I got scars on toppa scars."

When I first met Bill, I characterized his speech as proceeding somewhat like a car being driven by someone learning to use a clutch. This is still true, even as he has become more comfortable talking to me, a process that has taken a few sessions and continues. Our first working meeting was a disaster, at least in my opinion. We'd done the business stuff the week before, the formalities of filling out forms and meeting Madeline and letting the two of them talk about money while I hid in my office. I hate talking about money with my patients, clients, whatever you want to call them. If I find out what their annual income is, it might temper my care, for one thing. So, I don't ask. Nonetheless, money comes up in therapy all the time, but I try to keep the discussion to how they feel about it, not how much they have.

The next week, as agreed, Bill and I met at the city Starbucks — we only have one so far —for our first real session. It was apparent to me the night Larry introduced Bill and I that he would never be lying on the couch in inner sanctum. I'd have to get a bigger couch, for one thing.

I did find one that would fit him just the other day in another antique mall on the other side of downtown. Nice couch. But I don't need it because, like his buddy Larry, Bill likes to walk. Unlike his buddy Larry, Bill has a hard time walking and talking. Or more accurately, talking. He *can* do both at the same time, when he finally decides to say something. It's that he doesn't appear to have a lot to say. Which, for me, as his therapist who is supposed to draw him out verbally, is not quite maddening, but daunting. If Bill was paying me by the word — his own — I would go broke on him.

On our first walk around the downtown, he said maybe nine words in the first ten minutes, many monosyllabic, in answer to my opening questions.

"How are you feeling today, Bill?"

"Fine."

"Is there anything in particular you would like to talk about?"

Pause. "Nope."

I knew how old he was, already, but I thought, *What the hell?* and asked him anyway.

"Fifty-six."

"Where were you born?"

"Buffalo." This, perhaps, explains why he thinks today's weather is "nice."

"Any siblings?"

He looks at me with question marks in his eyes.

"Brothers and sisters."

"Oh. Yep." No further explanation is offered.

Finally, in desperation, at about the ten-minute mark, I fall back on the Freudian opening line. "Tell me about your mom, Bill." I didn't know, yet, what asking him about his father might lead to.

He gets a faraway look in his eye. "She left."

"What do you mean, 'left?' "

"Went away."

"Reticence" has been redefined in my personal dictionary. Today, there's a picture of Bill beside the word.

"*When* did she go away?"

He names a year. I do the math. Forty-four years ago. When Bill was twelve years old.

"Did she ever come back?"

He looks at me like I have two or three heads. "Hell, no," he says, as if he were explaining the obvious to an idiot.

We walk in silence for a while and I try to keep the nose of my mental kayak pointed at the berg. After about twenty paces, he says, "Sorry, Doctor," — he hadn't started calling me Doctor Mary yet — "Sorry for cussin."

Inside, I giggle. *That was cussing?* I think. *You should meet Hildegard the Horrific, Bill.* That is not her real name, of course, but as refined as she appears on the outside, she has a mouth like a sailor in confession — umm, I mean "session."

"No worries, Bill," I say gently. "The word 'hell' isn't going to offend me."

He nods.

I had to finally stop asking questions that day. In his short answers, there was so much hidden that I needed to sit down and write some notes before they escaped me. But I was worried about what the day meant to him.

"Bill," I said, "If you don't mind, I need to make some notes. Can we sit for a while?"

"Sure."

So, we sit on a bench along Fifth while I scribble down impressions of our session. He sits quietly, watching people walk by, being greeted by some of them. I'm blasting away on the note pad, trying to keep ahead of my own thoughts.

Out of nowhere, he says, "This is good."

"What's good?" I ask.

"Talkin,' " he says.

This is when I find out he's a bit thin skinned. To me, this is hilarious. I'm trying to get him to talk, and he *is* talking, by his own definition. I try not to, but I can't not. I start laughing.

"What's funny?" he says, like a little boy.

I am suddenly standing on thin ice. One wrong move, and I'm in over my head and Bill is never going to mumble a monosyllable at me again. I take a slow, deep breath.

"Bill," I say, "it's not so much funny as it makes me happy. I laugh when I'm happy. I'm happy that you think talking to me is good."

"Well, it is," he says, still on the defensive.

"I'm glad you think so," I say, and I really, really mean it. And he knows I mean it.

And the moment passed. Without any additional scars.

Whew.

Round 3
Salt and Pepper Shakers

Meanwhile, back at the antique mall, "Scars on top of scars," I say.

Bill holds out his hands, palms down. He closes his hands and reopens them. Between the second and third knuckles on his seven fingers are a myriad of marks and minor disfigurements, and the skin looks to be a quarter-inch thick. I want to touch it and see, but I resist. If I was seven, I don't think I could.

"Boxin' leaves scars," he says. "I still punch every day."

"Punch." I say.

He drops his hands and starts walking down the aisle toward the back of the store.

"I work bags every mornin," he says. He stops in front of a booth specializing in salt and pepper shakers. He picks up and inspects a pair of glass birds, one black, one white. "Speed bag and heavy bag." He returns the birds to their perch.

It's dawning on me why Bill is in such good shape.

"Every day?" I ask.

"'Cept Sundays. Day off."

Now, he has a pair of small, porcelain shakers in his right hand, shaped and colored like robin's eggs. He inspects them very carefully, holding one upside down between his thumb and index finger to look at the cork plug in the bottom. It looks tiny in comparison and I am reminded of how huge his hands are.

"I like 'em," he says, matter-of-factly. He continues in the same tone, "If I don't, I freeze up."

"Freeze up."

"Took a couple of weeks off once, right after I quit drinkin'. Took me a month to get flexy again."

"Flexy?"

He turns away from me, comes up on his toes and goes into a boxer's stance. He dances forward and punches the air — left, left, left — very quickly, so fast I can't imagine he isn't going to knock something off a shelf. Then, his body changes angle. The right follows in an extended arc, and boom, I imagine it landing. So does he, I think, as it pulls up two inches short of a book shelf I was sure was doomed.

He turns back to me with a grin on his face I'd not seen before, a big, wide joyous smile. "Flexy," he says.

"Is that a word you made up?"

"Nah. Had a manager when I's a kid. Said I's th' most flexy boxer he ever met. Said I had reflexes and I's flexible. Flexy."

We are far down the aisle, now, and he still has the robin's eggs in his right hand.

"Are you going to buy those?" I ask.

"Yep. Angie will like 'em."

"Angie?"

"My girlfriend."

"I didn't know you had a girlfriend, Bill."

"Yep."

"Does she live nearby?"

He turns shy. "We been together twenty-two years."

"Twenty-two years? You live together? Now?"

He is blushing. "Yep."

"You never got married?"

"Huh-uh." He's looking at his feet.

"Why not?"

"Never asked her," he says.

"Why not?"

He doesn't say anything. We know session time is nearly up and we are by nonverbal agreement — of course — approaching the cashier's stand.

The young woman at the counter looks up expectantly. "Hello, Bill," she says, with a big smile. "How have you been?"

"Good. You?"

"Just fine," she says. "Nice to see you."

"Thanks." He's shy again. "You, too."

Bill pays for the shakers and she carefully wraps them in newsprint and puts them in a plastic bag. He pulls the tam out of his pocket and replaces it with the packet of robin's eggs.

We are out the door and standing under the awning in front of the store. The rain is not letting up.

"You know lots of people," I say.

"Yep," he says. And nothing more. He's not being evasive. It's like he's confirming what is obvious. I stuff my questions back into the "none-of-my-business" file.

Then, he says to me, as I'm putting my hood up, "Never asked her 'cause I'm afraid she might say 'no.' "

I look at him in surprise. They've been together 22 years and he's afraid she might say no? He's staring at the ground, looking very, very pointedly at his shoes. He finally swivels his gaze and looks down at me — Bill is a lot taller than I am — and I see that he is ashamed. If he were really four or five, his lower lip might be quivering, and maybe it is, figuratively. I'm not sure.

"Let me see your hands, Bill," I say.

He holds them out to me again, fingers closed, and I indulge my seven-year old. I touch the skin on the face of his fists, and it *feels* a quarter inch thick, too.

"Bill," I say, without looking at him, "with hands like these, you shouldn't be afraid of anything."

He holds them up and looks at them himself.

"Maybe," he says. "Maybe so."

Round 4
Enter the Monster

With Bill, it's not so much of a smooth progression as it is a stutter step — like the way he talks, as a matter of fact, so maybe it's natural. Bill has more resources that I might imagine, Madeline assures me — the VA is involved — so there is no deadline, but measurable headway is important to me. I am accepting the fact that Bill's never going to be loquacious, but I love it when he puts two or three sentences together once in a while.

When he does, I also pay attention.

"Tell me about your dad," I say, two weeks after he confessed the reason for the loss of his left pinky. We are, by my design, back at the same spot, sitting on the same bench. Once a confessional is established as such, it's good to revisit it from time to time. Besides, it's a beautiful October day and we all know there aren't many left.

His eyes go bright and flinty, a look I'd never seen before. Not that his expression surprises me, knowing just one not-so-small detail of his relationship with the man.

"Dead," he says, "twelve years dead."

"What else?"

Bill pulls his lips together, sealing them tight, working them against each other. It's as if something is trying to break out of his mouth.

"Can't speak ill of the dead," he finally says.

"Pretend he's not dead, Bill. Just for a minute."

"Why?"

"So you can say what you're thinking."

"I'm thinkin' I'm glad he's dead."

I'm surprised by his vehemence. It must show, because he says, "Not good, huh?"

"I don't think," I say carefully, "that it's ever good to hate a parent, father or mother. Maybe you have good reason, but to continue to hate them — I think it's harmful."

"How come?"

"Because our parents are part of who we are. It's like hating part of yourself."

He doesn't say anything for a while. We just look out at the lake. A runner I know lopes by. "Hi, Mary," she calls out.

I wave and Bill pulls himself to his feet and begins walking after her.

"Hey," I say. "Wait for me." He doesn't slow down and I hustle after him.

He's looking very pointedly at the ground when I catch up with him, walking fast. I can keep up, but just, without actually breaking into a trot.

"He's a monster," he tells the bike path.

I'm surprised by his use of the term and the present tense. Until I put it into context. Bill, the little boy, is talking. Monsters are really in the closet and under the bed when you live with a mean drunk, and they never die. You never know when or which one's going to show up. Apparently — witness Bill's missing finger and missing mother and missing years — his dad was a mean drunk.

"What was his name?" I pant.

He stops suddenly and faces the lake.

"William." He spits it out. "William Warren."

"Same as yours?"

"Same as mine."

He's extraordinarily angry, now, nearly frighteningly so. I feel myself pulling back, ready to run. I point the kayak right at him and begin paddling hard.

"Not Bill?"

He strains the words through his teeth and they hit me in the face like wind-driven sleet. "Only when he's drunk. Drunk, he's Bill. Sober, he's William. God help ya if you call him Bill when he's sober or William when he's drunk. If Ma said it wrong, she got backhanded. We didn't call him nothin' 'cept 'Daddy,' and never even that 'cept when we was beggin' him not to hit somebody." His tone changes to that of a frightened child. " 'Don't hit me, Daddy! Daddy, stop hittin' her! Daddy, leave him alone!' "

He stops and pulls his lips together once more. I'm surprised he doesn't make the motion of zipping them shut, like a kid sealing in a secret he knows. He looks everywhere but at me, and his eyes are bright. He's breathing hard. But the storm is subsiding.

Finally, he takes a deep, shuddering breath. He starts walking slowly up the path. In a different, gentler voice, he says, "I's second oldest. My sis Meg's two years older than me, but she's small. I's always big. Bigger 'n anybody my age. Bigger 'n my mom by the time I's 10. I took more beatin' than anybody else, 'cause when he's drunk, I'd wade in and grab him. Distract him, and he'd forget who he's workin' on. When he's sober, ya couldn't distract him. If you interfered, you's just next."

He blows a big whistling sigh out through his lips, pulls a blue paisley handkerchief out of a pants pocket, blows his nose, wipes his eyes. "He ain't no parta me, Doctor Mary. Rather be an orphan found on the front porch than think he's parta me."

A question occurs to me, a sort of dangerous question, but I must ask. "When you were drinking, Bill, did you ever beat anyone?"

To his incredible credit, he laughs in the same gentle way. "See," he says, "that's how I know he ain't no parta me. I never beat nobody smaller or weaker. Nobody defenseless. Nobody 't all, 'cept it was a fair fight, even when I was drinkin,' 'cept one time."

"One time?"

"One time." He says it in such a way, I know who it was.

"Your dad."

He nods and walks for a while, and then begins to talk. The speech is the longest he's ever made in my presence.

"I's 16. Been boxin' in school for two years. Meg's gone soon as she got a job. Got me a job, too, and we got a little 'partment. My boxin' coach took in my brothers —twins two years younger than me. Mama — she's long gone. Nobody at home anymore he could hurt. He come one night — found us somehow — and told us ta come home. He's sober. Threatened ta beat us both if we didn't. Had a baton he thought he's gonna use on me. Meg and me. Somethin' cold came on that night. We went down in the street in front of our 'partment building. Never had a chance. Never even knew to put his hands up. I beat hell out him, first with these" — he holds up his fists — "and then with his own stick. 'til the police come and stopped me."

He goes silent and I count ten paces before I ask, "Did you get arrested?"

"They knew us. Been to our house lotsa times. The neighbors would call 'em when Mama started screamin.' They took him to the jail infirmary. Told me to stay away from 'im. Told 'im to stay away from us. Sergeant Tom told me later what they told 'im, that if he came back, next time they wouldn't rescue 'im. He never did."

"That was the last time you saw him?"

"Nah. Saw him lots of times after that."

"Where did you see him?"

He doesn't immediately answer. After a few steps, he stops and swings to where he's looking at the lake.

"He use ta come watch me box."

There is something in the way he says this, some sense of satisfaction, that gives me pause.

Round 5
Children

"Do you have children, Bill?" I ask one day.

"Kids? Nah. Not me. Never got around to it."

"What about Angie. Didn't she want kids?"

He laughs. "Angie *has* kids. Three. Good kids. One in the Army twenty years. Other two married with their own kids. One's in Seattle. Other in a little town in Oregon. Army guy is single. In Afghanistan right now. Special Forces."

I think about this for a while.

"So, it sounds like you do have kids in a sense."

He grins. "Sort of. They haven't always liked me. Now, we get along pretty good."

"How old were they when you met Angie?"

"Don't know." He squints. "When we moved in together, the oldest, the Army guy, was just in service. Eighteen, maybe? The girls were 12 and 15. Something like that."

"You don't remember exactly."

He gets this funny look. "Angie and me. We's drinkin' buddies before we's lovers." He laughs at the word, like he's never said it before. "There's lotsa things we don't remember 'xactly. Didn't meet the kids until I's livin' with her."

"Is Angie in recovery, too?"

"You mean AA?"

"Yes."

"Never sure if I should say or not."

"But she is."

He nods.

"Did you go to AA together?"

"You don't tell nothin,' right?"

"Right." I want to laugh at his innocence, if that's what it is. Not at it, really, because I applaud his determination to do this correctly, however he might define "correctly." His sense of honor, I suppose.

"We go together sometimes."

"Still."

"Yep."

"Did you quit drinking together?"

"Oh, hell — I mean, heck, no. She's got her 15-year pin."

"Fifteen years?"

He nods. By his look, he's very proud of her. I can see he loves her very much.

"So she started a long time before you?"

"She got sober a long time before me."

"Did you go to AA when she first started?"

"We started together."

"And you've been sober how long?"

"You know."

"Five-plus years."

"Get my six-year pin in four months." He stops and then walks to the nearest tree, a maple three feet through, and knocks on it with his knuckles. "Knock wood," he says.

Yeah, Bill, I think. *Don't jinx it.*

I realize, once again, how fragile abstinence really is, no matter how long you've been fostering it.

"So," I ask "did you go to AA for the other ten years while you were still drinking?"

"Yep."

I don't know quite what else to ask, so I let it rest for a while. We're walking through the park in my neighborhood, a few square blocks of lovely lawn populated by Norway maples, black locust, chestnuts, occasional black walnuts and obligatory Colorado blue spruce, looking out of place and lonely. They're beautiful trees, but I'll never understand why folks can't leave them in the mountains where they belong.

The leaves are nearly all off the hardwoods, now, and we rattle through a crunchy layer of red, gold, brown and silver castoffs waiting for the city crew to come rake them into the gutter so the big beeping sweeper can pick them up. I'm glad they haven't yet.

"She never said she'd leave me if I didn't stop drinkin'," he says, after a while, "but she would if I stopped goin' to meetin."

We swish through the leaves for a dozen more paces. He gets a grin and says, "Guess she knew it'd take, finally."

I find myself wanting to meet this Angie; wondering if Angie isn't short for Angel.

Round 6
Frozen In Time

Therapizing on the run — or the walk, as it may be — has its challenges. It's hard to take notes, for one thing. It's sometimes hard to hear and be heard. The Larry Experiment taught me to carry a small recorder so at least I could remember what I ask, which, thankfully, helps me remember what the answers were, though sometimes not exactly.

I could call it the Larry Experience, but it was really an experiment, and not a controlled experiment, mind you, but an experiment in giving up control. Now there is the Larry *Method*. Don't tell Dr. McElroy. Dr. McElroy uses more conventional methods than walking around town with a digital recorder in his pocket, listening to his patients go off about their life. And, of course, so do I with many of my patients. But, the Larry Method demands letting go. "Let go and let God," they say in Alanon. This could be the slogan for the Larry Method.

The Larry Method is totally appropriate for Bill's therapy, for there is no rushing it. We sometimes go a few weeks with nothing to report, no iceberg calving, no waves, no monsters jumping out from under the bed; just the minutia of his daily life. He works at the same gym where he works the bags every morning. He goes to three or four AA meetings a week, and we talk about what he learns there about himself and his disease. Sometimes, he talks about his brothers and sister. His sister lives here and he sees her often. His brothers are on opposite coasts and don't talk to him often or each other at all, which is painful for him to even think about.

"They's twins, fer cryin' out loud. When they's kids, they's joined at the hip."

The Larry Method takes agendas and schedules and expectations and throws them out the window. More accurately, we bring them along on our walks and they fall by the wayside as we whisk along Seventh or the bike path. They slide off the table when the weather's nasty and we face each other across some small table at Starbucks or Frozen In Time, the ice cream parlor in the lobby of my building. Which is where we are now, because it's 10 degrees and howling outside. Bill's from Buffalo, maybe, but I'm not.

It's the first visit to Frozen In Time for Bill, and there's a new girl behind the counter. Her name is Agnes, and she's not quite as good as Larry's young friend Sherri Lee was when she worked here. At least not yet. Agnes hasn't been here long.

Sherri Lee retired from the ice cream business and got a job as a waitress at the Neutron, a fast-moving club at the west end of Seventh with a deck looking out toward the lake for dinner in the summer and a good bar full of reddish gold light and semi-private, cushy booths where you can almost hide, but friends can find you if they want. Dr. McElroy and I do after-hours therapy there about once a week on average.

Usually on Wednesdays, which runs on the shorter of my two daily schedules, we meet there about 6 o'clock. Sometimes, we walk there together, six blocks through the heart of downtown. McElroy's office is in my building, too. But most often, we meet there because he's done at 5, Mr. Conventionality that he is. I lock up — Madeline also leaves at 5, lucky gal — at 5:50 or so, depending on if my last patient of the day is extra talkative or not.

One thing about McElroy, though, is that he can make an old-fashioned last a long time. He always has at least half of his first drink left when I get there after him, and he's always got us a booth, which at the Neutron, is a premium at 6:00 on a Wednesday night. So, bless you, Dr. McElroy. Bless you.

At Frozen In Time, Agnes is struggling with my hot fudge sundae. And, then, she will have to build Bill's banana split. It will take a while, so we have time to talk, which, of course, is good, because Bill takes his time about talking. And, today, as the Deepfreeze moves in from Canada, I want Bill to talk about his mom.

"So, Bill," I say, cannily sneaking up on the subject like a good therapist, "what happened to your mom after she left when you were twelve?"

"Twelve," he says. He is not at all phased by the question. "Nah. 'leven. Almost twelve, maybe. Let's see." He thinks for a minute, and ticks off some mental list on his fingers. " 'leven and a half."

"When's your birthday?"

"December 4th. Three days b'fore Pearl Harbor. That's how I 'member."

That's an odd way to remember your own birthday, Bill. I think it, don't say it.

"So she left in June?"

He nods. "June 9th."

"You remember the exact day?"

"Three days after D-Day," he says.

"D-Day."

"Invasion of Normandy."

"Another battle anniversary."

"Sort of. D-Day was more than a battle. A whole bunch of battles. Omaha Beach, Juneau Beach. Some went on for days."

"You know a lot about World War II," I say.

"Know a lot about 'merican war history."

"From . . . ?"

"French 'n' Indian War — lasted nine years —first European-based war in the 'mericas. Lots of European-native battles before, but they's pretty one-sided."

That wasn't the intent of my question. I wondered where and how he had learned this.

"History Channel?" I ask.

"Nah. TV's boring. Maybe not the History Channel all the time, but all sounds the same." He waves his arms "Everybody's all dramatic."

He gets a grin on and intones in announcereze, " 'Facin' the men landing at Anzio was the famous 101st Panzer Division.' Like we don't know how it turned out already."

"Not everybody does, Bill."

" 'spose not. I read a lot. Been reading about wars since I was reading.' "

Bill has never revealed the historian side of himself before. In fact, I'm surprised, and somewhat ashamed to be so. He has always struck me as a sort of simple guy — read "not so intelligent" — because of his manner of speech.

Note to self: *Reticence and intelligence have not so much to do with each other.*

I have a new appreciation of the big guy with the scars sitting across the tiny table from me, now digging into a banana split.

"So what happened after your mom left?"

He takes a bite of banana and does not talk with his mouth full. After he swallows, he says, "Old man had one less person to beat up on." He takes another bite, and I, who am learning to time my questions, wait until he is working at the dish for his next bite to ask, "What happened to your mom?"

"Don't know."

"She never contacted you?"

He sighs a big sad sigh. "Runnin' for her life. The old man's gonna kill her one day when me or Meg wasn't 'round. She's a tiny woman. The old man never gets better, just worse. He's not as big as me, but he's big, too."

He speaks of them both in the present tense. I think. Maybe he's contracting "she was" or "he was," like he does with "he is" and "she is" but I don't think so. I chew on that for a while, while he takes a couple of bites of his split. He looks sad and ashamed. At least, that's my translation.

"Don't like talkin' 'bout this," he mumbles, almost to himself, back to being five or four or however old he was when that finger was lost. I've watched him go back there a number of times, especially when the questions and answers get hard and personal and hurtful. I reach out and touch his hand, the big scarred-up paw that's holding down the banana split dish. I allow myself to do that now, after the antique mall. McElroy might not like it, but I like Bill. A lot. I can touch his hand if I want.

Neener neener, McElroy, I think.

"It's OK. Another time, then."

Bill nods and takes a bite of his banana split. He is working his way methodically from the strawberry end toward the chocolate end. He is rocking in the wire chair like the stressed out little boy that he is right now. I let him finish before I say another word.

Round 7 The Monster Revisited

The weather is wintry, but it hasn't started snowing yet and we're walking up Fifth, away from the lake. It's the day after Bill's birthday —two days before Pearl Harbor Day. We missed last week because of Thanksgiving. Bill's sessions are Thursday afternoons, same as Larry's were. Each of us has a Starbucks cup in one hand — Bill's birthday present is a caramel frappuccino —and we are really strolling. Several people have greeted us, but Bill is leading by a two-to-one margin.

The Christmas decorations are in the store windows and we are, by silent and mutual agreement, enjoying them as we walk by. The big old chain department store in town — still holding on by the skin of its corporate teeth — always goes whole hog at Christmas.

I've been coming here at Christmas since my mom and dad first brought me at four to see the big Santa's workshop display in the Fifth street window, the kind that moves, with elves and even a reindeer — Rudolph by the look of his nose — standing in the corner watching the progress. The store still has the display and they still set it up each Christmas season. Rudolph moves his head back and forth in animated awe in time to the elf with the hand saw who is perpetually cutting a board for some new creation. Only the toys in Santa's bag and sled have changed in the thirty-something years since the three of us held hands walking down this street in the red and green light of the season.

I'm thinking of my parents as Bill and I stand in front of the magic window — that's how I've always thought of it— and watch Santa tap gently away with his little hammer on a model train engine. I maybe should be working, but this place has drawn me away from it. Mom and Dad will both turn 80 in the next six months. They are — knock wood — both in really great health, mentally and physically. But still. Eighty years on the same planet is a long time, longer than the average bear hangs around, certainly.

Gazing through the window, I become aware of Bill's bulky reflection next to mine. He's turned away. *Back to work, Dr. Miller,* I tell myself.

"Sorry, Bill," I say. "Shall we go?"

" 't's OK, Doctor Mary. Just thinkin."

"About what."

"Ma."

That perks my ears up, even under my fleece cap.

"What about her?"

He starts strolling again, dropping his empty Starbucks cup in a street trash container. I pace him along the front of the store.

"She'd try to make Christmas, and the old man would tear it down after a few days — first time he come home drunk. Called it a waste. But she always tried."

"How did your folks meet?"

"How do people meet? She's a waitress. He's a gandy dancer. She serves him food. He asks her out."

"Gandy dancer?"

"Railroad worker. Never made nothin' but laborer. Guys he started with was in charge of him. He hated 'em. Railed on 'em every time he come home. Took it out on us. Our fault for bein' born."

His hands are clinched, and he's walking faster.

"You were thinking about your mom," I remind him.

He slows and then stops, opens his hands and rubs them together, warming them up. I've not seen Bill with gloves on yet, and this day his hands are bright red from exposure.

"Said I don't know what happened to her?"

"Yes."

He's standing facing me, looking over my head back the way we came. "I know where she is."

"You do?" I'm surprised.

He looks down at me. His expression is flat and guarded. "Didn't mean to lie to you, Doctor Mary."

"Well, Bill, knowing where she is and knowing what happened to her could be two different things, couldn't they."

He looks up again, over the top of my head.

"Yep."

"Where is she, Bill?"

"Albany."

"New York?"

"Yep."

"How do you know that?"

"Hired a detective. Year I quit drinkin,' finally, I's hot to figure stuff out. Like we're doin' now."

Glad you think so, Bill, I think. *I'm not so sure, myself.*

"Ma could tell stuff I don't know, and I's excited to know more, but the detective said she's married. With kids. 'n' grandkids. Never thought 'bout that. Maybe better left alone. I didn't get in touch."

I'm in the math mode. She leaves when her oldest is 13 or 14. She's already had four kids. Would she want more?

"How old is your mom now, Bill?"

He thinks for a minute. "Seventy-four, I guess."

Back to the math: She left 44 years ago. She was 30.

"She had your sis when she was how old?" I ask

"They got married 'cause they had to," he says. It sounds like confession.

"So your mom was pregnant at 16."

"Maybe. Maybe 15. Don't know."

"How old was your dad?"

He looks at the sidewalk, scuffs the bottoms of his wingtips against the concrete — I've never seen him wear anything else on his feet, and I wonder if he boxed in wingtips — and works his lips against each other. He cracks them open, reluctantly.

"Heard her tell her friend one time she didn't want to but he made her."

"He forced her to have sex."

He nods. I am incensed, and I am not careful when I ask the next question.

"How old was your dad, Bill, the first time he raped your mother?"

He's rocking back and forth, hands stuffed in his pockets.

"First time," he says. It's like a sledgehammer right to the chest for him, and I'm screaming at myself inside: ***Stupid, stupid, stupid! How can you be so stupid?***

To his credit, he doesn't stumble, doesn't retreat, just wades in, head hunched down between his huge shoulders.

"First time," he says again, as if he is assimilating the thought, the image, the whole concept. His head comes up.

"Maybe 30," he says. "Don't know."

He's a monster, I think. ***That's what Bill said. I didn't want to believe that. Too late now.***

Bill, who has never been a mind reader like Larry seems to be, steps up and takes a turn at it.

"Told ya," he says. "He's a monster."

Round 8
If I Let Him Die

On the Thursday before the Thursday before Christmas — if it were 1944, the Battle of the Bulge would be starting, Bill tells me — I say to Bill, "Do you always talk about your dad in the present tense, as if he's still alive?"

"Told me to pretend he was still alive," Bill says.

Way to go, Dr. Miller, I think.

I look at him and he has a funny smile on his face. I realize he's teasing me.

I accuse him of it and he laughs.

I'm surprised, and can't quite understand why; maybe because I don't expect Bill to be sophisticated enough to know how to tease someone. But, I join his laughter, and he gets all shy, like a little boy might after a successful foray into humor.

We are trekking cross town on Buckeye. I have my favorite Hudson's Bay blanket overcoat on and we are kicking through a few inches of fresh snow on the wide sidewalks of one of our old neighborhoods. Houses from the 1920s sit back from the street on big lots with big trees.

After another quarter of a block, I ask, "Is that really why?"

"Nah," he says. He heaves a huge sigh. "If I let 'im die, I might forget ta hate 'im."

This time, I've already got the kayak pointed into the wave. I knew this could cause a big swell. It was my intention.

"You do that on purpose, then." It's not a question.

"I guess."

"Do you think it's good for you, Bill, to hate someone who's dead? To purposefully hate anyone?"

"What *should* I do with him?"

Great question, Bill! I shout inside, and one word comes into my mind. *Forgive.* But for whatever reason, I don't think Bill's ready to hear that. His hatred is like the iceberg. Maybe it *is* the iceberg. It won't melt in a day. And, it appears to be precious to its possessor. Bill goes out of his way to keep his iceberg.

I ask the question that has suddenly appeared on the screen in my mind. Something is adding up here.

"When he used to come to watch you box, did you hate him then?"

He gets quiet, and his lips seal tight, so I know there's something important about to happen. I wait in the calm water, paddle across the gun'l.

He stops in the sidewalk and faces into the street. I see, for the second time, that hard glint in his eye. He looks right at me, and it occurs to me that the reason Bill can tease me is that he's starting to trust me. Does trust me. And that is a big, big deal for Bill. To trust anyone is huge.

" 'member I told you I never stayed down?"

I nodded.

"If I was on the mat, ta get back up, all I had ta do was think th' other guy was him."

The iceberg calves, but the chunk slides straight down into the water. It's huge, like a quarter of the main berg, it feels like. There is no distinct wave, but as the fragment slides under, I suspect there will be a disturbance when it breaches, comes back to the surface. How big, I'm not sure. Nor am I certain of when it might happen.

But, I'm thinking, *So, the decisions he lost, he lost to his dad? But the knockouts were all his. What does that mean?* The knot between my eyebrows might have been bigger, but I don't know how.

Bill noticed. "Make sense?" he asks.

"On the surface, it does." I smile at my own — private — iceberg joke. "But, I have a question. I think I do, anyway. I just don't know what it is yet."

"OK," he says, all patient.

I'm cracking myself up today.

We start walking again while I sort through Jung, Frankl, a little McElroy and even some Freud. Freud is not one of my heroes. I think of him as the guy who put "anal" in psychoanalysis. But he had some good thoughts, too.

What's here that I'm seeking? I haven't said a thing in four minutes, not a record between Bill and I, but it's getting close.

"Sorry, Bill," I say, "I'm ruminating."

"What?"

"Thinking."

"Oh. 'Bout what I said?"

"Yes."

"Me, too."

"Really." I stop. Across the street, a house is lit up for Christmas. I admire it as I ask, "So, have you reached any conclusions?"

"Conclusions?"

"Do you have other thoughts that came from the thought that the thought of your dad . . . " I stop. I'm hilarious today.

"Yep."

Holy logic, Batman! I think *He followed that?"* Bill may be a *lot* smarter than I think he is.

"And. . . ."

"Fights I got knocked down and got back up?" he says.

"Yes," I say.

"Won 'bout half of 'em." He's chewing on his lip.

"Go on, Bill. What's the rest of that thought?"

"Don't know if this makes sense."

"Try me."

"Maybe. . . ." Now he has his own knot between his eyes. "Maybe I should say 'Thanks' for that? Made me a better boxer."

"Who would you say thanks to? Your dad?"

"Oh, hell . . . heck no! Sorry. No. God, maybe. Yeah. God."

I'm still thinking of forgiveness. "That's a start, Bill."

"On what?"

I'm caught out. It takes me a few seconds to think of a reasonable answer. Finally, I just jump in. Maybe he's ready to start thinking about thinking about forgiveness.

"Getting things straight between you and your dad."

He nods and doesn't say anything for a bit. We start walking again. I glance at him after a few steps and he's got a little smile on his face.

"What?"

He grins and says, "He's dead, ya know."

I giggle and he laughs right out loud.

A little black humor is better than none at all, I always say sometimes.

He sobers soon and I note his gaze has gone inward. He's thinking about something I don't know what, and I don't think I'm going to ask him today. It's tied to that big piece of the berg that slid under the surface earlier in our walk. It will reappear. I hope I'm ready when it does. I hope Bill's ready.

Round 9
Meeting Angie

I wasn't prepared to meet Angie, even though I once wished that I would. Not that I was ***unprepared***; I just never expected one way or the other that it would happen. Period. I have quite a few patients who have spouses — partners — I know only in abstract. So meeting Angie was not in the plan, but in one of those out-of-the-blue moments, I do.

"Doctor Mary." I recognize Bill's voice from behind me in the grocery store. I'm standing in the produce section marveling at the price of broccoli. I can afford it, but I'm not sure how some other folks can. Maybe that's why there is such a big supply here. I turn toward the voice and there's Bill with an eggplant in his hand and a little grin on his face. Standing nearby, on the other side of him, hefting an avocado like she's thinking about how far she could throw it, is a small woman with a mop of shoulder-length lightly graying red hair. It's not bright red, but a deep, dark red; almost brunette; chestnut. She's small, but not tiny. He gestures toward her, pointing nearly over his shoulder.

"This's Angie," he says, and the way he says it leads me to believe that he expects me to be thinking, ***This explains*** everything***!***

Angie looks from behind her curtain of hair with one eye and smiles apologetically, almost as if to say, "Sorry to bother you." She waves the avocado at me. “Hi,” she says, in a squeaky little voice that falters half way through the word, breaks it in half, short as it is. She clears her throat and tries again. This time, she gets all the way through without incident. And I thought Bill was shy.

Bill turns to her and waves her forward. She comes nearly to his side, and stands just a little behind him and to his left, looking between him and the stacked eggplants at me. The top of her head is an inch below his armpit. Bill is the classic head-and-shoulders taller than she.

He points to me. “This's Doctor Mary,” he says. “Doctor Miller, I mean.”

When she nods, her head moves in an odd way. Her chin stays level rather than bobbing up and down, slides in and out as her neck flexes. Her gray eyes stay on me. They don't waver. “Plea . . . ahem . . . pleased to meet-cha,” she says. She keeps nodding for a few seconds, then stops.

“How are you today?” I ask, like she's a five-year-old I want to come out from behind her brother. At least Bill is partnered up with someone his own age.

She smiles a little wider. She has great teeth, or a good dentist. Probably both. She nods that odd nod again. “Fi . . . ahem . . . fine.”

“I'm glad to hear that,” I say. She keeps nodding.

I've thinking we've just about exhausted possible niceties when she steps around Bill and extends her right hand, which I reach out and grasp. She brings her left hand over mine and holds it. She stops nodding and looks right at me.

“Bi . . . ahem . . . Bill's been talkin' to you, huh?”

Her hands are warm and dry and calloused, strong, a gardener's hands, or some sort of laborer. I feel perfectly safe holding on to these hands.

“Yes, he has.” She's smiling big now.

“She's pretty,” she says to Bill without taking her eyes off me. “Like you said.”

I laugh. “Thank you, Bill.” I say.

He's staring at the floor, a small blush spreading from his cheekbones. He has a goofy grin on. “Ah, Angie,” he says, like she wasn't supposed to tell.

“You . . . ahem . . . you're nice, too,” she says to me, “aren'tcha?”

That's a hard question to answer, Angie, I'm thinking, ***without sounding like a self-centered dolt.*** My own blush comes to my rescue. She notices.

"I . . . ahem . . . I knew it," she says almost triumphantly, and squeezes my hand with both of hers. She lets go gently. "I knew ya had to be nice if Bill was talkin' to ya."

She's nodding again, but in a more traditional manner, and she still has that big smile. She goes back and stands with Bill, this time beside him. "Some . . . ahem . . . sometimes, ya know," she says, "ya know stuff about people before you meet 'em."

Yes, Angie, I think, ***you're right, but for me, you're pretty much of a surprise.*** It's not that I expected her to be any certain way. It's more that I would never have expected her to be the way she is. I imagine her during an AA meeting, nodding her own special nod and telling in her broken-but-not-really-broken voice about how it was and how she got sober and how it is now, and the thought makes me smile. She smiles back, not a grin, but a happy, lips-closed, I-have-nothing-more-I-need-to-say-but-I'm-very-glad-I-said-what-I-did sort of smile.

As we part company, I tell her, "It was nice to meet you, Angie." She nods and looks pleased.

They go back to considering their respective vegetables. I put a couple of broccoli stalks in my cart and move down the aisle. I stop at the romaine and look back. He towers over her, and they are looking at Bill's eggplant. She pokes at it with her right index finger and says something. They both laugh. I suddenly feel like a voyeur. I move on to the seafood stand to marvel at the price of wild-caught salmon.

I think about things I already knew about Angie: a.) Bill loves her immoderately, b.) they have been together for over two decades, c.) she has three grown children, d.) and she is 15 years sober.

Now I also know that she loves Bill in the same manner he loves her. And, I suspect that in her life I don't know about, she is somewhat of a force.

Round 10
Bill, The Zen Master

"She's somethin', huh?" Bill says.

It's the first thing he says the next time we meet, and he knows that I know who he's talking about. We're in the lobby of my building. The weather isn't too bad, a light snow falling and 20 above, so we will be walking today. I wrap myself in my favorite Hudson's Bay blanket overcoat and begin for the door.

"I think you're right, Bill. She's something. I like her."

Bill gets the door, nodding like an excited kid. "She likes you, too."

We walk out onto the sidewalk and turn left. I don't know why, but left seems to be a good direction to turn today, toward the lake. He falls in beside me.

"That's important to you, isn't it?"

"Uh-huh," he says.

I'm in an odd mood today, a little raw. McElroy and I had a tiff last night. Just a misunderstanding, but still. He's such a knucklehead sometimes. I assumed — yes, I know what "assume" does, makes an *ass* of *u* and *me* — that we were on for Wednesday after-hours therapy. I walk to the Neutron in 10-above weather, in a skirt, my favorite Hudson's Bay blanket overcoat and not quite enough else. I arrive semi-frozen to find him not there. I wander around with my coat over my arm looking for him, like I'm Joseph's drycleaner with his many-colored coat. Nobody's seen McElroy, and I ask way too many people if they have, being convinced that he ***has*** to be there.

Finally, I call him. When he answers, I blithely ask, "Where are you?" thinking he's hiding in some corner laughing and watching me walk around looking for him. Like hide-and-seek.

"Ummm," he says. "I'm at home."

"It's Wednesday," I say, like he doesn't know that.

"Ummm," he says again. "I know."

Now, I'm sort of half steamed.

"I'm at the Neutron looking for you. Why didn't you let me know?"

Silence. Finally, he says, "I didn't know we had a date."

"We always go to the Neutron on Wednesday. Almost always. Don't we?"

Silence. He's thinking. Analyzing, I bet. *Take the rest of the night off, McElroy. Just talk to me.*

"I guess we do. I go and you go. So, yes. *We* go to the Neutron." He gets careful in his speech, like he's picking each and every word. "But I never assumed" (I *hate* that word right now) "that our presence, umm, the presence of one of us was dependent on the presence of the other."

He's soooo logical.

"Oh." I say. Carefully. I say it very carefully.

"I mean," he says, or begins to say. That's as far as he gets. Mean.

"I *know* what you mean," I say, somewhat more carefully than I intended; so carefully he can hear each individual letter almost. But, I want him to know that I *know* what he means. And at this moment, I think he's mean. That's unspoken, of course, and I don't really think that — all the time. Just *right now!*

I want to hang up. But I don't. Not until I say, "Have a good night," not that I mean it. Then, I hang up. If it was one of those old-fashioned, ten-pound black Bakelite phones I was hanging up, he would have at least one broken eardrum, but it's one of those wussy little smart phones that you don't even get the satisfaction of flipping closed.

"Grrrrr." I say.

"Cocktail, Dr. Miller?" It's Bob the Bartender, who has been standing by for much of the conversation, I'm afraid. Hopefully, he can't translate half a conversation like he can a whole one.

"Double Bombay marti straight up, four olives," I say. No wussy little vodka martini lemon drop frufru drink for me tonight.

"Yes ma'am." Bob says. His left eyebrow is still raised when he brings it back.

"Thanks," I say.

"I assume you want to run a tab."

I pull my card out and slap it on the bar. "Never assume anything, Bob," I say, rather abruptly.

"Yes ma'am," he says, and goes and runs my card, which he brings back without comment. He lays the pen and slip on the bar and walks off like he sees me drink double martinis every day. After a self-indulgent crab dinner, I take a cab home. It's 5 degrees, for crap sake. Or crab's sake. Or something.

Today, I'm better. Quite a bit better. But not completely, so I should, I tell myself, be careful about what I say how to Bill. Still, I want to know.

"What if she didn't like me Bill? What if you liked me, but Angie didn't? What do you think you would do?"

I say it kindly, softly, gently, thinking I'm going to cause some sort of tidal wave by broaching the idea.

He laughs. He sounds a little nervous.

"But she does."

"And that's good. I know. But, I'm curious, Bill. What would you do if she didn't like me?"

He frowns and pushes his hands way down in his pockets. His pace picks up a bit. I can tell he's thinking hard.

"What has this got to do with anything?" I hear McElroy ask. "Are you looking for validation?"

McElroy, I think, *you stay the* hell *out of this.* At least I hope I thought that, didn't say it out loud. I look at Bill. He's still deep in thought.

OK, McElroy, I think, *I'm convicted. Self indulgence, assumption, seeking validation, having a slight hangover. Guilty as charged. You unfeeling bum!*

Boy, Dr. Miller, I think some more, *you are really, really pissed.*

And, I was right.

About that time, Bill pulls up and faces me, who is so engrossed in my own stuff that I almost don't notice. I screech to a halt, and slip on the icy sidewalk. Bill reaches out and rescues me from falling on my butt.

"Whoa," he says, and physically sets me back on my feet, like he's standing up a big doll. "All right?" he asks.

"Yes." I say. I'm sort of stunned by how quickly that all happened. "Yes. Thank you, Bill. Thanks."

"Welcome," he says. He looks at me. "Know what?" he says.

"What," I say.

"Don't matter."

"What doesn't matter, Bill?"

"Don't matter if Angie don't like you," he says, and I'm thinking, *So there, McElroy!*

" 'Cause she does," he continues, gleefully. "It's what it is already."

We begin again, me a little more carefully, and walk along for a while. Finally, Bill says, "See?" He really wants to know if I get it.

"Yes, Bill. I see," I say, because I really do. "And you are very, very right."

He grins and keeps walking.

So, there, Dr. Miller, I think. *Bill, the Zen master has spoken.*

Now. Perhaps I shall speak to Dr. McElroy.

Round 11
About Wednesday Night, James

Thanks to Bill's Zen lesson, Dr. McElroy and I are speaking to each other again. Not that McElroy ever realized that I had stopped speaking to him, however briefly.

Reflecting on Bill's it-doesn't-matter-because-this-is-how-it-is answer allows me see that how one Dr. James F. McElroy, M.D., feels about me is not the point, but how he treats me is. And, not speaking will solve nothing, but speaking might. And, if I am going to speak, the only way that the situation will resolve itself effectively is if I speak fearlessly.

So, even though I was kind and assertive and chose not to tear him a new one, Dr. McElroy did come to realize that I wasn't happy with his actions Wednesday night.

"McElroy," I say when I call him on Friday, "I want to talk to you."

"Talk away," he says, blithely.

"In person, Doctor, if you don't mind."

"Oh." I can hear him analyzing. "Umm, lunch maybe?"

"That will work."

"Neutron?"

"I think not." Too early to return to the scene of the crime. "How about Deli Vision."

"Umm, OK. Noonish?"

"Good. See you then."

When we have ordered our sandwiches at the counter and found a table, I say, "About Wednesday night, James . . ."

I've called him James three times in all the time we have known each other: today, once when his dog died and once when he was about to buy a Miata that would have spent most of its life in a garage.

"I'm really, really sorry you lost Beau, James."

"James, I think buying that car is completely excessive and silly."

He listened to me both of those other times, and he is listening again today. He doesn't quite twitch, but he wants to.

"Sorry," he says. "I . . . ummm . . . I was feeling a little punk, so I just went home."

"Feeling better today?"

"Yes."

"Good."

"Thank you," he says, and heaves a sigh. I know the unspoken additional phrase is "for not tearing me a new one."

"You're welcome."

Our lunches come and we set about eating them.

"Next Wednesday?" he says after a bit.

"Yes?"

"And on future Wednesdays?"

"Yes?"

"If I can't make it, I'll let you know."

"Thank you."

"You're welcome."

We eat in silence for a while.

"How's the sandwich?" he asks.

"Very good," I say.

"Miller," he says, "you are a fine, fine friend."

"McElroy," I say, "I'm pleased that you think so."

He gets a funny little smile. I reach over with my napkin and wipe the mustard off his upper lip.

I hear Bill say, "It's what it is already," and I bless him.

Round 12
Tugboat Mary

When I was in medical school at U-Dub and living next to a harbor, my main entertainment as a poverty-stricken student with no boyfriend and no time for a social life anyway was watching ships come and go. My studio looked out on a huge wharf complex where container ships came calling day and night. Watching the big, storky cranes was meditative, their long beaks casting back and forth, back and forth, regular as metronomes, moving Evergreen or Hyundai containers from deck to rail car, or back the other way, the ship buoying higher and higher or lower and lower as things progressed.

In this picture, the tugs were my favorites. Tiny when compared to the hulking *Maru Celeste* or whatever, they nonetheless had their way with the leviathans, pushing them around, towing them when necessary, or — my favorite — nosing into them amidships and pushing them into dock. Guys in bright vests stand by with the ends of hawsers as big around as Bill's neck, ready to drop them over cleats as big as Ruby — my car. Even as I worked on my anatomy, I always had to stop and watch. Water churns and boils behind the tug and through the double pane window of my apartment, I hear the big Cat diesels roaring as the tugs push the freighters around.

Tugboat Mary

When Bill and I are walking and talking, I sometimes feel like a tug working a big freighter into a wharf. Like the tugs, I'm supposed to be helpful, even directive. Bill's physically much bigger than I, but more importantly, he has a huge amount of spiritual, emotional and mental freight on board that might be better off-loaded.

I know. I know. Which is he, a freighter or an iceberg? Am I a tug or paddling a kayak? These metaphors better not get mixed, or I will end up trying to push the freighter with the kayak.

Maybe I need an ocean fix. I've been restless lately. We have a nice big lake here, but it's nothing like a good ocean for soul soothing.

Enough about me. Sorry.

Bill's "freight" is not quite so containerized as the *Maru Celeste's.* It's more like — what is it like? Everything is connected, as it is in most of us. Father. Mother. Sibs. Significant others. Experiences involving all of them and the rest of the world. All held together by the tangled, twisted cargo net of memory, too big to unload all at once; and it can't get unloaded until the ship is hawsered to the dock, anyway, without just throwing everything willy-nilly into the sea.

Not that that's a bad idea in the case of some of the cargo. But it's good to sort the valuable stuff out before jettisoning the rest.

So, what's the dock? And where is it?

I ask myself those questions one Thursday afternoon just after Christmas as I ride the elevator to meet Bill at Frozen in Time. The Polar Express is running full tilt this week. Bill from Buffalo might think about going out, but not this girl.

The answers to my questions aren't real obvious, or I don't think they are. Safe harbor seems to be Angie. She's been the constant anchorage in his life for 22 years. She's the one that stuck with him for the ten years she quit drinking before him and has now survived five, almost six years of his own sobriety. And that ain't hay, as my dad would say.

Much of what I know about recovery I learned from a.) Larry and b.) volunteering at an inner city clinic after I got out of school, watching patients enter 12-step programs. Some were successful first time, or within a relatively short time. Others fell out of the program or stayed in like Bill did for ten years; going to meetings but still acting out. Option A is better, most assuredly, but still, the process of the 12 Steps is not easy on relationships. What do you do with a drunk who suddenly gets sober, even if the drunk is yourself? Substitute any addiction you want for alcohol and it's very much the same. Recovery tears an old life apart and reassembles it, often in an almost unrecognizable way.

Some folks get to a certain place and stall, but to embrace the program completely takes two things: time and courage, particularly the courage to be someone other than who you thought you were. Recovery can be like diving off a ship you know is going to wreck on the rocks in a heavy storm, the ship being your out-of-control life. . . .

Ahh, dammit. Another ocean metaphor. Hmmm.

Bill is waiting in the lobby. I steer him into Frozen in Time. "Too cold today, Bill." He looks disappointed as a yellow lab that thought it was going for a walk on the beach.

"It's ten below!"

"Yeah, I know." he says. He's resigned. He looks out the window and sighs. "I like weather."

Go hiking with your friend Larry, I think. Larry has this crazy hobby of skiing across our frozen lake in blizzards.

"In the Coast Guard," Bill says, "I loved rough weather."

"The Coast Guard?" *I need to read my patient histories more carefully,* I think. "I thought you were in the Navy."

He looks caught out. He nods, and mumbles to the floor. "Four years Navy. Four years in the ring. Then the Coast Guard." He starts chewing on his lip, and I know something is stuck in his head that he's not sure he wants to let out.

I can't believe I didn't know he was in the Coast Guard. I'm looking at his patient history in my mind, and there's no mention of it. "Then seven years as a cop," he adds, which I knew about. I feel he's trying to deflect me from asking about the Coast Guard, but I'm not to be deflected. I rev up my tugboat engine.

"Did you tell about your time in the Coast Guard when you filled out your patient history?" I ask.

"Umm." He's chewing on his lip. "Maybe not."

I want to ask why not, but we're approaching Agnes standing behind the counter. I ask the next question that comes to mind.

"How long were you in?"

He says nothing.

"Single scoop of vanilla with strawberry sauce, please," I tell Agnes. I'm trying to keep the post-Christmas calorie count down. Five pounds is five pounds.

Agnes nods and looks expectantly at Bill. He's lost, looking out the window.

"Bill?" I say. "Want anything?" I'm starting to talk like him.

He shakes his head, and he looks a little misty.

"That's all, Agnes," I say, and hand her a few ones. "Keep the change."

I touch Bill on the elbow and navigate him to a table where he can see out the window but I don't have to sit by it. I'm warm and I want to stay that way. We sit down, and I say, as gently as possible, "How long were you in the Coast Guard, Bill?"

He's rocking, looking at the table top.

"Sixteen," he says.

"Years?" I ask. I must sound startled.

He nods.

"Sixteen years?"

Stop sounding surprised, Doctor, I tell myself. But I am. Here I am being a tugboat and the damned freighter has morphed into a calving iceberg. ***All hands on deck!***

He nods again and hunches up his shoulders. I add up his Navy time and his recently declared Coast Guard time. Twenty years of service. This explains why the VA is paying his bill.

The tug wallows through the wave. After it passes, I ask, in the gentlest way possible, "Did you retire from the Coast Guard?"

"Sorta."

"Sorta?" I say. He says nothing.

I rev up the engine on the tug and get pushy. I think Bill trusts me enough to let me push by now. I hope he does. I pray he does. "What do you mean by 'sorta,' Bill? And why didn't you tell about the Coast Guard when you filled out your patient history form? Sixteen years is a significant amount of history."

He snaps to, comes back from wherever he's been with bright eyes and zipped lips.

Agnes brings my ice cream. I take a bite and wait. Bill is looking at his hands, and I see he is ashamed. The light comes on.

Before I can stop myself, I say. "You had to leave because of your drinking."

We savvy therapists are not supposed to make assumption like that, of course. Our statements are supposed to be inquisitive, not declarative. *At least, Dr. Miller,* I think, *that was not said in an accusatory tone.* At least, I hope not.

Bill is nodding, still looking at his own, huge, scarred-up hands. "Yep," he mumbles, and a huge tear runs down his right cheek and drops onto the table with a splash. He stops the second one with the sleeve of his pea jacket.

Salt water, I think. *Maybe the ocean metaphors are some kind of message from God?*

"Yep," he says again, and a couple of more tears escape. He's rocking in the chair. "My favorite thing," he says, like a little boy who's lost his Texaco fire truck in the back yard somewhere.

If this man could let himself cry, he'd be sobbing right now. I'm trying not to.

"You loved the Coast Guard," I say, mostly to give myself something to do rather than cry. He nods and takes one of those deep, stuttering breaths kids get when they have finally stopped bawling their heads off. He takes a couple of napkins out of the holder and wipes his eyes, blows his nose.

He gets a wobbly little smile and looks at me. "No court martial, though. Just 'yer done.' Had to tell Angie."

"How long ago was that, Bill?"

"Long time," he says. He's still rocking. "Long, long time."

"But you knew Angie?"

"Oh, yeah. We's livin' together by then."

"When you got kicked out of the Coast Guard." So, it was less than 22 years ago.

"Didn't get kicked out!" he says. He's as animated as I've ever seen him. "Not a DD. Wouldn't let me reup. CPO Wilhelm said it was 'cuz I was drinkin' too much."

I dislike acronyms — this from the gal with MD behind her name — but the world is full of them. We're too lazy to say what we mean? Come on.

"What does DD mean, Bill?"

He looks toward the window, hesitant to tell.

"CPO?" I ask.

"Chief Petty Officer," he says. "He 's my immediate superior."

"Oh," I say. I finish scraping my ice cream dish.

He's rocking in his chair. "Dishonorable discharge," he says.

I nod. He looks at me like a guilty kindergartner. I try to smile like a benevolent kindergarten teacher. "It's OK, Bill. We're talking about stuff that happened a long time ago. I'm not going to tell you you're not eligible to reup."

" 'K," he says.

"What did you love most about the Coast Guard?" I ask.

He gets a faraway look, and the mist comes back into his eyes. He's looking across the top of my head and out the window.

"Beatin' the ocean," he says, in a high, tight voice. His hands are made into fists, and I imagine his nails digging into his palms and him centering on the pain to keep himself from crying.

"The ocean?"

"Beatin' the ocean," he says again. He has calmed himself. "Worked outta Portland. Maine. Not Or'gon. Roll out on distress call, winter, pull some poor crew off a sinkin' trawler, take 'em away from the monster. Get 'em home safe."

"The monster."

"North 'lantic."

"That's the same reference you use for your father, Bill. Monster."

"Yep," he says, as if he knew that already. "Beatin' the monster's always good."

"So, are there other monsters in your life that you try to beat?"

"Oh, yeah," he says.

"Name one."

"Alcohol," he says. He smiles at me shyly, like a kid who's trying to see if the teacher is still mad at him.

"Yes. And you seem to be doing well at that, Bill. That's good."

His smile gets bigger. Confession is good for the soul, and absolution is good for the appetite. He turns in his chair and says, "Hey, Agnes, can I get a banana split?"

He gets up and goes to the counter to pay her.

While he's gone, I do some math. Bill quit drinking five-plus years ago. Ten years before that, he started AA with Angie, who he moved in with sometime while he was still in the Coast Guard. He boxed for four years. He was in the Navy for four years. Ding, ding, ding! Something seems to be adding up here.

He comes back from paying Agnes, who is now industriously digging away with her silver scoop, constructing Bill's banana split.

"How old were you when you went into the Navy, Bill?" I ask.

There is no reluctance left. "Seventeen. Lied to 'em 'bout how old I's."

I finish my formula. "So, when you moved in with Angie, you'd already known her about four years. Is that right?"

He nods and Agnes, who has become almost as efficient as Sherrie Lee, brings his split to the table.

"And about three years later, you both started AA?"

He nods again.

"That's when we moved here."

"Was that a condition of your moving here together? That you go to AA?"

He nods. "Told ya that."

Yes, he had, in a sort of roundabout way.

He takes a bite of his split. After carefully chewing and swallowing he says, "Sorry for not tellin' 'bout the Coast Guard, Doctor Mary."

"All's well that ends well, Bill," I say. He looks down and sighs. I can see that's he's not sure it's all ended well, and not really sure he's completely absolved, but I'm not going to say more today. If I'm going to push him to safe moorage, he has to tell me the truth, and he has to know that.

Well, Dr. Miller, I think, *through no fault of your own, there's a significant chunk of cargo lying on the dock. Maybe we should pry the container open and take a look inside.*

Round 13
Cargo Inspection

After the docking maneuvers of last week, and my decision to open the container, the first box I come to is the one containing Bill's missing finger. At least that seems to be the one that demands opening. It's the piece of cargo that seems to me his heaviest.

"You told me that you've never told anybody about your finger before. Not even Angie? She never asked?"

"Told her I lost if to a car door."

"Like your mom told the hospital."

"Yep." He's beginning to rock in the chair, just a little bit, but I see the discomfort this is causing him.

We're once again in Starbucks, because, once again, the weather is not Mary Magdalene Miller compliant. Seven below with a stiff breeze out of the north.

"We could ride the bus to the Mall and walk around, if you'd like," I offer.

"Nah," he says. "Don't like the bus much."

"Why not?" Our little city has a great bus system.

He shrugs and says nothing, and I leave it at that. For now. There's something there, but meanwhile, back at the missing finger.

"How many people do you think you've told that you lost your finger in a car door?"

The rocking increases, and his lips seal together. I want to blast him out of this little boy place somehow. Not "blast," certainly, but somehow draw him out of there. That seems to be my job with Bill, to help him grow up and out of this arrested state that he retreats to when he gets scared, which seems to be often when he faces himself and his own story.

"Is that what I'm trying to do here, McElroy?" I asked at Neutron last night. Dr. McElroy and I discuss each other's cases from time to time, albeit from a distance, and sometimes ask for the perspective that distance affords. "And, if it is, how do I do it?"

"Well," he says, "I don't know the patient, but. . . ." He always starts that way, disclaimer first. Drives me sort of crazy. *Just talk to me, McElroy!* I think, but don't say. I purloin the cherry out of his Old Fashioned instead. Passive-aggressive garnish stealing.

He frowns at me, but not because of the cherry. He never eats them anyway. I asked him once why he doesn't just tell the bartender to hold the cherry, and he gets a funny look, like he's trying not to laugh. He says, finally, that he knows I will be disappointed if I can't steal his cherry on a regular basis, and then starts giggling in a delighted and embarrassed sort of way, like a little kid who just told his first dirty joke.

I give him "the look," set on medium high, and he subsides.

"Sorry," he says, and so am I for ruining his fun. But I don't tell him that, an act of cowardice on my part. Which causes me to blush, which he notices. "Sorry," he says again, and I say, "Me, too," which he, I'm sure, has not a clue of the real meaning. He's more Freudian than I. But that was a while ago. Quite a long while ago, back in the day when Neutron was brand new and not long after we began our almost weekly tradition.

"Maybe if you talk to the little boy. . . ." McElroy suggests in our most recent conversation. I nod and chew on that along with the cherry.

"Good suggestion," I say after a while.

He nods and looks pleased. "Thanks."

Now, here I am trying to imagine a small boy rocking in the chair on the other side of the table in Starbucks, rather than the big, scarred-up tough guy I see in front of me. As the image begins to coalesce, the iceberg forms too, looming large above the boy.

Holy kayak, Doctor, I think, *be careful here. You don't want to drown both of you.*

Ever so cautiously, I approach the child I see huddled in the chair. "Do you want to tell me?" I ask.

He shakes his head, makes no eye contact.

"Shall I guess?"

"Guess ya can if ya want." He's taking no control of the situation.

"Will you tell me if I guess right?" I'm trying to make a game out of this.

"There ain't no answer," he says. His voice is sullen. Game is *not* on.

"You've lost count," I say, in the most tender way possible.

He nods.

"Lots of people ask you what happened to that finger."

He nods again.

"And you're ashamed to tell them the truth?"

"Yep."

"But it wasn't your fault."

"I's stealin'!" The words hiss out of his mouth in a whispered scream.

Another chunk of iceberg roars as it peels off into the sea, and in my fervent efforts to keep the kayak from swamping, I forget I'm supposed to be talking to a little boy, even though there he is, right there, five-year-old logic and all. I'm angry and just about to cry.

"Jesus, Bill, you were five years old! If every five-year old that got caught filching something lost a pinky, not many of us would have all of our fingers."

"I know," he says, still the five-year old.

"Do you?"

"I wanta go home now," he says, and I know he means it. I'm totally disastrous as a five-year-old-blaster-outer.

"You can go home if you'd like," I say, sort of out of nowhere. ***Whoa! Did I just say that?*** I think. ***What am I going to say next, I wonder.***

He looks at me like he wants to know the same thing. I've already gone so far that I might as well go the rest of the way.

"Bill," I say, all grown-up like. "You're not five years old any more. And, it's not normal for a five-year-old to lose a finger for taking a quarter off the kitchen table. And, lying about it when someone asks isn't good for you. It's called 'denial,' which you know about from AA, I'm sure. It just reinforces the idea that somehow this horrible thing that happened to you was your fault. And it wasn't. Kids get a *spanking* for stealing, or a good talking to and sent to bed without dinner. No normal, loving parent takes a butcher knife and cuts their kid's finger off for stealing."

"Never stole nothin' again," he says in self-defense.

"But you've been lying about it ever since," I say. "Wouldn't you much rather be able to say that when you got caught stealing, you got sent to your room?"

"Ain't what happened," he says.

"It didn't get cut off with a car door, either, Bill."

He nods, but he's also stopped rocking. It appears that Bill the adult has showed up at the table. He's stopped chewing on his lip, and he's looking right at me with bright eyes. ***Hooray!*** I shout inside.

"What?" I say, on the outside.

"What *should* I say? Kid asks. Angie asks. What do I tell 'em? 'Oh, not much. My old man cut it off when he's drunk one night.' Do I say that?" He's almost crying. Almost.

"You could say, 'I lost it when I was very young, and I don't like to talk about it.' That's the pure truth, isn't it?"

He nods slowly and rocks just a bit, like his nodding is causing him to.

"But I still hafta tell Angie, don't I?"

"If you think so."

"Hafta make it straight with her."

"OK. Good that you know that. Anybody else you can think of that you need to get straight with?"

He thinks for a bit, and I can see him counting up.

He continues to nod and rock slightly. He takes a deep breath. "Yep. A few folks."

"The ones who love you. The ones you love."

"Yep," he says.

"Good," I say. "Good."

I reach out and touch his left hand on the third knuckle where his pinky used to be. "Your missing finger deserves the truth, Bill, and so do you."

He nods and rocks, just a little bit. "Thanks, Doctor Mary."

After a bit, he says, "Think I'll go home, now." There's something different in his voice, a tone of relief combined with resignation, like someone who has just won a huge victory but is so exhausted and beaten up that they can't bring themselves to celebrate.

I sort of feel the same way. I sit for a while after he's gone, staring at the backs of my own hands, saying "thank you" for each of my fingers.

"Nice to meetcha, Bill," I finally say. I finish my cold latte, put on my coat and head back to the office for my weekly match with Hildegard the Horrific.

Round 14
Thursday Night Fights

The morning after the day Bill turned into a grown up before my very eyes, however briefly, Angie calls the office. Madeline takes a message and on my first break, I call her back. She and Bill fought the night before, and he didn't come home after his AA meeting.

"What did you fight about, Angie?" I ask, even though I know full well. The wave from Bill's iceberg has followed him home.

"I . . . ahem . . . it was horrible, Dr. Mary. He tole me 'bout his finger, what really happened, like you said he should."

Uh-oh, I think. *I'm sure I told him he* could, *if he thought it was the right thing to do. I hope I didn't say "should."* Us savvy therapists try not to say, "should."

"An . . . ahem . . . an' all I could think was that if he lied to me 'bout that, he . . . ahem . . . he must have lied to me 'bout lots of things." Her voice rose to a wail. "Lo . . . ahem . . . lots of things."

I've done a bit of couples counseling, mostly pro-bono for organizations like the food bank or "my" church, but I'm not sure it's a good idea to have both partners in a marriage talking to the same counselor in different sessions, unless the goal is to get them together to talk to each other. I've seen it done, but I suspect that one or both might be wondering what the therapist might know already; worry about what the other might have told, which seems to me would get in the way of frank communication.

But Angie isn't asking me for counseling. She's asking for help.

"Do you really believe that he's lied to you about lots of things, Angie?"

"No . . . ahem . . . no. Maybe not lots of things. But if he lied once . . . I don't know. I don't know nothin' 'cept he's gone. He's go . . . ahem . . . gone, Doctor Mary. What do I do?"

That's Angie's picture next to "distraught" in my dictionary today.

"Where might he go, Angie?"

"I don't know." Angie's sounding a bit like a five-year-old today, and it feels like she caught it from Bill.

"If you were Bill, Angie, and you were upset, where would you go."

"A ba . . . ahem . . . a bar? God, Doctor Mary. I'm so scared he's out drinkin.' So. . . ahem . . . so scared." Her voice trails off. She's crying too hard to make much sense.

"Listen, Angie," I say, "are you listening?"

"Uh-huh," she squeaks.

"OK. Good. My guess is that Bill's not drinking," ***Please, God, please, please, please,*** I pray, "but I have an idea of a couple of places where he might be."

She sniffs, and then I hear her blow her nose. She's getting back under control.

"Whe . . . ahem . . . where do ya think?

"Maybe at Larry's? Or another friends? Or maybe at the gym working on the bags?"

"OK. I can call Larry. OK. Thank you!"

She's making like she's going to hang up. "Wait, Angie. Let's talk a bit more."

"'bout what?" she asks.

"Just a couple of thoughts," I say.

"OK."

I take a deep breath. "Did you accuse Bill of having told you lots of lies?"

It gets very quiet on the other end of the line.

"Angie?"

It comes out like a keening. "Yes!"

I wait until she has stopped sobbing. "Listen, Angie. Can you listen?"

"Ye. .. ahem . . .yes."

"You must know that's not true. Think about all the other things you and he have been through. Think about all the times you have been there for him and him for you. Think about all the times when you have told each other true things."

"Yes," she says. "Yep, yer right."

"OK. When you find Bill or he comes home, tell him you're sorry. Don't make it any more complicated than that. Tell him you're sorry and that you love him."

"OK."

"Then, ask him to call me. And, the next time he comes in, I'd like you to come, too. OK?"

"Um . . . ahem . . . ummm. OK."

"And, Angie?"

"Yes?"

"If you don't find Bill in short order, call me back."

"OK. I will."

On my next break, I get a message, which Madeline hands to me with a "should we be charging for this" frown. I ignore her, poor woman. Bill's at Larry's. *Thank you, God, thank you, thank you, thank you.* He's going to come home after a while. He'll call me then. Good. Very good. Not so great, but very good.

What hath Mary Magdalene Miller wrought? I wonder.

Sometimes, this job is harder than others.

Round 15
Two-For-One

The next week, we meet in inner sanctum, the three of us. Madeline isn't happy to see two patients traipse in when we're being paid for one, but Madeline, bless her pecuniary little head, isn't really the boss of me. She just thinks she is, and I let her think that most of the time because she's really good at what she does and, under her crusty outer shell beats a heart of gold that she shows when she wants to.

The two of them are sitting on the couch about two feet apart and looking at their shoes. I feel like the principal who has to give two kindergarten kids who have been fighting on the bus a good talking to.

"It's been a hard week, huh?" I say by way of opening the conversation.

They won't look at each other, but both of them nod.

"Have you been fighting? I mean have you fought any more since last Thursday?"

They both shake their head. I'm beginning to see why these two love each other so much. They are *exactly* the same age, emotionally. I find myself wondering what happened to the little girl Angie when she was five. I'm not sure I want to know, but it might be good for Angie if she were to get to tell someone. Not me, today, though. My job is to get them over the wave that followed Bill home from Starbucks last week.

"So, why are you still mad at each other?"

Nobody says anything.

"Bill?"

"Not mad," he says. That's Bill's picture next to "petulance" in my dictionary today.

"You're lying, Bill." Both heads snap up.

Doctor! I think. ***Be careful.*** Do I listen? No. I just carry on. Another declarative statement jumps right out there. And a bossy one at that.

"Don't lie," I say to him. Angie's looking, not at me, but right at him, trying to judge what this is going to do to him. "It's what got you into trouble in the first place."

"Ye . . . ahem . . . yeah, Bill. Don't lie."

"Angie," I say, in the same adult sort of tone, "don't you play the victim."

Now, she's looking at me. And he's looking at me. ***Now that I have your attention,*** I think. Time to go back to using curly punctuation marks. Sort of.

"You are both in AA, correct?"

They both nod.

"Not only that, you have both been in AA for quite a while, correct?"

They both nod.

"And, aren't honesty and non-judgment two of the tenets of AA?"

They both nod.

"So, where have you both been all week, since last Thursday?"

They both look confused.

"Mo . . . ahem . . . mostly at home," Angie says.

"Been at the gym a lot," Bill says.

"Yeah," says Angie, and sighs.

I want to laugh but I don't dare.

"Maybe I'm wrong," I say carefully, "but I think you might both have been at a big pity party."

Bill — God bless Bill — he snorts and then starts to laugh. I've never heard Bill laugh like this, like a grown up. "Yeah," he says. "Yep."

Angie is looking at her shoes again. She's sooooo shy. But she's very brave, too. She is nodding her own special nod and her lips are pursed against each other, slowly forming into that big closed-mouth smile I witnessed at the supermarket.

"Yer pretty good, Doctor Mary," she says, still nodding, not quite looking at me yet, but just about to. As she finally does, she says "Callin' us on our own sh . . . ahem . . . our own stuff." Now, she's grinning. "Th . . . ahem . . . that din't hardly hurt 'tal."

"Sorry," Bill says, and not to me.

"Me, too," Angie says. They look at each other like two kids in a Norman Rockwell painting. I try to suppress the ridiculous thought that these two might have had sex once or twice in their lives together.

They are both sitting on the edge of the couch now, both rocking slightly and both ready to run out of here, completely happy with the outcome of this little session.

"OK," I say, and almost unconsciously cast a big sigh. "That wasn't so bad, was it?"

"No," says Angie. Bill shakes his head.

"So," I say, "If you'd like, why don't you sit back and relax and let's talk about surviving recovery as a couple."

They both laugh sort of adult laughs.

"We have about 45 minutes left today," I say. "Is there anything you want to tell each other that maybe I could help with?"

Bill and Angie are both nodding.

Madeline, whose heart snuck a look at Angie when she came through the reception room, will henceforth refer to them, without prejudice, as the two-for-the-price-of-one couple.

Round 16
Madeline at the Beach

Bill and Angie don't start coming together every time, which is good. Madeline is fine with it once in a while, but she would be for adjusting the fee if it happened every time. Not that Madeline witnesses every session between Bill and me, for many — most —are not in inner sanctum, anyway.

I admit that I don't tell her about some of the personal time I dedicate to certain, um, clients, but Madeline and I are never going to have big secrets from each other that involve the practice. In our personal lives, that's not so true, but not with intention. We just don't know all there is to know about each other once the office door is closed behind us. And that's OK.

I know that Madeline is single, like me. Unlike me, she has a steady boyfriend she has been seeing for a long time. Like ten years. I've seen him several times in the seven years Madeline and I have been working together. His name is Ralph, and he works for the post office as a mail carrier. He has a dog named Terry — it's a terrier — and Madeline and he don't live together. But, they've been to Hawaii, Tahiti, Mexico, St. John's and several other tropical places together. Each winter, around the middle of February, Madeline takes 10 days off and they go somewhere warm.

Scars on Top of Scars

If I had a boyfriend, maybe I'd take the same two weeks and go someplace warm, too. But I don't. Not right now, at least. OK. I haven't had a real boyfriend since I got into med school, lo these many years ago. Twelve, to be exact. McElroy *doesn't* count.

I don't know what this means, but my mom and dad were both late bloomers, too. They didn't even start dating — I mean each other — until they were older than I am now. So. Maybe it's genetic.

Larry — my dear friend who used to be a client, not a patient — says it's because I'm such a spectacular woman that most men are terrified in my presence and it will take a true champion to take the golden apples from my lap.

"Like Cinderlad in *The Princess on the Glass Hill*," he says.

Sexual overtones of the story notwithstanding, it's still my favorite fairy tale, and how Larry knew that — oh, that's right, I forget sometimes that Larry is a mind reader.

So, Cinderlad, where the hell *are you?* I find myself thinking once in a while.

Sorry. I digress.

Madeline and Ralph are gone to Aruba, lucky folks. Terry is on vacation at the kennel, and I am managing things alone, which, thanks to Madeline's diligence, is relatively easy. If it's a money matter, I just say, "Madeline will be back on the 22nd." If it's a scheduling thing, I know where the calendar is and how it works. Today, a scheduling thing has come up. It's Thursday morning, and Angie calls and leaves a message.

"Doc . . . ahem . . . Doctor Mary," Angie says via voicemail, "Bill's down with the flu. He can't come today."

Between the first and second patients of the day, I call her — them — back. "How's Bill?" I ask.

"Re . . . ahem . . . really sick."

"Like go-to-the-hospital sick?"

"No . . . ahem . . . no, no. He's gonna to be fine. He . . . ahem . . . he's just really sick today. He has the flu, but hi . . . ahem . . . his fever is goin' down, and he's sleepin' real good right now. He . . . ahem . . . he'll probly wake up hungry."

This is a wise woman, this Angie. She's been on sick watch before.

"Good," I say. "I just wanted to check in with you."

"Tha . . . ahem . . . thanks," she says.

"Tell Bill I'll see him next week, then."

"O . . . ahem . . . OK," she says. There's a second of silence. "Doc. . . ahem . . . Doctor Mary?"

"Yes?"

"Wo. . . ahem . . . would it be OK if I came in his place?"

I don't answer immediately because I'm mentally debating whether it *would* be OK.

"I . . . ahem . . . it's, OK. Ju. . . ahem . . . just a thought," she says. She's assumed that I'm going to say "no."

"Angie," I say, "why did you assume I'm going to say no?"

"We . . . ahem . . . well, you know. I'm . . . ahem . . . I'm not really your patient. I don't wanta impose." She's being sort of whiney.

"You're being sort of whiney, Angie," I hear myself say. *Doctor! Watch it.*

To her great credit, she laughs. "Ye . . . ahem . . . yeah, I know. Sorry. But can I?"

I start to laugh myself. The wise woman is, emulating her boyfriend, about five years old this morning.

"Sure, Angie. Sure you can. Come early though, so you can fill out a patient history form."

"A what?"

"You'll see," I say. "Just come at 1:45. I'll meet you in the reception room."

At 1:45, I usher my 12:45 patient out of inner sanctum. Angie is sitting in the reception room, perching on the edge of a chair like she's about to get up and run away.

"Hi . . . ahem . . . hi," she says.

I say, "Hi, Angie," and walk around into Madeline's space and dig a patient history form out a file cabinet. Every time Madeline goes on vacation to someplace warm, just before she leaves, she shows me where all the important forms are, plus where to put the checks and find petty cash. In seven years, nothing has moved, but she shows me every time, just in case. I love Madeline.

I put the form on a clipboard, take it to Angie and give it to her with a pen. "I'll be right back," I say.

I go to the bathroom and when I return, Angie is sitting with the clipboard in her lap. The form is still blank.

"Do you need help?" I ask.

She nods. She's not looking at me.

"It's pretty easy," I say. "See where it says 'patient name'?"

Now she's looking at me. She holds the clipboard out to me, and says, "I . . . ahem . . . I'm literate."

Well, Angie. Congratulations. So am I, I think. I must look confused. "So, what's the problem?" I ask.

"I'm literate," she says more emphatically. She holds out the clipboard imploringly. Something is going "ding, ding, ding" in the back of my mind, something in her speech pattern. She contracts many of her words. *Literate. She's literate.* I see the word in my mind and an apostrophe appears in front of the "l". 'literate. *Holy reading and writing, Batman! She means "illiterate!"*

I take a deep breath. "You can't read."

She looks down, ashamed, and nods. "Or . . . ahem . . . or write. A little bit. Not very good."

"How do you get . . . ?" I'm flummoxed. "How do you survive?"

I really want to know.

"Bi . . . ahem . . . Bill helps," she says, simply. "He's a good reader."

"Let's go into my office, Angie," I say. I've got the clipboard now. "We can fill this out together."

"O . . . ahem . . . OK," she says.

Round 17
Who's On First

"Bill," I say the next week — after finding out Angie can neither read nor write beyond deciphering prices and being able to sign her own name by rote — "why have you never encouraged Angie to learn to read?"

"She said she told ya," he said. There is some sort of implication in the way he says it that I don't like. I feel my jaw set. *Careful here, Doctor,* I tell myself.

"Do you think she shouldn't have? She says she's mentioned taking adult literacy classes a few times, and you haven't really liked the idea. Is that true?"

"Thought I's the patient here," he says.

His picture is beside "surly" today, but he has me on ethics.

"You are," I say.

"Then why we talkin' 'bout her?"

I'm feeling a bit surly myself. "So let's talk about you, Bill. Are you angry because she talked to me?"

"No."

"Don't lie, Bill."

"Yes."

"Yes, what?"

"Yes, I'm mad she told ya she can't . . ." He breaks off.

"Why?"

"None of yer business."

I suddenly recall the "Whose-on-first" routine of Abbot and Costello. There are so many ways to interpret that last sentence. Sentence fragment, really, but. . . .

"Is it none of my business why you're mad or is it none of my business that Angie, in her 54th year of life in the United States of America, can't read or write?"

"Yeah," he says, "that." Like he's won the point. "I can read. I read for her."

I can't laugh, but I want to. Here's a great big guy with scars on top of scars who's been a cop, rescued people from sinking ships in the middle of storms, stood toe to toe with the best boxers in the world, and he reverts to five-year-old logic when he gets stressed. OK. Not funny, if you're the great big guy, I guess. But what else can I do?

Especially, what can I do with my own anger that he's kept Angie from learning to read? Now, it's not quite so funny.

Couples counseling has a way of getting complicated, Doctor.

We're walking in my neighborhood along shoveled sidewalks with several feet of snow stacked on both sides. It's a nice February day, 22 degrees and sunny. Bill tells me that the suffering was near its worst at Valley Forge in 1778, but here today, my favorite Hudson's Bay blanket overcoat is almost — but not quite — too warm. Madeline will be back to work on Monday, which I am feeling relieved about. It's hard holding the fort alone. Though I seem to be pretty good at it.

A line from that famous bit about love in First Corinthians comes to mind: "When I was a child, I spoke like a child, I thought like a child, I reasoned like a child. When I became a man, I gave up childish ways."

"It *is* my business, Bill," I tell him. "You said yourself that I'm a doctor of the mind. I'm here to help you think correctly, and in this, Bill, you have to think like a grown up."

"Whadya mean?" he says.

"Right now, you are thinking like the little boy who got his finger cut off. You need to think like an adult about this."

He squints at me and I see something in his eyes harden.

"Grownups never was much help to me . . . or Angie," he says.

"What about your coach?"

"Who?"

"Your high school coach who took your brothers in."

"There's always somebody better'n me. That's what he tol' me."

Yeow! This isn't getting easier. What next?

"What do you think he meant by that?" I ask as gently as I can.

"I wasn't good enough."

"Is that when you quit school?"

"I's fleet champ," he says. "Showed 'im."

"Is that why you left high school, Bill, because your coach told you there would always be somebody better? Is that what he really said?"

He's got his head way down between his shoulders, and his hands deep in his pea jacket pockets. It's as if he's covering up in a fight, trying to protect himself.

"Yes!"

" 'Yes,' that's when you quit school, or 'yes,' that's what he really said?

"Don't wanta talk about this," he says.

"OK," I say. "What do you want to talk about instead?"

"Nothin,' " he says.

I'm Ok with that, I think. I'm tired of dealing with the five-year-old, anyway. I want to trade places with Madeline, lay on a beach in the sun with my lover and a pina colada and 5,000 miles between me and these snow berms and this big guy who won't grow up to save his own soul.

Nice thought, Doctor, I think. *Now, get back in there and kick that five-year-old's spoiled little butt.*

"Bill," I say, "You can act like a five-year-old for the rest of your life, if you want. Your choice. But if you refuse to grow up and act like an adult, there's really no sense in wasting your money and my time and yours on these sessions."

He stops in the middle of the sidewalk and I keep walking. I start counting. *One-thousand-one, one-thousand-two, one-thousand-three, one-thousand-four, one-thousand-five. Dammit. He's gone home.*

"So, how do I do that?" I hear him call.

I swing around and face him. "Do what?" Even from where I am, I see his cheeks are glistening with tears.

"Grow up."

"That's a good start," I say. It seems that my cheeks are glistening, too.

Round 18
Liar, Liar, Pants on Fire

Now, *what have I done?* I think later. *How do I teach a 56-year-old five-year-old to grow up?*

After a round of apologies to each other, Bill has gone home. The first thing he will do when he gets there is tell Angie that it will be OK with him if she takes adult literacy classes. I explained to him on our walk back to the office that his resistance to her learning how to read is a way of holding her hostage to him, a way to make sure that she doesn't leave him by making himself needed.

"Grown-ups don't do that to each other, Bill," I say, *Liar, liar, pants on fire,* I think. "At least, real grown-ups don't," I disclaim.

Later still, after Hildegard has come and gone — proving me wrong *and* right about what grown-ups do to each other, and finally the last patient of the day — I start thinking about Bill again, and words like "accountability," "responsibility," and — and what? "Adaptability." "Durability." "Capability." "Lovability."

"Lovability." Is that a capacity of adulthood? Maybe it's the ability to love that is.

Old St. Paul has managed to piss me off a few times in my readings of him, but I have come to understand that some of the stuff attributed to him is not really his, and so have forgiven him for telling us women to keep silent in church, which it seems he didn't really say after all. Even when I was angry with him, though, First Corinthians 13 always struck me as true. And now, with Bill as my witness, I'm putting what he said about love together with what he said about growing up.

"When I was a child, I spoke like a child, I thought like a child, I reasoned like a child. When I became a man, I gave up childish ways."

The prelude to this is that few verses that a few jillion couples have used as part of their wedding vows. "Love is patient and kind. Love is not jealous or boastful; it is not arrogant or rude. Love does not insist on its own way; it is not irritable or resentful; it does not rejoice at wrong, but rejoices in the right. Love bears all things, believes all things, hopes all things, endures all things. Love never ends . . . "

I've always thought of my mom and dad when I read this as an adult — a grown-up, which, I guess is what I am. Yes. They taught me to be such, thank you very much. But, I've never made that hard connection before — that one leads to the other, that learning to love like Paul tries to teach us is part of growing up.

"Is growing up simply learning to temper our actions with love?" I ask McElroy the next Wednesday. I've been thinking about this all week, and the more I think about it, the more clearly the answer to the question is "yes." But, I want to hear what the good doctor has to say.

He looks at me over the top of his glass. His brows knit together above his handsome face. He puts the glass down, and purses his lips.

"I think you might be right, Miller," he says. "Part of it, anyway." He thinks for a while, analyzing, I'm sure. "Agape love, that is. Romantic love — not sure that's about growing up."

"Right," I say. "Of course." McElroy's cherry is staying in his Old Fashioned tonight. I don't think he'll even notice.

The next day, at 2:00, Bill and I head out for our walk, and I'm practically bursting with optimism. Bill's going to grow up! And I get to help!

"How's it been this week, Bill?" I ask, as a way of getting the ball rolling.

"Fine," he says, in a tone that really means "not-so-fine."

"What do you mean, fine?" I ask. "Did you talk to Angie about reading?"

"Uh-huh."

"And?"

"She wants me ta talk ta my mom." He's got that little-boy voice going.

"And you don't want to?"

"Never wanted me to before," he says. He's next to "pout" in the dictionary today.

"I thought you didn't want to."

He's got his head between his shoulders, and his lips are sealed up tight. He kicks a chunk of ice off the sidewalk and into the street. It skitters clear to the other side.

"You didn't tell me the truth about that, did you?"

"Nope," he says, mournfully.

Tit for tat, this for that, I think.

Bill relinquishes control of Angie's reading. Angie releases control over Bill's relationship with his mom. *Wow. What next?*

"Grown-ups don't have to lie, Bill, though sometimes they do. Kids lie to protect themselves from powerful others, parents, teachers, bullies. Grown-ups learn to tell the truth, especially to people they love. Grown-ups protect themselves in other ways."

"How?"

"By not caring so much what other people think of them, for one thing. By learning to trust themselves to know what's good for them and what isn't."

He thinks about this for a while and we turn up Ash, past what Larry assures me is the ugliest building in our little city.

"Sorry, for lyin,' Doctor Mary. Didn't wanta blame nobody."

"I understand. You were protecting Angie. You love Angie a lot, don't you?"

"Yep."

"Then don't protect her from the truth."

"You mean like reading'?"

"And how you really feel about things."

"But what if she don't like how I feel?"

"You'll have to trust her to understand that we don't all feel the same way about everything, and that doesn't mean we can't love each other."

He's ruminating, now, even if he doesn't know the word well. I let him.

Madeline is back in the office this week, all tan and happy. It's good to have her back. I take her to lunch at Deli Vision so she could tell me all about it. When we sit down, she holds out her left hand. I'm amazed that I didn't see it before. The Rock of Gibraltar glitters on her ring finger.

"Holy carats," I say right out loud. "Mail carriers must do alright."

She laughs and makes like the cat that ate the canary. *This is going to change things around the old office,* I think.

Ah, love.

Round 19
. . . Ahem. . .

Bill's — and Angie's — growing up lessons have been going well. I realized right away that one without the other would not work very well, because it's around each other and other folks that know them best — like me, for instance — that they most often act like five-year-olds. Plus, Paul's lesson was not just for guys, even though he might have thought so. Or some translator might have thought so. "When I became an adult, I gave up childish ways." I wonder if there's a translation that says that. The Mary Magdalene Miller translation would.

Angie understands this. She confesses that she was terrified Bill would disconnect from her if he were to reconnect with his Mom.

"Why would he do that?" I ask. We are in inner sanctum, and it's a Saturday, something Madeline would have skinned me for prior to the recently renamed Rock of Aruba. (Gibraltar is not a two-carat imperial-cut stone that refracts light like a disco ball.) But, she's fine with it right now. Hopefully, I will get the old Madeline back after the new wears off the ring, but for now, I'm taking a little advantage.

"I . . . ahem . . . I don't know." She's got her whiney voice on.

"So, Angie," I say, "why do you always clear your throat when you start to say something?"

"What?"

"Wh . . . ahem . . . why do you talk like this?"

"Oh," she says, "I . . . ahem . . . I don't know. I'm just not very . . . "

I wait. Finally, I say, "Not very what?"

"Not very sure of what to say?"

"I think it might be more that you're afraid to say it, because you always seem to know what to say. "

"Maybe," she says. "Maybe, you . . . ahem . . . you're right."

"Why is that, do you think?"

She puts her fingers over her lips, like she's holding the words in.

"You can tell," I say. She shakes her head.

"I'm not going to tell anybody, Angie. This is just between us."

She looks right at me and holds her chin up, like she's daring me to hit her. "Maybe 'cause momma would slap me if I spoke?"

"You mean if you spoke out of turn or said something smart?"

She looks away, rocking on the edge of the couch.

"No."

"She would slap you if you spoke at all."

"Sometimes." Her rocking has increased. "Lots of times."

"How old were you then,"

She's holding herself, now. " 'til I's ten."

"And then what happened?"

Her jaw is set now. She looks at me again and her eyes are dark with fury.

"She died. Died in the poor house with me and two others left behind."

"What do you mean, poor house?"

"The shelter home. San Diego."

"How did she die?"

"Heroine."

Holy I-don't-know-what, Batman. I think. I'm almost speechless. Almost.

"What about your father?" I ask, even though I think I know the answer to this one.

"Never knew who. They's all diffrent."

"What was all different?"

"All our dads. She was . . ." She takes a deep breath. "She sold herself. She's beautiful! They all wanted her. She'd bring 'em home, and if any of us made a peep in the next room, she'd come in an' smack us."

I don't say anything. My damned kayak is taking on water and I'm bailing as fast as I can. Bill and Angie have matching icebergs, for Christ's sake. ***Paddle, Doctor Miller, paddle hard!***

When you're growing up in Middle America with great parents and plenty to eat and lovely things and good friends, you never think about those other people who don't have all you have. You only know that what you have is normal because it's what all your friends have and what all your friends' friends have. We go to school and learn to read and write, and our parents work hard and scrimp and save and send us to college and encourage us to become what we want to be. And they never slap us just for talking or cut our fingers off with butcher knives.

But then, if we're really, really, ***really*** lucky, we meet people like Angie and Bill.

I hand Angie the box of Kleenex I keep by the couch. I take a few for myself. We sob and blubber and sniff and wipe our noses and eyes with one hand because we are holding on to each other with the other.

After a while, I say, "You must not have been afraid to say that."

"Why's that?" she asked.

"You didn't clear your throat once," I say. "You might want to learn to talk that way all the time."

She laughs a wobbly little laugh. "Ye . . . ahem . . . yes."

She laughs again, this time stronger. "Yes," she says, "I might want to do that."

Round 20
"Investigation"

It's been a while since that Saturday afternoon. Bill and Angie are learning to be grown up — most of the time. But, I don't think it's good for anybody to be a grownup all of the time. We should all get to be children on occasion. Childhood is the home of wonder and awe, and we should never get so jaded or pragmatic that we don't experience those.

Angie is learning to read, an interesting process. Read first, write later. Her writing skills lag way behind her reading. I think she will read *War and Peace* before she writes her first complete and grammatically correct paragraph. OK. Maybe not, but she's blasted through Dick and Jane, is now a Nancy Drew addict, and she still doesn't have the basics of writing down. And, she's stubborn about it.

"What do I have ta write about?" she asks. "And look at all the writin' that's already done." She has me there. She was amazed by her first trip to the library.

Once Angie got into recovery, I think she started having the childhood she never had, and she is taking her own sweet time about it. There is a saying: "Wizards live their lives backwards." Maybe Angie is a wizard.

Bill has been in somewhat of a quandary about his mother. He knows where she is. He has her telephone number, even. He suspects she has knowledge that would be helpful to him. Still, he's not sure he wants to open that door.

"What if I's to ruin her life she has now?" he asks me one afternoon.

We are walking in the park near where he lives on Ash Avenue, nearly to the opposite end of where Larry's ugliest building is. Brave tulips are beginning to push green shoots up out of the soil. Sometimes lately on Thursdays, I bring the car to the office and actually walk my 12:45 patient to the parking lot, where I jump into Ruby — she's red — and dash across town to Bill's park. He doesn't mind if I'm 5 minutes late. He doesn't have to walk all the way across town to the office for his session — he seems to be mad at the bus system — and I get a bit of an adventure. Plus, I have half an hour between Bill and Hildegard, so I have plenty of time to get back.

"Do you really think you might?" I ask. "I mean, ruin her life?"

He pulls his head into his shoulders. "Dunno."

"It's a risky thing," I say.

"Scary," he says, and laughs.

"Yes. What happens if she doesn't want to have anything to do with you?"

He frowns. "Never thoughta that."

"You didn't?"

"Huh-uh."

"Then what's scary?"

He purses his lips, drawing them closed. "What, Bill?" I ask.

He blows out, opening his lips with his exhalation. "All the feelin's," he says. "What'll we do with all the feelin's?"

I am really surprised by that question. Bill is more grown up today than I've ever seen him, I think.

"That's a good question, Bill. Feel them, I guess. If you dare."

"What about her?"

"That's another good question. That's a question a grown-up would ask, Bill."

He sighs. "Ain't easy, ya know."

"Growing up, you mean?"

"Yeah." He unhunches his shoulders, lifts his head.

"I'll figure it out," he says. "Angie an' me, we're talkin' 'bout what it might mean to us and her. Angie says it's totally up to me."

I haven't seen Angie in a few weeks. We talk on the phone more often. She calls me with reading questions, which is how I find out she's reading Nancy Drew. "I-n-v-e-s-t-i-g-a-t-i-o-n," she says. "Investi-what?"

"Investigation," I say.

"Oh," she says. She's surprised.

"What are you reading, the newspaper?"

"No . . . ahem . . . no," she gets her conspiratorial "this is just between you 'n' me," tone. "Nancy Drew. Investigation."

She says it slowly. I can see her with the book open in her lap and her finger tracing the syllables.

"Which one," I ask. I was a Nancy Drew fan back in the day.

"*The Secret at Shadow Ranch* —that's not how ***I'd*** spell 'investigation,' "

"English has some strange rules," I say. "T-i-o-n often — but not always — sounds like s-h-soft e-n. 'shen,' "

"Oh, really," she say. "Then I got 'nother ques-shen for you." She laughs and so do I. Not only is Angie one tough cookie, she is one smart cookie.

Bill's ques-shen, of course, isn't as easy to answer.

At the risk of projecting, I try to imagine how I might feel if I hadn't seen my mother for 44 years, but I knew where she lived and that I could pick up the phone any time and call her.

"Scary," I say, right out loud. And Bill actually guffaws. A real, hearty, heart-felt peal of laughter.

He subsides and sighs. "Yeah."

"Courage, Bill," I say.

Bill knows where his sibs are, as you know. His sister lives here, which is why he and Angie came here in the first place.

"Needed a place away from the ocean," he says. When I ask why, he gets that far-away look of his. "Smellin' it ever day reminded me that I wasn't in the Guard no more."

Which brings to mind another question for today,

"So, how did you get from Maine to San Diego, Bill?"

"Took a transfer," he says. His answer is terse.

"Because of your drinking?" I ask.

He sighs. "Yeah. Figured I could get a hold on it, movin' someplace completely new where nobody knew me. Get away from the crowd I was runnin' with."

"And that didn't work."

He laughs. "There's lots more places ta drink and people ta drink with in San Diego than Portland," he says, "and just's many reasons."

"Why *did* you drink?" I ask.

He looks at me like I've got a foot sticking out my forehead.

"Because I ***could***," he says.

I laugh. The answer is soooo obvious.

"What we learned in AA is lotsa alc'holics have genetic disp'sition. Somethin' miswired in our brain, or somethin' like that. My dad was alc'holic — never went to meetin,' though, that I know of — and maybe that's why I am." Then he says, sadly, "So, maybe the old man is part me, after all, huh?"

"It's OK, Bill. He's not all of you. Genetic disposition. Yes, that's true about many sorts of addicts," I say.

"Really? Not just alc'holics?"

"Research shows that people inherit addictive tendencies."

"Hmmm," he says, "maybe I should tell my sister. She 'dicted to television, I think. Can't get her 'way from it."

"Maybe you should," I say.

He gets quiet. We're approaching where I parked Ruby. Our time is almost up.

"Scary," he says, and laughs.

Round 21
Angie at the Beach

"We was in and out of foster homes so fast," Angie tells me one day, "I never was in school long enough to learn to read. Three months here, four months there. Nobody wanted to keep us all. No . . . ahem . . . not me, least of all."

"Why not you, Angie? Good, by the way. You only stumbled once."

Angie nods, smiling that big, closed-mouth smile of hers. She's knitting, and sitting in my living room. I can practically see McElroy's frown from here. McElroy is all about professional distance. But, my former client Larry and my current patient Bill are in my backyard with a chainsaw. The top blew out of my beautiful old maple tree a few days ago, and they are cleaning up. There is a big hole where the crown used to be, and it makes me sad. She sees me looking out the window.

"It's a old, old tree," she says, by way of comfort.

"I know," I say. "Still."

"Yer funny, Doctor Mary. You love lotsa things. Trees. Your house. Madeline. Ya love Madeline, I know."

She's only seen Madeline and I together once at the office, but somehow she knows.

"Ya love Larry, too," she says. If only she knew, but thank God she doesn't. "An . . . ahem . . . an' Bill an' me."

She looks at me shyly over the mitten she's knitting for the homeless shelter.

"Now how do you know all that, wise woman?" I ask. I don't have to confirm what she's said. She's not looking for a "hit." She's just saying what she sees.

"Been around, you know," she says conspiratorially. She gets a big grin. I just giggle. She nods her special nod.

"Those are great colors, by the way." The mittens are beautiful. She knits a pair a week, no matter the season. "Avoid the rush that way," she says.

"Glad you like 'em." Her smile gets bigger, if possible.

"I's a problem after momma died," she says. "Really mad, really scared. Like a scared cat. Nobody could talk me outta the tree. If they tried to come and get me, I scratched 'em bad." She's rocking a bit, not hard, just a little from the waist.

"When I's 13, they went to turn me over to Juvie, and then I ran."

"Ran away?"

"Yep."

"Where'd you go?"

"The beach. Lived at the beach for long time."

"How long?"

"Three years, maybe. Dunno, really. 'til I met Kevin. So longer, really."

"Kevin."

"Surfer guy. He'n I hit it off big." She laughs. "My first."

"Boyfriend?"

She giggles. "Everything. First everything."

I change the subject, because I know I can come back to Kevin, and know I will.

"How'd you survive three years?"

"It was a rich place. Lots of rich folks with big houses on the beach. I's dressed better than most folks with jobs."

"But what did you eat?"

She looks at me like I'm kind of stupid, which I know she doesn't think.

"Ate what they didn't," she says, as if I should have known that.

"You lived out of their trash cans."

"Yep."

"Nobody tried to help you?"

"Nope. I's invis'ble." She holds up a finished mitten. "Me an' lotsa others. It was a lot warmer there than here."

I go look out the window at my missing treetop. Larry and Bill have got most of it cut up now, and they are loading it into Larry's old pickup.

I imagine a 13-year-old girl digging through the trash bin at the curb. How do I not see her?

Angie works at a dry-cleaning place. She doesn't have to read there, as long as the customer has the ticket, which they very nearly always do. All she has to do is match the numbers on the ticket with the numbers on the bagged clothing hanging from the big rotating rack.

She just waits for those numbers, those shapes, to come around and then she takes them to the customer, who takes them to the cashier.

"Works good," she says. Now, though, she's starting to pick out letters and put them together, which is her secret thrill.

"Nobody knows, 'cept Bill. And you, course."

"You haven't told your kids?"

"It'll be a sprise," she says. She gets a big grin.

"They all read, ya know," she says proudly. "Kevin and me made sure they got schoolin."

"Kevin, your first." We're back there already.

"The kids. They's all . . . ahem . . . all his."

"Were you married, then?"

"Naw," she says, and then she laughs. "Well, he was."

"He was married? To someone else?"

She nods that special nod.

Just when you thought you might have this figured out, Doctor. Time to trim the kayak.

"And you had three kids with him."

" 'member, I tole you it was a rich place?"

"Yes."

"He's one of the rich ones. Had a beach cottage. Loved to surf. His wi . . . ahem . . . wife hated the ocean. Never came there. Almost never."

"So, you moved into the cottage?"

She laughs. "Moved in for 'leven years. Time I was 16 'til I was 27."

"You were 16 when you moved into Kevin's cottage. And how old was he?"

"Older," she says. "Lots. He made his own money. Lots of it."

I shake my head. "And then?"

She jerks her head to one side like she's been slapped. I reach for my paddle.

"Then one day his wi . . . ahem . . . wife comes. With policemen. Says we're trespassin' and we're goin' to jail. He's in the car, but he won't get out. He just sits there. She knows what's really happenin.' So do the cops. Won't let us take our clothes. Nothin.' The kids' books. Nothin.' Everything lost."

"Nex . . . ahem . . . next day, a big van comes and everything goes to Goodwill. Everything. Clothes, Furniture. Toys. Stuff we had for years."

She stops talking. She's rocking on the couch, knitting away on the next mitten.

"Wasn't right," she finally says, "livin' with a man who's married to someone else. Bit me good. But it wasn't the kids' fault. She shouldn't of taken the kids' things, too."

I'm suddenly very tired. This has exhausted me, all this paddling. I don't want to ask another single question, or hear another single answer. It's Saturday, and I'm thinking that Madeline is right. I need to not work on my days off. Even if I were to get paid for working on my day off, it wouldn't be good for me. *Sorry, Madeline,* I think.

I want everyone to be magically gone, and then I could go upstairs and get under my down comforter — I might not even take off my shoes— and sleep until I want to wake up. Maybe even clear through until tomorrow.

Bill comes up on the back deck. Larry the mind reader has gone already. He knows. And Bill knows, maybe by osmosis. He steps into the kitchen. "Ready?" he asks. Angie knows, too. She's already put her knitting away. She puts her coat on.

"Ya know what I did then, Dr. Mary?"

She has a funny little smile on her face, like she knows a really good joke. I decide to bite.

"I went to Goodwill and applied for a job and they hired me!" She giggles. "I wanted to get my kids' stuff back, 's all, but I worked there for 12 years. 'til we moved here."

I laugh with her. ***You are one tough cookie, Angie,*** I think, but don't say. "We'll talk some more, Angie," I do say.

I see them out the door, and as I'm closing it, I turn and see the mittens are still lying on the couch. I grab them and return to the door, waving them as I call after them, "Hey, you forgot the mittens."

"Those're for you," she calls back from the street, very clearly, without a hint of hesitation. She waves and Bill grins at me and off they go down the street, arm in arm.

"Thank you, Angie." I say to the mittens. "Thanks very much."

They're gone now. I've decided that before I go upstairs and get under the comforter, I will sit in *my* living room for a while, just sit. I love this house. Larry, who I also love, helped me buy it. The mittens are lying on the table by the front door. Before I go just sit, I decide to put them in the closet with my favorite Hudson's Bay blanket overcoat, ready for next winter.

They are a perfect match.

Not that I'm going to do it every Saturday, you understand, but working on Saturdays does have its rewards.

Round 22
Squares, Circles and Curves

While I was still in college, Bill became a patrol officer in this fair city who distinguished himself several times in his years as a policeman. I was out of the local loop, then, or I would have recognized his name. In fact, I think that if I could tell my dad Bill Warren was a patient, his eyebrows would go through his hairline. Mine did when I learned about a couple of his adventures as a policeman.

Bill says he was a "cop," but I've never been very comfortable with that moniker. My old-fashioned folks always insisted that I call them police officers or policemen. To them, "cop" was a disrespectful term. "Cop," to me, seems like sort of a dirty word.

Dr. McElroy might have a hay-day with that. Which is why I won't confide such a thing to him. He's sort of an interesting study himself.

I'm sad to think that. He and I have been friends for almost seven years — and we still are. But the old saw about familiarity and contempt has been working its way into our friendship of late and I don't like it. It's my own fault. I'm the one with expectations. He certainly doesn't seem to have any. I'm just "Miller," and he's just "McElroy." As you know, we've called each other by our first names so infrequently that I remember each occasion.

Scars on Top of Scars

We started our practices nearly on the same date, but three years apart. He was already working in "my" building when I arrived; came down a couple of floors and introduced himself during the open house at my office, looking all burly and manly — as he always does. Now, I'm really sad. I had such hopes back then. *Dammit.*

OK, how did I get over here? Oh, yeah. Cops. Policemen. Sorry.

It was Larry who first mentioned that Bill had been a policeman — Larry said "cop" — when he introduced us back last May, nearly eleven months ago, now. Five days before the anniversary of the Battle of Midway, Bill tells me, which, of course is how he remembers when we met. I'm not sure that I want to be remembered for that, but . . .

During a session in the middle of April, we are walking down Seventh and back toward the office, and he says, out of the blue, "When I's a cop, this's part of my beat."

Our city keeps the rather quaint tradition of foot patrol officers, particularly in the summer months — actually May through September — when tourists crowd downtown shops and flock to the beach. Besides being ambassadors of good will, giving directions and advice on what to see or not, the patrol officers enforce the parking ordinances and, occasionally, other laws.

Our tourists tend to park anywhere at any time, deluded by sunshine and our beautiful, friendly city, perhaps, into thinking that they would never get in trouble for such a thing as leaving the family van in a two-hour meter zone for most of the day. How much can a parking ticket be, right?

Actually, a first offense is pretty cheap: $20. But, if the ticket, with the car under it, is still there on the second pass by a foot patrolman — in other words, after about five hours — they bring the dreaded boot, and the price of parking goes up drastically. If you want to ruin your day, just leave your car all day on Seventh to save the lot fee. Maybe, if you're having a baby on short notice, or an emergency appendectomy — and you can prove it — you won't have to ransom your car.

"So, wasn't that sort of boring," I ask, "walking around checking license plates?"

"Nope," he says. "Always intrestin.' Patterns. Everbody's got patterns."

"Routines, you mean."

"Maybe. Patterns. Some folks move 'n circles. Some 'n squares. Some 'n curves." He is looking up the street. "See that guy?"

He nods toward a young man — young being relative; he's about my age — striding up the sidewalk toward us. He's dressed in jeans and a light jacket, and he moves like he knows where he's going. He occasionally casts a glance at the street over his shoulder.

"Yes?"

Bill stops and so do I. "Watch," he says.

Just as Bill says it, the guy in jeans veers left and crosses Fifth at a trot. An alley opens on the street at his point of intersection, and he disappears into it.

"Smart dog," Bill observes. "No leash."

"What do you mean, 'no leash,'?"

Bill points toward the traffic light we are approaching, now displaying an orange cautionary hand.

"Stay," he says, in a firm voice.

I laugh. Bill continues to surprise me.

"So, he moves in curves?"

"Yep."

The light turns green and we are told we can walk, which we do. A couple ahead of us does an almost military right turn at the corner and stop to wait for permission to cross Ash.

"Squares?" I ask, and it's Bill's turn to laugh.

" 'Squares' follow directions," he says.

I squint at him. I'm not sure if he's doing the double entendre tango on purpose, but even if he's not, it's an interesting point of view.

"What?" he says. He noticed my odd expression.

"What about circles?" I ask.

"Watch," he says.

We walk in silence for half a minute, and then he points at a car driving slowly along the far curb. I recognize the driver as an accountant who has an office on the floor below mine. He's doing what many folks do a couple of times a day, circling the block in search of a new spot so as not to violate the two-hour limit.

"Lots of circle folks," he says, matter-of-factly.

I get this image of dogs chasing their own tails, which turns into a gerbil on a wheel in a cage.

Hmmm. What am I? I wonder.

"Yer a curve," he says.

Whew. I think. And I realize he's right. I leave my car at home most of the time, even though I pay for a parking space in the building lot (maybe I should let the accountant use it when I walk to work). I often change the route from home to the office and back, though I do have a favorite. And, I have no problem crossing in the middle of the block.

Bill's a curve, too, I think.

"I wasn't always a curve," he says, confirming my thought. "I's pretty square once upon a time."

"When were you a square, Bill?"

"For most of my life," he says. "Always tryin' to follow the rules just right and stay outta trouble."

"Perfectionism," I say.

"Yeah. That's what they call it in group, too."

"Was that why you became a policeman? So you could enforce the rules?"

He stops walking and turns to look at me. He's got an "ah-ha" look on his face.

"Never thought of that before. Maybe so. Liked it, keepin' folks in line."

He starts walking again. I imagine him in his blue uniform, golden badge glimmering on his left breast pocket, shiny black shoes and military cap, night stick, gun, handcuffs and mace. He must have been iconic in his days walking the downtown beat. I wondered if the citizens might have called him Big Bill or some such thing. Or Officer Bill. And, I suddenly realize why so many folks know him. I shake my head. I'm somewhat obtuse on some days, even as a savvy therapist.

"Why did you leave the job?" I ask

He stops and looks across the street. "There's Smart Dog again," he says. "Goin' back ta work, I bet."

The young(ish) man in jeans comes angling across the street at a fast walk. "Walk" is not really a good descriptor of how he moves, though. Maybe "hike" would be better. He hits the sidewalk a few yards in front of us.

"Hey, Bill," he says and waves. Bill waves back.

"He knows you?"

"He's been movin' through here since I's a cop," he says.

"Who is he?" I hear myself ask.

"Don't know his name." Bill says. "He's just Smart Dog."

One of our city busses pulls up and it brings to mind something Bill said long ago.

"Why is it you don't like busses, Bill?"

"Driver turned me in for bein' drunk one time."

"So, that's why you'd rather walk."

His jaw sets. "Yep."

I can tell the subject is closed for now. But I wonder.

Round 23
Brevet Officer Warren

How did you ever get to be a policeman, Bill?"

Don't ask me why I asked the question, or why I asked the way I did, although I can tell you why I was thinking it. Here's a guy who has a hard time putting a verb and an object together; who's not been allowed to reenlist in the Coast Guard because of his drinking; who didn't finish high school, for that matter; and he gets hired to a fairly competent small city police force in an era when intimate knowledge of anyone is just a couple of knowing keystrokes away. The Internet knows all, and all it could tell the local police department was "Hire him?"

"Field promotion," he says, without blinking an eye.

I look at him across the table. We are at Starbucks because it's pouring rain. One of those damnable April "showers." It better live up to its billing, that's all I can say. I am sick of too much rain and not enough flowers.

Don't get me started.

OK. I'm feeling a bit testy. Madeline is all in love; can't take her eyes off the Rock of Aruba. McElroy is out to lunch. Sorry, but it's true. Hildegard the Horrific has a new lover, and even she is somewhat blissful. Larry and Anna are conferring and conspiring on wedding plans. Angie — God bless Angie — is so in love with reading that. . . . That what? I am completely jealous that anyone could be so much in love with anything. Or anyone! Dammit!

OK. Bless it, and bless them all. Even McElroy. But it seems like everyone is having fun except me.

Well, maybe Bill isn't having a lot of fun, either. He seems sort of moody of late. He's approaching his six-year pin, which may be part of it. Progress in recovery can seem glacial.

"What do you mean, 'field promotion?' "

"I's a brevet patrolman, for a while. Not really brevet, I guess, "cause I did get paid. After probation, I's a regular cop."

"Explain, please."

He gets a grim little smile. "The city ran out of real cops. Budget crunch. They couldn't pay much as other places. I's part of th' volunteer police auxiliary. When they ran short on patrolmen, they looked ta see who had real experience. I's number one in line. So, I'm an accidental cop."

He looks as if he just confessed to the biggest sin ever.

Now, I feel bad. I'm on the prod because I have no life outside of work and my house — *my* house — and I've taken it out on a client. OK. Patient. Who — God bless him, too — is about as transparent as a pane of glass, and just as blameless. What is the matter with me today?

Bill is wondering the same thing. "You OK, Doctor Mary?" he asks.

Time to buck up, Doctor, I tell myself. *Just put yourself away.*

"But you were a good cop, Bill," I say. I surprise myself sometimes. "You must have been to be on the force for, what, seven years? These folks you know on your old beat seem to love you. You must have been good at your job."

"I've been good at lotsa of jobs," he says, "just not good at livin' life off hours."

"An interesting thought," I say. Because it is.

"Why do you think that is?" I ask.

He looks ashamed. "I just keep failin,' I guess."

"But you haven't really. You stood up to your father as a kid even when you were sure to lose, and it didn't matter because you were right. You were fleet champ. You stood up to guys who were world champions. You rescued people from the sea monster. You have Angie. You have all the friends you made when you were on foot patrol. You have done so much good."

He sighs and looks out the window.

"I'm tryin' to believe that," he says.

I have to carefully consider what I'm thinking right now. I think this might be a critical moment, and I don't want to get it wrong. Too much depends on it, I think. Bill's self-image may be in the crux.

"I have a confession, Bill," I say, and I do. I've actually been feeling contrite about this, and my intuition has been leading to say something about it. *Good start, Doctor Miller,* I think.

He's looking at me across the table.

"Whe . . . ahem . . . when I first met you," — I'm talking like the old Angie, here — "I thou. . . ahem . . . thought you were — well — a little slow."

He's looking at his hands, now, but he hasn't started rocking in the chair.

"Yeah," he says, " but I ain't Lenny."

"Lenny?"

He grins. "The boxer guy in *Mice and Men*. Don't talk so great. Or so much, either. But, I ain't stupid. Just do stupid things sometimes."

I'm surprised he knows Steinbeck and even more that he hasn't latched on to what I said about thinking originally he was not too bright.

"One 'a the reasons I got hired on as a cop," he continues, "'s'cause I managed to do most of 'em on my own time. Held my breath when the force called the Guard. They just looked at my record and said "'xemplary service at sea" and "hon'rable discharge" Navy said th' same thing. Not that I ever was drunk on duty. CPO Wilhelm was just sick of me showing up hung over for work. And, I guess he could see where it was goin.' "

"So, Bill," I say, "I just confessed to you that when we first met, I didn't think you were very bright. You didn't bat an eye. Didn't that bother you?"

"Ya know better now, right? Besides, in group, you know how we take inventory?"

I search around through my knowledge of the 12 Steps, and come up with, "Made a searching moral inventory of ourselves."

"Close," he says, "Step Four's 'Made a *fearless* 'n' searching moral inventory of ourselves.' My sponsor told me, 'bout the fifth inventory I did, that I gotta count good stuff, too. One of the things I can say about myself is that I ain't stupid.

"Can you say you're smart?"

"That's a little harder," he says, and laughs. He's embarrassed.

"Well, I think you are. I wanted to tell you I was sorry for thinking otherwise."

"Thanks, Doctor Mary." He's nodding and looking out at the rain, upgraded now from downpour to monsoon.

"I use ta stand out in weather like this on ship. If there's half a gale blowin' and the cutter was pitchin' like a bad horse and cold water 's seeping in around the edges of my mack'naw, all the better. It's then I felt more 'live than any other time, partly 'cause I was half scared and partly 'cause I was 'pletely sober."

He looks at me and smiles. "You know, Doctor Mary, I feel the same way lots of times now."

"The same way?"

His smile grows into a grin. "Half scared and 'pletely sober."

I am suddenly aware that Bill possesses a profound humility when he's being an adult human being, which he is being right now.

Round 24
Hero Worship

It's now the month of flowers, and as promised, they are beginning to appear. In honor of it being May, I have asked Bill to show me his old beat, or at least as much as he can in our hour.

"Pretty simple," he says. "Startin' at the lake, eight blocks up Fourth t' Ash, left on Ash t' Tenth, left on Ninth t' Minnehaha and back t' Fourth."

I do some quick calculations. Five blocks wide and eight-and-a-half blocks long (Minnehaha veers inland at Seventh, where the main entrance to the beach park is, and don't ask me *why* the city fathers named our winding lakefront boulevard "Minnehaha"). Each block is about a tenth of a mile, give or take 50 feet. Bill's beat was a half mile wide by seven-tenths of a mile long; about two and a third miles around. But to walk each street in sequence? Ding, ding, ding — 8 miles, plus or minus.

"So, did you walk every street every day?"

"Always made two complete circuits 'less somethin' 'citin' happened — up and down and across — sometimes more, but never lots more. Walked up Fourth from th'lake one day. Then back down Fifth. Next day, I'd start at Seventh and Ash and go backwards. Then Ash and Fourth, then the lake and Seventh, then start over, but go the other way."

"Pattern," I say.

"Yep. Grid pattern." I hear pride in his voice for the first time ever, I think. "Way it worked, folks 'd see me almost anywhere anytime. Figured it out myself. Sergeant didn't like it much 'til he went with me one day. Then ever'body's doin' it."

At this point, as if we have manifested her, the foot patroller du jour comes around the corner and heads our way. When she sees Bill, she lights up.

"Officer Warren," she says as we approach. She's about 30, very pretty in a burly sort of police way and delighted to see him.

He blushes and leans over to let her give him a shoulder hug, "Ah, Amy, I ain't no officer any more. You know that."

"You were a damn good cop, Bill." She's looking at me expectantly.

"Mary Miller," I say and hold out my hand, as I was taught to do when I was ten years old.

She shakes it enthusiastically. "Amy McPherson," she says.

"You a friend of Bill's?" she asks.

"Yes," I say. "We go walking every Thursday."

"Yep," says Bill. He's got a funny grin on. We are having a private joke.

Officer Amy is gazing lovingly at Bill. "He trained me on the beat," she says. Her gaze begins to switch back and forth between him and me.

"I was his rookie!" Such avid hero worship is not often observed in our world. "Saved my life once, too. Has Bill told you how he saved my life, Ms. Miller?"

"Amy," Bill complains, "don't be tellin' secrets."

She looks directly at me. "Have Bill tell you sometime how he saved my life."

"I will," I say, and I really mean it."

She turns to him and pulls his head down and gives him a smooch on the cheek. "Love you, Officer Warren," she says. "Nice to meet you Ms. Miller."

"Mary," I say.

I hold out my hand, and she takes it again.

She grins. “Mary. See ya ’round,” and off she goes on her appointed rounds.

Bill looks after her as she strolls down the street. He is glowing from both pleasure and extreme embarrassment.

“Wow,” he says.

“You really like that woman,” I say.

Bill shakes his head, bringing himself back to being Bill, I think. He nods.

“Yep,” he says. And then he adds, “But not like that,”

“What do you mean, ‘not like that’?” I ask, even though I know full well what he means.

“You know,” he says.

“Yes,” I say, “I know.”

I also know you are lying through your teeth, Bill, I think to myself, *to me and yourself, but for you and her and Angie, it might be a perfectly acceptable lie. I will have to think about it.*

And, I will, later, but now I say, “So, Bill, tell me how you saved Officer Amy’s life.”

“Wish she hadn’t said nothin,” he says.

“Yes, but she did.”

He sighs.

“Fourth year on the force, Amy — Officer McPherson — come outta Academy. Put ’er with me on foot patrol down here. She’s gonna be evenin’ patrol after she got trained. I’s just moved to day shift. I still worked swing once in a while, but not all th’ time. They’s just puttin’ young cops on bikes at night, too, but they wanted ’em to learn the territory on foot first.

“They put ’er with another guy for a while, but they didn’t work out. Fact, he got disc’plined for comin’ on to her.”

He stops and seems embarrassed. “Know what I mean?” he asks.

He must think I’m a nun, I think. In spite of the name, which I made up myself, I’m not even Catholic. I’m Presbyterian, if anything, and a Jack Presbyterian at that.

“I know what you mean, Bill. Sexual harassment.”

He nods. "She never tolerated no nonsense. Still don't. First time, she warned him. Second time, she went to the sergeant. Other officer went to graveyard. Gone now."

OK, OK, Bill. Enough background. Get to the exciting part.

" 'bout the end of orientation — four weeks or so — we's at Sixth 'n' Maple. . ."

"Right there?" I ask, pointing down the street.

"Yeah. And we got a radio call — well, call came on the radio —there's a armed robbery in progress. US Bank."

"The one down the block from my office?"

"Yep."

Suddenly, a headline leaps into my mind directly from one of the local papers my folks sent faithfully to me each week — a package of six dailies and a Sunday arrived every Thursday — while I was in medical school.

"Cops foil daring daylight heist at downtown bank," was across the top in 100-point type.

The subhead read, "Veteran foot patroller blocks escape, saves rookie's life."

"That was you?"

"So ya know already." He seems relieved not to have to tell the story.

"Sort of. I read about it in the paper, but I didn't live here then. You and Amy were the officers that confronted the robbers when they were running through the alley."

"Yep."

"That alley!" I point across the street.

"Yep."

"And you pushed her out of the way of the shotgun."

"Yep. Caught us flatfooted. She's pretty much froze up. We's just goin' to see if we could assist. Had no idea where they was. Hadn't drawn weapons. Nothin."

"But you got your gun out."

"Pistol," he said.

"Pistol. OK."

"Yep. Both of us."

"Her, too?"

"Yep." He laughs. "Pushed her into a doorway. Shotgun goes off, hits th' wall. She's got her weapon out, lookin' 'cross the alley at me behind the car. Her eyes are this big." He holds up his hands, fingers and thumbs in semicircles.

"Patrol car come screechin' into the alley behind the bad guys. There's three of 'em. They turn. No place to go. I stand up and start yellin' at 'em to drop their weapons. Amy comes out of the doorway, points her pistol at 'em and starts screamin', 'Get on the ground! Get on the ground! Get on the ground!' "

"The shotgun guy starts to swing his weapon around and I'm thinkin' 'Here we go.' He looks over his shoulder at her, an' I see somethin' go 'click' in his eyes. She's standin' rock steady with a big pistol pointin' right at 'im. He tosses his shotgun up the alley and gets on his belly. Then the other two do."

"Wow." It's my turn to say it.

"We let her put th' cuffs on th' shotgun guy," he says.

"And you both got medals for that, right?"

"Yep."

"Wow," I say again. I suddenly realize that I'm looking at him sort of like Officer Amy was looking at him earlier. He's absolutely embarrassed.

Back to being a professional, Dr. Miller, I think.

"So, how did you feel when it was all over, Bill?"

He grins at me. He knows I've gone back to work.

"Shaky," he says. "Real shaky."

We walk back toward the office.

He's suddenly serious again. "Know the really good thing about that day?" he says.

"What, Bill?"

"One shot fired and nobody got hurt."

Round 25
Headshot

It turns out that heroics weren't always the case in the adventures of Officer Bill Warren, whose seven years on the force overlapped much of my time in college and medical school and internship. Bill left the force — over an incident caused by his drinking, of course — just as I started my second year of practice here. According to my calculations, it was about nine months after that that Bill quit drinking.

"Glad I waited," he says with a grin one day when I ask him if losing his job was the final catalyst to get him to stop.

"What do you mean by that?"

"Don't think I coulda been a cop if I hadn't been drinkin.' Lotsa stress. Odd hours. Angie didn't like it neither. Best times was summer foot patrol, but even that's hard. Never know what's gonna happen. Like the bank robbers."

"Does Officer Amy drink, too?" I realize that's a question outside of my purview as soon as I ask, but he doesn't quibble.

"Nah. Amy's got her head on straight. Good cop, but she's gonna start law school soon. Never lets it get t' her, 'cause she can see the future."

"That's an interesting way to look at it. Can you see the future?"

"Nope. Never learned how. In my future there's always some monster waitin."

He's really sad to say this. And I think about that little boy who comes to visit me quite often when Bill and I talk about his past, the one with the drunken, raging father.

"Maybe not always," he adds, "but seems like there's lots of times."

"Tell me about one of those times," I say.

It's well into May now, but it's turned cold and we're walking in a light rain through the park in Bill's neighborhood. His park is different from the one in my neighborhood. It's one of those new-fangled sculpted landscape parks populated by small hillocks covered with grass and recently planted trees and a bike path winding through, following the river, more or less, toward the lake. It's beautiful, surely, but not as dignified and mature as "my" park, which, of course, isn't really mine. But, it's also more interesting visually and when it grows up, I think it will beat my park, hands down, even thought it will be quite some time. Whoever designed this park can see the future.

Bill has been thinking about my request. His mouth is firmly closed, as it gets when he doesn't want to talk about something. I'm about to relent.

Today, as we walk through the rain, just before I say, "If you'd rather not today, that's fine," Bill decides to tell about a day when a monster showed up.

"While I's a cop, I killed a guy once," he says. His voice sounds different than I've ever heard it, almost muffled. He has his head pulled way down between his shoulders. I'm not surprised, somehow, that he has had this experience. I remember what he said about the end of the day when the robbers quit before anyone got hurt.

"How so?"

"I's on graveyard. It's winter and we're patrollin' on the other side." He waves his hand in the general direction of the poorest section of our little city, one built around what used to be stockyards and processing and rendering plants. They're closed now for years, and nothing has replaced those jobs, unless you count Walmart and the other big box stores along the highway that runs across that end of town. Poor people live there, and they have since I was little. The police spend an inordinate amount of time there.

"Been to this house lotsa times. 'mestic violence calls. Her or the neighbors callin' couple times a week. She threw 'im out. Welfare Services got a lawyer 'n' a restrainin' order. She wants to move to a shelter, but there ain't no room. She has to wait."

"We get a call, and dispatch has a tone in her voice I ain't never heard on police radio 'fore. She says 'hurry.' So we hurry. Get there. Front door is open. We can hear a woman screamin' . . . " He stops talking.

After a few steps, he says, "Don't know if you need to hear this, Doctor Mary."

I'm tough, Bill, I think. *I'm the gal you told about your finger, remember.*

"Do you need to say it, Bill?"

"Never talked about it this way before. Police doctor never asked me ta tell 'im about the whole thing."

"Go ahead, then."

He nods and takes a deep breath. It's like he's talking to his chest and I have to listen very carefully.

" 'tween the screams," he says, "there's a thumpin' sound. He's beatin' her with a baton or a baseball bat or somethin.' Heard the sound before — same sound as when I was hittin' the old man with his own baton. 'cept the old man didn't scream when I hit 'im. Not like she was."

"I go in, and he was standin' over her with a wreckin' bar."

"Oh, my God," I say. *You may not be as tough as you think, Miller,* I think.

"Oh my God is right," he says. "Point my weapon at 'im. Yell at 'im to drop the bar. He looks right at me. His eyes are all glassy. He's cranked up on meth, we find out later. Turns back and raises the bar over his head with both hands. I shoot him. Hits the floor dead. She keeps screamin' 'til the ambulance guy gives her a shot o' morphine or somethin' It seemed like a long time."

"How long?"

"Dunno. Seemed like forever. They got her in the box an' she died on the way."

"To the hospital," I say.

He nods.

"All that for nothin," he says. "Didn't save nobody."

"Were there any kids?"

"No kids. They's long gone. If she had kid's at home, the shelter woulda took her."

"How old were these people?"

"Fourties. He'd been beatin' her for 20-plus years."

"It's not your fault she died, Bill. You did exactly the right thing. The only thing you could do."

We're almost back to Ruby.

"Here's the part I didn't tell the police doctor," he says.

I instinctively reach for my kayak paddle. This feels like it could be big.

"Go on," I say.

"When the guy looked at me?"

"The man with the crowbar?"

"Yeah. When he looks at me, it's like he's gone and the devil's in his body."

"The devil?"

He takes a deep breath. "He's standin' over her with the crowbar, and he looks just like my old man."

For some reason, I think of that piece of iceberg that went missing last December just after his birthday, the day he told me about his dad coming to watch him box.

"Just like him?"

"To me."

"Did that change things?"

"Yep," he says.

"How," I ask.

"Changed my aim."

We're at the car now, and he leans against the trunk, looking toward the river. His head is hunched into his shoulders, and his body is bent forward. He looks completely beaten, as if he might fall over at any moment.

"I don't understand," I say.

"I went for a headshot."

That huge chunk of berg that's been under the surface since December breaches like a charging whale. It comes right up under both of us, it feels like, and I can only turn and run with the wave.

"You consciously decided to kill this man."

He nods. He's looking at his shoes, ashamed. I paddle hard.

"Because he looked like your dad."

He nods harder, and looks at me. His eyes are bright. He's about to cry.

"Wow," I say. The wave is beginning to play out. I slide down the crest into calmer water, but there seem to be some huge eddies left from the breaching. Time to be careful.

"Pretty crazy, huh?" he says.

I nod. "Pretty crazy," I say, even though savvy therapists are never supposed to use the "C" word.

I think for a moment, though I'm risking being late for Hildegard.

"Would you have still fired, even if he hadn't looked like your dad? I mean, to you?"

He nods. "Not for th' head."

"Which you knew would kill him."

He nods.

"What was your other choice?"

"Body shot."

"Wouldn't that have killed him, too?"

"Maybe. Probably at that range. But that ain't it. I killed this guy on purpose."

"With intent, you mean."

"Yeah. I guess."

"To save the woman's life."

"Not really. 'n' she dies anyway."

I'm trying to find a way around the whirlpool that is Bill's self-revealed culpability in the death of a man who might otherwise not have died.

There is a chance he could have survived if Bill had not decided to kill him. That's apparent. A small chance, but still. There's no way around it.

"That's a burden, Bill."

He nods and looks at me, and I can see he expects me to say something, which I am not really prepared to do. Not yet. Too much to process. And we're out of time.

I do as quick a sort as I can and come up with this: "Do you know what I like about this, Bill?"

"There ain't much to like," he says.

"I see three things to like."

His head comes up and I see a glimmer of hope.

"You haven't shuttled this off by rationalization, first of all. And, you trust me to keep it between us. And, you are working on healing yourself by telling me about it."

"Ain't easy," he says.

"You've never told anyone else about this? Not even Angie?"

"You gotta go," he says, and he's right. I'm now officially late, and of all my patients, I hate apologizing to Hildegard the worst. Not to mention Madeline.

"You've never told anyone else?"

He shakes his head.

"Well, thank you for telling me. It's a good start. We'll talk about it more, OK?"

He nods and I flee into my car, leaving him standing in the rain in the parking lot. In the rearview mirror I see what appears to be an aura of aloneness around him, and tears begin to escape me.

You're not as tough as you think you are, Dr. Miller, I think. *Now, keep your eye on the road. Dammit.*

Round 26
"You Don't Wanta Know"

"I have a hard question, Bill," I say.

"'bout what?" he says, but he knows. It's a week after he told me about killing the man who looked like his father. I've been carrying it around with me, as he has, both of us trying to figure out what to do with it, how to lay it down and leave it behind. That Bill feels incredibly guilty is apparent. He practically dropped to his knees under the burden of telling me. And, it's not like sharing the burden has made it any lighter. In fact, to me, it seems like it has doubled in weight in the telling. Now two people know, and the secret has grown larger to accommodate us both.

Just to reassure him — and myself — that this will work out, I call him on Saturday. Madeline needn't know, and I'm really concerned. It's an awkward conversation. I ask him if he's OK. He says he is, but it feels to me like I am intruding by calling.

I briefly considered consulting Dr. McElroy. Briefly. Somehow, it seems out of the question. For one thing, this is a highly volatile secret we have here. The fewer who know it, the better. For another, it's consummately clear what this means. There are no Freudian nuances to be ferreted out.

Bill, in a moment of high stress and familiar pain, literally, figuratively and purposefully kills his abusive father. I want him to talk about it.

"Did the woman who was being beaten look like your mother?" This isn't the question I had been planning for three days to ask him. It just popped out of me, from under my own Freudian nuances, maybe. What I had intended to ask him was if the man still looked like his father after he was dead.

Still, it must have been the right question. Bill's reaction is the most electrified I've seen from him since the day he jerked his pinkie-deficient hand out of my view and stuffed it into his pocket. It's like he's been shocked.

"Don't wanta think 'bout that." He's instantly five years old.

"You don't want to think about that woman or you don't want to think about your mom?"

His lips are sealed tight and he picks up the pace. It's warm today, getting ready to hit 75 for the first time. The leaves are set on the trees in his park, a huge array of flowers are blooming, and there's a nice breeze blowing up the river from the lake. For such a beautiful day, we are not having a good time. I try to stay with him for a minute, but then I stop and call after him, "Don't run away from this, Bill, or it might kill you, too."

He stops and turns to face me. He's angry, I can tell. I stay where I am. It doesn't seem prudent to approach him for some reason, though I know he wouldn't hurt me.

Good, Bill, good. Now talk!

"Ya can't know what th' woman looked like," he says. His voice is a low growl, a snarl I've never heard before. "Ya don't wanta know. He's tryin' to kill 'er, but she's already dead, an' I knew it."

"I thought you said she died on the way to the hospital."

He takes two steps toward me and I have to tell myself not to run.

"Don'tcha get it? Nobody's gonna live through what happened to her. Nobody should. Didn't want her to. Wanted her to . . . " he trails off and turns away from me.

I walk up beside him and stand quiet for a moment. I can almost feel his grief.

"Wanted her to what, Bill. Tell me what you wanted."

"You know," he said.

"Yes, I do, but I want you to speak it so it's not inside you any more."

"I wanted her to die. So she'll stop screamin,' so she's outta her body that's never gonna heal and . . . "

"And you're not supposed to feel that way."

He nods and swallows. This is hard on him. Me, too, but especially him.

"Whatta I do with that, Doctor Mary?"

"That's a good question, Bill." I let a small laugh out, relieved that he would ask such a thing. "That is a damned good question. And I think the first thing to do with it is put it into the light of the situation and you, particularly, in that situation."

"Whatcha mean by that."

"You're shaped by what happens to you, particularly what happens to you as a child." A dangerous question comes to mind, and I turn it over a few times. I still want to ask.

"This is a somewhat dangerous question," I tell him, "and if you don't want to answer, just tell me. OK?"

"K," he says.

I take a deep breath. "When you were a little kid and your dad was beating your mom, did you ever want to kill him?"

The question doesn't rock him back on his heels as I feared it might.

"Only every time," he says. There is that same grim tone he uses every time he talks about his father. I am glad to hear it.

"And now you have," I say.

"Wasn't really my old man."

"In that moment, he was. You told me yourself that you changed your aim because he looked like your dad."

"Don't make it better," he says.

"Maybe not in the light of you as an adult police officer making a decision to kill someone purposefully, but what about the little guy watching his father beat his mom or his sister or his brother. What about him, the five- or six-year-old Bill with the missing pinky? What would that kid do, given the chance?"

"Wasn't that kid," he says, and I almost laugh because he has become that kid, a little boy with a black and white view of the world. It's either right or wrong and there is no in between.

"You're that kid right now, Bill. What would he have done?"

"Don't know."

"Yes you do. You told me that you used to attack your father when he was beating someone. Were you trying to distract him or stop him?"

"Stop 'im. Never worked, though. Somebody always got beat anyway."

"Were you trying to stop him once or stop him forever?"

His jaw sets, and he says, "Forever."

"I can't absolve you of this, Bill, or of wanting that poor woman to die. Only you can do that. I can tell you that I see that your intentions were not bad, given the choices you had, and the circumstances of your life. Self-forgiveness is the hardest thing we have to do in our whole lives, I think, but in this case, it's critical for you to do so. It's the only way to put this away and go on.

"One thing that might have come out of that night is that you finally accomplished something you tried to do again and again as a helpless little kid. You should recognize it as such."

He looks confused. "What did I 'complish?"

"You stopped your father from beating anyone else forever."

I'm not sure he gets it, but it does give him pause. We walk in silence for a while, right into that warm breeze. To me, it feels like it's washing the last bits of winter away.

"Don't make it right," he says.

"We don't always get to do the right thing, Bill," I say, "but most of the time, given the opportunity, we do the best that we can. I think on that night, Bill, you were doing the best that you could."

"Maybe," he says. We take two more steps. "Maybe so."

Round 27
Perspective

Bill and I haven't talked about much for the past two weeks. We talk, but we don't talk about much important. Bill is grim and quiet, even for him. I'm waiting for something I know not what. In spite of that warm breeze of a couple of weeks ago, we are both still carrying around that chunk of iceberg, it feels like.

Angie, in the meantime, is blooming like the flowers in Bill's park. I don't think she notices how withdrawn Bill is because she is finding so much joy in opening up the world around her via reading. Bill, to his credit, is doing his best to not rain on her parade.

"She's havin' fun," he says one day when I ask. "It's good."

"But it seems you're not," I say.

He nods. "Not much."

"What are you thinking about these days?"

"You know," he says.

And, I do. He's having the moral dilemma of his life. And I get to watch. *Oh, boy!*

"Can't get around it, Doctor Mary," he says. "I did the wrong thing."

"OK," I say, "maybe you did the wrong thing. But if it's the wrong thing, what can you do about it?"

"I don't know."

"Ever been wrong about anything else?"

"Never this wrong. Never life 'n' death wrong."

"But you've done the wrong thing before."

"Course. Everybody screws up."

"And everybody but you gets to get away with it, huh?"

"Whatta ya mean?"

"Bill, the only way this is going to go away is if you can forgive yourself. And, while we are on the subject of forgiveness, the only way you are going to truly get over your past is to forgive others who hurt you or you think hurt you. Or at least wish for them to rest in peace."

"Talkin' 'bout my dad."

"And your high school coach, and CPO Wilhelm, and the bus driver who turned you in for being drunk. I'm sure there are others."

"OK. Maybe I c'n do that. Forgive those guys. Maybe even my dad. But how do ya forgive yerself?"

He is truly curious.

"I believe that part of forgiveness is perspective. Let's start with your coach. When he said there would always be someone better, was he being cruel, or offering advice?"

We walk along in silence while he thinks about that.

"Advice, and he 's right," Bill finally says, sadly. "I's a kid then, 'th a thin skin and a big chip. And, I been pissed at him ever since. Sorry. Mad."

He's beginning to mist up. "He 's a good guy. He 's just tryin' to warn me about thinkin' I 's bulletproof, which I pretty much thought I was. In the ring, anyway."

"There. Perspective."

He nods. "Wonder if he's still 'live."

"Would you go see him if he were?"

"Yeah," he says, and he heaves a big sigh. A tear runs down his left cheek. "Yep, I would. If he'd have me."

"You said he's a good guy. I bet he'd love it."

We walk along in the sunshine for a bit. He's thinking hard, I can tell. It's really a nice day, and I'm suddenly in a better mood than I've been in for a while. Something about perspective. I have a really good life, after all.

"Now," I say, all official like, "about your dad. . . . "

He looks at me and for just an instant, I think I have overstepped myself, but then he starts laughing. He knows I'm teasing and he's taking it well. Whew.

"That could take a while," he says. Then he adds, "But, I'll think about it."

When I became an adult, I gave up childish ways. Thanks, Paul.

Round 28
How About Those Packers?

We are walking slowly along the lake. It's Thursday, of course, and it's not high tourist season yet, so it's not too crowded; just the local moms and their kiddos enjoying the water and the playground. We have the bike path to ourselves, and sound of the kids playing seems to come from far away.

There is something in Bill's countenance that's shifted. He's been thinking about something, and not like when he gave me the Zen lesson. He is weighing something, perhaps the something I am waiting for.

"Do ya believe in Hell?" he asks.

"The Hell of the Bible, eternal damnation and fire and all that?"

"Yeah."

"Not really. No. I would sooner believe in Heaven, but I'm not much on that, either. Heaven actually sounds sort of boring. Golden streets and ivory gates and all that. Is there a lake there? There's no mention of a lake. Or an ocean. Or mountains."

Bill laughs at that, and it's a good sound.

"Are you worried you're going to Hell, Bill?"

"Maybe. Don't know. Somethin's cookin." He laughs at his own pun. "Good one, huh?"

I giggle. "Good one. What do you mean, 'Something's cooking?' "

"I been chasin' all this around in my head 'bout what you said about 'doin' the best that we can.' An' about gettin' perspective. Tryin' to step back and get a view."

"A view of what?"

"Me." He's frowning. "Never had no trainin' in thinkin' like that, ya know. It's hard. Hard work."

"Are you having any luck? I mean are you getting that view?"

"Little bit. Kinda sad."

"How so?"

"If I knew me," he says, with a sad smile, "I'd think I had a really rotten life so far. 'cept for Angie, course."

"And what would you say to you?" I ask.

"Can't say."

"Why not?"

"Ya know when ya have a friend who's really hurt and ya go to his house to cheer 'im up, how ya talk about everything but his hurt 'cause talkin' about the hurt hurts?"

That's quite the thought, Bill, I think.

"Yes, I know," I say.

"It's like that."

I laugh. "So, you'd say, "Hey, Bill. How about those Packers?"

He looks at me like I've grown hound ears. And then he starts laughing. For some reason, he thinks that's hilarious. And, it kind of is.

Oh, Bill. You grownup, you. I'm so proud.

"Yeah," he finally says. "Yeah, Bill, how about th' Pack?"

"But you know what that really means, Bill, right?"

"What?"

" 'Hey, friend. Sorry you've had such a struggle, but I'm here to help you through it. You can count on me.' Could that be what 'How about those Packers?' really means?"

"Never thought about tellin' myself that."

"What's it say on the back of the AA medallion, Bill?"

"Ta thine own self be true."

"Same thing, you know."

"Ya think?"

"Pretty close."

"Hmm."

I'm thinking of what Larry said about Hell once, that he'd been there and after that, purgatory's not so bad. And, now, he's even moved out of purgatory, it seems — now that he's met Anna.

"If there's a Hell, Bill, I don't think it's an afterlife place. That's more like something someone came up with to keep their kids in line, I think."

"Better'n beatin' 'em," he says.

"Or cutting off their finger, huh?"

He doesn't even flinch.

"Yeah. That too."

For the first time ever, I see him put his left hand up in front of him and purposefully look at it. He shakes his head.

"Little kids get their fingers cut off in Hell," he says.

"You're right. And sometimes, police officers are forced to make really hard decisions about horrible situations in Hell."

He nods. "Yeah. OK. That's a fair idea."

"What do you mean, fair?" I ask, though I'm secretly doing the happy dance. He's come soooo far. ***Thank you, God, whoever you are!***

"If I 's not me," he says, "and I found out what I did, and why I did it, if I 's bein' fair, I'd hafta say 'Sorry ya had ta do that, but there wasn't nothin' else ta do."

I hear that verse from Paul again. *I gave up childish ways.*

"That is one damned fine thought, Bill. That's a totally grown-up thought. That is the perfect thought. Thank you for thinking it."

"It's what it is," he says. "Nothin' to do but go on."

Bill, the Zen master, has spoken.

"Amen," I say.

Round 29
The Dream Beat

Summer is in full swing, and Bill seems to be at peace. We have endeavored to walk his entire beat over the course of the summer, which is fun for both of us. Bill knows lots of people and lots of people know — and love — Bill. It's good for them to see each other again. We see Officer Amy quite often, as well as the Smart Dog, who has stopped and talked briefly with Bill twice. His name is Adam Turpin and he's an architect. And he never wears a tie or shiny shoes. And he always moves like he's going somewhere. And he has blue eyes. That's all I know.

The circumstances of that horrific winter night six years ago were never mitigated by a summer of foot patrol, the police job Bill loved best, because just a month later Bill was arrested for public drunkenness — on a city bus — and it was found that he was also carrying his service pistol. First, he got suspended. Then, he got fired.

"An' that's all she wrote," he says. "Next stop, AA."

"So, it was good, in a way, correct?"

He gets a funny smile. "Good in lotsa ways."

Angie has noticed, also.

"Ya know," she says, "I don't think Bill's had a nightmare in a long time."

"Why do you say that?"

"Ever sleep with a guy who weighs 220 pounds?"

"No," I admit.

"When he has a nightmare, ya know it," she say, and then she laughs.

I don't know why I've never asked Bill about his dream life. It was hard enough, I suppose, to get past his waking life. But, better late than never, I think.

We are walking down Ninth and nearing Minnehaha. In our fourth week, we are going to make it back to the point of beginning. We have been on every block in the grid at least once, and many twice as we cross-check downtown.

As we turn down Minnehaha, and the lake opens on our right, I ask, "Do you ever have nightmares, Bill."

"Used to. Lots. Not so many any more."

"What did you dream about?"

"Somethin' after me, fer years. Then, the guy — you know."

"What else was after you?"

"Lotsa stuff. Big mean dogs, sometimes. Sometimes th' old man. Sometimes big waves 'n' I'm in a row boat." He laughs. "Sometimes, Joe Frazier."

"Joe Frazier?"

"Only fighter I's ever 'fraid of."

"Did you ever fight him?"

"Nope. Manager wanted me to spar with 'im once, but wouldn't get 'n th' ring with 'im fer a million bucks. He's a monster. That's when I quit boxin' pro and went in the Coast Guard."

"A monster?"

He laughs. "Not that kinda monster. Really a nice guy, but he'd knock yer head off in the ring and not blink 'n eye."

"And that man, the one you shot, came after you?"

"Only every night fer about a year. Then not so much. Slowed way down after I quit drinkin."

"Drinking didn't help you sleep through the dreams?"

"Nah. Made 'em worse, I think. Ya can drink yerself to sleep, but after while, that don't guar'ntee yer gonna stay that way. Alcohol's a fuel, ya know."

"Hmm. Never thought of that. But, do you still have nightmares?"

"Not for a while," he says. "Tryin' to remember the last time."

He gets quiet and we walk along Minnehaha past the big community garden and the new, brick-and-glass office building they just finished. It's really lovely, though lots of folks said it would be an eyesore on the water-front. Larry loves it, and that's good enough for me. I've heard that Smart Dog designed it, and it fits into our city very nicely. I've thought about moving the office there, but I think I'm going to pay down the mortgage on my house first. Then, maybe we'll move to Minnehaha. Madeline will like it there.

We pass the Neutron deck where last evening Dr. McElroy and I had cocktails and watched the light fade over the lake. It was a beautiful evening, but we didn't talk about much. Maybe McElroy and I have run out of things to talk about; not like we ever had deep discussions about important things. Lately, I get a sad feeling about Dr. McElroy, that he's self-contained to the point of isolation. I wonder if he's lonely in there.

Bill is quiet for all this way, and I don't mind. I know he's thinking about the question, and I'm thinking about Dr. McElroy and the new building on Minnehaha. Finally, he says, "Can't remember when, but I remember the dream."

"What was it?"

"The guy with th' crowbar was after me. I kept shootin', but he wouldn't fall down."

"And you haven't had that dream for a while?"

"Nope. Don't think I will, either."

We walk another few paces, and he says, "He's dead, ya know."

It's not a joke like it was when he said it about his dad what seems like a hundred years ago, but was really just before Christmas. I look at Bill, and he's walking with his head up. He glances at me and nods. There's a light in his eyes that tells me he's just fine. He's awake to the moment we are in, and he is done with being haunted by monsters with crowbars and butcher knives. He may even stop coming to see me on Thursdays, which makes me kind of sad and kind of happy at the same time. I know I will still be seeing him, though, because the idea of him and Angie passing out of my life is ridiculous. I can't imagine a future without them in it, any more than I could imagine one without Larry.

It's all Larry's fault, too, bless him.

"Ya know what I've been dreamin' about lately?" Bill asks, as we turn up Seventh and back toward the office.

"What?"

"My mom."

"Are you going to call her?"

"Yep."

"Are you going to be OK with all those scary feelings?"

He laughs.

"Oh, hell yes," he says. " 'f I c'n face the monster, I c'n face anything."

I know McElroy would frown, but I can't help it. I put my hand in the crook of Bill's big, scarred-up left arm and leave it there, all the way back to the office.

ROUND 30
Smart Dog

Bill is talking to his mom on the phone these days. They have much to catch up on. It hasn't been an easy reconnection for either of them. Angie's been a rock, though, and when Bill has wavered, she's pushed him back into the ring. When Ruth balked — Bill's mom's name is Ruth — Angie called her and begged her to keep talking.

Ruth is revisiting a past she thought was dead, and it must be terrifying sometimes, but she has a good family back there in Albany, where she has been ever since she fled Buffalo 45 years ago. She had three more children with her now husband, and once they all found out what was going on — especially her husband, who knew all about her past — they got on board the family reunion train. Bill and Angie — and Meg — are headed for Albany in September. Bill and Meg are going to meet two brothers and a sister who never knew they existed until about a month ago. Angie's got a mother-in-law for the first time in her life.

"Ya wanta thinka somethin' scary?" she says one day, "Ho . . . ahem . . . how 'bout meetin' the inlaws fer the first time when yer 55?" She laughs that special laugh of hers and I join her.

We're at Deli Vision having a girl lunch and she's showing me her first completed cursive writing project. It's a letter to California Department of

Social Services, inquiring about three children who were brought into the child protective system in San Diego about 45 years ago.

"Might find my sister and brother," she says matter-of-factly, "might not. But I gotta start on it."

It's sort of a primitive letter, but I'm going to let her send it as is. It's the sort of letter that someone sitting at a desk in San Diego County will read with interest because it's so different from all the other documents that cross her desk. I don't know why I imagine it will be a her, but it's my imagination, and I can imagine a her if I want to. I imagine her putting the letter on her desk and turning to her computer and typing certain criteria into a search engine. Now, she is frowning at the screen. Now she is writing something down and getting up and crossing the room and asking someone else a question. Maybe she will find what Angie, a half a continent away, is starting to look for. That's my imaginary gift to Angie today.

Bill and Angie both have found new each others, and they still love each other very much. In fact, I'm somewhat jealous. And, last weekend, to make things worse in the jealous place, Larry and Anna got married out at her lake place, where they met on her deck in the middle of a blizzard about a thousand years ago. Not really, but it seems much longer ago than the 18 months it really is.

I don't know what possessed me, but I asked McElroy if he would like to go. He demurred, making the not-so-illegitimate excuse that he didn't really know anyone who would be there. Too bad for him. It was a great party. Bill and Angie were there, and Anna's kids were all part of the wedding party. They *love* Larry, and well they should.

The Whitmores, at whose house Larry introduced me to Bill, are there, too. And, so is Smart Dog — Adam. He stays for the ceremony and another half-hour, and disappears. I find out later he's a friend of the groom's, because of the groom's amateur but sincere interest in architecture.

"I just stopped into his office one day," Larry tells me when I finally get up the nerve to enquire, "and we hit it off."

He wiggles his eyebrows in Larryesque fashion. "Wanta meet him?"

"Maybe," I say. "Let me think about it."

"Don't wait too long," he says with a grin. "I hear he's a hot item on the local market."

"Who says I'm shopping?" I'm trying to be cool and collected, like the good savvy therapist that I am.

"And, get this." he adds in a fake whisper. "He consulted on your deck."

Larry redesigned the deck on *my* house last summer.

"Really?"

He nods and gives me a kiss on the cheek. "For free."

He winks at me and leaves me standing on the edge of Anna's deck with a lemon drop in my hand. The party swirls around me. Anna's kids come bailing out of the house with their play clothes on, followed by a string of other kids, all headed for the beach. Soon, my lemon drop is balanced on a flat rock near water's edge, my shoes are sitting next to the rock and we are all skipping stones as far as we can toward my little city across the lake.

The next Wednesday evening, Dr. McElroy and I are sitting on the deck at Neutron. For the first time in a while, we walked there together, upon which walk I confirm a suspicion I've had for a while. McElroy, by Bill's rating system, is a "square." I did get him to jay-cross with me once, but while I trotted, he very pointedly walked.

"So, McElroy," I say, "Have you ever read *The Princess on the Glass Hill?"*

"The what?" he says.

"It's a fairy tale," I say.

"Oh," he says. "Then probably not. I never liked fairy tales."

"Why not?"

"I don't know," he says. "They just never interested me."

"What did you read when you were a kid?"

"Tom Swift," he says. He's serious.

"Sci-fi fantasy? From the generation before us?"

He nods.

"But you don't like fairy tales."

He shrugs. I've already stolen the cherry out of his old fashioned. I am *not* about to tell him about the golden apples. The sun is lowering behind us. Bill and Angie walk by holding hands. They don't see me, and I don't call out to them. They are happy enough today without my help. And probably tomorrow, too.

McElroy is looking at me like I'm supposed to say something more, but there is really nothing more to say. I look away.

Cinderlad, I think, ***where the*** hell ***are you?***

Just as I think this, Smart Dog comes trotting across the street from the direction of the lake. He spots me sitting on the deck, gets a big grin and raises a hand in greeting. My right hand lifts of its own accord and waves back. He strides up Minnehaha, tapping Bill as he passes. Bill says something to him, it appears, because he turns and gives them that same grin. I watch him until he disappears.

Final Round
Epilogue

It's nearly a year to the day since Bill and I sat on this same bench in the October sunshine and he began to tell me about his iceberg, the tragedies that haunted him and kept him from enjoying life as an adult much of the time. Bill and Angie — and Meg — have been to Albany and back. Angie confided to me that it was one of the hardest weeks of her life, and not because it was bad, but because it was so good she spent a great deal of time waiting for something to go wrong, some episodic meltdown that would ruin it all. "I 's the cause of all my own trouble," she confesses, with a small laugh.

She has also asked me to be maid of honor in December ("Matron" might be a more appropriate term, but I'm going with "maid." That's what she asked.). She and her boxer are tying the knot. At his request. Maybe Smart Dog will go with. He's pretty independent, but I like that. If I ask *just so*. . . . I laugh to think about it.

Bill called me early last week and asked if he could meet with me, that there was something he wanted to tell me. He's off my regular schedule now, replaced by a woman who is the angriest person I have ever dealt with professionally. We are just beginning to expore her rage, and I wonder if I am ever going to be able to help her moderate it.

Bill, on the other hand, may be one of my proudest achievements. The frightened 220-pound five-year old who confided one of his deepest, darkest secrets on this self same bench just twelve months ago seems to have been absorbed and assimilated by the man sitting calmly beside me.

"I wanted ta tell ya something my mom told me," he says. He laughs. " 'My mom.' It still feels funny to say that and know, really know, who I'm talkin' about."

"It's good though, huh?"

"Oh, yeah. Sometimes hard, but good. Real good."

"So, what did she tell you?"

"Things 'bout my dad that made me — I don't know what, really —it s'prised me and made me sad — and happy, too."

"And that was?"

He clears his throat, as if there is something catching there; takes my hand and puts it in the crook of his big, scarred-up right arm. "Said when they first met, he 's the handsomest, nicest man she ever saw. Treated her like a queen."

He stops and looks down that same bike path he took off on the day he said his dad was no part of him. He swallows and turns to face the lake. "Told Meg, with me sitting there, that the night she 's conceived was one of the happiest of her life, that it wasn't until later when he 's drinkin' — well, you know what I told ya."

"You asked her about that?"

"Yep."

"You are very brave, William Warren," I say, and he smiles a sad smile.

"Maybe," he says, "but not as brave as her." Now, he's beginning to weep. " ' 'ts alcohol that 's the monster,' my mom says to us— Angie, too. 'Got him by the throat and never let him go,' she says. She's real sad. 'He tried to quit every week and every way, sometimes every day, until he just gave up an' b'came the monster himself.' Says she stayed so long 'cause it was so good in the beginnin,' she thought it'd be that way 'gain. But it never was." Tears are pouring unhindered down his cheeks.

He pauses and catches a breath, wipes his eyes. I imagine chards of iceberg melting in his wake; just bits of leftover ice, now, melting fast in the warmer waters of now. He takes a deep breath, as if he's diving in.

"She didn't leave 'cause she 's afraid he 's gonna kill 'er," he says slowly. "She left 'cause she 's 'fraid he'd kill her in fronta us kids."

I sit a while and absorb that, and finally say, "From which there would be no redemption."

He nods. "None fer any of us."

I'm nearly crying myself. "She loved him very much."

"Yep. I'd say so. An' us, too."

We sit together for a long time in the sunshine of this October without saying another word, but I think this thought: *Love never ends.*

The End

Her Name is Lillian

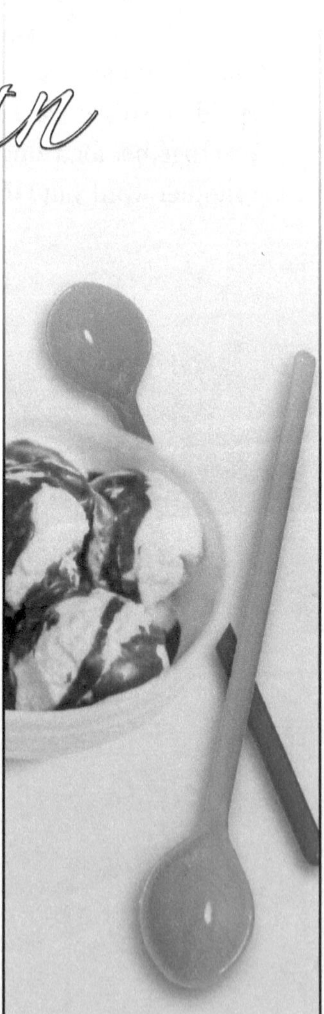

Mary Magdalene Miller, savvy therapist, is falling in love with two people at the same time. One is "the smart dog," an architect who may or may not be wooing her. It's hard to tell. The other is Lillian, a 15-year-old anorexic girl intent on becoming invisible by starving herself.

Two O'Clock On Thursdays

Batting Average

Once there was a girl who so wanted to fly away that she endeavored to make herself light enough that she could use her arms for wings. When it became apparent to her that this was not going to work, she decided instead to make herself invisible. Though the goal has changed, the method of approach has not. She tries to do this through eating. Or, more accurately, not eating.

Lillian is her name. When we first met, she had, for the past 18 months or so, been suffering anorexia nervosa; an eating disorder characterized by fear of becoming fat and refusal of food, leading to debility and even death. That's right out of the dictionary, by the way, a simple definition for a very complex problem. As that, it is not entirely accurate. Psychiatric textbooks, encyclopedias and the world wide web go on and on, including internet sites that encourage it, unfortunately. But the basic definition will have to suffice for right now, because all the other additional information won't fit and still leave room for Lillian's story.

My job is to root out the cause of Lillian's disease— and effect a cure — before the ultimate conclusion of the disease is reached. I'm her therapist.

At least, I am at this point. There are considerations that might nix that as I begin this, but I'm trying not to think about that too much, and just continue to do my job as best as I am able.

I've already said this in stories of other clients and/or patients, but you may not have had a chance to explore them: Please get don't get tense about tense. Some of this is written in retrospect. Some is transcribed from recordings of sessions. Some is lifted from session notes. And some is from my personal journal, which is where I am working today, because some of this has not so much to do with Lillian as it does with other, more personal "stuff."

But, it's all going on at the same time, and to say that there is an impermeable layer between my professional and personal lives would be a big, fat lie. Given that, I need to say that Mary Magdalene Miller is not my real name, any more than Lillian's real name is Lillian Ballenkamp. But, those will have to do because my credentials will get revoked by the AMA or the APA if I use our real names. Not that I don't take a few chances in that direction from time to time. But these names will work, just as the rest of the made up names in this story will, because the really important thing here is the story. And Lillian's healthy recovery. A miracle for which I hope. And pray. And some other stuff I hope and pray for.

I'm not sure psychiatrists are actually supposed to pray, though I'm sure that my psychiatric heroes, Jung and Frankl, did so on a regular basis. And sometimes, I bet, spontaneously. Particularly Frankl, who survived Nazi death camps of the Holocaust as a young, Jewish psychiatrist. His small and vital opus *Man's Search For Meaning*, might be one of the most important books of the 20th century. He went on to invent and implement logostherapy, a school of psychiatry founded on the premise that the belief that one's life has meaning might cure most neuroses, as well as many psychoses. That Frankl quotes Jung serves only to endear him to me more.

Frankl lived through years in a place where food — the lack thereof, actually —was used as a weapon; a method of abasement and intentional murder of others. Lillian, when I met her, was using her self-denial of its benefits as a method of self-destruction. And I didn't really know what to do about it. Still don't some days.

But, that's not an unusual place for me to be.

In recent times, my 2:00 p.m. patients on Thursdays, the space currently occupied by Lillian in my professional schedule, have been of special interest. Not that all my patients aren't of interest, but for some reason this time slot often — but not always — seems to be reserved for people who come to mean more to me than simple professional challenge and care. Part of the reason for that is that I really have had no idea of what to do with them; no clear-cut, cliché, clinical procedure that I can call on. It's more like a game of pick-up psychiatry in which I find myself making it up as I go.

Thus, the prayer.

But, so far, so good. Previous two-on-Thursdays have worked out well; some of them miraculously so, in fact. I'm not so sure about Lillian's prognosis, but I wasn't so sure about the others in the beginning, either.

I suppose I could worry about batting average if I so choose, but I do not. I have enough to worry about. Or, more accurately, to try not to worry about. At which I am sometimes successful.

"The Girl"
Lillian

I met Lillian for the first time in consultation with her parents, after I had first met with her mother alone. Marion Ballenkamp came seeking someone who would agree to take Lillian as a patient, and I got the impression that I wasn't her first choice, but some circumstance had sent her to me. After a half-hour interview with her, during which she talked mostly about herself, I agreed to meet with Lillian and both her parents. It was understood that I would make up my mind about taking Lillian after we all met, but after that initial thirty minutes, I was almost certain I would.

Marion, I came to know — forgive me my judgment — is a driven woman who needs success in the same way some need alcohol. She sells real estate, and she is the first one at her desk in the morning and the last one at her desk at night. Sometimes, when she is hot on the heels of a deal, the two merge. She does this, she tells me, "for the girl's future," though I think she is running from the past; perhaps a huge and unstated regret that she married Lillian's father and had a daughter in the first place. This is my assumption after meeting her husband, and we all know what "assume" does. Still, it's apparent — to me —that she is running from something, and as long as she is pursuing that other, she doesn't have to think about what the something is.

We haven't talked about that because, as she will point out in the meeting with her husband and Lillian and I, she is not the one going into therapy, though I think she might be well served to be. When I mention family counseling as a possibility, she laughs.

"I'm fine, Doctor," she says, "Unlike the girl, I have no trouble keeping my breakfast down."

This in front of "the girl," Lillian.

Lillian doesn't react visibly except to look away and out the window that opens on the street in front of my office building. We are in inner sanctum — my interview room, you might call it — and it's raining outside; not hard, just a cold, soaking rain that early April is famous for around here.

Mr. Ballenkamp — Joseph, not Joe — is sitting in the corner, silent and apparently bored. He's somewhat famous in our little city for his lack of discretion. He is known for his philandering. How the marriage survives is a mystery. Or why. I think he might be well served by some therapy, also, but that seems even less likely than Marion's chances.

He's a cold fish, something tells me. I look in his direction and he is looking back at me, as if sizing me up. I suppress a shudder. Not a fish, I tell the something, but definitely cold blooded.

We've not made much progress, the four of us. None of the others want to be here. I look at Lillian, who is, I know by the form in front of me, 15 years and 6 months old and 5 feet and 5 inches tall. She weighs, Madeline's scale tells me, 98 pounds. With her shoes on. She has high cheekbones and beautiful gray eyes that seem way too big for her face, like an anime drawing. A waif. She is behind in school, even though I suspect she is brilliantly intelligent. She is lovely and fragile and tough as nails, I think.

I say her name. "Lillian."

She turns from the window and looks at me full on for the first time. Her head tilts back, her chin points straight at me and her lids fall half-way across her eyes. It is apparent to me that she is, above all else, extraordinarily angry. Enraged, in fact.

"Would you like to come see me for a while? On a professional basis?"

For an instant, she looks startled, as if she is surprised that I would be asking her what she wants to do. Then the curtain comes down again.

"Not really," she says, as if the idea is revolting.

Marion starts to say something, and I hold up my hand. "This is between Lillian and me, please." The mother's jaw muscles stand out, but she holds her tongue.

"But will you?"

"I don't have a choice, do I?"

"Yes. You do."

"They say I have to." She doesn't look at her parents, but the implication is clear.

"You mom and dad," I begin, and I might have poked them all with the same red-hot iron. Interesting, I think. "Your mother and father," I say, and everyone twitches again, "want you to enter therapy for your eating problem . . . "

"I don't have an eating problem," she interrupts. "I just don't eat."

At this statement, I make the initial diagnosis of anorexia. Bulemics eat. They just don't keep it down. I knew that I might be wrong, but it seemed most likely. I would learn I was correct.

"Don't interrupt, please," I say. "It's not polite."

She looks surprised. I am not looking at her parents. On some level — many levels, in fact — I don't care what they think.

"I apologize for assuming you have an eating problem. That hasn't really been determined, has it? Although, I have my suspicions."

She says nothing, but she is still looking right at me.

"Let me begin again. Your parents want you to enter therapy. I think it would be a good idea, because, as a doctor, I can see that you are not in the best of health. But I won't ask you to come here against your will. In this state, your parents, as your legal guardians, have the right to place you under care against your will, but I won't take you on under those conditions."

"Then why should I come?"

"Because," I say, "I believe it could be helpful for you to talk to someone about the circumstances of your life."

Because, I think, *I want you to.*

CONSULTATION
Do I Really?

Do I really? Want her to? Or am I just being Quixotic?"

"The girl's not a windmill," McElroy says.

"She has a name," I say. My testiness surprises us both.

He frowns. "Yes she does, I imagine."

"Sorry. I know you don't know her name. 'The girl.' That's how her mother refers to her. Grrr. Sometimes the rules of this profession make me crazy."

"Yes, I know they do. Despite the compassionate basis of your desire to have her come see you, rules are for a reason," he says, all McElroyish.

Thanks very much for the lecture on ethics, McElroy, I am thinking.

"But, bending the rules a bit," he continues, "I think I know who you're talking about. Lillian, right?"

Just when I think Dr. McElroy can't surprise me, he does.

We're doing after-hours therapy at Neutron, as we have regularly ever since the place opened a few years ago. We don't do it as often as we used to — every Wednesday night, for a while, with certain notable exceptions — because James F. McElroy . . . let me just say I know another man that I would rather spend time with, given the chance. After-hours therapy sessions have moved out of the realm of indulgence and back into the realm of necessity.

Do I Really?

Today's necessity is my own doubts about my motivation for accepting Lillian as a patient, which she has not agreed to yet, and may not. I left it up to her, much to the displeasure of her mother. Joseph didn't seem to care one way or the other. I'm not so worried about Lillian's answer as I am about having to deal with her parents if she does say "yes." I do want her to say "yes," but I'm pretty sure that isn't going to solve the parenting problem, and if that doesn't get solved — I've already thought about that too much.

McElroy surprises me again. "They came to me first. I turned them down. Malpractice suit waiting to happen, I think."

He takes a sip out of his Old Fashioned. I only recently discovered that McElroy always orders a double, which explains how he can make one drink last so long. I had always thought it was remarkable restraint.

I stopped stealing the cherry out of his drink a while ago, which he has noticed, I'm sure, but has not noted aloud. Dr. McElroy is no fool, except about certain things.

The other man is due here any minute, and that thought makes my heart do a small forward roll. Thirty-something going on sixteen, I think. At least, my heart lands on its feet. I'm no fool either, and even less a fool is Adam Turpin, architect and man of interest in my life. We are not quite going steady, but we are steadily going in the direction of going steady. I really like Adam. And, he really likes me. I think. And sometimes pray. That's my picture beside "infatuated" in the dictionary today. At least, I know I am, and what it means.

There's that forward roll again, this time with a handstand and fancy landing. I catch myself smiling, and so does McElroy.

"What?" he says.

I say nothing, and then he says, "Oh." He's looking over my head, and I know the smart dog — Mr. Turpin — is headed our way. I slide over as he fronts the table and he sits down beside me.

"Hi," he says. That's all. He has a draft beer in his left hand and the Adam smile on his face. "Doctor," he says, and reaches across to clink his glass against McElroy's. "How goes the therapy session?"

It is a general question, pointed at both of us.

"Nearly concluded," McElroy says. "Just one more thing."

"Shall I give you another moment?"

"No need," McElroy says. He pats my hand on the table, a liberty he has seldom taken before, but maybe now that it's safe . . .

"Yes, Miller, you are being Quixotic. Maybe even a little idiotic. But I admire your courage. And I wish you success. But, just in case, I'll e-mail you my lawyer's name."

He laughs. "How are you, Adam?"

Therapy is over, but that's three surprises in three minutes. Holy cow!

Enamoration

James F. McElroy, M.D.

While we are on the subject, I might tell you that at one time I was quite enamored of Dr. James F. McElroy, M.D. Confession is good for the soul, they say. But Dr. McElroy has never returned the enamoration. He has, instead, consistently stayed behind his attractive exterior, as if his good looks are walls within which the real him hunkers while he analyzes all things. I would think that he who analyzes all things would have recognized that I was enamored, and maybe he did or does, but he has never spoken to it or acted upon it.

This, for a while, caused me some serious angst, which unacknowledged infatuation is prone to do. (I'm being a bit analytical myself, today). I found myself wondering if there was something wrong with me, but it turns out I'm just fine.

I thought this before I met McElroy (with occasional and normal spates of self-doubt), and after some months of suffering his lack of engagement beyond superficiality, I remembered that I was just fine, and relaxed around him. We had, after that, some good moments, enough to keep my hopes up, but after a couple of years of hope and patience and being my best self around him, it became apparent that he was never coming out from behind his good looks to meet me in any intimate way

This sounds like a report on a patient, which it sort of is. "Physician, heal thyself," a great man said once. I've not been completely brokenhearted over McElroy, but I have been sad. First, it was for myself, regretting all the time I put into a relationship that is really not much more than a sort of symbiotic pact. He helps me clarify certain challenges of the profession, particularly through what I think of as our after-hours therapy sessions, which involve having a cocktail and sometimes dinner together in a public venue.

He's not asked me for advice nearly as much as I have him. I'm not sure, but I suspect my role has been to be his public female friend to keep other females at bay. Maybe. I asked him once, in a semi-joking manner, if he was gay, and he just laughed. Still.

A year ago, I accepted the fact that Dr. McElroy was never going to come out to play in any meaningful way. Six months later — last October — my former and favorite "client" Larry Longquist introduced me to the smart dog.

I was already aware of Adam because of his relationships with Larry and my friend and former patient, Bill Warren — both two-on-Thursday "miracles." Maybe psychiatrists aren't supposed to think of their successes as miracles, any more than we are supposed to pray, but some days I can't help but think that Something — with a capital "s" — is operative in inner sanctum and in the other places I meet with people.

Adam is not by any means a dog, but Bill was familiar enough with him to give him the "smart dog" tag, based on the way he moves through our city. Since Larry introduced us, and ever so slowly, we have been moving toward each other. I think I already know more about Adam than I ever will about Dr. McElroy, even though Adam and I have known each other about one tenth of the time I have known James.

My sadness for myself has transformed into sadness for McElroy, which is probably projection on my part. He may be perfectly happy and fulfilled living inside his walls, but I get the idea that he is afraid to come out and join other people in any meaningful way. I may be his best friend, for that matter, and if that's so, maybe his only.

See, now I am about to cry. I don't like that idea. It seems like a big responsibility for me, and a sad state of affairs for McElroy.

But, I am extremely grateful for the time I spent in passive pursuit of him, because it gave me great practice in being hopeful, patient and my best self around a person I really like, and want to really like me as well. I am applying that practice to the smart dog.

The timing of all this has been a good lesson. It was after I accepted that McElroy was never coming out of his shell for me —maybe not for anybody — that I first saw Adam, though we live in the same small city and share several friends. Since then, he and I have been doing the "getting-to-know-you" dance, adagio. One little bit at a time. He hasn't met my folks yet, nor I his, but I am thinking of inviting him and my mom and dad to dinner at my house to see what happens. Full disclosure to all parties will be made.

Now, that is completely terrifying. But, I will be brave, as my good old dad taught me to be long ago.

But, I'm getting way ahead of myself; like four months. It's September. Let's go back to April.

Adam Turpin
The Smart Dog

It's a week after the consultation with Lillian and parents. Madeline the office manager informed me on Monday that Mrs. Ballenkamp called to say that Lillian has agreed to enter therapy with me. Purposefully, I told Madeline to put her into the 2:00 slot on Thursday. I'm not really superstitious, but if something seems to work, why not take advantage. The woman who occupied it after Bill is doing well enough that she's "on maintenance," which means we catch up as we need to, often with a phone call between visits with others in inner sanctum.

So, the two-on-Thursday slot is full again; of what may be the biggest challenge of my career. With the possible exception of anatomy class. All that interconnected stuff making up the human body — whew. Lift a finger and the whole thing notices in some way or another, even as the intellect takes it all for granted. It's all connected, and, for me, that thought got extended into the larger world. We are all connected.

Some wish not to be, and that seems to be the case with Lillian's parents when it comes to their daughter and each other, but it's too late for Lillian to isolate herself from them. Or maybe too early. Maybe with help, Lillian can separate herself from her parents' apparent lack of real care for her.

That's what I've been thinking about since Madeline gave me the news.

In the world of medical ethics, us doctors are not to speak to anyone else about a specific patient except with permission of the patient and in consultation with other professionals who might be handy in achieving healing for said patient. I'm not sure what percentage of us manage to keep that confidence absolutely. Most after-hours therapy with McElroy has had more to do with my doubts and challenges than it has been about those of my patients. Sometimes, though, the discussion has turned to a patient's troubles.

As the smart dog and I move closer, I find myself consulting him about my doubts and challenges, which at first was somewhat scary, but after his first few responses, I came to know that this was perfectly fine. And he has actually asked for — and accepted — advice from me. Adam's advice is at least as good as McElroy's, and delivered without McElroy's analytics; less logic and more compassion. Which, when I think about it might not be the right combination for me, because I am less logic and more compassion myself. Maybe we need someone to balance our nature, so we cover all the bases.

When it comes to Adam, I think I have thought more about our relationship than a.) I need to and b.) I have ever thought about any other single thing in my life. Well, maybe anatomy is a tie. But still. This isn't a college class, though maybe it should be. If it were, maybe the divorce rate would be lower. There I am, thinking about it again.

Adam Turpin. 40-something. Not tall. Not short. Just right. Blondish. Very blue eyes that get bluer when he gets excited about something. Architect. Grew up near Yellowstone Park. He's lived here for about eight years —why he left the mountains, I don't know yet — long enough to have designed three of the most attractive buildings in town, and some others as well. Single, and not divorced — important distinction. He's not slender or skinny or slim. He is lithe, in a muscular sort of way. He's an occasional runner — a couple of miles about once a week, which he says helps him think. He also walks (or hikes) almost everywhere he goes.

I was beginning to suspect that he didn't even own a car, but it turns out he does: a silver Volvo C30, which is sort of like him. Lithe. Attractive.

Efficient (35-plus mpg). And sort of rare. It will hold four folks in a pinch, but it's much more suitable for two. He bought it new, I will find out, and after a decade plus, it has just over 50,000 miles on it. I have yet to ride in it, and I wonder if he ever goes anywhere.

He's had two serious girlfriends, who he doesn't talk much about. I only know this much, so far. One broke off with him after she and he disagreed about an architectural project he was involved in. Interesting reason to break up, I think, but he seems to feel like that was the right thing for both of them. The other was while he was still living in the mountains. He has hardly mentioned her, but I get the idea that their parting was painful for him. I am being patient with that. First of all, he's not a patient. And it may be, like Larry Longquist's former wife Mary, none of my business.

He seems to be pretty even-tempered. I've not seen him angry yet, though I've seen him aggravated a time or two, but not without justification We walked to the post office together today and he pulled out of his box a handful of those horrid mega-sized postcards trashing electoral opponents without saying a word about why you should vote for the person it was sent in support of. Our May primary is coming up.

Try ripping four of those in half at once sometime. Mr. Turpin has no problem with that, and slam-dunks the remains into a trash can by the door. I say nothing, just keep up as he strides down the sidewalk. After a bit, he slows down, and then he stops and looks across the street.

I think he is looking at something in particular, but after a moment, he says, "It would be good if people would start thinking with the parts of their brains above the stem."

I understand that. "Yes," I say. "You're right."

"What's really sad, and somewhat maddening, is that both sides use attack ad tactics. It's disgusting. And what's even more disgusting, it seems to work. Grrr."

Yes, he really growled. So, I am not alone in growling.

Then, he sighs and looks at me. "Sorry," he says. "Those things irritate me."

"I can tell," I said.

He laughs. "Maybe we will learn to think someday, huh?"

"Some of us seem to know how already."

He gives me a look that I can only think of as appraising. "Yes," he says. "You're right." He nods and gets the Adam smile, and we walk back toward my office. We aren't touching, but I can still feel him and I think he can feel me.

Tomorrow is Thursday, and there are two things I could be worried about: Will Lillian show up for her first appointment? (I'm almost willing to bet not.) And will I be able to gracefully handle my weekly encounter with Hildegard the Horrific? But, I am not going to worry about those things right now. I am going to enjoy the presence of the smart dog and let him enjoy me.

Maybe less logic and more compassion squared is a good thing.

Get over yourself, Doctor, I think. *Be brave and quit overthinking the whole thing. Grrr.*

Session One
Legions of Lesions

I am surprised and pleased when Lillian does show up for our first appointment. On time. She showed no enthusiasm for beginning in our consultation with her parents, and I already said I would have bet she would skip the first session, just because. I am glad to have lost the bet.

I see by her body language as she huddles in the waiting room that she doesn't want to be here, but she is, curled into herself in one of the big chairs.

"Come on in, Lillian," I say.

She looks at me as if she's never seen me before, which she hasn't often. This is just our second time in each other's presence. It's an open look, though somewhat hostile and trepidatious. For some reason, I think of Jesus' demoniac, possessed by spirits whose name were Legion. Her look asks, "What have you to do with me?" Maybe.

I'm not Jesus or really Mary Magdalene — though I admire both. I'm not even religious, but I appreciate the mythic and archetypal elements of Biblical stories. The stories in Mark and Luke about evil spirits leaving the man for a great herd of swine have always fascinated and intrigued me.

When I was a twelve-year-old in Sunday School, I felt sorry for the poor pigs. Still do, for that matter, but why pigs? Something to do with being unclean in the eyes of the culture of that day, I suppose. And why did Legion have to ask to be allowed to enter the swine and then why did the swine rush off into the sea and drown, all two thousand of them? And then, why did the neighbors freak out instead of celebrating with this guy who was suddenly sane and free? OK. I might know the answer to that question best of all — they were the neighbor's pigs — but they are good questions all, I think.

My Sunday School teacher did not think so, and shortly after the theological discussion that ensued — it wasn't our first — took up almost all of her carefully planned session on Messianic miracles, I stopped attending Sunday School. I'm not sure if it was because I asked my parents if I could be excused from the weekly exercise in futility and frustration or if it was at the teacher's request, but I always knew somehow it was by mutual desire.

I still hold that Sunday School teachers and preachers — and their audiences — might be better off if they were to confine themselves to telling about their own experiences of God — the Spirit, the Something — and leave the miracles untarnished by their speculative tellings and translations.

Though I am almost certain that no herd of swine will be involved, Lillian's disease might also be called Legion, as it seems many-pronged and rooted in multiple places, each one a psychic wound, a lesion in her soul, if you will, that allows the disease purchase. That's how I perceive it, anyway. Finding the lesions — legions of lesions! Oh, God, I'm not sure I wanted to think that thought — is one challenge. Applying healing to as many as possible is the other; closing up the wounds before her soul oozes out and her self shrivels up and disappears. Before it — and she — becomes invisible.

What kind of box am I opening here? I think, as I usher her in.

I point her to my couch, where she perches on the edge like a sparrow ready to take flight. She is wearing black exclusively, and in the fashion of the day, a pair of lycra tights under a short skirt with a loose-fitting slouchy sweater over a close-fitting, long-sleeved top.

I ask her to stand and take the sweater off.

"Why?" she says.

"One of the things that I am, Lillian," I answer, "is a medical doctor. I specialize in mental health, but I am a doctor of the body, as well. I want to look at your body so I can better understand what is going on with you."

"Can I show you a picture instead?"

"No," I say. "That won't work."

The idea that she has pictures of herself in her current state is not an alarm bell. What kid who has a cell phone doesn't have pictures of themselves? But it does tip me to the possibility that she might be sharing those pictures on internet pro-ana sites.

After deciding to take Lillian as a patient, I began researching anorexia, and discovered through the know-all aspect of Google that these exist — in fact, there are many. They are, in my opinion, dangerous places for young women to hang out — women of any age, for that matter — but particularly preteen and teen-age girls. They normalize malnutrition and glorify anorexia. Girls compete to see who can be thinnest, lose the most weight in the shortest amount of time, and give the best hints about not eating. They even have recipes, for Something's sake. Sharing pictures is part of the deal on many of them, and the pictures are downright frightening. I make a note to ask her to show me that picture at another time, but not right now.

"Fine," she says. She gets up and takes the sweater off, and then she keeps going. I don't stop her. In less than a minute, she is standing naked in front of me, her clothing on the floor around her.

"There," she says. "You can see everything. Happy?"

I take a good look at her. I try to memorize what I am seeing, and it won't be all that hard. She is, as I already knew, extraordinarily thin. Not quite like the pictures of the residents of Auschwitz or Dachau, but a few more weeks or months of this regimen she has put herself into will lead to that. Because of this, her head appears to be outsized.

"I'm not unhappy, Lillian. Turn to the side please."

She complies. Her breasts are shrunk against her ribs, which all show. Her arms, hands and legs are pale and bony, like an old woman's.

"Turn your back to me."

She does, and her head drops. I intuit she is looking at herself, but she looks defeated. Her buttocks are shrunk and somewhat saggy, and her hipbones show distinctly, as do her shoulder blades and the points of her shoulders.

She is not a box, and she is not "the girl," I think. *She is Lillian. And when she is healthy again, she will be extraordinarily beautiful.* I am somewhat amazed that I have let myself think the words "when she is" instead of "if she is ever." But, it is a good thought, and I will keep it.

"Have you seen yourself in a mirror lately?" I ask.

Her head comes up and she turns around.

"Just this morning, as a matter of fact."

"What do you think when you see yourself?"

"I'm getting fat." She sounds disgusted, but she also seems unfazed by her nakedness. I let her stand there while I make more notes about what I have seen. I don't look at her.

She asks, finally, with a hint of anger in her voice, "May I get dressed now?"

I look up. "It was your choice to undress. Do as you see fit."

I see a flash in her eyes, and for just a second, I'm afraid that this session is going to go on with her in the nude, but then it's gone and she picks her clothes up off the floor and begins to put them on.

Session Two
You're Funny

Anorexia nervosa is one of the most interesting psychoses. And challenging. And destructive. And insidious. And confusing. Lillian's mother, for instance, has confused it with bulimia nervosa, also all of the above, but quite different. Anorexia is characterized by a refusal or reluctance to eat. Bulimia is characterized by binge eating and then purging. Both are connected to body image, particularly an obsession with weight. Lillian's refusal of food is anorexic, at least on the surface, but I find myself wondering if it's more of a symptom than the real disease.

That Marion doesn't know her daughter is not throwing up after breakfast, as opposed to not eating breakfast at all, is indicative of the true nature of Lillian's problem, I think. A mom who pays so little attention to her daughter as to be ignorant of her true eating patterns . . .

Hold up right there, Dr. Miller.

A classic case of anorexia often goes undetected for a number of reasons. The sufferer — very often female — might purposefully wear baggy clothing to hide her true physical condition. This might be because she is hiding the disease or because she is ashamed that her body isn't perfect. Or because it's the latest style. It's almost impossible to say with certainty.

Whatever the reason, anorexia often manifests at the time a girl begins the tricky process of becoming a woman. Particularly in our highly visual, image-conscious American society, there is a huge amount of pressure to be physically perfect, an unrealistic expectation that can lead to some pretty interesting mental and emotional trauma.

On the other side of that coin is what I perceive as an epidemic of obesity in the world, and particularly in the United States. In a reversal of obsession with body image, there is a trend that seems to make it OK to be grossly overweight. And not just a few pounds. My body mass index ain't perfect, that's for sure, but I can climb the stairs in my building to my floor and dog-trot across the street without chancing a coronary.

I see more and more people of whom that is not true. The very thought of exercise might kill some of the more extreme cases. It seems a combination of "convenience" food, lack of personal restraint and societal acceptance have created a perfect storm of morbidly overweight men and women who, besides harming themselves, also stress the health-care system by their tendency to suffer heart problems and other general health issues. As a doctor and mental health specialist,

I find this all very interesting — in a distressing sort of way — and wonder some days how all this will play out in the future of our country and the larger world.

There's that word again: "interesting." Lillian's second session was indeed that.

She has decided to come see me on a regular basis; not without some parental pressure I'm sure, but she says she is here willingly. I question her motives, but not publically and not too closely. She is here, and that is a good beginning. Two o'clock on Thursdays, for one thing, gets her out of school an hour early. Not sure what class she is missing, if any. High school isn't like it was when I went, I don't think. OK. I know it isn't. Even though it doesn't seem that long ago that I was at Fillmore High.

Millard Fillmore seems to me to be a ridiculous president to name a high school after, but the laws of chance seem to dictate that someone will go to a school named after our thirteenth president. My classmates and I were chosen by fate to do so.

Lillian doesn't go to Fillmore, but to Minnehaha Alternative High School, a laid-back sort of hall of learning for the kids who used to hang out on the corner across the street from my school, smoke cigarettes, wear black and have children at an early age. Demographically, Lillian doesn't fit in. Her parents have way too much money. But by attitude and demeanor, she's a natural.

She has died her hair since our first session. It is naturally a little on the chestnut side, now jet black. She is sitting stiffly on the couch, knees tightly together, arms folded across her chest, leaning forward as if she is about to rise to her feet. I am making a few notes to begin the interview.

"Aren't you supposed to be asking me questions?"

"Maybe," I counter. "Maybe I will just wait to see what you want to tell me."

I am determined to be somewhat of a hardass with Lillian. I believe that it's important to establish and maintain some real boundaries with her, one being that I run the sessions, not her.

I do this for the simple reason that she seems to have none in the rest of her life. I wish for her to trust me, and will not to try to be her friend or even inordinately kind, but to be fair and present. If there is one thing that Lillian needs in her life, it's some real boundaries, hard walls of behavior — even if set by another — that she can trust to be there when she needs or wants to lean on them.

I continue my notes, mostly about my perception of her physical being. She is, if possible, thinner than she was a week ago.

"I don't want to tell you anything."

"Then this is perfect, isn't it?" I don't look at her.

She begins rocking a bit, which many of my clients do when seated and trying to speak to their pain — or, in Lillian's case, not speak to it. She starts to look around the room, curious, perhaps, about my curiosities. I keep beautiful things in inner sanctum.

"Feel free to look more closely at anything you wish," I offer. I'm curious to see what she might pick.

She snaps back to her original pose, stiff as a board.

The standoff continues, but after a bit, I catch her looking at something behind me and to my left. She is looking at it quite openly, with enough attention that she doesn't see that I am looking at her, or if she does, she doesn't seem to care. I mentally inventory the glass-fronted bookcase on that wall, a lovely piece I found in an antique mall when I was out walking with Bill, my second-to-last two-on-Thursday.

On top of the case is a realistic carving of a wooden platter piled with sliced apples and cheeses. I'm not sure what the wood is, but it is hard and dark and of one piece. Maybe walnut. The artist was talented as a carver and a painter. Replicated are different sorts of apples and a variety of cheeses. As a crowning touch, he — his name was Frank Argot — imbedded an antique paring knife that had been sharpened down over decades in a chunk of what appears for all the world to be bleu cheese.

"Are you hungry?" I ask. My own voice intruding on our silence surprises even me. Lillian jumps as if she has been shocked.

"Yes."

"Do you want something to eat?"

"No."

"Why, if you are hungry, wouldn't you want something to eat?"

She shrugs and looks away from the carving. "I don't know."

"Is that true? That you don't know?"

"You wouldn't understand all the reasons."

"That's true. Maybe not all the reasons all at once, but perhaps I could understand them one at a time. Do you understand all the reasons?"

Her arms tighten around herself.

"No."

"Maybe we could figure them out one at a time."

"Why?"

"Good question. Why do you think we might do such a thing, figure them out one at a time."

"So my parents will continue to pay you?"

Her cynicism is searing, as deep as her anger. Well it should be, as they are likely based in the same thing, but I'm surprised at its depth, and at the depth it intrudes into me, like that paring knife embedded in the replicated bleu cheese.

I'm not quite prepared for it. I need to catch my breath. Silence returns to inner sanctum.

After a while, though, I ask, "Assuming that your parents continuing to pay me might be one answer to my question, what might be another?"

"I don't know."

"May I make a suggestion?"

"If you insist."

"I don't insist. I'm asking your permission."

She squints at me with eyes as hard and piercing as kleig lights — as if I'm some sort of wraith that she can't quite focus on.

Take a chance, Lillian, I think.

Give us both a chance, God, I pray, *or this little girl is toast.*

Something changes in her eyes. She looks away, back at the carving.

"Suggest away," she says.

"If we were to figure out a few reasons — one at a time, even — you might be able to have something to eat when you're hungry."

"But that would interfere with my plan to become invisible."

"Invisible. That's your plan?"

She nods. And puts her hands over her eyes. "You can't see me," she says. She takes her hands down and grows a grin that is real, but more like that of a three-year-old than a 15-year-old.

"Invisible."

She nods with enthusiasm.

"Are you afraid of being seen?"

She looks at something out of the corner of her eyes — nothing, but something, if you know what I mean.

"If nobody can see me, nobody can hurt me."

"Who wants to hurt you?"

She looks away, out that same window. "Who doesn't?"

"Well, there's me," I say.

She laughs.

I wasn't sure why Lillian laughed, and still may not be, but it was a good sound, one that took us both somewhat by surprise.

"You're funny," she said. There is not a hint of sarcasm in her voice.

"Yes, sometimes I can be."

LAUGHTER *Good For The Soul*

"You're funny." Adam says. He's grinning and I can see he means that in a good way.

"Some of my patients think so, too," I say.

We are, for a change, strolling — as opposed to hiking — through the park near the river on the outskirts of town. It's not my favorite park, which is a stately old thing in my neighborhood across town, but it's still a pretty nice park. It's only about ten years old, so it's still growing up. I can imagine it as an adult park, and it will be spectacular. In fact, I have made it a goal to live long enough to see it when it becomes adult — say in 50 years.

In the meantime, it's late April — May is next week — the sun is out and all the adolescent trees are just unfurling their new leaves. The older trees in my neighborhood park have been busily doing the same, but these upstarts are ahead of the game. Ah, youth.

"So, you have them cracking up on the couch?"

"Not all the time. But we have some good moments."

"Good moments," he says.

"I don't know who it was, but someone once said, 'Laughter is good for the soul.' "

"Abraham Lincoln?" he says, and this makes me laugh.

"So," he asks, "do you consider yourself a doctor of the soul?"

I know the answer to this question, though I have never even asked it of myself.

"Yes. Not always, but sometimes. And, for God's sake, don't tell the world."

He laughs again. Maybe I *am* funny.

OK. I can be pretty funny when I let myself be. My father once called me a natural smart-aleck when I was a teenager running my mouth about something. I try to keep things a bit lighter in inner sanctum than some people expect. More than once, someone has asked me, "Are we supposed to be laughing about this?" Maybe not right out loud, but by some sort of expression.

Some folks aren't immediately ready to laugh about their problems, and I can't say that I blame them. But when they are, I see that they are healing. Maybe that's why Lillian's laughter has been so much on my mind for the past couple of days. What does *that* mean? I find myself wondering. Is she *really* getting better this quickly, or am I having false hope?

"Hey, Doctor," Adam says. "Where are you?"

'Just wandering around in my mind," I say, and he laughs again. "Sorry. Thinking about a patient. Madeline would tell me to take the rest of the day off."

"Madeline?"

"My office manager; guardian of all things pecuniary as well as timekeeper and advisor on keeping my life in balance. In other words, she makes sure I don't work too much, so I have time to do these kinds of things with . . . "

I realize I have talked myself into a corner. I'm not wanting to be proprietary with Adam at this point. Maybe never, for that matter. He's not mine, after all. He is his. And I am mine. And we are both of such a nature that it will work best if we kind of keep it that way. I think. Maybe. Arggh!

"With?" he says, and there are like twelve question marks on that question. OK, at least six.

"My friends," I say, standing on the edge. Then, I jump in. "With you."

He decides to tease me. I think. Maybe. Again.

"Am I your friend?" He asks like a six-year-old, which he certainly isn't in any way, manner or form.

"Let me think about that," I say, much to my own surprise. Teasing runs both ways.

I remember what Larry Longquist taught me about friendship. A friend is someone you know, like and trust. We stroll a bit farther. He's not hanging on my answer, which I think is extra good. I like this guy. I'm getting to know him. Above all else, I trust him.

"Yes." I say. "Yes, you are."

He gets the Adam smile. I'm not sure if all friends hold hands, but I suddenly want to. I settle for putting my left hand through the crook of his right arm.

"Whew!" he says, in mock relief.

It is possible to stroll and crack up at the same time.

A few hundred yards down the river path, he says, "Back to the original question. Or the answer to the original question. Why wouldn't you want the world to know you are a doctor of the soul?"

I think that's a good question, and say so. I add, "I may have to think about that."

"Now or later?"

I giggle. "I think later. Madeline doesn't like it when I think about work too much on my days off."

"Fair enough. But I will be interested to know what you discover."

"Duly noted." For some reason, I am suddenly famished. All this strolling and laughing. "I'm hungry."

"Food. Good idea."

We *hike* back to the Volvo, which I met just today, and head for Deli-Vision, a big, fat meat-lover's pizza and a beer. We are both glowing. Inside and out, I think.

FOOD STUFF
A Clear Assignment

When I was a waitress, back in the days of pre-med college, I met many people who had some issue or another with food; some small, some large. Most young kids who won't eat anything green will eventually get over it, but not all. Some folks are very determined to finish everything on their plate, even though there are perfectly good to-go boxes at their beck and call, and even though they are in no way hungry after finishing half their dinner. Some purposefully leave one bite as a symbol of their personal restraint. Some gobble up the protein and leave everything else. Some pace themselves so that all the elements on the plate are finished at the same time.

One of my patients surprised me when they confessed they were addicted to food, or more accurately, eating. But they were also deeply into recovery, and hadn't acted out in years. And now there is Lillian, who is not addicted to not eating, I don't think, but simply determined to starve herself to invisibility.

"You do know that if you achieve invisibility, it will be because you are dead?" I say in session number four. I have not asked her to show me the picture of herself she offered, yet, and I may not. Her physical presence is enough to let me know the state of her body. I'm trying to figure out the state of her mind.

She looks at me out of the corner of her left eye. "An unfortunate side effect, but yes, I know that."

"So, in your effort to escape those who wish to hurt you, you are instead hurting yourself."

"Yes."

"How does that make sense?"

Lillian is, I think, even more intelligent than I initially believed. Somewhere around genius, would be my guess.

"It gives me control of the situation," she says.

Yes, I think. That's the mantra of several of the pro-ana sites I've gotten a look at. A lot of these are closed groups that one has to apply to get into, which I am not compelled to do. I can learn enough distressing stuff by reading the stories of people who had been active in them or investigated them. One investigator wrote about the "goddess of malnutrition," noting that some of the people in the group she got into seemed to actually worship "her."

A slogan from the Twelve Step programs comes to mind: "In control means out of control." When addicts try to manage their own addictions — "I can only have two beers today." — the management plan might last a few days or a few months. Then, it comes undone, and the planner has another reason to drink or eat or whatever: their own regret and guilt that the plan failed. Denial on steroids, you might say.

But what is Lillian addicted to, if anything? Or is she so without hope that she can't see beyond her pain to anywhere that might make sense.

She is looking at the carving again.

"Are you hungry?" I ask.

"Yes."

"Does being hungry all the time affect how you think?"

"Yes."

"How so?"

"It allows me to see things very clearly."

"So, you see your only future as death by starvation?"

"No," she says. "There are other possibilities."

I feel this is somewhat hopeful, so I ask, "What might one be?"

"I could get hit by a truck."

Some big hope that is, I think. This is making me tired. And sad. And, when I think about it, angry.

"You see no reason to live," I say. Declarative sentence. No question mark.

"Correct."

"Then why are you here?"

She is still looking at the carving.

"If I tell you, will you promise not to tell my parents."

"Yes."

My immediate response surprises me, but it doesn't seem to surprise Lillian. She looks at me full on for maybe the third time ever, and I see again how beautiful she will be if she were to give up trying to become invisible.

"Maybe you can save my life," she says.

I look away. I want to cry, but I don't want to cry in front of Lillian, at least not right now, so I ram the nails of my left hand into my palm. That succeeds in stopping any unauthorized flow.

After a long half-minute, I ask, "Do you want to be saved?"

"Yes. I think so."

Her usually reserved manner is showing signs of breaking, and I'm not sure I want that to happen, either. I would rather that no huge emotional outburst happen to either one of us. Not right now, anyway. Maybe later, for me. Probably later, in fact.

"How does your exceptionally clear thinking indicate that could happen?"

She pulls back into her shell.

"You're the one who has to figure that out."

We are saved from drowning in each other's tears, and I have a clear assignment.

Rearrangement
Some Miracles Take Longer

"So, Lillian," I ask on the next Thursday, "A few sessions ago, when I said 'There's me,' why did you laugh ?

"You said, 'Well, there's me.' "

"OK. That's what I said," (I make a mental note that she remembered exactly what I said.) "Still, why did you laugh."

She is not any thinner that I can see, which is a good thing. Maybe she's in a holding pattern. I will ask her later, but now I am interested to know why she laughed.

"It was funny," she says. "The way you said it. You sounded like a kid."

"I'll take that as a compliment," I said.

From her expression, I think she is not sure what that means, but I'm sincere in that. Nothing wrong with being as honest as a kid from time to time. That's what I say.

I have done a little rearranging in inner sanctum this week. Nice to freshen up the look once in a while. I've moved paintings around, switched out two for two from home, and moved some of my "knick-knacks" around. Some may really be a bit too valuable to call a "knick-knack," but that's what comes to mind.

With Lillian in mind, I deliberately put the apple and cheese carving somewhere else. She can still see it from where she normally sits, but it's at a different angle than what she's used to. In its place, I placed a glazed pottery rendition of the Mayan fertility god, a plump and well-endowed female holding corn in her arms, a sort of anti-anorexic symbol. I'm not sure Lillian will get it, but at least I do.

I have done this sort of thing with patients before, moving some object they seem to be interested in to a new place in the office, and timing how long it will take them to re-find it, if they do so at all. Many, but not all, will search out the moved piece within five minutes of arrival (I don't try to hide them). Some settle in without comment or action. Once in a while, someone will ask, "What happened to the 'whatever?' " But not often.

But, I often ask them about what the object might mean to them.

I'm not always sure what I learn from doing this — sometime the answer is just, "It's pretty," — but it's an interesting exercise. Sometimes, I learn something very important. In the case of one woman — the last two-on-Thursday before Lillian — her favorite object was an enameled vase with an intricate floral design. In the first session after I moved it, I was afraid I had made a big mistake, because she was almost panicky. Her eyes darted around frantically, and she couldn't focus on our conversation until she found it. It took her only two minutes, but it was a long two minutes.

She visibly relaxed, then, and seemed to come back to herself.

"I moved the vase," I said.

"Yes," she said. "I see that."

"Is that vase especially important to you?"

She bit her lip and didn't answer right away. I waited.

Finally, she said, "It reminds me of the urn my mom's ashes were in."

I knew she had lost her mom relatively early in life, when she was in her twenties, to a car accident. She was now in her forties, and angry about almost everything in her world.

"What happened to the urn?" I asked. It was somewhat apparent that something had.

"I threw it in the ocean," she said, and she was suddenly incredibly angry. Her hands were fists and her teeth were set together so hard I was afraid she might crack one.

"Why did you do that?"

She is looking at her hands, and she slowly releases them. I can see the marks the nails made in her palms.

"So she would go away and leave me alone. Quit intruding on my thoughts all the time. Quit talking to me. Let me be." She is beginning to cry.

Now, we are getting somewhere, I think. Tears are as good a sign as laughter.

"Did it work?"

She is almost sobbing. "No! She still won't leave me alone. She's always in my head, telling me what to do. How to do it. When to do it. I hate her!"

"Did you hate her when she was alive?"

"Sometimes. Yes. She had to be in everything I did. She ruined my first marriage. It feels like she's trying to ruin this one, as well."

"You know she's not real," I offer.

"She feels real! She never shuts up."

"Well," I say, "I think what you and I need to do next is start figuring out how to get your mom out of your head and into your past."

"Is that possible?"

"I think so. First thing to start with is asserting to yourself when she comes to visit that she is not real. She is certainly not in that vase. Would you like to look?"

She stands up and walks across the office and picks up the vase.

"Empty, right? Except for maybe a cobweb or two?"

She nods.

"Let's see if we can empty your mom out of your head."

She nodded again. It took a few months, but we managed to banish her mom to memory. She called it a miracle, which maybe it was. I can't tell. Seemed like good, old-fashioned analysis to me. But, there's something about miracles in my work, too. I am always grateful when one seems to appear.

Today, Lillian began looking for the carving a few minutes after we started the session. I knew when she finally found it. She didn't relax, as I thought she might. She just kept looking at it as we talked.

She seems to have drawn back from last week and her confession that maybe she wanted me to save her life. She is not quite hostile, but she is definitely not as open as I thought she might be. Hoped she might be. *So, here we are again,* I think. Not quite square one, but still.

"Are you hungry," I ask. Back to basics.

"Yes," she said.

"How much have you had to eat today?"

"An apple."

"That's it?" It's 2:30 in the afternoon.

"Yes."

"Do you plan to eat anything else?"

"No."

"Do you know what will happen when you finally fall over from starvation?"

"I'll become invisible."

"No. You will be put into a hospital bed and fed intravenously. Against your will, perhaps, but that's what will happen. There goes the control, right?"

She doesn't answer, but I can see she doesn't like that thought.

"What would have to happen for you to allow yourself to eat again?"

"I can't say," she says.

"Can't or won't?" I ask.

"Either one."

"Is it stuck in your head? Will it not come out? Or do you not want it to come out?"

She is getting agitated.

"I can't say."

I decide it's best to relent on the question. For now.

"OK, Lillian. If and when you can say — will say — will you tell me the answer to that question?"

"Maybe," she says.

I don't push it. That's sometimes as good as it gets in inner sanctum. Some miracles take longer than others.

Ask McElroy
Professional Challenges

One challenge of my profession is keeping professional distance. In my case, this is difficult only in the case of certain patients, clients, whatever you want to call them.

Many of my patients are pretty much in my care to hear themselves work out their own angst, with me asking directive questions. If you're looking for a doctor who will prescribe your way to better mental health, you best look elsewhere. I'm here to work with you, but I want you to be willing to work, too. Drugs are last resort for me.

But that means we have to get to know each other, and getting to know each other can mean becoming attached. I actually like most of my patients on some level or another, even when they sometimes don't like themselves very much. With most, though, I have no problem staying detached.

In some cases, there is negative attachment to overcome. Hildegard the Horrific, for instance, is never going to intrude on my personal space, nor will I into hers. It's bad enough that we have to spend an hour together every week. IMHO, there is not much more wrong with her than that she knows no one else who will listen to her bombast and so has contracted with me to be her vent on a regular basis.

That she feels lonely and isolated, I understand, but perhaps if she were to shut up and listen once in a while, she might meet people who are willing to spend real time with her. Maybe. See. There I am, feeling sorry for my most difficult patient. I'm evidently a softie. And somewhat judgmental.

Why I entered this profession is unclear to me some days. Most — OK, many — psychiatrists I know seem to be trying to work out their own "stuff." I sometimes feel slightly guilty for not having more "stuff," but I don't think I do. I'm sort of boring, in fact, because I seem to be relatively healthy, mentally and physically, and kind of "normal." I'm an only child of good parents whom I love and who love me, nurtured me, gave me a good life and let me pay for my own college education. No traumatic incidents of abuse or unusual drama in high school. Somewhat deficient love life, in my opinion, but no heartbreaks or psychic meltdowns that lasted, no obsessions, no stalkers or stalking. I did find myself loving a client — umm, patient — once, but for darned good reasons, in my opinion. He was — and still is — a man worth loving. Luckily, he found someone else before I figured out how much I love him. Or the smart dog — Adam — and I would not have come to be almost maybe a couple, a prospect that is infinitely more appropriate, for a number of reasons more or less pertinent.

In a small city like ours, we all know each other, almost. Larry, the client who is the man worth loving who met someone else, introduced me to Bill, who became a patient. Bill pointed out Adam as the smart dog. Then, Larry introduced me to Adam, but he didn't know that Bill knew Adam or even knew of him.

Maybe I should have been an anthropologist instead of a psychiatrist, because I find these sorts of connections fascinating. How we fit together as a community and within the larger culture is very interesting. And, this sometimes makes keeping professional distance more challenging.

Dr. McElroy has no problem with this. As handsome and witty and intelligent as he is, he is also so incredibly self-contained he seems incapable — or perhaps un-needful — of having a relationship deeper than professional consultation. I assume he has other friends, but I never see him with anyone else in a social setting that might indicate an intimate relationship. He had a dog he was fond of when we met, but did not replace after it died. Or hasn't yet. I know where he lives, but I have never been there — a condominium on the shores of the lake in an ultramodern complex that Larry says is attractive in a sleek sort of way, but not a compelling building. Hmm. Sort of like Dr. McElroy, in fact. Sorry, friend. Just ruminating here. I will never share that thought with you, as it might hurt your feelings.

Larry went and introduced himself to Adam because Larry is an architecture aficionado. He consulted on my house several times — with Adam's help, unbeknownst to me until well after the fact — and was an enthusiastic supporter of my buying it. And, as noted, he introduced me to what I am cautiously beginning to think of "my" architect. The smart dog.

"Smart dog" is Bill's designation for Mr. Turpin, risen out of his impressions of Adam in encounters downtown when Bill was walking a beat as a policeman. Adam travels through cityscapes somewhat like a smart dog, always watching traffic and ignoring traffic signals, using shortest route strategy to get from point A to point B.

I love walking with Adam, though "walk" is hardly the right term. "Hike" is better, for he doesn't often stroll, but moves with direct purpose and sometimes at a trot. A journey from my office on Seventh to his building on Minnehaha can take several forms and include alleys, parking lots and the occasional walk-through lobby. This makes me smile, just thinking about it.

Walking — urban hiking — is an important part of our developing relationship, and I think our first walk together was somewhat of a test. Perhaps not intentionally, but on some level, I believe he wanted to know if I could keep up. I could. I did. And, I didn't have to stretch myself to do so. We had so much fun, it was somewhat frightening to a girl — a woman — who hadn't had a good first date in — let's see — well, waaay too many years. When I got home that evening, I probably glowed in the dark.

So there is the counterpoint to my developing relationship with the emotionally distant Lillian, who, for various unprofessional reasons, I already love too much to be objective all the time. Which is part of my reason to play the hardass. But, she so needs someone to love her.

An idea has been hovering at the edge of my consciousness for a few weeks, since Lillian unwittingly gave me the assignment to save her life. I have resisted thinking the idea fully, because around the edges it seems outlandish and unprofessional, as well as possibly impossible. But, still, it has stayed there, waiting to be thought.

So, today, I thought the thought. *What if I were to seek custody of Lillian?*

Would I be able to take her away from her parents — or, better yet, get them to give me custody — and would that be effective in saving her life?

The latter is the real question. Will getting Lillian out of her family situation and fully under my care and supervision allow her to stop becoming invisible? That is a distinctly ambiguous question, whatever that might mean, and I don't know the answer, but I want the answer to be "Yes." So, for right now, I will pretend it is, perhaps at risk to my heart and professional license. I can always go back to being a waitress.

But, just in case, maybe I should ask Dr. McElroy what he thinks.

Not Your Job
Professional Differences

McElroy and I are in consultation — to be differentiated from after-hours-therapy — and he is being logical, ethical and somewhat of a jerk. I have asked him what he thinks about the idea of my seeking custody of Lillian, and although he started off with an "That's an interesting idea," he then went into a series of "buts," which all reflect his own ideas of staying detached.

I have responded with what I think are good reasons to do this, including Lillian's ultimate future, and he has been getting more frustrated with my basic refusal to see things his way. Logic has fled the conversation, and I think it might be because he is feeling threatened, that his own views of the profession are being challenged. Finally, it comes down to this.

"You can't just adopt a patient, Miller," he says.

"I'm not adopting her. I'm thinking of asking for legal custody," I say. Again.

"On what grounds?"

"On the grounds that I care about Lillian and neither of her parents really give a good goddam about her." My frustration with McElroy's attitude is causing words I don't generally use to jump out of me.

"That's not your job as a psychiatrist," he says. Again.

"No," I say, "That's not *your* job as a psychiatrist." I pull up short because what I want to say next is unkind — and true. *Your job,* I want to say, *seems to be to remain detached, analytical, and somewhat remote and assure that the patient is not going to sue you.*

"What do you mean by that?"

I try to soften what I am feeling right now. "I mean we do our jobs in very different ways, McElroy. We use different methods and . . . "

"Adopting a patient is not a method, Miller."

"I think we're done talking about this now, James."

Dr. McElroy and I very seldom call each other by anything but "Doctor," our surnames or the combination there of. In fact, even I am surprised that I have invoked his first name, but I have had some pretty important buttons pushed this evening. We have always been at odds about treatment to some extent, and this conversation has revealed a huge gap that I may never be able to bridge. I may have suspected this for some time, but having it truly revealed and seeing the futility of trying to reconcile the two has caused me to snap at him, for which I am immediately sorry.

It also has an immediate effect. He clamps his mouth shut and bites his upper lip, as if trying to keep his next words inside. I am grateful that he manages to do so. We have been friends for a long time.

Finally, he says, "Good luck, Doctor." He downs the remains of his Old Fashioned in one big swallow, something I have never seen him do before, and slides out of the booth.

"Good night, Doctor," I say.

He walks away.

At least, both of us managed to keep from saying "Goodbye, Doctor."

I sat there for a long time after, wondering if I am as wrong as McElroy seems to think I am. I even wandered back out into the realm of "What if?", a place I don't often go without a guiding premise. What if McElroy was right, that this was a huge ethical violation that would not only get me in trouble with the Association, but cause some sort of irreparable harm to my reputation?

What if I were to lose my license? My practice? I have a mortgage on that lovely home of mine. How would I pay that? Waitressing probably won't do it.

The main question though, is what if I take the risk and it doesn't help the patient at all (*Her name is Lillian,* I reminded myself)? What if she just dives back into her misery?

Her biggest problems seem to be manifestations of her parents' inability to care about her. What if Lillian sees their acceptance of a request for custody as the ultimate rejection and completely regresses? What if I am, as my dad might say, "rushing in where angels fear to tread?"

What if this is a really, really, really stupid idea?

Sheila Says
Emancipation 101

"I don't think it's a stupid idea," Sheila says. "Novel, yes. Somewhat chancy, yes. I mean, what if the judge says 'fuggedaboutit' and puts his hammer down? Then what? It seems that both you and your patient would be hit pretty hard by that. But it's not a stupid idea."

I take a sip of my cosmopolitan and think about "fuggedaboutit." That would be harmful, especially if Lillian had her hopes up as high as I might. But, I haven't talked to Lillian about this idea yet.

Sheila McNair is not "my" lawyer, but when I need one, she will be. She and I graduated Millard Filmore together, lo these many years ago. We were speaking acquaintances then, traveling in circles that didn't have a lot in common except year of graduation, gender and GPA. She was Miss Popularity and I was Miss Semi-Invisible. She was a cheerleader and I was a Thespian who preferred backstage to the footlights. We knew each others' names, because you couldn't go to Millard F. and not know who Sheila was and because she is an incredibly nice person who remembers everybody's name.

I once wished out loud that I was more like her, but my mom said, in her best mom way, "You just keep being like you already are. You're good at it. Besides, if you were like Sheila, you'd never be home, and I like it when you're at home." Thanks, Mom. Good advice.

While I went to med school, Sheila went to law school. We reconnected at our ten-year high school reunion. Or should I say, "connected?" It's interesting how a decade can change the view we have of others and ourselves.

I overcame my shyness, and she managed to conquer her desire to be involved in everything. She had moved home and hung up her shingle, and I was still two years from finishing my residency, but we stayed in touch. She has become one of my best friends.

So, I have asked her about the legal details of guardianship and she has been graciously telling me — for free. Sort of free. Dinner and drinks are on me for consultation. She has argued this, but I have insisted, and she has graciously relented.

"The parents," she says, and then pauses.

"What about them?" I say.

"Tell me about them."

"That might construe a breach of confidentiality," I say.

"Not their names. How do they fit into all this? Are they going to fight you on this, or just roll over?"

"Well," I say, "the mother seems to think money can cure anything, which colors the patient's view of our relationship. She's twice said something to the effect that the only reason I continue to work with her is because her parents are paying me. And the father looks at me like I'm on the menu."

Sheila snorts at this last.

"And how do they treat the patient?"

"Like an object. And one they don't find very valuable, at that."

"Why are they even bothering to have you work with the patient?"

"Good question," I say, and it is.

Hmmm. Why indeed? As little as they seem to care about Lillian the person, why are they trying, in their own oblique way, to take care of Lillian the object?

"There are legal requirements,," Sheila says. "They are responsible for their child's life and actions until emancipation."

"Emancipation."

"When a person is no longer responsible to or under the care of their parents. In this sense. Which brings to mind a question. How old is the patient?"

"Fifteen. Sixteen in October."

"Your life just got a bit easier," Sheila says.

"How so?"

"At age 16 in this state, a person can petition to be emancipated from their parents. Judges often grant that request, particularly in an abusive family situation, or one in which there is an obvious reason that the child would be better off living on their own, or at least not in the family home. Which means there has to be some sort plan in place; a job, maybe, or a friend who is willing to take them in until the reach the age of majority.

I think about that.

"Who does the petitioning?"

"In this case, I do," Sheila says.

She has a funny smile on her face, which I could attribute to her own cosmo, but she's only half-way through the drink and I happen to know she holds her liquor better than that.

"What's funny?" I ask.

"Funny you should ask," she says, and we both crack up. Maybe the cosmos are doing their work more quickly than usual, but it's more likely because we suffer from similar senses of humor.

After the giggling subsides, she says, "Remember Marcos?"

I dig around in my memory filing system and come up with a skinny Latino kid who went to Millard F. with us. He was a wonderful actor and a pretty good basketball player, second string varsity. He was actually one of the best players — high school basketball, I understand and like — but he was only about five-foot-seven, so he didn't start. But he got a lot of playing time.

"Marcos. Yes. I remember."

"Emancipated," Sheila says.

"Really."

"His family was huuuuuuge, and he decided that it would be better for him to take some of the pressure off by moving out and getting a job. At least there would be one less mouth to feed. It worked out for him. His mom was set against it, but the judge saw the logic and need and granted his request."

"Even back then," I say.

"It was soooo long ago," Sheila says.

When we stop laughing, I ask, "How much is this going to cost?"

"I have very reasonable emancipation rates," she says.

A person who grew up with a disorganized attachment often won't learn healthy ways to self-soothe. They may have trouble socially or struggle in using others to co-regulate their emotions. It may be difficult for them to open up to others or to seek out help. They often have difficulty trusting people, as they were unable to trust those they relied on for safety growing up. They may struggle in their relationships or friendships or when parenting their own children. Their social lives may further be affected, as people with secure attachments tend to get on better throughout their development. Children with secure attachment are often treated better by peers and even teachers in school. On the other hand, those with disorganized attachment, because they struggle with poor social or emotional regulation skills, may find it difficult to form and sustain solid relationships. They often have difficulty managing stress and may even demonstrate hostile or aggressive behaviors. Because of their negative early life experiences, they may see the world as an unsafe place. — Jennifer Schindler, Ph.D

Self-Consumed Disorganized Attachment

"Do your parents fight a lot?"

This question was the first that came to mind in our next session. Besides doing homework on legal matters, I've been doing more on anorexia.

I won't tell Madeline how much homework, because my office manager is just as concerned about my private time as my professional time. Though she would have me believe it is from a purely pecuniary point of view, I know it is also a personal interest in my personal health. Madeline is a fine office manager, but I don't tell her everything. Which is just fine. There are some things she doesn't need to know.

So, I've been burning a bit of midnight oil on anorexia — not an unreasonable amount — and disorganized attachment has come up several times. And parent-child relationships are most often the source of disorganized attachment.

"They hardly speak to each other," she says.

She is looking at the carving of the apples and cheese again.

"Do they talk to you?"

"About what?"

"Anything."

"No."

"They don't ask about school or your social life or . . . ?"

"My parents are self-consumed idiots."

"Wow. Is that really true?"

She is warming up. "My mom is concerned about one thing: money. My dad is concerned about one thing: sex. And not with my mom. Neither one of them is concerned about me, and never have been."

"Never?"

"Never in my experience. I've spent more time in day care or with *au pairs* than with them. The *au pairs* don't stay very long, because my dad . . . "

She pulls up short.

This confession stabs me right in the heart. No wonder she's trying to become invisible. She seems to have been mostly invisible to her parents for most of her life.

It occurs to me that Lillian, for a person her age, has a better than average grasp of language and vocabulary. I make a mental note to ask her about that.

"So, why do you suppose they have sent you to see me?"

"Because they can afford to?"

Good answer, I think. But do not say. I change tacks.

"A couple of weeks ago, you told me you were trying to become invisible through not eating. Is that a correct interpretation?"

She is looking at the wooden fruit and cheese tray.

"Yes."

"You also told me that if nobody could see you, nobody could hurt you. Is that correct?"

"That I told you that?"

"Is that how you feel?"

"Maybe."

I don't like that answer, but I continue on my tack.

"When I asked who wants to hurt you, you said, 'Who doesn't?' Do you really think that everybody wants to hurt you?"

"Maybe."

I don't like that answer again.

"Do you think your parents want to hurt you?"

She looks right at me. "They must want to, because they do it all the time."

"Do they hurt you physically?"

"Oh, no," she says. "I take care of that myself."

My heart heads for the ground at breakneck speed. I didn't see any marks of self-mutilation when she was naked a few weeks ago, but that was a few weeks ago.

"What do you mean by that?"

"Becoming invisible is painful," she says.

"You mean starving yourself."

"Yes."

"Are you harming yourself in other ways?"

"No." She is emphatic.

"Good."

"Do you believe me?"

"Should I not?"

"My parents don't believe anything I say."

"I'm not your parent."

She doesn't answer this.

"Do you think I want to hurt you?"

She is quiet for a long time, as if she is thinking. Finally, I close my notebook.

"No," she says. Her voice is barely audible.

"Good," I say. Again.

Going Crazy Loving Lillian

I am going crazy! I want so badly to talk to Adam about Lillian, which would be a big breach of conduct, which would be something I could probably live with if I thought his counsel would help save the girl, of which I am not sure enough to take the step. And I am loathe to talk to McElroy about this anymore. It's bad enough where we left it last time we talked. He is not going to understand that I have allowed myself to become enamored of this waif, this wasting-away wastrel, even though my love for her is, I believe, completely merited. She not only needs someone to love her, but she deserves it.

I know. I KNOW!

So do a whole huge bunch of other children and adults and dogs and . . . WHATEVER! But Lillian is the one I know. And, she has walked right into my heart. Of course, I opened the door for her. She didn't even have to knock.

Smart dog and I have been on hiatus, sort of. I recently found out that he does indeed go places. Right now, he is in South America, working on a project with UNESCO. They are teaching impoverished people how to build shelters that won't fall down at the least provocation, and are at least somewhat fire resistant. In other words, he is working in a slum in Rio de Janeiro, which ain't the safest place for a white guy from America, and I worry about him a bit.

We have communicated via e-mail, but we haven't talked for a couple of weeks. I miss him. I haven't told him that, nor has he told me that. We are being "careful," here, which is also making me a little bit crazy. But not as crazy as Exhibit A.

So, I am saved from having to make a big decision for at least another few days. He'll be home on Wednesday. With no jetlag to worry about, we have a date for dinner.

We also have a place to go that isn't the Neutron. I am feeling sad about the situation with McElroy, which is Exhibit C in *mi* currently *vida loca*. Something tugs at my heart when I think of where we left it — or he left me — last time we saw each other. We've been friends for a long time, and I don't want our differences to cause that to fade away. I also recognize that he is not getting that regular bit of social time we have enjoyed for lo, these many years.

This also makes me sad, especially when I consider that he might not have any other outlet. So, OK. I love McElroy, too. But not *that* way, as the teenagers say. He needs someone to love him, too.

I suddenly have a furrow between my eyes. I have never talked to McElroy about where he grew up, though I know he grew up in Boston. Or his folks, though I know they still live there, and he goes to visit them once in a great while, seemingly less frequently than Adam goes someplace. We have known each other for, what, almost ten years, and I don't have a good clue about those sorts of details. I know he went to Southern Cal for his M.D., but not where he went to school for premed. To me, this is good evidence that even when he was a man of interest, some part of me recognized his monolithic nature.

Now, I am thinking about doing something really crazy: calling McElroy and asking him if he would like to have dinner at Neutron tomorrow; on a Monday! And not for after-hours therapy. We need to make up, after all. And, maybe it's time to really get to know Dr. McElroy. And, maybe he will be ready to let that happen. Now that it's safe. Ha!

That's crazy.

MAUVE
More Surprises

Dr. McElroy agreed to meet me for dinner. He also expressed his regret for leaving so abruptly last time we talked. And, I've admitted my own culpability in the incident. So, here we are, sitting in our regular booth on an irregular night.

Arlene, the hostess, looked a bit confused when I walked in, but then said "Dr. McElroy is at your regular table."

Bob the bartender, who seems to work here seven days a week, raised his right eyebrow when I stopped by the bar and ordered a drink on my way to the table.

Surprise! I want to laugh.

McElroy, who usually beats me here, has his double old-fashioned in hand and looks at me quizzically when I slide in across from him. Bob himself brings me the cosmo I just ordered, as if the check to see if it's really me. I want to laugh even more, and it must show.

"What's so funny?" McElroy wants to know.

"It seems we are messing with the order of the universe by being here on a Monday."

He looks a bit confused.

"We most often come here together on Wednesday," I say.

He smiles. "True. But, I come here on other nights, as well."

Surprise! Again. So, I am not McElroy's only social outlet. Whew. That's a good thing to know.

"You're not my only friend, you know."

He sounds somewhat defensive, but it's good to know he thinks of me as a friend. Still.

"Sorry, James," I say. Which makes him twitch. Now, I suspect he thinks I might be angry with him about something else, which I don't want him to think.

So, I just jump in.

"It occurred to me, Doctor (he relaxes) that for as long as we have known each other, I don't really know a huge amount about you. We have always kept things on a pretty professional level (he seems to be tensing up). And, I am curious as to the why of that."

He looks studiously at his old-fashioned, and I can see that he is in analysis mode. I can practically hear him thinking, *What does this mean?*

"This isn't a test, James. I am truly curious about why I don't know you better."

Now, the furrow between his eyes gets deeper. "What do you want to know?"

A silly question comes to mind. "What's your favorite color?"

"What?"

"Do you have a favorite color?"

He lets out a small laugh. "Yes. Mauve." He's relaxing a bit.

"That's pretty specific," I say. I'm grinning.

"I suppose so. What's your favorite color?"

I'm kind of surprised that he is reciprocating, but I'm also grateful. *You have to start someplace, right?* I think.

I'm also thinking about what my favorite color is. I have so many. "I suppose if I were to pick any single one, it would be cerulean."

"Talk about specific," he says, and we both laugh.

Wow, I think. *This is going better than I expected.*

"Where did you go for premed?" I ask.

His grin fades. "UCLA."

A logical question comes to mind, knowing what I know. "Why not Boston U?"

"Too close to home," he says, and the way he says it tells me that it is not a good idea to delve deeper into that at the moment.

"I understand that. I went to State for my premed, but when it came time for med school, I wanted some real space. Florida seemed too one-dimensional weather-wise, so I picked U-Dub."

"Seems like your parents are pretty supportive," he says, which surprises me. He knows my mom and dad a little bit, but not intimately. "I've seen you and them together. You get along nicely."

He's right about that.

"What about your folks?" I ask

He takes a sip of his old-fashioned. "Not so much."

"How's that?"

He gets a funny smile and says, "Mauve," which makes me laugh and tells me that we are not going any further into Dr. McElroy's familial relationships. At least not tonight.

"You have a good sense of humor, James," I say.

He picks up his glass, clinks it against the edge of mine, and takes a long sip.

"You have a good sense of propriety, Doctor Miller."

The rest of the evening is spent in small talk about local details: the weather and our new mayor and the fact that he is going to have his office remodeled soon. I tell him, in all innocence, that someday I might move mine to Adam's building. He gets a funny look on his face.

"I suppose that would make sense," he finally says. "But I would miss you."

Wow. Talk about surprises. Good surprises, though. We are still friends.

Blair's Smart Dogs and Horses

Adam and I are sitting at the back table in Blair's Seventh Street Pub, Grill and Coffeehouse. It's not quite "our" table, yet, but we seem to be working on it. The pub is just "Blair's" in the local parlance, but that longer moniker is what the sign hanging over the door proclaims. No hard alcohol here. I am sipping on a pilsner, which is about as far into the beer world that I have ventured. I have tasted Adam's IPA, but he is in no danger of me pilfering it. I could have a glass of wine, but that seems counter to the pub atmosphere.

I've already jumped into deep water this week with McElroy, so I figure I may as well continue with Adam.

"I missed you," I say.

He gets that funny smile of his. "I was too busy to miss anything," he says, which sort of confuses me, but at least it's a reasonable answer. "Until I got on the plane for home," he continues. "Then, I missed you." He pats my hand somewhat in the same manner McElroy did a few weeks ago, but the result is a bit different.

I laugh, and a goofy grin comes out of nowhere and settles on my face. I am glad it's sort of dark at the back table, because I can feel my face starting to glow. Adam notices anyway, and giggles. Yes, giggles. Not exactly like a little kid, but sort of like a little kid. I've only heard this sort of laugh from him a couple of times, but I am coming to understand it as a sign that something has amused him beyond just being funny, but also touching.

An example from a few weeks ago, just before he left for South America: we are walking —hiking — and exploring a neighborhood across town from mine. We come across a girl and a boy harnessing a huge Bernese mountain dog to a two-wheel cart. The dog is bigger than either of the kids, but they are industriously — and expertly — getting it between the draw bars. It's apparent they have done this before. We stop to watch until the dog is in the traces, after which the girl climbs up on the seat and picks up the reins. They are attached to the dog's harness at the shoulders, one on each side. The boy climbs up behind her to stand in the box of the cart. He puts his hands on her shoulders.

"Giddup, Fletcher," says the girl, and off they go up the sidewalk. The boy looks like a Roman centurion standing behind his chariot driver. He points forward with his right arm. As they approach a cross street, the girl calls, "Gee, Fletcher. Gee!" and around the corner they go. All this makes Adam giggle. A couple of times.

"Wow," he says. "Wish I'd had one of those when I was a kid."

"Never too late," I say.

He grins. "It would have to be a bigger dog."

"Maybe a horse?" I say.

"Hmm. Already had a horse," he said. He doesn't sound too enthusiastic.

"Really?"

"Yep." He laughs. "Where do you think I learned to say, 'Yep?' "

This makes me giggle.

We slow down a bit, and he tells about the horse he had as a kid. "Jughead recovering packhorse," he calls it. "Took me the better part of six years to come to an agreement with him about who was in charge."

"Six years?"

I must have sounded surprised, because I was.

"Yep. From the time I was eight until I was 14. Probably then only because I was strong enough to hold him and he had taught me to be a good enough rider to stay on when he wanted to argue."

He gets a sad smile. "Then, when I was 15, he died."

"What happened?"

"He got pneumonia. And then he got down. We couldn't afford a vet. We had to . . ." He hesitates. He has grown a bit misty. "Yeah. It wasn't a good day. For any of us."

"Sorry," I say.

"Me, too," he said. "I think that's when I decided that maybe one horse was enough."

I imagine how a 15-year-old might feel about losing his pet horse, even one who was a "jughead recovering packhorse." And this makes me think of Lillian, the 15-year-old who is in the continuing process of losing her childhood.

Suddenly, I am sort of misty myself. Adam notices.

"Thanks," he says.

I nod, and we continue on our walk. Soon, the dog cart comes back into view. The boy and girl have switched positions. They are not quite careening down the sidewalk, but I would guess their mom might freak out a bit if she were watching. Fletcher is loping, the boy is driving and the girl is riding in the back now — with no hands on the boy's shoulders — just free-standing in the cart. The girl sounds the full-charge call — "Da-da-dah-da-da-da-daaa!" — and the boy yells, "Yo, Fletcher."

"Whoa," I say.

"I don't think so," Adam says as they come rumbling past. We turn and watch them as they roll away. He giggles again, and says, "Oh, man."

Meanwhile, at the back table in Blair's, our food comes. Caesar salad with prawns for me; a big, fat bacon cheeseburger with fries for him.

"Oh, man," he says. "I missed this as well."

Well, at least I know that I'm up there with good old American cuisine in his priorities.

Willie
"Next Dog."

Lillian is not looking at the carving today. She seems distracted and unfocussed. I have tried to call her back from wherever she is by asking some pretty specific questions about what's going on with her this week, but her answers are monosyllabic grunts of assent or dissent. Finally, I ask, "So, where are you, Lillian? What are you thinking about?"

"What do you mean?" she says.

"You don't seem to be here, today. Where are you?"

She seems to know the answer, but she also seems not to want to answer. She looks away, and out the window.

Finally, she says, "Willie died this morning."

"Willie?"

She sighs, and then she starts to cry. "My dog."

It's the first time I have seen her cry. I don't know why I thought this, but I thought it would be a long time before I would see her cry. She is one tough customer, Lillian is. But, she also obviously loved her dog.

I want to hug her, but I don't think I have permission to do that. Not yet.

"I'm sorry, Lillian. I didn't know you had a dog."

I let her cry. She isn't sobbing, just weeping and rocking and holding herself. After a bit, she stops rocking and leaking and sniffs a few times. I hand her the requisite box of tissues every savvy therapist keeps handy. She takes it without a word and begins dabbing at her eyes.

"How long have you had Willie?" I ask. "Did you have Willie?"

"Forever," she says.

"All your life?"

"Forever."

I take it that Willie was around when she became self-aware, whenever that was. So, Willie would have been an old dog.

"He was the only one who listened," she says. "Nobody else."

She gulps and I see that she might start to cry again, but she manages to get hold of her tears and keeps them in.

"So, you lost a really good friend."

"Yes."

"What kind of dog was Willie?" I ask.

"Want to see a picture?"

"Yes."

She pulls her phone out of her pocket. "Can I?"

It has been understood that cell phones are not to be turned on in inner sanctum; hers, mine or anyone else's.

"Yes."

She turns the phone on and it goes sort of crazy, signaling all the sorts of stuff that cell phones signal these days. To her credit, she ignores the signals and starts scrolling through pictures. She finds the one she is looking for and shows it to me. It's a selfie of her and a happy-looking dog of indiscriminate breeding; maybe part yellow lab, part Australian shepherd, part something else. It was obviously taken before she started her starvation program. She is a red-cheeked, sort of gleeful-looking girl of ten or eleven, very healthy looking and obviously happy to be with this dog.

She holds the phone up to me for a bit, and then turns it toward herself and looks at the picture. I suspect that she might break down, but she doesn't. She just looks at the picture for a bit more, and then turns off her phone.

"Willie was a beautiful dog," I say.

She nods.

"And you were a beautiful little girl."

She nods again. She is rocking on the edge of her chair.

"Not so much any more, huh?" she says.

"What do you think happened to that girl?" I ask.

"She found out that life sucks," she says, and she means it. She is caught between grief and rage, I think, and doesn't know which way to go. In her emotional holding pattern, she has become cold and remote. I can almost feel her moving away.

"And today proves it," she says.

I am silent for a while, parsing out what I might and might not say to her. Tipping her one way or the other emotionally might be either cathartic or catastrophic. I'm not sure which.

"If Willie could talk," I finally say, "do you think he would have told you that he loved you?"

She moves toward the grief side. Tears well in her eyes. "He didn't have to talk to tell me that."

"What do you think he would have said about you becoming invisible?"

"He thought it was a good idea."

"Why's that?"

" 'cause he got lots of stuff I didn't eat." She smiles a sad smile. "I didn't let him get fat, though."

"Was he your dog to feed, then?"

"Oh, yeah. From when I was five." She grows grim. "They wanted to give him away."

I understood that "they" were her parents, but I wanted to make sure.

"They? Your parents?"

She nods.

"So, you took care of Willie from the time you were five until now?"

She nods. "I promised."

"You promised you parents you would take care of him?

She shook her head. "I promised Willie."

It occurred to me that one of the things anchoring her to this world might be that promise, and now it was moot.

"You kept that promise for ten years?"

She nods.

"That's a wonderful thing, Lillian. Keeping a promise for all that time is terrific."

"But he left anyway."

"That's what happens to dogs. They don't live as long as we do. But even knowing that doesn't help, does it?"

She shakes her head. She is leaking again.

"Where is he now?"

"You mean his body?"

"OK. Yes. His body."

She swallows and closes down the leaks. "At the vets."

"Was that where he was when he died?"

She nods and swallows, keeping her tears to herself.

"I made my mom take him. He couldn't get up anymore."

"You made your mom?"

She nods. "Yes. She was going to have the gardener shoot him, but I wouldn't let him."

"How did you stop him."

"I laid down on top of him."

"You laid down on top of Willie?"

She nods.

I am close to tears myself, but if she can't cry, then neither can I.

"The vet put him to sleep," she confides. "They're going to cremate him, and I'll get his ashes."

"Your parents are going to pay for that?"

"I have to. They wanted to give him away."

"How can you afford that?"

"I get an allowance. The vet said I can make payments. And I will."

I can't imagine how long it might take to pay to have Willie euthanized and cremated on a 15-year-old's allowance, and I don't ask.

"Who's your vet?" I ask.

"Dr. Franks."

I make a mental note to talk to Dr. Franks about what it might have cost to have Willie euthanized and cremated. I'm not sure what I can do to help there, but maybe something.

In the meantime, I have a mourning teenaged anorexic in my consultation room. What do I say to her? Particularly now that what may have been one of her biggest reasons for continuing to live is gone.

She is looking out the window again.

"Lillian," I say, as I did the first day we met. Once again, she turns to look at me, and once again, I can see how beautiful she is, gaunt or not.

"You are still beautiful," I say. "Willie thought so. I think so. And, your next dog will think so, too."

She grows an odd look. "Next dog," she says, like she never considered that.

"Next dog." I say.

The Push

Speaking of Dogs

Speaking of dogs, I have decided to breach confidentiality and talk to the smart dog about the idea of becoming Lillian's guardian, emancipation plan, whatever it turns out to be. I have been in a huge quandary about this, both the breaching and the idea of guardianship, but I'm obviously not wanting to take McElroy's advice, and I think I need a fix of some good, old-fashioned common sense. There is another doctor I could talk with, but he's a close-to-retired, old-school Freudian who likes to overthink things to infinity. Talking to him about Lillian seems to be an opening on the world's longest consultation.

"I will have to think about that," he will say, and then he will. Forever.

So, here I am, ready to jump, but I'm also waiting for something to push me. Maybe Something, with a capital "S." I may not be what some call a believer, but my experience is that prayer is a good practice. I think there is Something out there that listens and provides answers to hard questions, even if It doesn't always grant our random requests for gratification. My answer comes during a call with Dr. Franks.

I had trouble getting his receptionist to put him on the phone with me, but when I told her that I was a friend of the girl who had brought her dog in to be euthanized last Thursday, she knew immediately who I was talking about.

"Lillian, correct?" she said.

"Yes."

"I'll have him call you on his next break," she said.

Ten minutes later, Dr. Franks called.

"What's your connection with Lillian?" he asked, first thing.

"I'm a psychiatrist."

"Her psychiatrist," he said.

"Yes."

"It's good to know she's under someone's care," he said. "In fact, I have been wrestling with my concern for her since she brought Willie in. I was going to call Child Welfare Services today, in fact, and ask them to check on her."

I let that sink in.

"We are working on her problems," I say.

"I can tell you what her problem is." He sounds angry. "Have you met her parents?"

"Doctor," I say, "I'm a doctor. I can't really tell you the answer to that. What I want to know, if you can tell me, is how much Lillian is having to pay for your services with Willie."

"We're going to write it off," he says.

A thought comes to me, an interesting memory.

"The vet said I can make payments," Lillian said last Thursday. "And I will."

"That's admirable, Dr. Franks," I say. "Thank you for caring about her. But, I'm going to ask you to let her make payments for a while."

"Why's that?" He sounds surprised.

"At the risk of giving too much information, I will tell you that I believe it will help keep her alive. It will give her something to live for, at least temporarily."

"Hmm. Interesting thought. Sad, but interesting."

"Yes. I can't say too much more, but we have been making progress. Willie's death was, as you know, a big blow, but her sense of responsibility to him is real and, I think, grounding for her."

"Alright, then," he says. "I'll let bookkeeping know. But they won't like it, I don't think. The whole clinic . . . Well, we are all a bunch of softies around here. She has been a subject of conversation."

"I take it that your staff trusts you," I say.

"Yes. Yes, they do. Why?"

"Then, you can tell them that you have knowledge that indicates it will be in Lillian's best interest to let her pay. It would also be in Lillian's best interest for you and your staff to let her know that you care about her. A sympathy card or maybe an invitation to come visit under happier circumstances."

I will find out later that Dr. Franks and his staff sent Lillian flowers and a card. Lillian showed me the card a few weeks later. It was signed by at least a dozen people, and contained a notice that they had reduced the amount she owed by half. Perfect, Dr. Franks. Perfect.

In the meantime, Dr. Franks and I ended our conversation like this:

"Good thoughts. Alright, Doctor. You're on. It must be hard to work with someone like that girl. Just between you and me, I'd take her away from her parents if I thought I could. I mean, who can you talk to about her?"

"We have moved into the realm of consultation, Doctor," I say. "I can't really answer that."

"Well, I hope you talk to somebody about it. About her. I understand the confidentiality thing, but that young lady needs as much help as you can give her."

That was the push I needed.

Dream About It
Thinking About It

I can't believe it's already September. But it is. Lillian has been faithful about coming to see me through the summer, but we haven't made a huge amount of progress beyond helping her work through the death of Willie, which actually seems like a sort of blessing in disguise. Her commitment to paying Dr. Franks seems to have tethered her to the planet for now. She will make monthly installments for another six months, through March, at which point she will have been in my care for nearly a year.

On the home front, Madeline and her mailman boyfriend of forever got married on the beach our little city faces sits on, in a sort of reminiscence of where Ralph asked her. They got engaged winter before last on a beach in Aruba, back before Adam entered my life. I think it might have been because Madeline said, "Ralph, the waiting is over," but it might have been Ralph who said it. Who knows, except them. It's none of my business, really, except that I like them both.

The smart dog and I and a few other folks, including Larry and Anna — Larry might be Madeline's favorite client of all time — attended the ceremony, which was short, sweet and presided over by the Justice of the Peace. It was basically, "Madeline, do you . . . ?" and then, "Ralph, do you . . . ?" and they both did. Bam, off for a weekend somewhere. For a real honeymoon — number 11 or 12 — they will go back to some south seas destination in February, as they have been doing for 11 or 12 years.

I am conscious that this is not the kind of wedding I want, but they have been together for so long, I guess they didn't really care. I refrain from thinking about it too much, but Adam says, after it's over, "Whew. That was fast."

I laugh and so does he. He says, "Seems like it should take a bit longer to pledge your undying love, don't you think." He's grinning, though, and I know he's making a joke, not being judgmental.

"Yes," I say, "but they've probably said all that a whole bunch of times in the last decade."

"They've been together that long?"

I nod.

"Well, no wonder, then." This makes me laugh again. It is also good to know that we might share similar views on weddings. I will not think about that too much, either.

This is Saturday morning, and Adam and I take time after the ceremony to go find a good breakfast. He and Larry are going to work on Larry's house this afternoon, and I am going to stay home and clean mine and take a nice long hot bath and a nice long nap. Yay, me!

In the meantime, I am going to ask Adam for his advice about Lillian. Part of the reason for the nice long nap is that I spent some hours tossing and turning last night, wondering if Dr. Frank's push was really a push, or if I just wanted it to be. I have done that for several nights, as a matter of fact, and I don't usually have trouble sleeping. This week, not so much.

My last session with Lillian was not great. She has drawn back further into her shell than she has been for a couple of months. Willie's death pushed her there, as much as anything else, and she is also constantly hungry, as you might imagine. It wears on her. It wears on me, as a matter of fact. She is also agitated about something else, I suspect, but she's not sharing. Conversely, I suspect that she might be eating a bit more than usual. Maybe. But I don't want to deter her from that, if it's true. I don't ask. Not yet. Maybe next week.

Anyway, last night, I had a sort of fitful dream in which Lillian and Willie and I are walking in the new park across town. It's a nice day, and Lillian is not bony thin. Adam appears on the sidewalk ahead of us and Willie and Lillian run to greet him. As I catch up with them, Adam looks at me and says, "See. I told you it would work."

I woke up knowing what to do, and then fell asleep and slept like a rock until the alarm went off.

So, now we are at breakfast and I say to him, "Adam, I am about to break a big rule and ask you about one of my patients."

He gets a serious expression on his face. "You're sure you want to do that." It's not a question, really, but a sort of confirmation.

I sigh. "Yes. Believe me, it's been a struggle to come to this conclusion, but for the patient, it might be a matter of life or death."

"What does Dr. McElroy think?" he asks.

"That I am completely wrong."

"What do you think?"

"That Dr. McElroy and I don't see eye to eye on this."

He sits silent for a full minute. "Alright," he says. "A matter of life or death. That's a bit of responsibility."

"Yes." I am beginning to think he will decline.

"I mean for you," he said. "OK. How can I help."

I suddenly want to cry, but I don't. Instead, I tell him about Lillian, and her parents, and her recently deceased dog, and her anorexia, and my thought that maybe it would be good idea for me to become her guardian, which might be the only way to save her life.

This takes me about 15 minutes, during which he listens pretty much without comment, and during which I become more resolute in my desire. Listening to yourself talk can be very helpful, right? I mean, that's what I think therapy is often all about.

Anyway, after I finish, he says, "Very interesting."

And, I say, "What do you think?"

And he says, "I will have to think about it for a while."

Which is not the answer I wanted, of course.
Then, he said, "I promise not to think about it too long."

Frozen in Time

Having Faith

It's now Monday, and Adam and I are sitting in Frozen In Time, the retro ice cream shop in the lobby of my building. We are having dessert for lunch, a sure sign that we have similar priorities, in my mind. Adam is eating a big bowl of raspberry sorbet. I am working on a hot fudge sundae. We have different metabolisms, my guy and I. I am taking liberties by wondering how we would do eating regular meals at home together. I am also taking liberties by thinking of him as "my" guy.

He hasn't shared his thoughts on Lillian, yet, but it's only been since Saturday, right? OK, that seems like forever, right now. He knows I've been thinking about her, and I think I know him well enough to be able to trust him to tell me what he thinks within a reasonable time. Besides, it's my dilemma I'm on the horns of. I'm really the one who has to bulldog it.

"I love raspberry sorbet," he says. "Makes me think of summers at home. Mom had a huge raspberry patch and a recipe for sorbet that was a summer staple. Kids from three miles around would come in the evenings with hopes that Mom would be making a batch. Never a problem to find someone to turn the handle on the ice cream mill." He has his Adam smile on.

"This" — he points at the bowl — "is almost as good as Mom's."

Silence descends, but after he has a few more bites, he says, "Once I had a client who was intent on designing his own building. He drew it out with a mechanical pencil, a ruler, a French curve and graph paper. He just wanted me to do the technical drawings and spec out materials to achieve his vision."

He takes another bite of sorbet. I wait. I know something is coming.

"I asked him to explain the purpose of his building; what it was supposed to be and do. He didn't quite understand the question.

" 'What's going to happen there?' I wanted to know.

"He said he wasn't sure. He just wanted a really beautiful building that he could build on a piece of property he owned downtown and rent out to business tenants.

" 'What kind of tenants?' I asked him.

"He didn't know. Or care. 'So,' I asked, 'why not just build a utilitarian building that can house any kind of business?' "

" 'Because my name is going to be on it,' he says, 'and I want it to be beautiful.'

"In reality, he was building a monument to himself. Which might seem egotistical and vain, but this guy is a humble sort, very open to suggestions and ideas about details. Also, his drawings were very thoughtful and kind of elegant. It was obvious he wasn't an architect, but he knew what he liked and was able to express it through his drawings. Lots of open public space wrapped around very efficient working areas. His offices are not palatial, sort of stoic in some ways. Room to turn around, but everything is available in that space. Desk, worktable, file storage. Room for a couple of visitors. But right down the hall on each floor in the corner suite position overlooking the lake is a big, shared conference room. Available to schedule in one-hour increments for all building tenants. No charge."

"Your building," I said. I knew by his description it was the building on Minnehaha where he had his office.

"Very good," he said, as if I had passed a test. "But, you are not quite correct. It's more like 'our' building. After I saw his plans and heard his intentions, and after I had thought about it for a good while, I asked him if I could invest. He was pleased as hell, and I was too when he accepted my offer."

I thought it very cool that my (maybe) guy was partial owner of his own office building, but I was wondering why he was telling me all this. It's not like the smart dog to brag about anything, and this seemed sort of out of character.

"I suppose you wonder why I'm telling you this," he says. He's another of the mind-reading men in my life, it seems, which pleases the hell out of me, for I really like having my mind read by certain people. Under most circumstances.

"You're right. I do."

"That offer was one of the scariest things I've ever done in my life. There were all sorts of 'what-ifs' attached. What if it sat empty for years? I was still on the hook for 40 percent of the mortgage. What if construction costs were underestimated? What if the guy turned out to be a shyster. If he accepted the offer, I was going to clean out my life savings and work mostly for free for about six months on a project that much of the downtown community saw as a boondoggle. My girlfriend at the time was totally against it, and my Dad didn't exactly tell me not to, but I know he wanted to. One of my closest friends told me I was crazy.

"After the initial barrage of negative input from the few people I trusted to tell about the idea, it took three weeks to screw up my courage and begin to talk to the guy about the prospects of being a partner. Even as I did, I was very cautious, but every time I felt like backing out, I would go back to the plans — his initial drawings — and imagine what the building would look like finished. Or take them down to the lot and visualize the construction process, from groundbreaking to grand opening. In my visualization, there were always a great number of people at the grand opening."

"And there really were," I said. "I was one of them. I nearly moved my practice there, but . . . "

"But what?"

"I wanted to pay the mortgage down on my house first."

"Good plan," he says.

What I didn't say was, *And I still had great hopes for McElroy.*

"Plus, Dr. McElroy's in this building, right?"

Be careful what you think around this guy, Dr. Miller, I think.

"Right," I say, without much enthusiasm, but then I add, "And, Frozen In Time!"

He gets a funny look on his face. "Don't tell, but we're wooing Frozen in Time."

What about me? I think, almost involuntarily. *Are you wooing me? It's hard to tell, you know.*

To cover up that thought, I say, "I would miss this place. It's an important part of the neighborhood."

He pats my hand. "Don't worry. I'll let you know if they decide to take our offer. Maybe we can make a package deal." He has the Adam smile on again.

"Maybe." I'm suddenly sad. Frozen In Time has also been an important part of my life, even my practice. Many sessions with some of my most important clients have been conducted over some permutation of ice cream, some of them absolutely cathartic. This is where Bill confessed his time in the Coast Guard, and where Larry told about skiing across the lake in a blizzard and began the story of Ulla, his lost Russian love. I haven't attempted to bring Lillian here yet, but I have been thinking of it.

"You really like this place, huh?"

"I do."

"Interesting. I never thought about that. And the shop in our building would be more of a touristy place, with the lake and all. It would be mad in the summer. This is more like a haven."

"Exactly," I say.

"Maybe I should talk to them about opening a second shop instead of moving this one. I think both could be successful."

"Would you do that?"

"Would you feel better about it if I did?"

I'm thinking of melting and sliding off the chair onto the black and white checker-board of a floor.

"That would be wonderful," I say.

"OK. I will," he says. The Cheshire Cat has nothing on me, right now.

"I'm telling you all this because," he says, "I know that you are trying to decide what to do about becoming Lillian's guardian. It's a risky thing, financially, professionally and personally. If it doesn't work, if Lillian doesn't respond in the way you hope and think she might, if someone calls you out on the professionalism of such a move, if you allow yourself to show how much you care about her and she responds by rejecting your care and love . . . well, you know what can go wrong."

I nod. "I do."

"I am not going to tell you what I think you should do. I am going to tell you what happened after I finally tendered my offer to Mr. Whitaker, though. He was very touched. And he one-upped me. 'Adam,' he said, 'you're going to outlive me by a long shot, so what if we do this? You get your choice of space, and pay no rent, but you get no share of the rents. Your share is applied completely against the mortgage and maintenance, gaining you a percentage of interest as measured against the original mortgage until the building is paid for. By then, my share of the rents will have returned my investment, plus interest, I'm sure, and you will have become owner.' "

"I was stunned, and expressed that fact."

" 'Well,' he said, 'I happen to know that many folks think this project will not work. Evidently, you are not one of them. I believe that people should be rewarded for their faith in themselves — and others.' I guess the question you might ask yourself is if you have faith that you and Lillian can make this work?"

He finished his sorbet.

"I have to go to back to the office for a while," he says. "Want to have dinner later?"

"Bailey's?"

"Let's go someplace new," he says.

"You pick," I say.

"OK. I'll come by about 6:30." He knows my schedule pretty well.

He leaves and I walk back to my office through the stairwell. I climb the stairs slowly and ruminate on Lillian and where to go next with all this. I am very sure I am going to explore the possibility of emancipation — with Lillian's permission. The other thing I am sure of is that we will have our next session at Frozen In Time.

Someplace New
Rolling Fish Company

It occurred to me after our conversation at Frozen In Time, but before we began dinner at "someplace new," — which happens to be the new sushi restaurant in the lobby of Adam's building — that Adam has not met my parents. Which is a completely terrifying thought. Not the meeting-my-parents part, but the asking-him-to-dinner-with-my-folks part.

What if he says, "Ummm. I'm pretty busy right now." ?

Not that I think he will, but some part of me knows that an invitation like that unaccepted would mean, sort of, "The End."

Here I am, being crazy again. And at the same time, discovering that I am crazy about sushi. In all my life, I have never had such a thing, and having it now is only because I want Adam to at least think I am always brave enough to try new stuff — which ain't always true. I've eaten gallons of Ivar's clam chowder, but never once while I was living near the ocean did I use chopsticks to pick up a pink piece of sashimi ahi with the intention of eating it. Raw fish? Ewww!

What a fool I have been!

This "someplace new" is called Rolling Fish Company, and features a lot of tile, teak and stainless steel and a kitchen where everything is visible from the dining room. Two people — a man and a woman — dressed in white and wielding large knives and bamboo roller-uppers, or whatever they are called, send divine gifts over the pick-up counter. I lived in Seattle for how long and didn't try this? Arghh!

The silver lining, of course, is that my maybe guy is getting to take delight in my own. He has been grinning since I tried my first bite, guiding me through the ritual of tamari, wasabi and ginger, showing me how to hold the chopsticks, and cluing me to the fact that dainty eating of a sticky-rice-wrapped piece of salmon is not required. Cutting it in half, which might seem more polite, risks dismantling the whole thing, and is not nearly as satisfying as just lobbing the whole thing in.

"Like this," he says. He demonstrates, and tamari dribbles from the corner of his mouth.

I catch the runaway soy with my napkin, an intimacy that I think surprises us both. But it is also something I know we both appreciate.

"Thanks," he says, with a funny smile on his face.

"This place is awesome," I say. "Thank you."

We eat in silence for a while, and then, just out of the blue, I say — sort of to my own surprise, in fact — "I'm thinking of inviting my folks to dinner on Sunday afternoon. Would you like to come?"

He is halfway through processing his most recent bite, and I have to wait until he swallows.

Then, he doesn't say anything for a few seconds. Then, he says, "What time?"

And, I say, "Late afternoon. Probably after 3."

And he says, "I think that will work."

My crazy self thinks, *He's giving himself an out, just in case.*

My sane self says, "That would be great."

I explain that it has to be late afternoon because the Packers are playing, I don't have a television and my Dad can't miss a game.

Adam says he understands, which I take to mean it makes sense that I would defer to my dad's preference, but I will find out it means a lot more than that.

And then he says, "What can I bring?"

And my sort-of-crazy-in-a-good-way self says, "The best bottle of red wine you can find for under 15 dollars."

He laughs out loud.

"Deal," he says.

"I'm pretty sure the folks will be able to come," I say, "but if they have another plan . . . "

"I'll take a rain check," he says, still grinning.

I almost couldn't wait until morning to call my Mom and ask them to dinner, but by the time I got home from the Rolling Fish Company, it was nearly 10, and my folks were probably in bed by 9. But now, it's Tuesday morning, and I'm on break after my first session of the day. I call my mom and invite them to dinner. My crazy self has been arguing about how to word the invitation without causing parental alert signals to sound. But my sane self prevails.

"My friend Adam is coming to dinner on Sunday," I say. "Would you like to join us?"

"Have we met this Adam?" my mom asks, so I know the signals are sounding.

"Not yet," I say, which to me, has the unstated message, "But you will, whether it's this week or next or the one after that."

"We'll be delighted," Mom says.

"Do you want to check with Dad?" I ask.

"Nope," she says. "He'll be delighted, as well." And we both laugh.

"Three-ish," I say.

"What can we bring?"

"Your world-famous dinner rolls," I say.

"See you Sunday, honey," she says.

Whew! I think. *That was easy.*

QUESTIONS
Can I Have A Bite?

I have some questions for you, Lillian," I say.

It's the Thursday after the Monday I invited Adam to dinner with my folks, and as I sort of foresaw that day, Lillian and I are sitting in Frozen In Time. If she is curious about why we are here instead of inner sanctum, she hasn't asked.

I am having a small bowl of vanilla with chocolate sauce, a bit of a reduction in what I might otherwise order, but when the other person at the table has ordered nothing, it seems improper to eat a banana split. Also, Mr. Turpin, the smart dog, may never judge me by my weight, but I never want to give him cause to be tempted.

"You always have questions," she says. She is not being dismissive, but funny.

"True," I say, and I laugh, which makes her smile a genuine, beautiful, undefended smile, which wrenches my heart. *God, I love this person,* I think. But, I say, "These questions are a bit different than the ones I've asked so far. They aren't about your anorexia. They are about some legal stuff."

She grows a frown and looks straight at me.

"Are you going to sue me?"

I laugh. "Where would you get that idea? What would I sue you for?"

"Just checking," she says, smiling again. Then, she grows serious. "Are my parents suing you? I mean, my mom?"

"Why would your mom sue me?"

"That's what she does when she doesn't get what she wants. She sues people. Or she fires them."

There is nothing Mrs. Ballenkamp can sue me for, and I figure she is smart enough to realize that, but the other option is possible. She can fire me.

"What is it that you mom isn't getting that she might want to fire me for?" I'm truly curious, and I'm also feeling like we might be on to something here.

"She's pissed because I'm not all healthy and happy yet."

"Yet," I say. "What do you think she expected?" I want to add, *Some sort of miracle?* but I don't.

"She thinks money can cure anything," she says, "but if it takes too much money, she gets pissed."

"And, she's pissed now?"

Lillian nods, but doesn't say more. She's looking at the ice cream and chocolate sauce in my bowl.

"Want a bite?" I ask.

She jumps as if caught stealing.

"No!"

"It's pretty good," I say.

She gulps and I see tears form.

"Don't tease me!" she says. She sounds intensely angry, but then a tear escapes.

Holy you-know-what, Doctor! Let's be careful here.

"I'm sorry, Lillian. I didn't mean to tease you. I ask your forgiveness."

Another tear escapes. And then it's a mass prison break. They are running down her cheeks and jumping onto the table. She tries to break up the escape with her hands, but she can't stop the salty little devils. She is sobbing.

I want to reach out and touch her, but something tells me that this is not the time. But, something also tells me that the time may be coming.

Lillian has allowed herself to full-on cry in my presence, something she managed to control even when telling me about Willie, and that is, in my opinion, one heck of a breakthrough. That is, in my opinion, a sign of significant trust, even though it might be temporary. But for this moment in Frozen in Time, she has let me see her pain.

After the prison break is over, she has pulled herself back toward her shell — though I believe she is not quite fully imbedded yet. I say, "Thank you for your tears, Lillian."

She sniffs and looks at me from red-rimmed eyes. She looks like a three-year-old.

"What do you mean?"

"It takes some trust and courage to show someone your tears, doesn't it?"

She looks away and nods. I can see that there might be another prison break, so I stay silent and let her deal with that. She rounds up the potential escapees and gets them back inside. She looks right at me, then, and her grey eyes are lit from behind. I can see she is angry, but I know she is not angry at me.

"I never cry when my dad teases me about food," she says.

"How often does that happen," I ask.

She doesn't answer.

"I'm going to guess. Is that OK?"

"If that's what you want to do." She's enraged, and almost back into her shell, now.

"Often."

She doesn't say anything, and I see she is struggling with her composure. She bites her lower lip so hard, I fear she's going to draw blood. Finally, she relents, but I can see the red marks her teeth have left. I look away, afraid that I'm going to have a mass escape of my own to deal with if I'm not careful. One of the rules of a savvy therapist is to not cry in front of a patient, but to save that for after they have gone home. I am close to breaking that rule.

"Almost every day," she says.

My body and mind and soul get together and decide it's just fine to let one escapee over the wall of my left lower eyelid. It runs joyously down my cheek and jumps straight into my ice cream. I've always loved salted chocolate, anyway, right?

Lillian has witnessed the escape. She is staring at me like I have suddenly grown an extra pair of ears. She opens her mouth as if to say something, but nothing comes out. Her mouth just stays open, as if in total surprise, and maybe that is what she is experiencing. Maybe she is surprised that someone might care enough to cry for her. Then, her mouth closes and the moment is over. She pops back into her shell. But she doesn't slam the door.

I ask, as gently as I can, "Does your mom tease you about food, as well?"

She is still incredibly angry. "No. She just lets my dad do that."

The next question pops out uninvited. Even as I try to reel it back in, it jumps off my tongue and onto the table, but sometimes things uninvited belong.

"What else does your dad tease you about?"

Lillian doesn't miss a beat.

"My lack of what he considers appropriate boobs and butt," she says.

"Your dad teases you about your body." It is not a question.

"My dad is a sexist jerk," she says. "He only thing he thinks about is getting — you know."

I do know. And I will still know for a long time. A very dangerous question comes to mind. And it comes out somewhat haltingly.

"Has your father ever acted . . . umm . . . touched . . . uhh . . done anything physically inappropriate with . . . urr . . . to you.

"Do you mean sexual stuff?"

"Yes. Yes, that's what I mean."

"Are you kidding? Look at me. Why would he even think about it?"

"I assume you are talking about the state of your body."

"No boobs. No butt."

"How old are you, again?"

"Fifteen," she says.

"How on earth . . . ?" I stop myself from finishing the question.

She answers anyway. "No need to make matters worse by tempting him, right? When it comes to sex, he's a reptile."

A pretty good answer to an unfinished question, which was, *How on earth does a 15-year-old become so wise and so cynical at the same time?*

The answer that comes to mind is "survival." I decide that I will save the legal questions for later. And do some research in the meantime.

But Lillian is curious enough to ask, "What legal stuff do you want to ask about?"

"I think we might have answered enough questions for one day," I say. She nods and sniffs. I think she is relieved that no more will be forthcoming.

I am trying to enjoy my ice cream, but it has become difficult to do so.

"I have a question," Lillian says.

"What's that?"

She has a very interesting look on her face, a cross between fear and hope, maybe. I'm not sure.

"Can I have a bite?"

I am so surprised, I can't respond in any way but to get up and go to the counter and ask Agnes for a spoon. I try not to hurry visibly, but I'm afraid she might change her mind. I hustle as casually as I can back to the table and hand her the long-handled plastic spoon.

She takes a deep breath and scoops a medium-sized pile of vanilla and chocolate sauce up and without hesitation puts it in her mouth.

I don't know quite what to expect, but a number of things run through my mind as possibilities: that she will immediately spit it out; that it will make her sick; that she will want more. None of this happens. She holds the bite in her mouth for a moment and then swallows.

"Now, when my mom tries to fire you, you can tell her you saw me eat something."

Holy ice cream!

I am stunned enough that I might fall out of my chair, but I have something compelling enough to do to prevent that. I have to round up that herd of salty little prisoners again, and manage to do so. For the time being.

Later, after Lillian has gone and after my mental wrestling match with Hildegard the Horrific, I go to Madeline and ask her to dial up Mrs. Ballenkamp and ask her if she has time to meet with me sometime soon. Then, I go into inner sanctum and turn the salty hordes loose.

Fellow Fans

Touchdown!

Oh, my God. No!

That was my thought when it became apparent that Adam, like my dad, is a football fan. OK. Maybe he's not as practically rabid as my dad, who would buy a car that matches the colors of the Packers if he could find one. I don't think Adam has anything like the cheese-head hat my dad keeps in the TV room, but I haven't been invited to Adam's home yet. Dad doesn't wear it for every game, I don't think, but Mom says he does once in a while, when it's an extra important game or the Pack is behind in a tight one or he has a few buddies over to entertain.

The revelation about Adam's football fandom happened as Dad was passing the fried chicken to Adam, who traded him the mashed potatoes and asked, "Do you follow football?"

My dad's response was to light up, and offer the enthusiastic comment that the Packers had come from behind to beat the Vikes (whoever they are) that very day.

Then, Adam lit up, and over cherry pie, they went into a post-game analysis of the contest and then the season so far, during which it was revealed that Adam is a Broncos fan, for which my father forgave him. All this blah-blah-blah allowed Mom and I move to the living room and talk about whatever we pleased.

Of course, she asked me all the Mom questions. Where did you meet him? How long have you known him? What does he do? And the big one: Where do you think this is going? I knew all the answers to the Mom questions except the big one.

"I'm not sure, Mom," I confessed. "I think I know where I would like it to go, but I also know that sometimes our thoughts are not in line with reality. And, that we can't always get what we want."

"Like the Rolling Stones," she said, and we both laughed. It has been ages since we watched The Big Chill together, but that line from the Stones, "You can't always get what you want," had been a constant in our lexicon ever since.

"I still hate that song," I said, and we laughed again.

"Well, in this case, I think it would be good if you did."

"Did what?"

"Get what you want."

"You like him," I said. It wasn't a question.

"What's not to like?" she asked.

"There's gotta be something," I said. But I'm not sure I believed it.

"Well, he's definitely a football fan," she said. She knows I don't understand or care for the game.

"There is that," I said. Being a specialist in mental illness, I have a hard time finding justification for the semi-controlled violence of some sports, and our obsession with it. Boxing? One of my favorite patients was a boxer, but I don't get it. Cage boxing? Uuuugh! OK. Compared to that, football looks somewhat benign, but still. I much prefer baseball.

I looked toward the dining nook in the kitchen, where the discussion continued. Mom patted my knee. She then stuck two fingers in her mouth and did her very good impression of an umpire's whistle. Kids in our neighborhood always knew when it was time for me to come home. "Gentlemen," she called "The game is over. Come join us, please."

I heard my dad say, "We've been flagged for unnecessary neglect." Adam laughed and they came through the arch from the kitchen into the living room. Adam had an expression on his face that made me laugh out loud, which made him grin, which made my dad grin even bigger.

My mom, one of the most calm and matter-of-fact folks I know, patted my knee again and said, "You have to be able to speak their language," which made me laugh again.

Adam was looking at me intently. I held his gaze for a long moment and realized I was beginning to blush. He chuckled, almost to himself, and then turned to my mom and said, "So, Mrs. Miller. Where did you get that recipe for dinner rolls?"

I swallowed my heart, willing it back into its proper place in my chest. *Be still, my foolish part,* I thought, which made me chuckle to myself. And got my pulse rate back to semi-normal.

Sunday dinner was a success. I may not know much about football, but I wanted to stand up and raise both my arms.

Lack of Progress
Mrs. Ballenkamp

Lillian tells me that you are unhappy with our progress."

"More accurately, I am unhappy with your lack of progress. She is still . . . well, look at her."

"Actually, Mrs. Ballenkamp, we have made quite a bit of progress. Yes. She is still acting out. But, I think we are getting somewhere with that. She has become more cooperative in sharing what's going on with her and that's good. But this is not a short-term proposition. Realistically, this might go on for a couple of years."

I am NOT going to tell her I saw Lillian eat something.

"A couple of years." She sounds irritated.

"Yes. And depending on what happens in her life going forward, it could be longer than that."

She pulls herself to her feet. "Then we will just have to find another doctor."

"Sit down, Mrs. Ballenkamp. Marion. Sit." I am surprised at the firmness in my voice, and so is she. She hesitates. "If you change doctors now — if you can even find someone else — it will be a huge setback for Lillian. She is beginning to trust me enough to take some suggestions about process and future."

"But why so long?" She is still standing. "This is going to cost thousands."

"I'm pretty sure you have thousands. You are well-known as the most successful broker in the state. And your daughter — any human — is worth more than that, though I admit that many might agree, but don't act that way."

I don't tell her that I am willing to work with Lillian for free, if that's what it takes. For one thing, I know she can afford much more than I am charging, and for another, Madeline would be after me. Madeline would relent, I know, because under her pecuniary little hide lies a soft heart, and Lillian is her current favorite patient. She hasn't told me that, but it's apparent by the way she inquires about her progress.

Marion has a pained expression that seems to say, "I don't like what you're saying, but I can't disagree."

"At the risk of hurting your feelings, it's taken fifteen-plus years to make Lillian the way she is, and you and your husband are the main architects." She turns and looks out the window. Her jaw muscles are set. I am expecting some sort of outburst, but she says nothing. It's as if she's waiting for the other shoe to drop.

"I think that Lillian's problems may be addressed in a shorter time than that, but not without your cooperation. Now. Please sit down, and let's talk about how to help Lillian together."

"I suppose it's a fair assessment," she says. She is still standing.

"What's that?"

"That we — Joseph and I — are the main architects." She swallows hard, as if that chunk of information has trouble going down. She turns from the window and returns to the chair she had been sitting in.

"Yes. I suppose that's true."

She sits.

"Thank you," I say. Inside, I am saying that very loudly. The Universe is cooperating today.

"May I ask you a few questions about you?"

"I suppose," she says. She has gone from defiant to somewhat despondent in record time.

"Before I do, Marion, I can tell you — is it alright to call you Marion?"

She waves her hand in permission.

I continue, encouraged. "Lillian's condition is not all your fault, Marion. There is her other parent and there are other factors than her parents. Our culture of perfectionism is partly to blame as well. We know too much already, I think, and modern media keeps stuffing more into our heads. But much of what we know — or think we know — is the result of someone else wanting to sell us something. Lillian has been sold on a method of self-destruction. There is even support for it on the internet. It's hard to know, really, who all is responsible for giving her a reason to try to kill herself, but it is modern culture that has given her the gun."

"Kill herself."

She doesn't sound shocked, but as if she is in shock. Her voice is flat and somewhat distant. I think she might still be processing that idea of being an architect of Lillian's current state. That's two big blows in a few minutes, but I'm encouraged by her reactions. She does have a soul under there somewhere, it appears. I may have used the jackhammer method to break the surface, but I determined before this session began that I wouldn't have much mercy in pointing out her and Joseph's culpability in this.

"Do you really think that? That's she's trying to kill herself?"

I mentally invoke doctor-patient confidentiality. There is, first of all, the trust that Lillian and I have built over these past months. And, second of all, I don't want Marion to overreact. I just want to see if I can to wake her up a bit. With Mr. Ballenkamp, I have not much hope for that; not until he can come to grips with his own stuff, which he may never have the impetus or wherewithal to do. I suspect that he is a full-blown sex addict. His acting out has already cost him the respect of this community, and he will likely soon be assigned pariah status, which may send him elsewhere to indulge his stuff. I don't think he is dangerous physically; spiritually and emotionally, not so much. It may be better for Lillian if he were completely out of the picture.

I am making assumptions and judgements here hand over fist, which I will keep to myself. For now, at least.

"That seems harsh, doesn't it? What I know is that she is starving herself, and the final stage of starvation is death. Whether she has the will to actually carry that out (*Careful, Doctor,* I think. *Don't reveal too much*) is another matter."

"On a professional note, we need to remember that Lillian is not suffering from bulimia — binging and purging — but from anorexia. They have similar symptoms, but they are not the same disease. Bulimia seems to be more about body image and cultural acceptance and expectation. Anorexia is partly about that, but more about self-destruction. Bulimics eat and throw up their meals over and over again. Anorexics just don't eat."

She doesn't respond, but she seems to be absorbing this. She is alternately slightly nodding and shaking her head, as if trying to decide whether she agrees or disagrees with what she's hearing, or maybe fluctuating between belief and disbelief. Her reality has been shaken today.

"So," I say. "My first question for you is this: Why have you and Joseph stayed married?"

She doesn't stiffen up, as I feared she might. Instead, she seems to soften a bit. She takes a breath and then lets it out slowly. "That's a good question, Doctor, but one without a very good answer."

I wait. She bites her lower lip, as if she might try to keep the answer in. But, then, she tells me.

Let's go 'Nauts!
Personal Questions

"May I ask you a personal question?"

"Fire away," Adam says. I'm not sure that he really wants me to do that, but I've been tempted to a few times in the past 24 hours. I've alternated between being reasonable — trying to assure myself that there must be a good explanation for what I saw at Blair's last evening — and feeling that cross between grief and outrage that many people suffer when they find out that their significant other is being unfaithful. Or think they have found that out, which is where I am, I suppose.

And, OK. I guess he's not really my significant other. And maybe he's not going to be, or doesn't really want to be, but that kiss we finally shared on Friday night seems to have been a huge step in that direction.

High school football teams play on Friday night. And Millard Fillmore was, by some miracle, playing for the state title last Friday. As you know, I don't much like or even understand football, but when the alma mater is playing for a state title, there is some reason to go, and when your male friend (I will not call him boyfriend) is a football fan, there is reason to invite him to go with you.

Adam was surprised, and allowed he had already planned to go, but he didn't think I would be interested. I just said, "Let's go, 'nauts!" This made him laugh, and we agreed to walk to the game together. The Millard Fillmore Argonauts never played for a state title in anything while I was attending there, but the city has grown and so has the sports program. The girls' volleyball team took state a few years ago, and now the boys football team had the same opportunity. How could I not go?

The game — during which I learned a lot about football, courtesy my companion — was a cliff-hanger. To make it even more interesting, there were quite a number of fans for the other team who had driven half way across the state to watch their Vandals play, so it was noisy, boisterous and actually quite a bit of fun. Sheila sat with us, and, much to Adam's amusement, we enthusiastically joined the Argonaut cheer team in chants that haven't changed much since we were in school.

The lead changed hands often. At the break, it was tied 31 to 31, and as the game progressed, even I began to realize that it was likely to boil down to whoever had the ball last.

So, when the Vandals had the ball and were "marching," as Adam called it, near the end of the game — it was tied 48 to 48, and I think there were 90 seconds left — the Argonaut crowd, us included, was chanting "Defense, defense." Adam said the Vandals were "eating up the clock," and "trying to get close enough to kick a field goal."

His predictions are correct. There are only 12 seconds left, and it isn't completely noisy when the Vandal kicker comes in to try. The Argonaut fans are grim-faced, looking less than hopeful, and make a sort of unenthusiastic response to the cheer team yelling "Block that kick."

Adam points out that the kicker has yet to miss, and that this is probably the game, outside of a miracle. And then, the miracle happens.

As seems to be the case in all football plays, the ball is thrown backward to somebody — counter-intuitive at best — and the world goes crazy for a few seconds. In all the confusion, I am not sure exactly what is going on, but all of the better informed Fillmore fans have gone crazy, as well. One of our boys — Number 13 — comes streaking by us with the ball in his arms and several Vandals chasing him. They don't catch him.

Adam explained to me later to me that the "holder," whoever that is, had trouble handling the "snap," whatever that is, so the kick was blocked, and Number 13 was able to scoop up the ball and run to the "end zone," which I actually understand.

Now, there are only five seconds left, we are all standing up and over the roar of the Argonaut fans, he yells at me, "They're going for two!" He has a manic expression of joy on his face, and so do a lot of others. I can't help but join them, even though inside I am going "Huh?"

I still have not much of a clue what that meant, except that Adam explained to me later that "going for two," — which they did not get because the guy with the ball just ran around without trying to go toward the goal until the gun went off — allowed the Argonauts to "eat up the clock," which they evidently did, because the game ended right after that.

So, maybe I understand football a little better. Maybe.

Adam and I live in different parts of town, and my house is closer to the football field than his place, so he drove the Volvo to my house and we walked from there. We were pretty giddy on our walk home, what with the glow of vicarious victory and the happy presence of one another. I had my hand through the crook of his arm, and I allowed myself the fantasy of doing that again and again in the coming years. He gave me a bit of tutorial in football as we walked, but not obsessively. We moved on to talk about his next project — he's designing a new courthouse for the county seat — and the fact that Frozen In Time is going to take his advice and open a second outlet in his building and leave the one in my building as is. Hooray!

When we got to my house, I took a deep breath and invited him in for a cocktail. He frowned and said, "I'll take a raincheck. I have some things I need to take care of early tomorrow."

Before I could be too disappointed, he said, "But, I have a question before I go."

"What's that?"

"May I kiss you?"

I laughed, right out loud.

"Does that mean yes or no?"

He asked the question with a big grin on his face.

"Yes," I said. "Yes, please."

As he climbed into the Volvo and I stood on my front porch and waved him goodbye, I could still feel that kiss, and I could conjure it up the next day as well. And now, it's Sunday, and it seems like that happened about a million years ago.

YESTERDAY *One More Miracle*

Yesterday, Saturday, I spent a lot of time thinking about what Marion told me as to the reasons she and Joseph are still married. And, the amazing fact that during the telling, she kept her composure to the end. Marion is somewhat emotionally stunted, in my opinion. Many other folks I have dealt with in that room would have been bawling their eyes out at such confession, but she just told me in a calm and clear voice that Joseph was her business partner, and in fact, the majority owner of the real estate company. Fifty-one percent doesn't seem like an overwhelming edge, but it is enough of an advantage that he, should he want to, can call the shots. He doesn't really want to, but he holds that sword over her head, and has for some time.

It was an inheritance from someone in his family that allowed them to buy a piece of land on the lake to develop well before Lillian was born. His family's money. Her drive for success. The equation worked.

She also confessed that Lillian was a mistake. An accident. A moment of unguarded passion. After she and Joseph had been married for seven years and business partners for five, she knew she had no intention of having a child with him. In fact, she was trying to figure out a way to buy him out and divorce him.

"Joseph couldn't manage his way around a budget to save his soul," she said. "I was the golden goose, am the golden goose."

Her control of her emotions is remarkable, and I say so.

"When you live with a man like Joseph" she says calmly, "you learn never to express yourself emotionally. He will take immediate advantage."

"What do you mean?"

"He will call you out on your lack of logic, your bleeding heart, your 'oh-poor-me' attitude. He will be as slyly cruel and manipulative as — as he can be. There is no good comparison."

"And you've allowed this for how long?"

"Allowed. Hmm." She paused, as if considering that for the first time ever. I expect her to defend herself, but she just swallows as she did when thinking about being an architect of Lillian's current self. "You can do the math."

I did. Somewhere around 20 years.

"I had a plan. Once Lillian was out of high school and I had squirreled away enough to start over, I was going to leave him."

"How's that working for you?"

She gets up and goes to the window. She remains stoic, but I can almost hear the wheels turning in her head.

"I can tell you one thing, Marion."

She continues to look out the window.

"It's not working for Lillian."

She nods. "Yes. You're right. I know that. And it hasn't for a long time, right?"

"Right."

She turns to me, and for the first time, I see emotion. She is not crying, nor do I expect her to, but she looks decades older than she did when she came to the office today. She looks incredibly sad, defeated. She reminds me of the woman in the famous photograph taken by Dorothea Lange during the Depression; except that the child the woman in the picture is holding is missing. I imagine a little Lillian sitting in her mom's lap, and I have to stop myself from leaking. I don't want to leak in front of Marion, and she saves me from it.

"What do we do?" she asks.

Suddenly, I have no reason to leak. Inside, I am close to jumping up and down with joy that a.) she would ask such a question and b.) she would use the pronoun "we."

Wow, Dr. Miller. *It's another miracle!*

I do not jump up and down. My savvy therapist takes over and says, "Have a seat, Marion, and let's talk about that."

She does, and we do.

And now, it's Sunday evening, and time to talk to the smart dog about what I saw last night. I pray for another miracle, still.

Telltale Timex *Trauma at "Our" Table.*

Saturday afternoon, after an exhausting and exhaustive discussion with Marion Ballenkamp about what "we" can do with and about Lillian, I went for a long walk alone in the new park across town, thinking about what we agreed to and how to approach Lillian about it. Marion has allowed me to — well, I'm getting ahead of myself. Let it be said that I had a lot to think about, and spent about three hours doing so. By the time I got back to Ruby, my little red car, it was almost dark. I drove toward home, and along the way, I passed Blair's, and, lo and behold, there was Adam's Volvo sitting on the street nearby.

I was almost elated. It was serendipitous, I thought, that the guy I wanted to talk to most about the day was in "our" restaurant just when I wanted to talk to him. I parked and went in the back door (the "in" crowd knows where the back door is). I had butterflies in my stomach, which immediately died and sank, dragging my gut to the floor. The back door opens on a short hallway where the bathrooms are and then there is an inner door. The inner door has a small window in it, and through the window, "our" table can be seen. As I approach the inner door, I realize Adam is sitting there, and I get ready to play "guess who?"

In preparation, I stop and look through the window. I focus beyond the back of Adam's head — I absolutely know it's him — and there is a quite good-looking woman facing him across "our" table — and he has his hand on top of hers. She is looking at him with an odd expression on her face, slightly bemused. I can't translate it, but I can understand hand-on-top-of-hand and direct eye contact when I see it. I stop dead. I want to think this is just a guy who looks like Adam from the back, but I know I am wrong. For one thing, Adam wears his watch on his right wrist, a black Timex Ironman. This person has a black Timex Ironman on his right wrist.

The quite good-looking woman senses someone is looking at her and looks at me. She is really, really quite good-looking. Our eyes meet for just a second — hers appear to be green — and then, I am out of there. I don't quite run back to Ruby, but I am in quick step. There is so much going on inside that I am having trouble catching my breath.

First of all, I am incredibly angry, perhaps as angry as I have ever been about anything.

" 'Our' table, my Aunt Fannie!"

I say that loud enough that a couple on the sidewalk look at me in surprise.

Then, I'm in the car, and just barely miss getting hit by a city bus as I pull out of my parking spot. City buses have, thank goodness, LOUD horns. I don't look at the Volvo when I pass it, and manage to get on to a circuitous route home that doesn't involve any high-traffic spots. I rage my way home, all the while trying to tell myself to settle down and quit jumping to conclusions.

Well, Dr. Miller, I think, *that conclusion doesn't require a huge leap. Goddamit!*

And I hardly ever think that word. But there it was. And it came up again once I was properly ensconced in my house and began to cry. I cried for a while. Quite a while. Then, I got angry again. And so forth and so on. I spent the better part of a perfectly good Saturday night and part of Sunday morning, alternating between grief and anger and hoping there was some sort of acceptable explanation for what I viewed as unacceptable.

What I didn't do, though I had to talk myself out of it about ten times, was pick up my phone and a.) let Adam have a piece of my mind, b.) call my Mom, or c.) call Larry and yell at him for introducing me to Mr. Turpin in the first place.

Nope, I would tell myself. *This is yours to handle, and you will.*

Which didn't help a lot, even though I knew it to be true. Sometimes, I hate being a grownup.

At 3 this afternoon, after I figure all football stuff is about over, I call Adam, and ask him to meet me at Neutron. *No Blair's for me for a while,* I think. *Maybe never again.* The very thought brings tears, which I allow. It might be good to be completely wrung out by 5 o'clock.

"Sounds good," he says, as blithely as if nothing at all could be wrong in the universe.

And, now, it's 5:15 and we are seated in the very same booth that Dr. McElroy and I have habitually occupied for a number of sessions of after-hours therapy, which, I am thinking, we will be indulging in this week, unless I get another miracle. I'm not sure how many miracles we are allowed per week, but I'm hoping for just one more, even though the image of the hand connected to the wrist wearing the Ironman over the hand connected to the quite good-looking woman with the green eyes is damping down any miraculous dreams.

"May I ask you a personal question?" I say, just as calm and cool as I don't feel at all.

"Fire away," he says.

"Who were you sitting with at Blair's last night?" I am aiming for a direct hit.

He gets a very peculiar look on his face, one I at first want to think is guilty surprise, but it isn't quite that. It's more like amused surprise, and I think, This guy has had me completely fooled. He thinks getting caught with another woman is funny.

Then he start to laugh. Right out loud.

Here it comes, I think. *The "logical" explanation.*

And guess what. I was right.

"It was you," he says, throttling down the laugh.

"What was me?" I ask.

"You were the woman Jackie saw through the window in the back door."

"Jackie."

"The woman I was sitting with. She said someone looked through the window at her, and turned around and left. "

"Yes, I did," I say.

It was better than murdering you both outright, I don't say.

"What about her?"

He still has the grin on, but I know he knows that the ice has gotten thin. He picks up his hand as if he is going to put it on top of mine — something that could get him killed in the current situation — but instead he scratches his head.

"Jackie is my ex-girlfriend. The one who broke up with me over the Whitmore project."

"And?" I say. *This better be good,* I'm thinking.

He sighs. "We were together for quite a while, and the breakup was pretty hard for both of us. About two weeks ago, she called and wanted to talk. I said, 'About what?' And she said, 'About us.' I didn't know exactly what that meant, but I also knew it might be good for both of us. I said I would think about it, and after a few days, I agreed to meet her and talk."

My stomach is tightening up, but I am also remembering the Adam that I knew Adam to be: an honest, straightforward, kind man. I want to believe this is the same guy.

"And?" I seem to know only one word, right now.

"She expressed her desire to give it another try."

My stomach is doing barrel rolls.

"And?"

He sighs again. "It's an interesting idea." My heart joins my stomach. "But . . . "

"But what?"

He's smiling at me now, and his hand does reach out and cover mine, and all of a sudden, I know it's all going to be just fine.

"Practically at the same moment you saw us?"

"Yes?"

"I was telling her about you, which made her sad, but not inconsolably so."

So. There it is, all logical and everything. All I can do is nod, and look at his hand on mine, and then I start to cry. So much for being wrung out.

He laughs, in self-defense, I think. "Been a hard 24 hours?" he asks.

I sniff and wipe tears away with my uncovered hand and grow a wobbly smile.

"More like an eternity," I say.

He grins his best Adam grin. "Good to know you care."

Care? Holy avoided heartbreak! My maybe guy was comforting his ex at the news that he was my maybe guy. Maybe "maybe" is not necessarily "maybe" any more.

"Let's get out of here," I say. The only things on the table are two glasses of water and menus. The staff has had the good sense to leave us to ourselves for a while.

"Where to?" he says.

"Let's go to Blair's," I say.

And we do.

But not before I kiss him — right in front of God and everybody in the Neutron dining room. He does not protest.

Winter Warning

The Real Lillian

Lillian and I are in inner sanctum. Outside the window, it is just beginning to snow, an early November warning about December. It won't stick today, but pretty soon the Arctic Express will come blitzing across our lake and pile frozen waves on the city beach. Larry will be waxing up his cross-country skis for expeditions on the lake, once it freezes over. He won't be venturing as far from shore as he has once — or twice. His newish wife Anna won't have it, and he is glad she won't.

Madeline and her newish hubby will be headed for some tropical island in a couple of months. I don't know exactly what the smart dog and I will be up to, but he has mentioned a passion for lift-assisted skiing — something I have almost no experience with — and the ski "hill" nearby will be open as soon as they get enough coverage.

I called Aspendale a mountain once, and he laughed.

"Two chairs and a rope tow do not a mountain make," he said. "But, it can still be fun."

Hmm. Do I see a ski lesson in my future? Maybe.

In the near future, though, I see that it's time to ask Lillian a few pertinent questions about her future. She is, I believe, ready to consider these questions, if not make some decisions about the answers. Time will tell.

Marion is getting ready to file for divorce from Joseph. There is plenty of evidence for a case built on his infidelity, including eye-witness depositions my lawyer friend Sheila's team has been gathering from various restaurant and hotel employees. In my opinion, he doesn't stand a chance, but it's probably going be messy and definitely expensive. The twist, Sheila says, is that if he resists too much, Marion can sue him for damaging the reputation of the realty company and probably win at least half of his interest, which will still give her control and get him out of the picture.

Marion is, by the way, almost ecstatic at the idea of letting him keep 25 percent just to get him out the door. This is tempered by her growing acceptance of her responsibility in her daughter's condition. We have met several times, verging on many, now — don't tell Madeline. Even though I think she has a lot of her own "stuff" to deal with — her obsession with fiscal success, for one — she has proven herself not as emotionally unconscious as I first thought her to be. For one thing, when she told me early on that she was "doing it for the girl," it appears she was not excusing herself, but declaring herself. This is good, I think, but there are a lot of other things she could be doing for "the girl" than assuring her financial future. Still. OK.

Of course, the divorce might be more complicated than just showing Joseph the door, and pretty ugly, to boot. Small city. Big scandal.

Part of the mess could be the idea of who gets custody of Lillian. And that's what I am going to talk with Lillian about today. She turned 16 last week, and so, is legally eligible to become emancipated. Marion and I have talked this over, and she is almost quivering with relief that her daughter might be able to get out of her house (read, "away from Joseph").

So, Marion has begun to redeem herself. Joseph, however, seems beyond help at this point. Somewhere back there, before he began indulging his addiction, he may have been a nice man. At least, Marion says he was when they first met. But, he might also be very good at hiding his true nature, as many sociopaths seem to be. It's really hard to tell, and I am not in a place to make that judgment. I only believe that it will be to Lillian's great advantage to get completely away from her father — and distance herself from her mom until some real healing can begin between the two of them.

To her great credit, Marion agrees, although I think she is hedging her bets on making the divorce as simple and straightforward as possible. If there is no question of custody, Joseph has one less lever to use to get what he might want out of the deal. Not that I think a judge would give him custody beyond visitation, but even that might be enough to keep Lillian on her quest for invisibility.

Speaking of the quest, Lillian seems to have relented somewhat. I'm not sure, and I'm not ready to ask quite yet, but I think she has been eating enough to maintain some semblance of health. On intuition, I asked her a couple of weeks ago when her last period was. She was a little shocked that I would ask her, and I had to remind her that I was a medical doctor, as well. The good news is that she had just finished menstruating — for the first time in a long time.

Hooray! I said inside. Active anorexics often don't have periods. Their bodies don't want to give up anything they don't absolutely have to. As long as I've been studying our anatomies, and as hard as that subject is for me sometimes, I am still sometimes flabbergasted by how our physical selves defend themselves, even against the mindful wishes of their owners.

As I think this, Lillian turns away from the window and her eyes finds the carving of cheese and fruit.

"Are you hungry?" I ask.

She gets a little smirk on her face, one I have seen a few times before, a look that reminds me that Lillian has a sense of humor, one somewhat stilted by her upbringing and condition, but still present and piquant when she reveals it. I am always honored when she lets me see it.

"Yep," she says. "Maybe I should have a bite of that cheese."

"Lots of fiber there," I say.

"True," she says, and she laughs.

"I've asked this question before, Lillian. Maybe in another form, but still. What situation do you think would allow you to actually enjoy a few bites of real cheese and an apple as well?"

She sighs. "I can't imagine that."

"Can't or won't?"

She looks at me with one eye. "What do you mean?"

"You've never expressed much hope about the future in my experience. A little, which I find encouraging, but not much. You've told me that the reason you don't eat is because it gives you control over your situation. What if—this is a serious question, not just an exercise in "what if"—what if you could take a lot more control of your life than you think you have now?"

She's looking at me, now, and not the carving.

"What if I could?" She is thinking. I can see the wheels turning. Lillian, as I have said before, is very smart. She looks back at the carving. "I think a better question might be," she says, and her eyes return to me, "is how could I?"

I told you. She's smart.

"I think I might have a good answer to that," I say.

My explanation of her right to become emancipated from her parents did not cause her to immediately embrace the idea. Or accept it. She wanted to know more about process, and who was going to help her do this. But the biggest question she had was, "Where will I live?"

And, when she asked that, I had a huge attack of uncertainty, bordering on panic.

What if she says she doesn't want to live with me?

I had asked myself that question about a thousand times since Marion and I agreed that I would make that offer. I have always honored Lillian's free will, and I knew that I couldn't pull any kind of card in this deal that would disallow that. There were some ground rules to be laid out if she was going to live with me, some basic guidelines that she would have to agree to if it was going to work.

One, that she would begin to take sufficient nourishment to regain her health.

Two, her absolute promise that she would do her best to stay away from pro-ana sites. A total ban was not really practicably enforced without taking away her phone and all other internet access — nearly impossible in our world — so I gave her some wiggle room.

Three, that in regular sessions "at home," she would keep me updated about how she was doing with number two, and how she was feeling about life in general and her life in particular.

Four, that she would continue to attend school and keep up with her studies.

Five, that after a few months, she would begin to meet with Marion and work out a healthier relationship.

And, then a bunch of semi-negotiable stuff, like keeping her room clean, helping around the house, participating in home life; stuff that I have taken for granted because that's what I did when I was growing up.

Working out these rules in my own mind, and getting Marion to agree to them as well, has taken some time, an extra month, in fact; and number five was the hardest one to agree on. I think Marion is terrified of loving another human being — or being loved. Maybe this is a result of having once loved and been loved by Joseph — or at least believing she was — and then being betrayed by him serially. I'm not sure.

But, I have insisted that number five be part of the deal, or no deal. This was not bargaining in good faith, to tell you the truth, because, no matter what, I want Lillian to come live with me — or someplace other than where she lives now — for her own good. Even if her mother never wanted to see her again, I would still want that. But, I also think — know — that it will be good for Lillian and her mom to have a chance to work some stuff out. That could become a new two-on-Thursday, depending on Lillian's response to the offer of my downstairs bedroom.

Another worry has been about how having Lillian living with me will affect the growing relationship between Adam and I. Will there be some kind of competition for my time that I'm not prepared for? Will Adam and I be able to have private time without me constantly worrying about what

Lillian might be up to? For that matter, will they like each other? And how are my folks going to take this? Is my mom going to smother Lillian or keep her at arm's length?

And what if she agrees to live with me, but then won't agree to the ground rules? Those are the thoughts rambling around in my mind.

Basically, *Oh, my God. What am I getting into?*

Meanwhile, back in inner sanctum, I take a deep breath and jump into the void. "How about with me?" I ask.

She has been looking at the carving off and on, but I know that she has also been listening as I explain the process and her right to leave her parent's home, that the judge will want her to have some sort of plan in place, that there may be some hard questions to answer. When I answer the question about where she might live, though, she snaps to.

"With you?"

"Yes."

"Do you want me to?" She sounds puzzled.

"I do."

"Why?"

Because, Lillian, I love you, I think, but don't say. I don't want to scare her to death.

"Because I think it would be very good for you if you got out of your current situation and had a safe place to start recovering yourself."

"What do you mean, 'recovering'?"

"That's a good question," I say. And I have to think about that myself. What do I mean? And, it turned out I had a pretty good answer.

"Will you show me that picture of Willie again?" I ask.

She nods, and pulls her phone out, turns it on and scrolls until she finds it. She holds it out to me. I look at it, and savor the image of the healthy little girl with the happy dog.

"Look at the picture, Lillian," I say.

She turns the screen toward herself.

"See that little girl?"

She nods. Emotions flicker across her face like lightning and tears form.

"That's you, Lillian. There is the real Lillian. She doesn't want to be invisible. This is your opportunity to reclaim that beautiful little girl.

The salty hordes assail her eyelids, and begin to escape. For the first time, I feel like I can do what I've wanted to do time and again. I hold out my arms, and she lets herself be folded into them.

After she has cried for a while, and I have leaked a little myself, I ask, "So, what do you think? Want to come live at my house for a while?"

She pulls away, sniffs and pulls a few Kleenex out of the box. She looks at me, then, and nods. "OK."

Let the negotiations begin, I think to myself. "Good. I'm glad. So, here's what we have to do, and some things we need to agree on."

Kinda Scary
Scary in a Good Way

Things have been happening quickly in Lillian's life. And mine, for that matter. First of all, last Monday, Lillian appeared in court with Sheila and I and asked the judge to allow her to become emancipated. The judge was a woman, for which I will be eternally grateful to both Something and Sheila. After she came out of her chambers and took her seat behind the bench, and we had all been seated, I looked at Sheila, who smiled at me and wiggled her eyebrows. My buddy the lawyer is a good one, both buddy and lawyer.

Both Marion and Joseph were in the courtroom. Marion, I expected. Joseph was a surprise.

"The father is here," I told Sheila.

She got a funny look.

"Where is he and what's he look like?" She had never seen him, but she also didn't seem to want to look directly at him.

Marion was seated right behind us, but Joseph was in a far corner, in which I could see him without being too obtrusive.

"To your right, sitting in the corner. Dark hair. Clean-shaven. Shaded glasses. Jeans and a white snap-button shirt. Leather jacket. Way too tan for this time of year." If there was a picture beside "playboy" in the dictionary that day, it was Joseph's.

Sheila turned and whispered something to one of her staff seated behind us, who nodded, stood and made her way out of the courtroom. Joseph's eyes followed her.

He seemed as he was the first and only other time I had seen him: alert in a sort of reptilian way. No emotion showed, and even when Lillian stood to tell the judge it was her wish to leave her home and move in with me, he didn't respond much more than to glance in my direction. In that, he caught me looking at him, and raised an eyebrow, like he was somewhat surprised at my attention. He then got a little smirk, and I had the idea that he was thinking, *You think you're so smart*.

I suddenly felt incredibly sad for him. He was, whether he knew it or not, about to lose everything of real importance in his life. That it was by his own doing was not the point, really. At one time, he was as innocent as any child can be. Somewhere, something went wrong and now that something was hanging over his head like Damocles' sword. Together, his daughter, his wife and I — with the able assistance of Sheila — were going to snip that thread.

I turned away just as the judge put her hammer down, granting Lillian's request.

Both Lillian and Marion turned toward me at that moment, and both were looking a little misty. I must have been, too, because Lillian gave me a wobbly grin and came over and touched my arm, as if in comfort. I held out my right hand, and she took it in hers. We shook.

"Congratulations."

"Kinda scary," she said.

"I imagine," I said, but I didn't really have to imagine. I knew. But it was scary in a good way.

As we filed out of the courtroom, Sheila said, "Watch this." She nodded to Joseph, who was not far ahead of us. In the hallway, the young woman Sheila had whispered to approached Joseph, and I saw him perk up.

She said something to him, and he nodded. She then handed him a sheaf of paper, which he looked at and then turned toward us. His reptilian gaze was transformed to something I can only describe as a combination of fear, anger and surprise.

"What's this about, Marion?" he said, "It seems you have forgotten some important details."

Marion didn't answer, but turned to Sheila.

"Mr. Ballenkamp," Sheila said, "you have been served. My client prefers not to talk with you directly, so you will have to communicate with me or a member of my firm or through your own attorney, which I advise you to acquire."

"This is not going to work," Joseph said.

"It will, Mr. Ballenkamp," Sheila said. "Our offer for settlement is part of the documents you just received. Please consider it thoughtfully. You will also find a restraining order, restricting you from contacting Marion — or Lillian — except through me or a member of my firm."

We made our way out of the courthouse. My last sight of Joseph was of him rustling through the summons, and I got the idea that he was looking for the settlement details. He would find that they were relatively generous, but I felt like it might be better for him if he were to get nothing. At least, then, he would have opportunity to face himself naked.

It was Marion's hope that he would just sign and they would be done. If it went to court, and depositions were read and witnesses called, it would be very messy for all of them.

A Tangled Web
A Dinner Invitation

What a tangled web we weave. . . " And, I'm complicit. I'm not really proud of helping to plot all this, but in this case, I believe the end justifies the means. Sheila, Marion and I had put together a timetable to emancipation — for both mother and daughter — without Lillian's input. Once Lillian agreed to the terms I set out — which was relatively easy to negotiate — we "pulled the trigger," as Sheila put it. And our aim seems to have been true.

So far, so good.

Marion acquired an apartment before we went to court with Lillian, which she has moved into temporarily — until the divorce is settled. Joseph has dropped out of sight, it feels like. I suppose that being blindsided like he was might have caused him to do a reality check. Maybe. Hopefully.

I feel bad for him, really. His whole world is fractured right now. I'm somewhat tempted to ask someone reach out to him — there is no way that I can — because I suspect he is a "hurtin' unit," as my guy would say.

"My" guy! Woohoo! Yet another miracle is wrought, one I'm trying not to think about too much, somewhat unsuccessfully.

Adam has actually invited me to dinner at his place, where I have never been. He's only been to my house a few times, for that matter. Our courtship, if you can actually call it that, has been slow and easy. OK. Slow. Our mutual attraction seems to have been in place for quite a long time, but our mutual caution has kept it from exploding prematurely, if you will. At least, I believe that we both know what we're doing here, even if it's also apparent that we may have both wanted to arrive "here" a bit sooner. But, I think that makes it all the sweeter. Delayed gratification can be the best kind.

He's going to cook. I always knew that he probably could, but the reality is very intriguing. But, there is a complication. It seems I have a roommate, and I'm a little trepidatious about leaving Lillian at home alone right yet. The "what if" monster has been at me. So, I am going to have to impose my new status as "guardian," — which I'm not really, officially, but certainly feel like one — on our dinner date.

We are in Frozen In Time when he invites me, and I crunch all the "what-if's" as quickly as I can. Final answer is "Yes, but . . . "

"May I bring Lillian?" I ask.

Adam looks at me with an odd, sort of blank expression, and I'm thinking, *Damn! There goes dinner at his house.* After a long moment, he gets the Adam smile, and then he laughs.

"Yes. You may bring Lillian."

I'm grateful that he has agreed, but I also sense there is something else going on behind that smile.

"What?" I ask.

He looks down at his sorbet as if he is thinking, which he is, I find out. He clears his throat, and chuckles. He's stalling.

"C'mon, Adam. What's up?"

"Well," he says, and "well" is about three seconds long, "Uh," he continues.

I'm considering timing all this.

"To tell you the truth," he finally says — and he always has, I think — "I was going to ask you to spend the night." He giggles that special giggle of his.

I begin to blush, which I hope doesn't send him the wrong message.

"Uh," I say. "Well." Mine outlasts his.

I am not averse to the idea, by any means. I am just totally surprised. It's not as if it has never crossed my mind. I have thought about the possibility of having sex with this man a number of times — the euphemism "sleeping together" is not an accurate description of my desire — but it seems this opportunity is trumped by quasi-parenthood.

He's looking at me with an expectant expression, and I know I better say something.

"Rain check," I say. "Pretty soon, but not yet." But, I really want to race him up to inner sanctum and have us have our way with each other. But, then, we would only have about 15 minutes before my next patient. A couple of hours would be much more appropriate. *Then*, we can sleep together.

"OK," he says. "At least you know, right?"

"Right. Yes. I know. Whew!"

I am totally blushing now, and I fan my face. He cracks up.

There's that delayed gratification thing again. And both of us will remember for a long time the embrace we shared in the stairwell before we went back to our respective offices.

A Deal is a Deal

Working Things Out

Lillian has come to call me "Mary," which I think is grand. It is a good reflection of our relationship, for one thing. She even asked if that was OK. She very seldom called me anything before she became my house mate. I can only remember a few times that she called me "Dr. Miller," in fact, and the last time was when she asked permission to call me "Mary."

"Dr. Miller?" she asked, around a mouthful of toothbrush. "Is it OK to call you Mary?"

It was her third week in the house. Things were still a little awkward. She was learning that a deal is a deal — eat and stay away from pro-ana sites or go back to your mom's house. She had tried a tantrum or two, and several crying jags. Then, that afternoon, she was not waiting at the library as we had agreed. I had to find her via text.

It was OK to find her hanging out at a friend's house, which she was used to doing quite often before moving to my place. But the deal was that she was to meet me at the library or let me know that she was going to do something else. She resisted waiting for me at the end of her friend's sidewalk, trying to get me to come knock instead, but I insisted, and she grudgingly gave in. The drive home was quiet and uncomfortable. Neither one of us said anything for 10 minutes. She didn't want to say anything, and I didn't know what to say.

I dug back through time to see what my mom or dad might have had to say in a case like this, and I remembered the time that I decided to walk to our house from school instead of taking the bus. I was in sixth grade and knew the town well enough to know I could find home.

I loved to walk then, as I do now, but I had misjudged quite badly how far home was. Instead of getting off the bus on my corner at 3:20, I dragged in about 5:30. And, I absolutely knew I was going to be in trouble. It was all I thought about for the last dozen blocks.

My mom was on the phone when I walked in the front door, and I knew she was probably talking to my Dad, who worked until 6 at the hardware store. It was his store to work in, after all, and he was the first guy there in the morning and the last to leave.

"Here she is now," she said, and I heard his garbled answer rattle through the phone. I had no idea of what to say, but my mom did.

"How was your day, Mary?" she said. That was all, but she was looking at me with a look that demanded an answer.

"It was OK," I said. "I'm sorry I'm late."

"Where did you get off the bus?" she said, "Hoboken?"

It was the closest I ever heard my mom to being sarcastic.

"I didn't ride the bus. I walked home."

"You did?" She was genuinely surprised.

I nodded, waiting for the other shoe to drop.

"Well, the next time you walk home, please have someone at the school call and tell me your plans so I don't have the city police out looking for you. OK?"

"OK, Mom." I was close to crying, but I didn't.

She turned back to the phone, and dialed a number. After a few rings, someone answered and she said, "Sergeant? This is Mrs. Miller. The prodigal has returned."

The voice on the other end of the line squawked something.

"Yes. She's fine." She looked at me. "I think. Just a little beat and hungry, I imagine. Thanks very much." She hung up.

"You have inconvenienced a number of people, Mary. You may go to your room and wait to be called for dinner."

After apologizing again, I did. I heard Dad come home and the murmur of their conversation in the kitchen, and my dad's laugh. He called me for dinner, and I went downstairs a-worrying, thinking I would get at least a scolding. He gave me a hug instead and said, "How's the feet, wanderer?"

They were sore. But that was all. We were done, and I knew better.

"How was your day, Lillian?" I ask, when we are about five minutes from home.

"It was OK," she says.

"Next time you want to go visit a friend instead of waiting at the Library, call the office and tell Madeline where you are going to be. I had several librarians running all over the place looking for you. You inconvenienced several people today, including me."

She's looking at the floor at her feet. "Sorry," she says, and I think she means it, but it's hard to tell.

After another quiet minute, we pull into my driveway.

"What are you going to do?" she asks, and I can hear fear in her voice.

"Make you eat some dinner," I say.

She doesn't look at me, but I see her relax. She doesn't move to get out of the car, and we sit there for a few moments.

Finally, she looks at me and gives me a small grin. "A fitting punishment, I suppose."

We laugh our way into the house. And she eats some dinner.

A Baker! *My B-b-b-boyfriend*

It's been three weeks since dinner at Adam's. It was a simple affair. He made spaghetti and meat sauce (and some vegie marinara for Lillian) , a big green salad and — get this — dinner rolls made from my mom's recipe. A baker! Holy waist-line, Batman!

Lillian resisted coming along, but I reminded her that this is part of participating in home life; that Adam was my b-b-b-boyfriend — there's a term I haven't used for a long time — and we would probably be seeing a lot of him.

She has been living with me now for six weeks, and things are going OK. Not great some days, but OK. She is, after all, a 16-year-old who is trying out her own ideas, and I seem to be the one she is trying most of them out on. We've had a couple of arguments about food, for one thing, and I've had to remind her — again — that food was part of the deal. We have negotiated a specific calorie intake that she has to achieve daily. It's hard for her to let go of her habit of not eating. She gets anxious when she eats, for one thing, which I believe is the old mental setting about control fighting off the new paradigm we are trying to establish.

I am being generous with the word "we," for sometimes, she seems to want nothing to do with it. The roots of anorexia are grown deep, and they can't just be jerked without causing some serious damage, I don't think. Still, I insist that she eats. And she grumbles and messes with her food like Calvin, the little stubborn kid in the comic strip.

Her biggest challenge seems to be keeping away from the pro-ana sites. I believe she is being truthful when I ask if she has visited one lately, because she sometimes answers "yes," "sometimes" being way too often, in my opinion. But then I insist that we talk about what she saw there, what she might have learned from her visit, and what she might have posted. She is forthcoming in these conversations — I don't judge or condemn — and I've learned that she is most often an observer, and very seldom a contributor, which I know to be a change from her past behavior. We have talked about this in depth a couple of times, and she has told me up front that she became an active member of several pro-ana groups beginning when she was 13.

I asked her if that was when she began puberty — a "doctor question," as she refers to them. She seemed somewhat embarrassed, but allowed that was indeed the case. Lillian hasn't quite gotten used to my blunt questions about medical concerns, and I don't want to treat her like a lab guinea pig, but I also want to know as much about her disease — her struggle — as possible. The more I know, the better able I am to help her heal. And, maybe this knowledge will come in handy with someone else in the future.

The bad news is that she still visits these places. The good news is that the frequency has been dropping. The other good news is that if we can have honest conversations about things like this, we can probably talk about anything.

I've had to rearrange my work load a bit to accommodate her school schedule. I drop her off at Minnehaha, and then pick her up at the local library branch or at a friend's house when I'm finished. This works pretty well, but it's cutting into my social time, big time. I haven't seen McElroy except in passing forever, it feels like. We did get a moment in the lobby of our building a couple of days ago, and he asked me how it was going with Lillian. It wasn't a skeptical question, either, but one of real concern. This made me happy, for him and me, both.

THREE BITES
Neutron Confrontation

Marion called this morning while I was with my first patient of the day. I called her back between sessions, and she told me the good news that Joseph signed the divorce papers without resistance. She is moving back into their — now, her — house day after tomorrow. She had the good sense and foresight to take a lot of pictures before filing for divorce, and Joseph was made aware of that, so his leaving should be relatively non-intrusive.

Of course, he's also walking away with a 27-percent interest in a seven-million-dollar real estate company, which, according to the decree, Marion will buy back from him in 3 percent annual increments over the next nine years. That's his picture beside "set for life" in the dictionary this morning. Unless, of course, he blows through it, which he just might. Whatever his demons are, they are still chasing him. Or he is chasing them. With addiction, it's never very clear which is which.

Adam, Lillian, McElroy and I were at Neutron last night — Dr. McElroy and I are friends on better terms than we have ever been. When we walked in, Joseph — "Joseph" sits better with me than "Lillian's dad" — was sitting back in a corner of the bar with what I took to be his latest "conquest." I am making assumptions, and jumping to conclusions. Maybe, I should be kinder.

But he is not being kind to me. The whole thing — divorce and Lillian's emancipation — according to him, is all my doing to gain "control" of Lillian. At least that is what the state ethics committee says he has told them.

When Marion called, I already knew what she had to tell me, though I didn't tell her so. She was so happy to share the news — I think the word is "ebullient" — I was loathe to rain on her parade with my concerns.

I already knew because I had been in conversation with my now lawyer, Sheila, who was the first person I called after I got the call from Dr. Trujillo. As chair of the state board of ethics, she asked me to come and appear before the board "in regard to your relationship with the minor patient Lillian Ballenkamp." That's how she put it. It was all pretty formal, as was the letter I got shortly after. Arggh!

The only other person beside Sheila that I've told about this upcoming "event" is my guy. (I think I might be getting used to the "my" thing when it comes to Mr. Adam Turpin.) He's a rock. A smart, funny, good-looking rock. The first thing he said was, "No advice unless you ask. I figure you can defend yourself well enough, but I'm here is you need me. Venting is just fine, though."

So, I vented. And cried a little. And got cuddled. There has been some relatively serious cuddling going on of late.

"It's all gonna be fine," he says in my left ear.

"What if I lose my license?" I say, right out loud.

"My guess is that won't happen," he says. "But if it does, I hear the new Frozen In Time is looking for counter girls who know how to make a great banana split."

This makes me laugh, and him, too.

"OK for your help, mister," I tell him, which makes us both laugh again.

Laughter is good for the soul, a friend told me long ago, and I have never found a reason to prove her wrong.

Adam says, "Whatever happens, we'll figure it out."

The implication in those half-dozen words are both thrilling and terrifying. "We."

Oh, my goodness.

Meanwhile, here we are at Neutron. My meeting with the board is next week. They have not suspended my license, so it's sort of business as normal — if living with a 16-year-old who is learning to eat again can be called that. There, right in front of her, is a small Caesar salad. No anchovies. She is determined to be vegetarian. Tofu has invaded my refrigerator. She is still bony thin, but she is, as we agreed, taking nourishment on a regular basis. Yogurt. Cottage cheese. Half a grilled cheese sandwich. Carrots. Broccoli. Apples. I think of that carving in my office, which she has not seen for a while.

We are continuing with her therapy at home, which pretty much consists of staying current about how she is feeling about the present. Eventually, we will venture back into her past, I think, and she knows that she has full permission to bring that up any time. In the meantime, the present is enough. The future? One day at a time is plenty for both of us. At least she is not on an all-white diet like a little kid might be. I am not "making" her eat any particular thing. I just praise her lightly for whatever she does eat.

Lillian didn't see her dad when we came in, I'm pretty sure. And if she did, she has not said anything about it. I am somewhat trepidatious about how she might react if she does see him. He didn't see us, either, I didn't think, and I was somewhat tempted to move our dinner date elsewhere, but something — Something? — said, "Let it be." So, I did.

Adam has wondered out loud if I wanted to tell Dr. McElroy about the upcoming meeting with the board. I was not enamored of the idea at first, but the more I thought about it, the more I realized it might be helpful. And, it would probably be a damned sight better than letting him find out through the grapevine, or on the six o'clock news, for that matter. There has been some local media attention to the divorce, particularly because Ballenkamp Realty is one of the biggest agencies in the state, and certainly the largest in our little city. I don't think there is any public hint of my upcoming meeting with the board, but I wouldn't put it past the guy in the bar with his young friend to mention it to the local paper if he so decided.

So, Lillian has finished her salad, and the rest of us are done as well. Adam says, "I bet I can beat you at Space Invaders, Lillian."

"Huh-uh!" she says. And off they go to the arcade next door. There is something completely natural about how they fit together. He doesn't try to be her dad. She accepts his friendship as part of the deal about living with me, and willingly. He can make her laugh. She can return the favor. Lillian is possibly the most honest person I know; about herself, about her life, about the world as she sees it; and she has an ability to express that in sometimes hilarious terms.

They have disappeared for a while, as Adam and I plotted. McElroy and I have our respective after-dinner cocktails, and I dive in.

"James," I say, and he perks right up. "The ethics board has called me to have a talk about my relationship with Lillian. As you warned me they might."

"I'm sorry, Doctor — uh, Mary. I don't know what to say."

"Well, at least you didn't say 'I told you so,' " I say.

"That's funny. You know, at one time, I might have. But I've learned a lot about letting some things be from you. I told you earlier that I admire your courage when it comes to what you think is right. I look at that little girl, and think to myself, 'Miracle.' You spend a lot of time with her, so you might not notice so much, but the difference between her now and when her mom brought her to see me is astounding."

"You think?"

"I know."

"Good. I'm glad to hear that. Sometimes, it feels like slow going."

"At least you're going." He holds up his glass, and I touch mine to his.

"If you would like, I'll attend your meeting with the board. If that's allowed."

"I'll check," I say. "Thanks very much. For everything."

He clears his throat, and then, again. Something seems to be stuck there. Finally, this is what comes out: "When this blows over, which I think it will, maybe I could consult with you about some family stuff."

"Sounds like a plan, Dr. McElroy," I say, as calm as you can please, as if I'm not a bit flabbergasted.

At this moment, Joseph Ballenkamp heaves into view from my left and stations himself at the end of the table. He did see me. I reflexively look at the dining room door to see if Adam and Lillian are in sight. His "date" is standing there waiting. Dr. McElroy, who has only met Lillian's mom, doesn't have a clue who he is, but he's about to find out. Joseph has had a drink or three, and he has something to say, it seems.

"So, Doctor," he says. "Have a nice time talking to the board?" He seems to think things like that are instantaneous.

"That will be next week, Mr. Ballenkamp."

"Well, I hope they do as much damage to your life as you've managed to do to mine."

Now McElroy knows who he is, and I expect him to say something, but he just looks on.

Joseph isn't happy with walking away yet.

"Your pretty girlfriend is gonna get censured," he says to McElroy, in a sort of juvenile, taunting voice. He has a half-smile. "You stepped on the wrong tail when you started messing with me. And I ain't done yet."

I open my mouth to respond, but nothing comes out.

"What else do you plan to do?" McElroy asks.

"I can hire lawyers, too. How about a big fat malpractice suit?"

"I doubt that will come to any good for you, Mr. Ballenkamp," McElroy says. "It will just cost you the rest of whatever reputation you have and a lot of money, particularly if she were to sue you for defamation of character."

I want to say, "Yeah. What he said," but I don't.

What I do say is, "Mr. Ballenkamp. This is my friend Dr. McElroy, who will be with me at the meeting with the ethics board next week, and likely will share this conversation with them. He is also a psychiatrist, and a good one. He believes I have been doing a very good job working with your daughter — Lillian — that we are making good progress. You may want to think about making an appointment with him to help address some of your own issues."

He looks at me like I'm some sort of alien. His face contorts, and I'm afraid he might spit on me, but instead he starts laughing.

"My issues?" he says, in a voice that is definitely not an indoor voice. "Mine? At least I don't wander around ruining lives, like you are trying to do to mine. Who the hell do you think you are? Little miss perfect?"

McElroy is trying to decide whether to get up or not, which I am willing him not to, but Bob the Bartender arrives before he can.

"Excuse me, sir. Is there something I can help you with?"

Bob the Bartender isn't a very big guy, but when he asks a question in the manner that he asked that one, people seem to calm right down. Joseph calmed down.

"I was just leaving," he says.

He turns and starts out, and I realize that Adam and Lillian have been standing in the door of the dining room where Joseph's date had been. She is gone.

Oh, blink! I think — and rest assured that "blink" is not the word I thought.

Lillian has a panicky look. I'm afraid she's going to run when Joseph turns to leave, but what she does is step behind Adam, which seems to me to be instinctual. Joseph, half drunk and all mad, doesn't see her. For which I am eternally grateful.

How much of Joseph's tirade she has heard, I don't know, but I know she heard part of it. Joseph storms by them. They make their way to the table, and I notice that Lillian has not looked after Joseph, but is looking instead at me.

They sit as they had been before they went to the arcade; Lillian beside me and Adam beside McElroy. Lillian looks at me, and says, "You OK?"

"Just a bit shaky," I say. I am amazed that she is so calm. "How about you?"

"Oh," she says, "I've seen him a lot madder than that."

I can only giggle, and Adam does, as well. McElroy can only shake his head.

"So," she says, calm as can be. "Adam beat me two games out of three. He says I have to have two bites of dessert."

I look at my guy, who winks at me. He stacked the deck on the video game. Space Invaders was invented a long time before Lillian was born, and he was ace at it. Still is, evidently. He calls our waiter over.

"We'll have the crème brulee," he says, "and three spoons."

"Two and four," says McElroy, and we all laugh.

Lillian has three bites.

Tiny White Box

What's For Dinner

It's nearly May, and I have known Lillian for just over a year, a year so remarkably full that it seems more like a decade. And, it feels like I have known Lillian forever. Time is relative, Dr. Einstein asserted, and he was right.

A single year doesn't seem large enough to contain the changing relationship with Dr. McElroy; the lovely, progressive, exciting, sometimes scary and maddeningly slow dance with the smart dog; the emancipation hearing; a session with the ethics committee; the emergence of Marion as a person I am coming to admire; and Lillian's continuing progress in healing.

In the five months we have lived together, Lillian has moved even more securely into my heart; so much so that I am a little jealous that she and her mom are beginning to bond, but only a little.

The three of us have been spending the two-on-Thursday time slot together for a month, and the last two sessions have been cathartic to the point of near-emotional overload for all of us. I may have to start buying Kleenex in bulk.

It's Saturday afternoon, and I have been at the office doing a little research on disorganized attachment. Don't tell Madeline. It's a phenomenon worth knowing as much as I can about; one that a whole bunch of people suffer from. Including, maybe, Dr. McElroy. It's sadly common, and results in children that never have a chance to be as successful in life as their genes might dictate.

Parents, take delight in your babies. Don't be afraid of them, and don't make them afraid of you. That might sound simple, but it's also essential to making kids secure in themselves and the larger world.

Lillian has been home alone today, and she has offered to cook dinner, a big surprise. I've been wondering what concoction she might come up with, not without some concern, but the house smells great when I get home. She's in the kitchen, standing at the stove, tending to a couple of pots.

"What's for dinner?" I ask.

"Spaghetti."

"Anything else?"

She gets the joke and laughs.

Lillian holds a spoon out to me, full of frothy red sauce. I take it, taste it, pronounce it delicious, which it is. She grins and goes back to the stove, hovering like a conjurer over the pot. Her hipbones disappeared back into her flesh in the past few weeks. I noticed sometime, but I can't remember exactly when.

"Is Adam coming?" she asks. She has requested his presence.

"I'm not sure. I asked him, and he said he would try, but that he has something he needs to think about. Evidently, I'm a distraction."

I don't like the way that last sentence came out, but there it is, sounding sort of pissy. But Adam has been sort of reserved this past week. We've not seen much of each other, and I get the idea that he has something on his mind that he doesn't want to discuss with me. I know better than to intrude where I'm not welcome, but it's still worrisome. Part of me realizes, though, that recognizing this as such is not all bad. If and when it becomes a serious gap, I will not hesitate to try to bridge it. If, as I wish and pray, we commit to partnership, we will each have the right and responsibility to know what's up with the other partner.

Lillian is grinning again. "That's not all bad," she says, as she dumps hot spaghetti into the sauce and begins to mix them together.

"OK. True. Thanks."

God, she's smart, I think. *And wise.*

I note that there are three places set, and that tugs hard at my heart. I'm not sure how much to burden this newly freed spirit with, so I keep my worries to myself. *One triumph at a time,* Doctor Miller, *I tell myself, and there she is, right there.*

I fix myself a drink. Gin on the rocks, three olives. Lillian pours the contents of the pan into a serving bowl and carries it to the table. As she sets it down, the doorbell rings.

"I'll get it!" She yells, and sprints for the front door, sliding the last few yards on the hardwood in her bunny slippers, pure joyous teenager. She pulls the door open, and the smart dog steps in with a bouquet of flowers in one hand. The timing of all this is making me begin to suspect that I have been set up by the two of them, which makes me wonder what's next.

Lillian leads him to the table with a huge smile on her face. Adam has the Adam smile on, and in the hand that doesn't have flowers in it is a small — tiny in fact — white box. It's so tiny it's huge. It is the biggest, heaviest, most massive tiny white box I have ever seen.

And, suddenly, I am terrified in the most wonderful way I have ever been scared in my life.

EPILOGUE
Something About Miracles

Doctor Franks called me a few weeks ago and told me about a young dog in their care he thought I might like to look at. His offices are next to the city animal shelter, for which he does quite a bit of *pro bono* work. I was somewhat confused, because I hadn't told him I was looking for a dog, and I certainly wasn't considering getting one.

When I asked what he was thinking, he said, "This dog looks extraordinarily like a young Willie."

It's summer now, and Lillian concluded her payments to Dr. Franks for Willie's euthanization and cremation two months ago. She hadn't said so, but I got the idea that she was sad about that. I asked her why, and she just said, "I like the people there."

She had been making the payments in person, and now that she was done, she didn't feel she had reason to visit.

"I think the people there like you, as well."

She nods. "Uh-huh."

"So, what can you do to stay in touch?"

"I don't know."

"Think about it," I say.

"OK."

And I knew she would. She's a thinker, Lillian is. About a million years ago, it feels like, I wondered about her command of English, and it has been revealed that she has read voraciously since the day she learned how. It was an escape from her then reality that was encouraged by a couple of delighted teachers who discovered she preferred the printed word to video games or social media.

A few days later, we are sitting at the table eating breakfast — really eating — and she says, "I'm going to ask if I can help walk the dogs at the shelter. Would that be OK, you think?"

I've tried my best not to be too authoritative with Lillian, so I'm kind of surprised that she seems to be asking permission.

"OK with who?" I ask.

"With the people at the vet's," she says.

"I think they'll love it."

She nods and finishes her Raisin Bran. A few minutes later, I hear her on her phone, talking to the vet's office staff.

She reports the outcome gleefully. "They say I can start any time," she says. She is absolutely lit up. "I can ride my bike."

It's interesting to me how much of a sense of responsibility Lillian has, in spite of her traumatic earlier life. It might be that she figured out early on that she was the one who had to be responsible for herself when others weren't stepping up. And, her decade of caring for Willie probably helped.

The vet staff must have seen it, as well. A month ago, after she had faithfully showed up to walk shelter dogs for a few weeks, they offered her a job walking dogs who were kenneled in their dog "hotel."

She was conflicted. "What about the dogs in the shelter?" She has a huge heart.

"Maybe a little of both?" I suggested.

She worked out a schedule with Dr. Franks. Two days walking shelter dogs for two hours. Two days walking kenneled dogs for two hours, for which she gets paid. And, the big bonus: Saturdays, she works a near full shift helping in the clinic, for which she also gets paid.

I really like this person, this Lillian. I mean besides loving her. She's a good one, and I am really, really, really glad she is in my life and I am in hers.

Speaking of dogs, the smart dog and I are — holy I-don't-know-what — getting married in October in the courtyard in front of Adam's building — or the lobby, depending on the weather — on the anniversary of our first, post-football-game kiss. We're going to honeymoon in and around Yellowstone, where we made a quick trip recently to meet his folks. He tells me that the crowds will be much lessened.

My guy grew up in a gorgeous place, one which he left after his first love left him for someone else, something we still haven't talked much about, and maybe never will. He says, in passing, that she did him a favor, because if she hadn't jilted him, he would never have met me. And, that is plenty for me to know.

His mom Ariel — she's a retired fifth grade teacher — still makes the best raspberry sorbet on the planet, which I can attest to. His dad, Tom, is a remarkable person. Still mountaineering at 73, guiding younger folks climbing and skiing in the Tetons. He quit setting routes a few years ago, he confesses, but still knows where most of the existing ones are. After we had been there for two days, Tom told Adam —in front of me — "You're on the right track with this gal, son." His mom was at the kitchen sink, looking out the window, but I could see her nodding. So, I'm in. Hooray!

Adam and I consulted about the dog Dr. Franks invited me to look at, and we both went to see it. The look was good, so we asked Lillian if she thought she might be ready for another dog. She said, "Maybe." It turned out she had already met the dog in question — one-year-old Clancy — which Dr. Franks, of course, knew. She thought he belonged to someone else, but Clancy was really being "rehomed" by some folks who couldn't keep him. When she learned Clancy was the likely candidate to succeed

Willie, she was ecstatic. I found it very interesting that she had already allowed herself to love Clancy, even though she thought he belonged to someone else. We are in the process of building a kennel in the back yard.

So. A dog in the back yard. A teenager in the kitchen. A wedding to plan. What else?

Oh, yes. McElroy. McElroy is leaving our little city. I am simultaneously sad to see him go and happy for him.

Long, long ago, on the back deck of my house, after everyone else had gone home from my housewarming party and before I even knew Adam existed, in sort of self-defense, I asked James if he was gay. It was meant as a joke, and he laughed, and said, "Who wants to know," but that was his only answer. Well, it turns out that he is, revealed to me in the consultation he alluded to the night Joseph accosted me at Neutron. McElroy doesn't go home often because his parents can't accept the idea that he is homosexual, and visits always lead to confrontations about his sexuality.

He and his sort-of-secret partner — another James, I was amused to find out, have decided to move to a bigger city where they can be completely open about their relationship without jeopardizing their respective careers. They are off to Portland, Oregon, in a few months. His patients — and his office — are being taken over by a young woman who just finished her residency. I've not met Emily Portsmouth, MD, yet. but I've heard good things about her.

"After the wedding," McElroy tells me.

James did go with me to the meeting with the ethics board, and he did stand up and tell them that, in his opinion as a psychiatrist, Lillian's life was saved by my efforts, which included my offer to host her in her emancipation. The "hearing," if you can call it that, was over in about 45 minutes.

Joseph Ballenkamp has disappeared. Someone said he moved to Las Vegas, but nobody knows that for sure. After he signed the divorce papers, he seemed to have vaporized.

Something About Miracles

Lillian and her mom are working things out, with me as coach and referee. I focus on getting Lillian to release her pile of latent anger and Marion to drop her load of guilt, sometimes with great success; other times, not so much. But baby-step by baby-step, I see them getting closer. Lillian got her sense of humor from her mom, a surprise for me when Marion began to relax enough to reveal it, and there is often laughter in inner sanctum to help absorb the tears.

Last week, as the session with the two of them was beginning, Lillian walked over and picked up the carving of apples and cheeses. She looked at me with her shy grin and said, "Too bad this isn't real. I'm hungry." We moved the session to Frozen In Time.

It's quiet in my kitchen and I am writing in my journal. Dishes are done and Lillian is in her room reading — Ambrose's *Undaunted Courage*, for goodness sake. I am thinking about all this, while trying not to think about it too much. Lillian comes scuffing out in her hilarious bunny slippers and dives into the refrigerator and comes up with a cup of yogurt. Low fat, of course.

"Mary?" she says

"What's up?"

"Is it OK to tell you that I love you?"

"Yes, Lillian. It's very OK." I say. I have a huge smile and sudden tears. "And I love you."

She shows her shy grin and nods.

"I knew that," she says, and shuffles back to her room, spooning in yogurt as she goes.

There's something about miracles here. I will not try to define it or even understand it. I will just be grateful.

Amen.

The End

About the Author

Sandy Compton lives in Western Montana. He is a writer, editor, publisher, photographer, back packer, world traveler. and jack-knife carpenter He inherited the house he grew up in and has been rebuilding it — with the help of friends — for quite some time.

He is also an adventurer who loves to go, and does, as often as he can.

Other books from Sandy Compton

Fiction & Poetry

Archer MacClehan and the Hungry Now

Archer MacClehan and the Girl Who Wouldn't Stop Running

The Dog With His Head On Sideways and Nineteen Other Sappy, Sentimental Stories

The Friction of Desire: A Mary Magdalene Miller Case Study

Scars on Top of Scars A Mary Magdalene Miller Case Study

Her Name is Lillian: A Mary Magdalene Miller Case Study

Jason's Passage and Other Stories

Elisba's Search for Water (Children's)

Caleb's Miracle (Children's)

34 Poems

Nonfiction

Side Trips From Cowboy Revisited: Addiction, Recovery and the Western American Myth

The Addiction Antidote: Surrender (a companion to *Side Trips From Cowboy*)

The Scenic Route: Life on the Road Between Hope and Paradise

Other Books from Blue Creek Press

Memoir

Camping in Wyoming: A 1910 Wedding Trip to Yellowstone Park
by Mariam Lawton Clayton

Hunting Tigers and Other Adventures on Christ's Mission in Old India
By Herman and Mildred Reynolds
— compiled by Frank and Joyce Coupal

Journey to the Slice of Life **by Helen Carrol**

Five Years on the Inside: Life as a Recreation Therapist at Salinas State Prison **by Garth D. Fisher**

Voices in the Wilderness: A Collection of Wild Essays
Compiled for Friends of Scotchman Peaks Wilderness and Montana Wilderness Association

My Road Trip: From Religious to Spiritual and Back Home **by Stanley D. Norman**

Social Commentary by Richard Sonnichen

All Fish Have Bones

A Leaf in a Stream

A Church in Peril

Why Don't Men Like Women

Adventures in Good Living

Enlightening Amercica

Fiction

Run, Naomi, Run, **by Pauline Shook**

Jumping Skyward **by Stan Tate**

Whipsawed **by Richard Sonnichsen**

Tumbleweed **by Richard Sonnichsen**

Travel Agent Escapades **by Pat Seiler**

My Grandma Has a Boyfriend (Children's) **by Pat Seiler**

Poetry

Any River **by Sam Olson**

www.ingramcontent.com/pod-product-compliance
Lightning Source LLC
Chambersburg PA
CBHW031741180726
48283CB00005B/1622
* 9 7 8 1 8 8 6 5 9 1 3 5 6 *